To Larry, who encouraged me and shared my excitement in finding my passion for writing.

And to Marilyn, Melanie and Iris, who happily read and critiqued my work long before I became a "real" author.

MAKING LOVE

"Will you sit still for a few minutes?" Dale said, laughing. He poured her a very full glass of champagne, and then walked around to the back of her chair.

"What are you doing?" She felt his fingers on her shoulders.

"Trying to get you to relax," he said, as he massaged her neck and shoulders. "Is this helping any?"

"Yes," she purred. "It feels great."

He smiled with pleasure. "I told you I was good with my hands."

Dale slowly walked around her, then taking her head firmly in his hand, he kissed her on the mouth.

She shrank back from his embrace, disturbed by her own feelings. "Dale!" she said. "I thought we were friends."

"We are friends," he assured her. "But I want more."

She felt a surge of panic. "What do you want?"

Dale looked at her as if she were a naive young girl. "I want to make love to you, Susan."

She gasped. "Dale, I'm flattered by your proposition, and I appreciate your honesty. I just don't think I could handle a casual affair."

His next words took her breath away. "I'm not interested in a casual affair."

WATCH AS THESE WOMEN LEARN
TO LOVE AGAIN

HELLO LOVE   (4094, $4.50/$5.50)
by Joan Shapiro

Family tragedy leaves Barbara Sinclair alone with her success. The fight to gain custody of her young granddaughter brings a confrontation with the determined rancher Sam Douglass. Also widowed, Sam has been caring for Emily alone, guided by his own ideas of childrearing. Barbara challenges his ideas. And that's not all she challenges . . . Long-buried desires surface, then gentle affection. Sam and Barbara cannot ignore the chance to love again.

THE BEST MEDICINE   (4220, $4.50/$5.50)
by Janet Lane Walters

Her late husband's expenses push Maggie Carr back to nursing, the career she left almost thirty years ago. The night shift is difficult, but it's harder still to ignore the way handsome Dr. Jason Knight soothes his patients. When she lends a hand to help his daughter, Jason and Maggie grow closer than simply doctor and nurse. Obstacles to romance seem insurmountable, but Maggie knows that love is always the best medicine.

AND BE MY LOVE   (4291, $4.50/$5.50)
by Joyce C. Ware

Selflessly catering first to husband, then children, grandchildren, and her aging, though imperious mother, leaves Beth Volmar little time for her own adventures or passions. Then, the handsome archaeologist Karim Donovan arrives and campaigns to widen the boundaries of her narrow life. Beth finds new freedom when Karim insists that she accompany him to Turkey on an archaeological dig . . . and a journey towards loving again.

OVER THE RAINBOW   (4032, $4.50/$5.50)
by Marjorie Eatock

Fifty-something, divorced for years, courted by more than one attractive man, and thoroughly enjoying her job with a large insurance company, Marian's sudden restlessness confuses her. She welcomes the chance to travel on business to a small Mississippi town. Full of good humor and words of love, Don Worth makes her feel needed, and not just to assess property damage. Marian takes the risk.

A KISS AT SUNRISE   (4260, $4.50/$5.50)
by Charlotte Sherman

Beginning widowhood and retirement, Ruth Nichols has her first taste of freedom. Against the advice of her mother and daughter, Ruth heads for an adventure in the motor home that has sat unused since her husband's death. Long days and lonely campgrounds start to dampen the excitement of traveling alone. That is, until a dapper widower named Jack parks next door and invites her for dinner. On the road, Ruth and Jack find the chance to love again.

Available wherever paperbacks are sold, or order direct from the Publisher. Send cover price plus 50¢ per copy for mailing and handling to Penguin USA, P.O. Box 999, c/o Dept. 17109, Bergenfield, NJ 07621.Residents of New York and Tennessee must include sales tax. DO NOT SEND CASH.

SEPTEMBER SPRING

LINDA STEINBERG

ZEBRA BOOKS
KENSINGTON PUBLISHING CORP.

ZEBRA BOOKS are published by

Kensington Publishing Corp.
475 Park Avenue South
New York, NY 10016

First Printing: February, 1994

Printed in the United States of America

One

Nothing to it, Susan thought bravely as she started the Jaguar's engine and was rewarded by a harmonious purr. I should have learned how to drive this car years ago. She hugged the steering wheel confidently, unaware that her elbow had just nudged the gearshift. Now all she had to do was let it warm up a bit, and then—

Susan gulped. The red convertible was starting to sail backward down the steep driveway. She tapped the brakes, but it didn't slow down. She braked harder. Nothing. Was she supposed to be doing something with the clutch? In a panic, Susan jammed the gearshift into first. There was a sharp grinding noise as the Jaguar jerked forward and stopped momentarily, then continued rolling down the hill again, at increased speed.

A frightening flash appeared in the rearview

mirror. Susan turned to see two cars approaching in the street behind her. Her neck muscles tightened like a taut guitar string. Where the hell was the emergency brake? She pumped the brakes, unsuccessfully, and leaned on the horn as she searched frantically for the hand brake.

The first car just cleared the Jaguar's path as the sports car careered backward into the street. The driver of the other, a silver Mercedes, slammed on his brakes a second later. At the same instant, Susan finally found the emergency brake and pulled it as hard as she could. The smell of rubber assaulted her nose as the Jaguar jumped the curb of the esplanade that divided the residential street, squealing to a stop just inches from the trunk of a twenty-five-year-old tree.

"What the hell were you doing, lady?" the driver of the Mercedes sputtered angrily, slamming his door as he got out. "Are you blind or just stupid?"

Susan, still seated in the Jaguar, raised her hands sheepishly. The man threw up his hands in exasperation, got back in his car, and peeled away.

Knees knocking in relief, Susan got out and inspected the Jaguar. God takes care of fools and little children and middle-aged ladies who can't drive a stick shift, she thought gratefully.

Not only was she unhurt, but, except for one bashed-in tire, there wasn't a single scratch on the car.

She reached in and flipped on the emergency flashers. This was her own fault, she thought guiltily as the red convertible blinked at her accusingly. She had neglected the Jaguar. This was the first time she had even tried to start it up since Mike died. Like a jealous wife spurning her husband's mistress, she had let it languish in disuse, bereft of Mike's loving attention. A tear fought its way to the corner of her eye. In his last years, her husband had doted on that car as if it were one of his children. He had kept it in perfect condition, washing and waxing it every week, servicing it regularly, protecting it from dents and scratches. Mike's toy, Susan smiled sadly, through the lump in her throat. Who could understand the love affair between a man and his car?

It was time to get rid of the Jaguar, she decided as she leaned pensively against the blue and white tile counter of her ranch-style kitchen. It was silly to keep it cloistered in the garage as if Mike might one day return to drive it. With trembling fingers, she poured a cup of gritty coffee from its under-the-cabinet decanter and reviewed her options.

She had thought that Joel might want to

have his father's car. But her son already had his own car, an economical Toyota, and he would not be at all enthusiastic about taking on the high cost of maintenance that the sporty Jaguar required. Joel had never been impressed by flashy cars or flashy clothes. Or flashy women. He had always preferred substance over style. Anyway, Susan had to admit, a chic convertible really wasn't very practical in downtown San Francisco, where Joel lived and worked. It was much more suited to cruising here on the southern California freeways.

Andrea, on the other hand, had always enjoyed driving the Jaguar. Mike didn't really like the kids, or anyone, driving his car, but he was a soft touch for his daughter's smile, and Andrea had managed on a number of occasions to cajole him into letting her take it out for a drive. Andrea would love to have it for her own. But she was still in her last year of college and wouldn't be able to afford it. Besides, they had just bought her a new Buick last year. It wasn't a sports car, but it was more practical, Mike had said, and he had insisted on a practical, trouble-free car for his daughter.

The only solution was to sell it. Hopefully it wouldn't be too expensive to fix whatever was wrong with the stupid brakes. Susan scrounged around the dump-in-everything kitchen drawer for Mike's address book, flipping through the dog-eared pages until she found the number of the car repair shop with which he had traded. Mike had always sworn by his mechanic. "Dale can fix anything with an engine," he had asserted.

After having the Jaguar towed to the repair shop, Susan entered the waiting room that sunny March morning feeling apprehensive and slightly intimidated. The shop was just outside Beverly Hills and even smelled expensive. The fragrance of Giorgio dotted the wrists of the well-dressed clientele, and the furniture exuded the aroma of real leather. Volvos, Mercedes, and BMWs lined the entrance. They probably wouldn't even work on *my* car, she thought.

Although she could well afford a newer, more expensive model, Susan was quite content driving her five-year-old Cutlass. It was comfortable, it still ran well, and she didn't see any need to replace it. Her fellow attorneys, however, teased her about it incessantly.

"When are you going to get rid of that old heap, Susan?" they joked. "It looks bad for the firm."

"I'll let you guys in Corporate worry about the firm's image," she teased back. *"My* clients are turned off by an attorney who drives a big fancy car. They don't like to think that their lawyer is getting rich off of their hard-earned money."

Susan's eyes swept across the waiting room of the repair shop, appraising the decor in the same brisk, facile manner she employed in skimming a law brief. She nodded approvingly at the beige stucco walls, sparsely but tastefully decorated with paintings that didn't look like they'd been bought at K mart. Susan also noted that the coffee table included copies of *Vogue* and *Working Woman* in addition to *Popular Mechanics* and the usual assortment of sports magazines. The big picture window afforded a generous view of the service bays. So you can make sure they actually *do* something to your car, not just keep it here for eight hours, she thought wryly.

Susan glanced at her watch and started tapping her foot impatiently, then caught hold of herself and forced a deep relaxing breath. She didn't have to be at the office until ten this morning, and it was an easy case, just a simple prenuptial contract to draw up. At least this part was simple; the hard part had been convincing Emily Weinman to do the contract in the first place. Although Emily's late husband Abe had left her a substantial sum from his dry-cleaning business, Emily had resisted asking her new boyfriend to sign a prenup because she feared it would look like she didn't trust him. Susan was amazed that an otherwise intelligent and mature woman could be so vulnerable to the charms of a good-looking, sweet-talking man. And so trusting. One thing Susan had learned in fifteen years of handling divorce cases was that no matter whether the marriage was about love, companionship, or money, the divorce was always, always about money.

The rockin' sounds of Bruce Springsteen flooded the room as the door from the work area opened. The man who entered was about six feet tall, thirtyish, and very handsome, with a medium brown mustache just a few shades darker than his golden brown hair. The men in the waiting room raised their eyes expectantly but did not change their position. The women, however, sat up straighter and almost imperceptibly brushed their hair back with their hands, preening themselves. Susan smiled to herself in amusement. The appearance of this handsome young man had obviously sent the females, old and young, into automatic flirtation mode.

The man wiped his hands on the rag that hung from his pants pocket. "It's bad news, Mrs. Grant," he said to a young woman in a designer T-shirt. "I'm afraid it's the transmission."

Worried lines filled the woman's fair-skinned face. "How much?" she asked, biting her lip.

The serviceman took the woman's hand and sat down beside her at the far end of the couch. "I'm going to make you out a list of everything we found needing attention, including the prices of new and/or rebuilt parts," he said patiently. He spoke very slowly and deliberately, as if giving instructions to a child. "You can talk it over with your husband and let me know tomorrow if you want to fix it or go in another direction. I'm sorry." He helped the woman to her feet.

"I hope you're not going to tell *me* that," a silver-haired lady sniffed petulantly.

"No, I'm not." The mechanic smiled a bright, engaging smile. "There is really nothing wrong with your car, Mrs. Fine. You keep getting soot in the engine because you don't drive it enough. You've got to take it out on the highway and let that baby run. You can't keep a Mercedes restricted to trips to the shopping mall."

Susan watched the man with interest as he made his rounds about the room, dispensing diagnoses like a doctor reporting on the condition of patients. Something about him looked so familiar. Her eyes followed him curiously. It wasn't just his looks that intrigued her. His style seemed familiar as well. He was easygoing, even flirtatious, with all the women customers, not just the young and pretty ones. With the men he was curt and businesslike, yet when he was questioned about a mechanical problem, he discussed it with the customer in great detail.

A harried, high-heeled woman in a business suit banged open the entrance door. Ignoring the clients already seated and waiting, she rushed up to the handsome serviceman. "How are you doing, Melissa?" the man asked pleasantly. Presumably the rude, line-cutting woman was a regular customer.

"Not so good," she complained. "I've got three appointments this morning and I'm already late for the first one and the damn Volvo starts giving me problems. And your little guy over there told me I'd have to leave it all day." She pointed to a short Hispanic man who stood in the drive-up area overseeing the incoming cars. "Can't you drive it for me, Dale, and tell me what it is?" She looked up at him helplessly, almost seductively.

He took the keys she held out to him. "Back in five, Terry," he yelled over his shoulder to the young woman in the cashier's booth.

"Well, I don't think it's the brakes," he said when he returned. "Or the steering. It could be a loose connection or something in the engine. Or," he winked, "it could just be the loose nut behind the wheel." He patted her shoulder solicitously. "I don't think it's anything dangerous. You can bring it in Saturday if you like and I'll check it out for you. Make an appointment with Terry so you won't have to wait all day."

"Thanks, Dale," the woman said gratefully.

The man had charm to spare. He was probably the service manager or public relations man. Susan couldn't imagine anyone storming out of here angry. Dale's broad smile and smooth manner seemed capable of soothing the most irate customer. Still, he seemed sincere. It was hard to keep from liking the man.

"Mrs. Riesman." The young man was looking at her now and Susan rose to stand beside him. He held out his hand to her. "I don't recognize the face," he smiled, "but I do recognize the car." He had a large hand, which enveloped Susan's completely when he shook it, yet it seemed quite delicate, almost like a surgeon's hand. "I'm Dale Clemens."

"Nice to meet you," Susan said politely. Dale's starched white shirt had his name handsewn in blue over the pocket. It looked like it had been spotlessly white earlier this morning, but now held several grease stains, as did his blue work pants. He obviously did more than just smile at the customers. He might double as the service manager, as Susan had originally surmised, but Dale looked as though he was not afraid of getting his hands and his clothes dirty.

She raised her eyes to his face, to the intelligent, gray-green eyes that riveted the attention of her whole being. That was it, of course. The eyes. It was his eyes that had made him seem familiar. The shape, the color, that intense, all-knowing gaze. She knew she had seen those eyes somewhere before. She wondered if Mike had ever noticed Dale's eyes and recognized whose they resembled. If he had, he had never said anything about it.

"I haven't had a chance to look at the car yet," Dale was saying, "but I doubt that it's anything major. Mike takes very good care of that car. I haven't seen him in quite a while. How's he been doing?"

Susan bit her lip. Although it had been almost six months since Mike's death, she was still running into people that didn't know about it. The experience always unnerved her. She still wasn't used to telling people that he was gone.

"I guess you didn't know," Susan said quietly. "Mike died last September."

"Oh!" The charming, all-purpose smile was suddenly ripped from Dale's face. His brow furrowed and he appeared genuinely distressed. "I'm very sorry," he said somberly.

"Please have a seat in my office. I'll be with you in a minute."

He pointed to the solid wood door marked "Private." Susan went inside and stationed herself on the large plush sofa.

Dale came in a few minutes later. "I'm very sorry to hear about your husband, Mrs. Riesman," he said as he sat beside her. "Mike was a wonderful man. I had a great deal of respect for him. Was it his heart?"

Susan nodded. Dale's eyes brimmed with warm sympathy. "Did you know Mike a long time?" she asked.

"Almost ten years. We played golf together occasionally." Dale stood and walked over to the large desk at the other end of the room. He opened a drawer and took out a handkerchief and handed it to Susan. The embroidered initials read *M.R.* "He left this on the course last time we played. It seems like only a little while ago."

"I'm sorry you weren't notified," Susan apologized. "I guess I wasn't aware of all of Mike's friends and acquaintances."

Dale waved off her apology. He sat down at his desk and rifled through his papers. When he looked at her again, his expression was all business. "So what can I do for you, Mrs. Riesman? You've been having problems with the Jag?"

"Well, I certainly did this morning!" As she told him what had happened, Dale's eyebrows knitted in concern.

"You were lucky you weren't hurt. The car can be fixed. Sounds like you may have messed up the gears, though, when you panicked. Don't feel too bad," he said kindly. "A lot of women don't understand how to operate a manual transmission."

Susan's eyes flashed. She felt like wiping the chauvinistic smirk from his face. But then he added, with a twinkle in his eye, "As a matter of fact, a lot of men don't, either. That car is a beautiful machine. If you like, I'll teach you how to drive it."

Those eyes could be as charming as they were disarming. Where *had* she seen that look before? "I don't want to drive it," she said flatly. "I want to sell it. I can't bear to look at it anymore. Mike was the only person who ever drove that car."

Dale nodded. "I understand. All right, Mrs. Riesman, we'll get it fixed and cleaned up for you, and unless it's in worse shape than I think, we'll bring the car to you before we close tonight. Will that be all right?"

"Fine," Susan acceded.

Dale opened the office door and motioned for her to precede him out. He tapped on the glass separating the waiting room from the service area, signaling to a young man on the other side. The mechanic put down the tool he was holding and came in immediately.

"Jose, will you drive Mrs. Riesman to work, please?" Dale reached into his pants pocket and tossed the young mechanic a handful of keys. "Take my truck."

"Thank you very much, Mr. Clemens," Susan said, shaking his hand warmly.

"Dale," he corrected. He pushed open the glass door and walked outside with her. "I'm so sorry about Mike. Please let me know if there is anything I can do."

She had heard that glib expression from a lot of people lately. This time it was from a man she didn't even know, yet, she felt instinctively that he really meant it.

As Susan waited for Jose to bring the truck, the young professional woman who had seemed so distraught scurried past her, then skidded to a stop. "You were in Dale's private office?" she smiled knowingly. "What's it like?"

"Like an office," Susan answered, surprised by the question. "A desk and a file cabinet. A sofa and a table. You know."

"Oh," the woman said, sounding just a little disappointed. "I'd heard he had a bedroom in there." Without waiting for Susan to reply, she darted away again, disappearing into a late-model Volvo.

Something about her words hit Susan in the gut like a one-two punch. Her gaze flitted back to the service area. Dale was still standing in the yard, his body angled slightly toward her. He appeared to be supervising the workers, but his eyes still lingered on Susan like a parent who watches from the front porch until his child is safely on the school bus. She couldn't help noticing what a powerful body he had. His stance was unassuming, yet confident. The slight breeze blew his hair against his brow like a casual caress. In the sunlight his hair looked much lighter. It had probably once been yellow-blond, the color of the sunlight itself, the color of a million marigold memories.

Susan gasped and her bones began to quiver. Suddenly she knew why Dale's eyes looked so familiar. Suddenly she saw another face under the golden hair, another body inside the strong physique. A slighter build, a smaller frame, but the same determined, almost arrogant, posture. "Jeff," she whispered.

Two

"Nice of you to join us, Susan," Ron Davis greeted her as she strolled into the office a little after nine. Despite the sarcastic words, his voice was playful and his eyes twinkled. "Is everything okay?"

Ron Davis was the managing partner of the law firm of Davis, Dobbs and Engels. Always a kind and considerate boss, he had been especially solicitous of Susan these past few months. He understood better than most people what she was going through because he had lost his wife of thirty-five years to cancer several years ago. He had allowed Susan as much time off after Mike's funeral as she needed and, when she had returned to the office three months ago, had pretty much let her make her own hours.

"Everything's fine," she assured him. "I just

had to take Mike's car to the repair shop. Is Mrs. Weinman here yet?"

"No, but the Archers are here. They asked if you had time to squeeze them in."

Unfortunately she did. George and Sheila Archer were going through a very hostile divorce. And George's attorney, Jim Slater, was not an easy man to negotiate with. After a confrontation that lasted an hour and a half, Susan's hair was damp with perspiration, and her linen suit felt like she had taken a bath in it.

She left work a little early that afternoon, begging a ride in Ron's metallic silver Lexus, but it was well after seven before the red Jaguar squealed to a stop in her driveway. "Well, it's about time!" she said as she opened the back door to admit Dale Clemens. "I thought maybe you'd forgotten about me."

"No, ma'am," Dale said as he handed her the keys to the Jaguar. "No way I could do that." He glanced in at the untidy kitchen, the counters of which held scraps of cut-up vegetables from the soup Susan was cooking.

"Well, come on in for a minute," she said, as Dale remained awkwardly in the doorway. He had changed out of his work uniform and was now wearing a red knit sport shirt and black denim pants. The casual clothing clung to his body as if custom made. "Would you like a cold drink?" she offered. "Coke? Beer?"

"Cold water would be fine, Mrs. Riesman." Dale moved inside and settled himself on a barstool next to the counter.

"My name is Susan." She handed him a tall glass of water with ice. "What time does your shop close, anyway?"

"Six o'clock. But I couldn't get away until just now. I had another car to finish up and some paperwork to do."

"They keep you pretty busy, don't they? Working on the cars *and* paperwork? Not to mention flirting with the customers."

He smiled a slow, beautiful smile. "Yes, well, it's a tough job, but somebody's got to do it."

She leaned over the bar which jutted out into the center of the kitchen. "You like what you do? Fixing cars, I mean."

"You bet. I wouldn't work so hard at it if I didn't. Actually I got off early tonight. I usually work much later."

"I'm impressed," Susan said. "Are you that dedicated or do you just have a tough boss?"

Dale laughed, displaying a full mouth of white pearly teeth. "I have the toughest boss in the world. There is no tougher boss than working for yourself."

Susan grinned. "So you're the owner. I should have guessed." She reached for her purse which sprawled open on the kitchen counter and took out her checkbook.

"You don't owe me anything for today," Dale said, waving her hand away. "It's the least I can do to honor Mike's memory."

"That's very nice of you, Dale, but I'm sure you're a better businessman than that. It must have been a pretty big job. Come on, how much?"

He hesitated, then shrugged in acquiescence. "Five hundred and eighty-nine dollars."

Susan raised her eyebrows.

"I know that seems like a lot, ma'am, but it *was* a lot of work. The problem with the brakes was minor, but somebody who didn't know how to drive that car messed up the gears big time."

He had Jeff's way of being overly polite, almost deferential, to cover up a supercilious attitude. He was looking down on her, she decided. He thought she was an overprivileged idiot who couldn't drive a simple car without breaking it. Susan wrote out the check and handed it to him. He stood up and folded it into his shirt pocket without taking his eyes from hers. His sharp green eyes bored relentlessly into her soft brown ones, as if they could plumb their depths and discern any secrets within them.

"I guess I'd better take you back," she said

awkwardly, jerking her eyes away. "I'm sure your wife must be holding dinner for you."

Dale smiled, apparently enjoying her discomfort. "I'm not married, if that's what you're asking. But I do have an eight o'clock appointment." His body was pointed toward the back door, but his eyes cast subtle glances at the chunks of meat and vegetables simmering in the eight-quart stewpot. Susan interpreted that look immediately. It was one she had often seen on the faces of Joel and his friends as teenagers, as they hung around her kitchen, sniffing out its delicacies. It had obviously been a long time since Dale had eaten a home-cooked meal.

She scooped several ladlefuls into a bowl, comfortable and in charge once again, ignoring Dale's halfhearted protest. "It's faster service than McDonald's, I guarantee you," Susan said in a motherly tone.

"Tastes a lot better, too," he commented, as he slurped it up eagerly. His eyes strayed to the large pot which was still filled almost to the top. "You always cook this much just for yourself? You *do* live here alone, don't you?"

For an instant, Susan was frightened. After all, she had only just met this man and she didn't know anything about him. He could be casing the house, making plans to rob her, or worse. "My son and daughter come and stay here frequently," she said guardedly. "In fact," she lied, "I am expecting my son to arrive shortly."

Dale's expression didn't change at the release of this information. She decided that she had been silly to think he might have criminal intentions. His eyes made her want to trust him.

"Would you like to go and wash up before your date?" she asked when he had finished his second helping of soup.

Dale smiled, apparently amused at her not-so-oblique way of routing out information. He hadn't said he had a date. "No, thanks, Mrs. Riesman," he said. "I showered at the shop."

Susan's eyes widened. "You have a shower at the garage?"

He nodded. "In my private office."

"So it's true, then," Susan mused out loud.

"What's true?"

She blushed slightly. "Somebody told me that your office was a convertible bedroom."

Dale's face turned a rosy shade of pink. "As a matter of fact, the couch *does* open up. But it's not what you think. I work a lot of nights, and most days I open the shop at six in the morning. Sometimes I just sleep at the office so I won't have to make the commute. It's a two-hour drive each way."

"Why do you live so far from your work?" Susan asked.

"It's the closest house I could afford," he replied simply.

"Why don't you live in an apartment? There are plenty of nice places very close to your garage." This is really none of your business, Susan, she admonished herself.

"I don't like apartments. When I *do* get home, I enjoy my comfort and privacy. I like playing my stereo as loud as I want, and I like having a private swim at four in the morning before I go to work."

"You have a swimming pool?"

"Uh-huh. You don't?" He seemed surprised at her denial. "That's unusual for this neighborhood."

"It wasn't when we first came here. Mike built this house himself, twenty-five years ago. We didn't dare to add on a pool when the kids were small, for fear of drowning accidents. We almost put one in about five years ago, but Mike decided he liked the social atmosphere of going to the club to swim instead."

She fell silent, her eyes focused on the repetitive geometric patterns of the vinyl flooring. When she looked up, Dale was staring at her intently with those serious green eyes. "You miss him a lot, don't you?"

"Mike? Of course. You live with a person for

28

a lifetime and then suddenly he's not there. Every room, every item in this house reminds me of him."

Dale stroked his mustache as he spoke. "Maybe you should sell the house. Move into one of those apartments you were telling me about."

"I could never sell this house. It has too many memories. Not just of Mike. Of my whole life." She ladled herself a cup of soup and sat down next to him at the bar. "It took me all these months just to get up the courage to sell the Jaguar."

"I understand." He placed his large palm, just for a second, over her hand, then removed it. "How much are you going to ask for the car?"

"I have no earthly idea," Susan confessed. "How much do you think I can get?"

Dale twitched his nose thoughtfully. "I shouldn't tell you this, but if you put an ad in *Car Classics*, you can probably get twenty-five to thirty thousand for it."

"Really? That's great!" Susan exclaimed. Her eyes narrowed. "Why shouldn't you have told me that?"

"Because I'd like to buy the Jag myself," Dale said candidly. "I've always loved that car. I've never let anyone else touch it since Mike first bought it. But I can't raise that kind of money."

"How much *can* you pay?"

He thought a minute. "Eighteen thousand. Maybe twenty, tops."

"Sold for twenty thousand."

He stared at her. "Are you serious? You're not joking with me?"

"Of course I'm serious."

"But why?" He was dumbfounded. "I just told you you could get at least five thousand more for her, maybe a lot more than that."

"To tell you the truth, I don't relish the thought of placing an ad and having people call here at all hours of the night. And I'm even less crazy about total strangers coming to the house and finding I live alone."

"Would you like me to sell it for you?" Dale offered. "I could have them call at the garage during business hours."

"That's very generous of you, Dale. Why don't you try to sell the car for twenty-five thousand and keep a twenty percent commission?"

"Oh, no, I couldn't take any money for it. I—"

Susan watched Dale's eyes as he did the mental arithmetic and realized what she was telling him. "Buy the car, Dale," she said. "Life's not just about money. Mike loved that car like it was his own child. I'm sure he'd like to see it go to someone who cares about it as much as he did."

"Thank you," Dale said simply, with gratitude in his eyes. "You are one classy lady." He rose and placed his bowl and spoon in the sink. "It might take a week or two before I can get the money together."

"Take as much time as you need," Susan said generously.

Dale reached into his shirt pocket and ceremoniously tore up the check she had given him. Pretty impressive gesture, Susan thought as he handed her the two pieces. The man was not without class himself. "Dale!" she exclaimed, as her gaze fell on the clock over the stove. "It's almost eight o'clock! I hope your girlfriend doesn't live too far from here."

"She lives pretty close, actually," he said, relinquishing any pretense of having a business engagement. "But I've still got to go back to the shop first to get my truck."

"Oh my gosh, I forgot. I'm sorry. We'll go right now." She was scooping up her keys when a thought occurred to her. "Dale," she suggested, "why don't you just take the Jaguar? I'm sure your date would rather ride in a sports car than a truck, and you won't be late."

"I can't do that," Dale protested. "I can't

use a customer's car for my own personal business."

"Don't you think I trust you to drive my car? I trust you to take it apart, don't I? Besides, it'll be your car soon," she pointed out. "Consider this a test drive."

"Well . . . thanks," he said reluctantly. "I'll bring it back to you first thing in the morning." As he reached to take the car keys from her, Dale's fingers lingered a half second longer than necessary over her soft white palm. And as he slipped out the back door, his hand brushed accidentally against Susan's back and slid slowly down until it touched the firm flesh of her hip.

At least she assumed it was accidental. She was almost twice Dale's age; surely he hadn't been intentionally flirting with her.

Nevertheless, when the red Jaguar drove up into the driveway the next morning, Susan felt an involuntary flutter in her chest. She told herself it was just heartburn, caused by gulping her coffee too fast. But as she rose eagerly to answer the knock on the back door and found Jose standing there, the unmistakable disappointment that washed over her forced her to admit that the flutter had been caused by something else. Excited anticipation at the thought of seeing Dale again.

She was embarrassed by her immature display of emotion. She was a little too old to be going gaga over every good-looking car mechanic she met. As she drove to work in her very unsporty Cutlass, she resolved to conduct any future business with Mr. Dale Clemens in a strictly professional manner.

Susan had two divorces pending, one of which was going to court that week, a child custody case, and a legal separation. She had also been working for several months with a young doctor's wife who was trying to get up the courage to divorce her internationally prominent but domestically abusive husband. Lois Webster was typical of many of Susan's clients: a woman who knew that her marriage was over but had so much invested in it, she could only allow herself to take one step at a time. She had finally thrown her husband out of the house, and Susan had gotten a restraining order issued to keep him away, but Simon Webster was determined to hold on to his property, which, in his mind, included not only his house but his wife. So when the phone rang early that evening, Susan was afraid it might be her client reporting that her husband had once again violated the restraining order.

It wasn't Lois Webster. "Susan?"

Her fingers began to tremble and her breath caught slightly in her throat as she recognized the low-toned, mellow voice. It was the first time Dale had called her by her first name.

"I made some phone calls this morning," he informed her. "I should be able to have the money for you early next week." There was excitement in Dale's voice as he discussed the arrangements, but Susan didn't delude herself that it was over the thought of seeing her. She knew he was brimming with the anticipation of finally owning the sleek Jaguar convertible.

"That will be fine," she said politely. "Whenever you're ready."

There was an uncomfortable pause. Dale cleared his throat. "Thank you for letting me use the car last night," he said. "And for the soup."

"You're welcome. Thanks for returning the car today." She was not about to be one-upped in the politeness game.

"Thank you for driving Jose back."

He was stalling, Susan noted with some pleasure. She sensed that he was as reluctant as she was to end this conversation, but there was nothing else to say. She smiled to herself as she hung up the phone.

When Dale arrived at her house the next week to sign the papers for the car, he brought a bottle of champagne with him. "I think we should drink to my new car," he said, as Susan gave him a quizzical look. He raised his glass over the living-room coffee table. "Skoal."

"*Lechayim,*" Susan said, touching her glass to his. "It means 'To Life,' " she explained, as Dale looked at her blankly.

"That's a Jewish word, right?" he asked.

"Hebrew, yes. It's a traditional toast said at all weddings, Bar Mitzvahs, any special occasion."

"Le Kayim," Dale said, trying unsuccessfully to mimic her pronunciation.

"Le*KH*ayim," she corrected, emphasizing the guttural sound. "It's the same sound as in German."

"I'm afraid I'm not very good at languages," Dale admitted. "My talents have always been in my hands."

Susan looked up expectantly, presuming a double entendre, but Dale's face was impassive. He seemed unaware that his innocent words could have another meaning. "Have you always liked working with your hands?" she asked him.

"Always. Since I was a little kid on the farm. I used to take tractors apart and put them back together again. I once had my grandpa's new combine practically all in pieces when he found me—then he started taking *me* apart. I've always liked working on cars best, though. Especially sports cars."

He took a long, slow sip of champagne as his eyes made a long, slow sweep of her face. His gaze made Susan nervous. She downed the rest of her glass.

Dale stood up and reached for the bottle. "Would you like another?"

"No, thanks. But you go ahead if you want."

"Not me either," he demurred. "I've got to go back to work. We can finish it up later. If you're free tonight, I'd like to take you out to dinner."

Susan was surprised by the invitation. "That's not necessary, Dale," she protested. "Bringing the champagne was a nice gesture, but it was more than enough."

"I'll take you to a nice place," he said, a little defensively. "I may not live in Palisades, but I can afford better than hamburgers. Is it because you don't want to be seen in the company of a grease monkey?"

"Oh, no, not at all," she said quickly, realizing she had offended him. "It has nothing to do with you. It's me, relative to you. I'm old enough to be your mother!"

He smiled a winsome and slightly seductive smile. "It is possible," he said, "but I doubt it. I don't usually ask ladies their age, but since you're making an issue of it, how old *are* you?"

Susan knew she was making a fool of herself, but she couldn't resist the coy response. "How old do you think I am?" She held her breath in anticipation. People usually guessed that she was quite a bit younger than her years.

He studied her face again. "Do you want me to be polite or honest?"

For an instant, she could have sworn that she saw another face, heard another voice, saying those words. "Which do you do best?" she parried.

"Honest." She nodded her permission. "I'd say early fifties," Dale said thoughtfully. "If I had to pinpoint a number, I'd have to say fifty-three."

Susan blinked her eyes in surprise and obvious disappointment. "You are cold and cruel. But exactly right. Most people tell me I look younger."

"Oh, you *do* look younger," he assured her. "At least ten years younger. I wasn't going by the way you look. I was going by Mike, and by the things you said about yourself." He grinned apologetically. "I guess I should have gone with 'polite.'"

"No, it's okay. I prefer honesty. Even when it hurts. So then you must realize that I'm way too old for you."

"Not necessarily. How old do you think *I* am?"

Susan resisted the urge to ask "Honest or polite?" She thought that he was probably in his early thirties. "Between twenty-eight and thirty-five," she said diplomatically.

"I'm forty-one."

Susan was surprised but not displeased. "You look younger."

"I'm twelve years younger than you, Susan. Not a lot, at our ages. I know you don't go out socially yet, but if you did, wouldn't you go out with a man who was twelve years *older* than you? Anyway," he asserted without waiting for her answer, "this is not a date. I just want to celebrate my ownership of a fine Jaguar convertible with the woman who made it possible." His eyes turned serious. "You did something very nice for me, Susan, that you didn't have to do. You've got to at least let me thank you for it."

She realized that he wasn't going to take no for an answer. "I suppose that arguing any further about this would only be wasting my breath," Susan said.

"You suppose right," Dale agreed, apparently relieved that the matter was settled. "I know a place that serves great prime rib. How does that sound to you?"

"Fine. Wonderful. Whatever you say."

"Now you're humoring me."

She had been, but in a way it was nice, although it went against her feminist grain to admit it, to have a man take charge of her life

38

again. Even just a simple decision like dinner. She was so tired of having to make every single damn decision, big and small, by herself.

"I'd be honored to go to dinner with you, Dale." She smiled at him brightly, and there was no sarcasm in her voice this time.

He grinned and lifted her hand to his lips and kissed it Continental style. "Later, 'Mama.'"

Rifling through her closet later, looking for something suitable to wear, Susan felt like a teenager getting ready for her first date. Of course, this wasn't a date; Dale understood that as well as she did. She was still in mourning for her husband, and even if she weren't, she would never consider going out on a date with a man twelve years her junior, no matter what he said about it not being a big age difference.

Still, she did want to look nice tonight. Dale was an extremely handsome man, and she didn't want to embarrass him by looking dowdy or frumpy. Or too matronly. Susan stared into her closet and surveyed three or four possibilities. She knew that not even the most expensive designer dress could make her look twenty-one again, or even thirty-one, but for God's sake, please let her not look her age. She really didn't want to look like his mother.

She was tempted to call her daughter and ask her advice. Andrea always knew what was in fashion and what was proper for any occasion. But Andrea would probably think her mother had taken leave of her sanity if Susan told her where she was going tonight and with whom.

She finally settled on a slimming black after-five dress with a flared, tiered, very short skirt and a rather low-cut bodice. Perhaps a little too revealing considering the circumstances, but she could wear it with a pink, filmy, blouselike scarf that didn't conceal what was intended to be revealed but did make it look less accessible.

When Dale arrived at the front door that evening, he looked her up and down. "Do I look all right?" she asked anxiously.

"No," he said slowly, his eyes still focused on her body. "You look better than that. You look fabulous."

"You don't look so bad yourself," she said, admiring the way he carried himself in his Armani suit.

"Well. All my overalls were in the wash." She could almost have expected him to say something like that. It was Jeff's style of humor, self-deprecating but arrogant at the same time. She wondered again how two men could be so alike.

He glanced around appreciatively at the tasteful furnishings and the classic art that lined the walls. "I guess this is the first time you've come in this way," Susan said apologetically.

"I usually use the servants' entrance," Dale said, his eyes twinkling. "I'm a back-door man."

I'll bet you are, Susan thought to herself.

She gave him a tour of the main-floor rooms. "It's very nice," Dale said. "Very well laid out. Mike was a good architect."

"He was the best," Susan affirmed. "I always loved the houses he designed. I wish he had done more residential." The name Michael Riesman had been almost a synonym for quality design and construction in Los Angeles area office buildings and shopping centers. Highly respected not only for his financial success but also for his many civic and cultural contributions to the Los Angeles community, Mike had enjoyed a reputation few real estate developers shared. He had financed business projects in inner city neighborhoods and had donated the profits from one of his shopping centers to building a community center in East L.A.

"Commercial is where the money is. Mike knew what he was doing." As Dale wrapped Susan's shawl around her and escorted her to the car, she was very much aware of the light pressure of his fingers against her back. It was a pleasant sensation.

"Would you like me to put the top up?" Dale asked politely, as the convertible cruised through the streets.

"Of course not. That's the main reason why you wanted to buy this car, isn't it?"

"Yes," he answered candidly, "but a lot of ladies don't want the wind to mess up their hair."

"You mean *old* ladies, don't you?" she challenged him.

"That's not what I said. And it's not what I meant."

"Well, I like the feel of the wind in my hair. Although it will probably look like hell when we get to the restaurant."

Dale smiled appreciatively at her use of the mild invective. Mike Riesman had been one of the wealthiest men he'd ever met, and one of the most powerful, but Dale had never known him to act the least bit pompous or self-important. Apparently his widow was the same casual, down-to-earth type.

Before entering the restaurant, Susan checked her hair in the visor mirror. "Your hair looks great," Dale assured her, as Susan looked at him questioningly. "It's fine," he repeated. "Come on."

The restaurant was fashionable but not ostentatious. Dale had three scotch and waters to Susan's one daiquiri before he even asked for the wine list. Susan rarely drank more than an occasional glass of wine with dinner, but Dale was apparently used to ingesting alcohol in much larger quantities and on a more frequent basis.

"Mike told me you were a lawyer," Dale said, as he poured Chardonnay into Susan's glass. "That must be pretty glamorous work."

Susan laughed. "It's not like 'L.A. Law,' if that's what you're thinking. Most lawyers rarely, if ever, do trial work, but you'd never guess it to look at what they show you on television. I do family law mostly. Child custody, adoptions, child abuse, child neglect, stuff like that. And divorces, of course."

"Aha!" His eyes flashed. "So you're the dragon lady responsible for fleecing us poor guys out of our hard-earned money and handing it over to opportunistic gold diggers."

"Certainly not." She sniffed affectedly. "*My* clients are usually poor innocent housewives who get dumped after twenty years of marriage when the husband finds a new, young mistress. You don't think a woman's entitled to get something after giving up the best years of her life to take care of a man and his children?"

"I don't have any problem with that," he said. "If a woman makes a home for a man, I believe she deserves some compensation when the marriage ends. I paid my first wife alimony for five years, and I still make child support payments every month. My second wife was a different story. We were only married nine months, but she still took me to the cleaners at divorce time."

She looked at him curiously. "How many times have you been married, Dale?"

"Two." He looked into her eyes. "You look surprised. What were you expecting me to say, six?"

Susan stared at him intently as if he were an interesting sociological specimen. "I don't know what I was expecting. You do seem to have a way with the ladies."

"You mean because I flirt with my customers? They love that. I think some of those women come to me more for the attention that I give them than for the attention I give their cars."

"I think you're right."

He shrugged. "So what's wrong with that? If I can brighten somebody's day, what harm does it do?"

"Is that why you invited me out to dinner? To 'brighten my day?'"

"Maybe," he said cryptically.

"I thought it was because you wanted to thank me for selling you the Jaguar."

"That, too."

Susan eyed him strangely. "Dale," she said slowly, "I just remembered the weirdest thing. Mike wanted you to have that car."

He looked confused. "You mean it was in his will?"

"No, nothing like that. But I just remembered a conversation we had. Mike knew he was dying; he didn't want anybody to lie to him about it. We talked about everything, including funeral arrangements. I remember teasing him about the Jaguar, asking him if he wanted to be buried in it." Her voice choked up a little. "He kept his sense of humor till the end. He said, 'No, of course not. You can just bury it in the plot next to me.' Then he got serious and said, 'You can sell it to my mechanic. He's always wanted to buy it. Be sure to give him a good price.' I swear I didn't remember that until just now."

"Then I have both of you to thank," Dale said quietly. "And since Mike can't be here with us, we'll just have to have a drink in his honor. To Mike," he said solemnly.

"To Mike," Susan repeated.

They had just been served their entrees when the scenario Susan had most dreaded materialized. She saw someone that she knew.

"Susan!" Betsy Handelman cooed as she and her husband stopped on the way to their table. Betsy gave Dale a covert glance as she pressed Susan's hand warmly. "How have you been? I've been meaning to get over to see you, but we've just been so busy. How have you been?" she repeated nervously, and a little guiltily, Susan thought. "Time passes so quickly. It seems only a few weeks since the funeral." She lowered her voice as she uttered the last two words.

"It's been six months, Betsy," Susan said stiffly. She knew that she should introduce Betsy and Greg to Dale, but she couldn't think how to handle it. "This is my friend, Dale"? "This is Mike's mechanic"? No matter what she said, from the way Dale looked, they would probably think she had hired an escort service for lonely women.

Betsy and Greg were staring at Dale curiously but pretending not to. "I'm Dale Clemens," he said, rescuing Susan from her dilemma. Greg introduced himself and his wife, and woodenly shook hands with Dale. Betsy resumed chattering with Susan, but suddenly she glanced at Dale more directly.

"You look very familiar," she said, almost accusingly. "Where have I seen you? At the club?"

"I don't think so," Dale said evenly.

Betsy started to turn back to Susan but was obviously still bothered. "I *do* know you, don't I?" she said to Dale. "Do I look familiar to you?"

Dale smiled. "You do if you drive a tan Mercedes."

Betsy's face broke out into a relieved smile. "Dale. Of course." She turned to her husband. "Greg, this is the mechanic I've been telling you about. The one who did such a marvelous job on the Mercedes."

Greg nodded disinterestedly.

"I'm sorry I didn't recognize you before," Betsy apologized to Dale. "You look different."

"It's all right," he said sweetly. "People often don't recognize me without the dirt under my fingernails."

Betsy accepted the remark without noticing the sarcasm, but Susan saw the hurt in Dale's eyes. "How do you two know each other?" Betsy asked Susan.

It was Dale who answered and explained. He invited them to join in the celebration, but the Handelmans politely declined. "Dale, I'm sorry," Susan said shamefacedly, after they had walked on. "I was very rude to you. I just didn't know how to introduce you."

"You really *are* ashamed to be with me, aren't you?" he asked bitterly. "No matter how

47

hard I scrub my hands, I still have dirt under my fingernails."

"That's not true," she protested. "There's nothing lowly about what you do for a living. It's honest work, and you're good at it, and you're doing exactly what you want to do. Not many people can say that about their jobs. I do feel awkward about being with you, but it's not because I'm ashamed of you. It's because of how we look together. Dale, I felt like my friends thought I'd hired a gigolo."

He gave an exasperated sigh. "This is the age thing again, right?"

"Of course it is. Twelve years may not seem like a lot to you, but it's a whole generation. You and I grew up watching different television shows. We have different tastes in music."

"Maybe," he said, watching her eyes. "What kind of music do you like to listen to?"

"The Rolling Stones," she rattled off immediately. "The Beatles. Bruce Springsteen." She grinned sheepishly, recalling the stereo sounds blasting at the garage. "All right," she admitted, "maybe we're *not* so far apart in some ways. But I still feel like I could be your mother. I have grown children!"

"So do I."

This surprised her. "You do?"

Dale wiped his lips with his napkin. "Uh-huh. My son is nineteen and my daughter is twenty-one, the same age as your daughter. Susan," he said, as she remained silent for a moment, "I don't know why you're making such a big deal out of this. It's only dinner. I'm not asking you to marry me."

Suddenly Susan felt like a colossal fool. "I'm so embarrassed," she said. "I really have been talking stupidly."

Dale reached across the table and touched her cheek, forcing her to look into his sapient green eyes. "Susan," he said incisively, "I think maybe you're a little afraid that you might get to like me too much."

Susan lowered her eyes to her plate and began stabbing at her steak with her fork and knife, cutting furiously, as if all her concentration were required toward that object. Dale turned his face away, politely allowing her to recover her dignity, but he couldn't hide his triumphant satisfaction.

Three

"I'm sorry about what I said before," Dale said as he walked Susan to her door that evening. "It was rude and a little bit cruel."

And very perceptive, she thought to herself. She had been projecting out of this simple business dinner a relationship that was as ridiculous as it was impossible. It wasn't embarrassing enough just to have those feelings; his recognizing it only increased her discomfort.

"Would you like to come in?" she asked politely.

"I would, but I don't think you want me to."

"Well, you can't forget to take your champagne. You left almost a whole bottle here this afternoon."

Dale leaned casually against the muted red brick. "I wasn't intending to finish it by myself. Will you help me drink it?"

The champagne was smooth, but not enough

to cover Susan's uneasiness. She kept jumping up to go to the kitchen for chips, nuts, any excuse not to keep looking for long periods into Dale's beautiful green eyes.

"Will you sit still for a few minutes?" he said, laughing. He poured her a very full glass of champagne, and then walked around to the back of her chair.

"What are you doing?" she asked nervously, as she felt his fingers on her shoulders.

"Trying to get you to relax," he said, as his fingers massaged her neck and shoulders. Susan didn't want to relax. She wanted to keep alert and in control of her body. She was afraid of losing herself under the hypnotic power of those caressing fingers. But eventually she had to close her eyes. When she did, she felt herself on a beach in Galveston, forty years ago, with another set of nimble fingers massaging her body. She heard the murmur of the ocean and smelled the damp salt sticking to a young boy's sleek, tan chest . . .

"Is this helping any?" Dale asked.

"Yes," she purred, leaning back in her chair and propping her feet up on the ottoman. "It feels great."

He smiled with pleasure. "I told you I was good with my hands."

He continued to massage her muscles for a few more minutes, then took his drink and sat down on the section of the couch nearest her chair. After another minute he rose and removed his jacket, folding it neatly over the back of the sofa. Then he pulled off his tie and unbuttoned the top two buttons of his shirt.

"Does this bother you?" he asked, as he noticed Susan staring at his throat.

"No," she said, turning her head away from the tan smoothness of his exposed chest. "Make yourself comfortable." Susan would have liked to have gotten comfortable herself, as the dress was *very* short, and it was impossible to cross her legs without being unladylike or to remove the shell pink wrap for fear of exposing too much cleavage. But she couldn't excuse herself to change into something more comfortable. She would feel like a character in a predictable old romantic movie. And she certainly didn't want to extend to Dale any unwarranted invitations.

He noticed her restlessness, as he noticed everything. "Susan, why don't you go change into more comfortable clothes?" he suggested kindly. "You look like you're wearing a girdle that's stifling you."

He had a way of being direct, and maybe a little too personal, yet his intimate manner did not offend her. It reminded her so much of Jeff that she knew instinctively that Dale's presumptuousness had been intended as a courtesy, not a come-on.

She stood up and smoothed down the flared skirt until it brushed her knees. "I thought you liked this dress."

"It's not the dress I like; it's the way you look in it. If you were not a lady in mourning and I were not a gentleman, I would have been all over you by now." He examined the half-empty bottle of champagne. "But I don't want you to pass out from suffocation before we have a chance to finish the bottle." He stood and put his hands on her shoulders. "Go change. I'll keep your drink chilled for you."

When Susan came down again, wearing jeans and a loose, flowing T-shirt, she heard the strains of John Lennon's "Imagine" being played on her piano.

"You play very well," she said as he finished. "Did you take lessons when you were a kid?"

"No," he said, wheeling around on the bench to face her. "I can't even read music. My grandmother had an old spinet piano in her parlor, so I just taught myself. A few of the keys were broken, but they were at the high and low ends, and didn't matter very much. I used to play Beatles songs all the time until she threatened to throw me out." He grinned. "So I learned to play Cole Porter and George Gershwin tunes in self-defense." He turned back to the piano and played a very moving rendition of "Night and Day."

Susan noticed that the half-empty bottle of champagne was now, inexplicably, three-quarters full. Either her eyes were deceiving her, or Dale had finished off that bottle while she was upstairs and started another one.

"It's nice," Susan said softly, leaning against the piano. "I can't believe you play so well just by ear."

She meant it as a compliment, but Dale didn't take it that way. "You don't need a college degree for everything," he said stiffly. "You didn't think a dumb mechanic could teach himself to play piano?"

It was a damned-if-you-say-yes, damned-if-you-say-no question, the kind that lawyers like to spring on hapless witnesses. Susan avoided the trap by ignoring the question he'd asked and answering the challenge he had really thrown out to her.

"You're not dumb, Dale. Education isn't the only measure of intelligence. I envy your mechanical ability. I can't even change a fuse. It took Mike six hours to put together a Barbie dollhouse. To us, the three most frightening words in the English language have always been 'Some Assembly Required.' "

Dale smiled. This compliment he could handle. "Well, anytime you need help with your

54

fuses, just call me, Mama. I'll be glad to fix anything you have that needs fixing."

He said it with a straight face, not flirtatiously, and Susan assumed, at first, that it was an ingenuous remark. But then she noticed the subtlest twinkle in his eye. He did know what he'd said; he'd said it on purpose. Probably he had been just as aware of the suggestiveness in his earlier remarks.

She responded to his statement at its face value. "Don't tempt me to take advantage of you, Dale. This house is twenty-five years old and things are constantly falling apart. I'll be calling you up every week."

Dale closed the piano and stared at her seriously with those somber green eyes that seemed to read her true feelings. "That doesn't scare me, Lady," he said deliberately.

Susan looked, hypnotized, into his eyes for a long moment. Dale's eyes remained fixed on hers. He didn't even blink. Susan sensed with a strange certainty that she was looking into Jeff's eyes once again.

Dale moved back to the sofa, and Susan was about to resume her position in the chair, but he patted the space beside him and motioned for her to sit there. She stretched her feet over the rolled arm of the sofa and rested her head drowsily against Dale's shoulder. He didn't seem to mind. "You must have been very close to your grandparents," Susan remarked.

"My grandparents raised me. My mother was only sixteen years old when I was born."

Susan blinked. "Sixteen? My god, how old was she when she got married?"

"Twenty." Susan turned around and looked at him curiously. "I'm a bastard," he said cheerfully.

"Are you also illegitimate?" she asked with a straight face.

Dale laughed appreciatively. She was quick, this lady, even when she was drunk, and it had been a long time since he had been with a woman that sharp. He was enjoying this evening a lot more than he had expected.

Susan took another sip of her drink. "Why did your parents wait so long to get married?" she asked, then apologized. "Forget I said that. I'm getting too personal."

"I'd hate to be cross-examined by you on a witness stand," Dale chuckled. He downed his own drink and poured himself another glass. "It's all right, I don't mind. My mother was never married to my father. She was an innocent little farm girl who went to the city to live with her sister and brother-in-law and go to high school. Some lowlife took advantage of her and got her pregnant. She tried to raise me herself for a while. When she met my step-

56

father, though, he wasn't crazy about the idea of having a little kid around, so she dumped me with my grandparents."

"How awful for you!" Susan exclaimed.

"It wasn't awful," he declared. "My grandma was a great lady. She died two years ago, but I still miss her. Don't feel sorry for me, Susan. It was great growing up on the farm. We had one of the nicest spreads in southern Illinois. You ever been to Illinois?"

"No," she said. "Unless you count East St. Louis. I went to college in St. Louis."

"I was born in East St. Louis," Dale said darkly.

Susan's eyebrows raised for a second as a long-forgotten memory surfaced in her mind. She forced it back into her unconsciousness. "Did you ever see your mother again?"

"Oh, sure. But my stepfather and I never did get along, so it's just as well I didn't live with them. I probably would have had my butt beaten raw by the time I was eight." Dale emptied another glass and pushed it aside. "My mother lives in Kansas City now with her third husband. I think he's two years younger than I am."

Susan leaned her head into his shoulder. "No wonder you're not bothered by age differences. Have you ever met your real father?"

"I don't even know who my father was. My mother always told me I didn't have one."

Susan smiled. "And you believed her?"

Dale laughed. "Not after I passed the age of five. Growing up on a farm, you figure these things out early. But she obviously didn't want to talk about it, so I never asked her."

"Weren't you ever curious to know who your real father was?"

"What is this, Twenty Questions? No, I never was. He was some bastard who knocked up a teenage girl and then dumped her. Why would I care who the hell he was?"

"Maybe he didn't know," Susan mused softly, almost to herself.

"What?"

"Maybe he didn't know that she was pregnant. Maybe he wasn't a bastard. He could have been an innocent, stupid, teenage kid himself." An image from the past flashed across her brain, then disappeared.

"He could have been the President of the United States for all I care," Dale said flatly. "As far as I'm concerned, my mother was right. I never had a father."

The only hint of agitation in his face was a light twitching in his cheeks, but as he finished his glass of champagne in one swallow, bounced it on the table, and poured another, Susan guessed she'd hit a nerve.

"I guess we'd better call it a night," she said. "I think I've had a little too much to drink."

"You've hardly gotten started," he protested. "I'm way ahead of you." His eyes twinkled seductively as he held out another full glass to her.

"No thanks," she demurred. "That's all I can handle. If I don't quit now, I might do something that I shouldn't."

"That would be nice," Dale smiled. But he accepted her refusal. "Okay, Lady, me and my new Jaguar are out of here."

He didn't stumble as he rose to his feet, but Susan almost did from the potent stench of alcohol that washed over her face. She suddenly realized just how much Dale had had to drink. Besides the cocktails he'd had before dinner, he had consumed at least half of the bottle of white wine they'd had with their appetizer, and almost all of the Cabernet Sauvignon they'd had with their main course. Plus a couple of glasses of brandy after dessert. And who knows how many bottles of champagne he had stashed away tonight and replaced when she wasn't looking.

"I don't think so, Dale," she said peremptorily. "You're too drunk to drive home. Do you want to crack up your new car on the first day you own it?"

His smile was almost patronizing. "I've

driven a lot farther when I was a lot drunker than this. Anyway, I wasn't planning on driving home. I'm going to go back to the shop and sack out there. I *can* drive," he said firmly, although his tongue slurred lazily over even those three words. "Anyway, I have no choice."

"Yes, you do." She heard her next words as if somebody else were saying them. "You can spend the night here."

Dale looked at her silently.

"Oh, no!" she said, suddenly embarrassed and nervous. "I didn't mean . . . I meant downstairs . . . the couch . . . or a guest room . . ."

"I know what you meant. The couch is fine," he said gratefully. "If you're sure that's okay with you."

She started up the stairs. "I'll get you a pillow and some blankets."

"Don't bother. I don't need anything. I could sleep on the kitchen floor tonight and not feel a thing."

She watched him sink into the couch. "Good night, Dale."

"Good night, Suse."

She wheeled around sharply. "What did you say?"

He sat up, surprised by her tone. "I just said good night."

"I know. I mean, what did you call me?"

Dale looked quite confused. "Susan."

"No, you didn't," she said flatly. "You called me Suse."

"I guess I just shortened it a little," he said apologetically. "Was that a childhood nick-name you hated or something? Oh, I get it," he said softly. "That was Mike's name for you, wasn't it?"

She sank down on the bottom step of the stairwell. "No," she said almost to herself. "Not Mike's."

Dale got off the couch and went over and knelt on the floor a few feet away from her. "Do you want to talk to me about it, Susan? I'm a good listener." He reached out to touch her quivering fingers. "And I can keep a secret. If there's something bothering you that you can't talk to your friends about, talk to me."

It was so tempting. She had held these feelings in for so long. Susan sat holding her knees and rocking them, biding her time before she spoke. "It's not only Mike that I'm in mourning for," she explained finally. "My best friend was killed in a plane crash seven years ago. It may seem like a long time, but I still miss him."

If Dale was surprised by the gender of her best friend, he didn't show it. Instead, he sat silently, his face practically devoid of emotion, waiting for her to continue.

"I know this is going to sound like I didn't love my husband," she said, "but that's not so. I loved Mike very much. It's just that—"

"Susan," he interrupted softly, "I'm not going to judge you. I liked Mike a lot, but he's gone now, and nothing you say can hurt him. You don't have to make excuses or apologies to anyone—certainly not to me."

She looked up at him gratefully, then lowered her eyes to her knees again. "It's not that I don't feel grief over Mike. In the beginning I felt it so bad that I actually had chest pains that lasted for hours at a time. When you lose someone that close to you, it hits you like a ton of bricks. Everything you see, everything you touch, reminds you of him and makes you expect to see him there as always. When you don't, the pain of remembrance hits you. Not once, but a hundred times an hour. It's like signals bombarding your every waking moment, telling you he's gone, only not so nicely; screaming at you 'He's dead!' and forcing you to face it. Even when you sleep, you can't get away from it. I never used to reach out for Mike at night. I didn't need to; I knew he was there. Now I do it all the time, or I did, after it first happened. And every time you reach and feel nothing but air, it wakes you up and reminds you again.

"When this happens to you hour after hour, day after day, month after month, it sinks in. I know Mike is dead. I hardly ever expect to see him anymore. I still miss him, of course, especially when I hear a certain song on the radio or do certain things that we used to do together. But the pain is beginning to dull. It's not a constant throbbing anymore, just a little, whining ache that makes you feel empty all the time and reminds you how lonely you are."

She paused for breath. "At least with Mike, we knew it was coming. We had time to prepare ourselves for it and say our goodbyes. With Jeff it was different. It was like in one second a light switched off and he was gone forever." She reached for Dale's hand to steady herself. "Dale, he was my best friend for thirty-five years. We were closer than brother and sister. I knew him for ten years before I even met Mike. He was always there for me. And suddenly, just like that, he's not there anymore. I feel like I never got to tell him goodbye. You know how you hear about these haunted houses where the ghost of some murdered person remains in the bedroom because it didn't die properly and move on to the next world?" Dale nodded. "Well, that's how I feel. Like he's still around here, haunting me, asking me to let him go, and I can't." She burst out sobbing. "I loved him so much!"

Dale moved closer to her and took her head in his hands. Knocking her from her first-step perch, he pressed her face to his chest and let her cry warm, copious tears into his shirt. Just as Jeff would have done.

After a few minutes she sat up and reached her hand around his waist to the back of his pants. Dale gave her a questioning look and flinched a little as she dug her fingers into his back right pocket. "I hope you don't mind," she said, as she dried her eyes and blew her nose into the handkerchief that she found there.

"No," he said, slightly amused. "I just didn't know what the hell you were doing at first. How did you know I had a handkerchief there?"

His eyes widened at her simple, matter-of-fact answer. "Jeff always kept his handkerchief in that pocket," she said. "You remind me of him so much, Dale. The resemblance is sometimes uncanny."

Dale grinned. "I guess he must have been a really good-looking guy," he teased.

"Yes, and he was conceited, too." She folded the corners of the handkerchief over themselves as she watched his eyes. "It's not just your looks," she confessed. "It's your personality, your gestures, your sense of humor. That's why I came unglued when you called me 'Suse.' Jeff was the only person who ever called me that."

Dale phrased his next question delicately. "Am I hearing you say that you think Jeff's presence is still around and that you think I'm his ghost?"

"You think I've really flipped out, don't you? No, Dale, I'm not crazy. I know Jeff is dead. And I know you are you, not him. It's just that I've had such a hard time getting over him."

She sighed and stretched her legs out to increase the circulation. "Jeff and I were very close emotionally, but we didn't actually spend that much time together. For most of those thirty-five years we were living in different cities, sometimes even different continents. So his death didn't hit me as forcefully at first as Mike's did. Even now, I sometimes forget. I'll be reading an article in the news and I'll think, 'I ought to call Jeff and tell him about this.' And then I'll have to remind myself that he's gone. It's like every time it happens, I get stabbed in the heart all over again!"

Susan's voice got softer and weaker. "I miss him so much. It's been a long time, but I still need him, especially with Mike gone. Now I feel like I need Jeff more than I ever did."

Her voice broke, and her chest heaved helplessly with dry tears. Dale put his arm around her. "I know I can't replace Mike, Susan. But if you'll let me, maybe I can try to fill some of the void that Jeff left."

She put her arms around him and hugged him tightly. His body felt like Jeff's once had, warm and inviting and nonthreatening.

Dale helped her to her feet and moved her with him into the darkened living room, keeping one arm around her as he placed a romantic Natalie Cole CD on the player. "Would you care to dance, Mrs. Riesman?"

Dale was a wonderful dancer. Susan had known that he would be. She had known that her body would follow his like an echo. He held her respectfully at arm's length, but his grip was firm and supportive.

She placed her arm tentatively around Dale's neck. "You can hold me tighter if you want to," he said kindly. Susan hated herself for doing it, but she pressed her body against the warm expanse of his chest, letting him guide her to the music. His arms felt so good. They were strong and warm and sheltering, encircling her easily as if they knew her body belonged inside them. Susan closed her eyes, concentrating only on the music and the feel of Dale's masterful hands on her body.

Intense yearnings began coursing through her loins. Guiltily she closed her eyes even tighter and tried to pretend that she was dancing with Mike. To no avail. Mike had never danced like this. She had never danced like this with Mike. She had never been able to dance in such perfect harmony with anybody before, except one person.

Suddenly it all came back to her again. Suddenly she was no longer a fifty-three-year-old woman in a comfortable living room in suburban Los Angeles. She was a teenager in Houston, Texas, waltzing to Natalie Cole's father's "Unforgettable," in the arms of the boy who first taught her to dance. If she let her heart remember, she could feel Jeff's magic fingers on her waist; she could smell his shampoo as he drew her close to his body and twirled her away again.

Susan moved as if in a dream, her body mimicking flawlessly Dale's fluid, graceful steps. There was no denying now whose arms Dale's felt like. The way he held her, the way he moved her, the way her feet followed his without even thinking about it.

"You're a terrific dancer!" Dale said in surprise.

"I'm not," Susan said dispassionately. "I'm

just following you. *You* are the wonderful dancer. You dance just like your—"

She gasped and her knees buckled under as she realized what she had almost said.

Four

"Susan!" Dale caught her just before she hit the ground. "Are you okay?"

"I'm fine," she mumbled, although the walls were spinning around her and the floor was sliding away under her feet.

"No, you're not." He raised her to a standing position, keeping his arm braced at her back for support. "You *have* had too much to drink, and it's my fault. I've been egging you on to match my speed, and you're not used to it." His right arm glided down her back and tucked under her arms while his left slipped under her bent knees.

"Dale!" she shrieked, as he lifted her in his strong arms and started to carry her up the stairs. "What the hell do you think you're doing?"

"Putting you to bed," he said calmly. "Don't worry, Mama," he winked. "I don't have any bad intentions. Even if I did," he added rue-fully, "I doubt I could do much about it in my condition."

For some reason, his assurances calmed her completely. Maybe it was because of his half-joking, half-respectful reference to the difference in their ages. Or maybe it was just that Dale Clemens appeared to be a man whose word could be trusted. She let her body go limp in his arms.

Dale stopped expectantly at the top of the stairs. "Well, tell me which way, Mama," he said. "I don't mind carrying you, but you're a little heavy for me to be standing here holding you all day."

"Sorry." She pointed toward her bedroom. He carried her to her bed and tucked her under the bedspread. "Good night and sleep tight," he whispered, in the manner of a father tucking in his child. His face hovered over hers momentarily as he brushed a lock of brown hair out of her eyes. He closed the bedroom door quietly behind him.

Susan listened intently as his footsteps ech-oed down the stairs. She knew she should get up and lock the door. There was, after all, a strange man in her house, a man she had known less than two weeks. She tried to raise her shoulders from the bed but her body sank back into the mattress like a tree felled by an ax. She was a granite pillar that could not be moved.

Sleep eluded her. Memories she had tried to bury pounded her consciousness like surf against the sand. She willed herself back to the present, but when she tried to conjure up a vision of Dale's handsome face, she couldn't remember what he looked like. Whenever she closed her eyes, it was Jeff's face she saw in front of her, Jeff's arms she felt around her in a warm, wonderful embrace. She forced herself to concentrate, to rip away the intruder's face, and suddenly she saw Dale again. Then he disappeared. The faces kept changing, from one with golden brown hair and mustache to one with silky blond hair and smooth skin; everything kept changing except the eyes. Everywhere she looked she saw the same gray-green expressive eyes watching her, taunting her. Her head spun like a pinwheel from Jeff to Dale to Jeff. And then to Mike. Mike was sitting in some kind of lawn chair, levitating off the ground, laughing.

Susan wasn't awakened by her alarm the next morning. Instead, she felt, rather than heard, a shadowy presence enter her bedroom. "Mike?" she asked automatically, still half-asleep, not at all frightened.

"It's Dale," said Jeff's voice. He leaned over her and tucked the covers up to her chin, kissing her softly on the cheek. "I'm going to work now. Go back to sleep. I'll be in touch."

She didn't see or hear from Dale the rest of the week or the next week either. There was no reason why she should, Susan reminded herself. Their business relationship was over; he had paid for the car and owned it free and clear. There were things in her house that needed repair, and she considered calling him to fix them. But she was afraid she would look like a middle-aged matron with a schoolgirl crush on a much younger man, which she was.

Not that age was any longer the sole impediment in the strange relationship that had developed between them. If Dale was who she thought he was, the problem was a lot bigger than she ever could have imagined.

She threw herself into her work, determined to put the infatuation out of her mind. Work had always had a stabilizing effect on her. The law was so precise and predictable, a comforting respite from the vagaries of her often erratic personal life. When the kids were younger and had driven her crazy with their whining or sibling fights, she had often retreated to the privacy of her office in the late hours of evening, there to find sanctuary in simple, methodical research. By the time Susan had cleared her head and was ready to return home to face real life again, Mike usually had the kids tucked away in bed and a glass of chilled wine waiting for her.

She smiled wistfully and gazed at the photograph on her desk, one of Mike when his hair was still black and curly, balancing both children on his knees. He had been a wonderful father. A wonderful husband. There was no way that she could ever replace him. A woman would have to be crazy to even think about trying.

"How's it going, Susan?" Ron Davis knocked politely at her open office door. It was after seven on a Saturday evening, and the few other attorneys who had come in that day had long since left. "You've been putting in a lot of hours lately." He leaned lazily against the doorjamb. "Are you starting to get back in the swing of things?"

"I guess so. Thanks, Ron. Thanks for understanding."

"No problem." Her boss smiled and sauntered to the window. "Glad to do anything I can to help." He angled his hip against the windowsill and propped his outstretched leg on the square black trash can next to the file cabinet. "You've got a nice view here. Better than mine," he grinned. His eyes scanned the Los Angeles skyline as his fingers stroked his graying temples. "Reminds me of watching the sunset over Tokyo on my last vacation with Peggy." Ron's eyes turned somber and his lower lip curled down sadly.

Susan stared at the photograph on her desk and felt her own eyes go misty. "How long does it take before you stop missing them, Ron? How long before you feel normal again?"

His eyes turned away from the window and scanned her face and hair, taking in the still-youthful features and the healthy brown roots mingling among the few straggly gray ones. "You never stop missing them, Susan. The pain goes away slowly, but the loneliness never does." Moving toward her chair, he placed his hand on her shoulder. "Not unless you find something or someone to fill up that empty place in your life."

Susan was still gazing at Mike's picture, so she didn't notice the expression in Ron's eyes. She might not have been able to read it even if she had. It held sympathy, but also wistfulness. And a flicker of hope. Without turning around, she laid her hand silently over his. Two lonely souls who understood what was in each other's heart shared a moment of comfort together.

Ron dropped his hand abruptly and moved

to the door, cutting by his stride the sentimentality that had suddenly embarrassed him. "How long were you planning to stay tonight, Susan?"

"Maybe another hour or two. I've got a custody hearing on the Bryan children on Wednesday."

He nodded. "I've got a bit of paper shuffling to do myself. I'll stay awhile and follow you home. I don't like the idea of you driving to that empty house alone after dark. That Gentleman Rapist is still on the loose."

Susan thanked him with her eyes. There had been practically nothing else on the local news lately. The Gentleman Rapist, so called because he dressed nicely and spoke in a refined manner, had thus far assaulted six women in Susan's area of town.

She was watching the latest updates on the twelve o'clock news that night when the doorbell rang. Susan caught her breath apprehensively. She switched off the television and listened more closely, thinking perhaps it had been her imagination. The bell rang again. Wrapping her robe around her pajamas, she crept quietly to the door. The Gentleman Rapist didn't usually force entry into houses; generally he posed as a stranded motorist and was admitted willingly by unsuspecting housewives. The most prudent response, she decided, was no response. Unless it was a burglar checking the house. In that case, ignoring the bell just might be an invitation to enter.

"Who is it?" she rasped harshly, trying to peer out the peephole into the darkness.

"It's Dale," came the voice.

"I'm sorry to disturb you at this hour," he apologized, after she had undone the chain latch and unlocked the two deadbolts. "I was driving by and saw your lights on, and I thought that you were still up."

"I *was* up, I was just watching TV," she said. "Is anything wrong?"

He shook his head as she ushered him inside. He wore jeans and a solid black T-shirt under a casual plaid jacket, the sleeves of which were rolled up to his elbows, Don Johnson-style. "Nothing's wrong. I was just about to drive home, and I thought maybe you wouldn't mind if I just sacked out here on your couch instead. If it's a problem," he added hurriedly, glancing about in the sudden realization that she might have company, "just tell me to go away. I won't be at all insulted."

"No, it's no problem. I didn't hear the Jaguar drive up," she said suspiciously, peeking out the blinds to see if it was parked out in front.

"I've got the truck. I parked farther down the street. I didn't want to taint the reputation of a respectable widow." His voice was teasing, but his face was serious.

"You knew I'd say yes, didn't you?" Susan smiled.

"No, I didn't. But it doesn't hurt to be discreet."

I'll bet you know all about that, she thought to herself. "Do you want some coffee?" she asked, and was already plodding toward the kitchen to make a strong pot before he answered.

"No, thanks. Why would I want coffee at this hour?"

Why indeed? Just because Jeff had often showed up at her house at this same hour of the night and consumed three or more cups of black coffee while they talked on into the wee hours? "I'll get you some linens," she said practically. "But you don't have to sleep on the couch. I mean," she added hastily, blushing just slightly, "there are three guest bedrooms upstairs. I could put you in my son's old room."

Dale's eyes roamed over the expanse of her green silk pajamas, clinging smoothly to her still-firm breasts. "I think I'd better stay down here," he said prudently.

He sank down on the couch wearily, his eyes barely focusing. Susan wrapped her robe about her more securely this time and sat down beside him. "So what happened tonight?" she asked curiously. "You struck out on a date?"

Dale smiled faintly. "Lady, you really have a way of cutting right to the chase. Must be the lawyer in you. Why don't you just kick me in the gut and get it over with?"

She grinned. "Sorry. Do you want to talk about it?"

He closed his eyes as if the effort of speaking made him tired. "There's not much to talk about. I was dating this woman for about four months. We broke up tonight."

Susan patted his shoulder sympathetically, startled by the electricity that shot through her fingers as she touched him. "I'm sorry, Dale."

"What's to be sorry about? These things happen. We had some good times. They ended. So did we."

"Is that what it's all about?" she mused thoughtfully. "Good times?"

"No, that's not what I think," Dale said seriously. "I think it's about more than that. But more than that is very tough to find." His eyes took on a dreamy expression, then closed again.

He wasn't shy about expressing his thoughts, but he was less comfortable sharing his feelings. Susan sensed that the evening's breakup had affected Dale more than he was admitting.

"Do you think you'll ever get married again, Dale?" Susan asked gently.

"Go for number three? With my track record? No. I'm a two-time loser, Susan. It's time I cut my losses and tried something else."

"Like what? A life of one-night stands? A different girl on your arm every night?" Suddenly she saw Jeff in front of her again.

"I don't do that. I've never done that. No, I wouldn't mind getting involved in a serious relationship. Maybe even a permanent relationship. But it has to be just right next time. I feel old, Susan, and I guess I'm getting lazy and selfish. I'm tired of working hard at relationships. I'm bored with all the stupid chatter you have to do to get into one, and I'm disgusted with the song-and-dance routines you have to go through to get out of one. I know it's the impossible dream, but I'd like to find myself suddenly transplanted into a relationship that had already been developed over a number of years, with a woman who knew me well, someone I didn't have to play games with. Somebody I could feel comfortable with, just being myself."

His eyes were half-closed, but Susan could still feel them staring at her, studying her, undressing her with their X-ray vision. She grabbed her robe, certain it had come loose again, but it was still snugly wrapped around her.

At last he looked up. "How about you, Susan?" he asked. "Do you think you'll ever get married again?"

"Me?" She looked at him as if he were joking. "I'm too old to get married again. Who would want me?"

"Don't be coy," he said. "Women older than you get married every day."

"Well, *I* wouldn't want to get married every day," she joked. "Seriously, I can't see getting married to some old codger, moving in together, and pooling our social security checks. I wouldn't want a marriage of companionship. I'm a big girl. A woman doesn't need to have a man in her life in order to feel fulfilled."

"Do you really mean that, or are you just saying it because you think that's what you're expected to say?"

She glared at him. This man could really be incisive, even cocky. He barely knew her, and yet he acted like he understood everything about her. Jeff all over again.

"I really mean it. I had a good marriage. I don't know if I could ever duplicate that."

"You don't believe that lightning strikes twice? You don't think that you could ever fall in love again?"

It already has struck twice, Susan thought to

herself as she fetched some linens and a pillow from the hall closet. *I've been lucky enough in my life to love and be loved by two wonderful men. It couldn't happen again.*

Dale's body was already easing itself into a horizontal position on the couch. He raised his head willingly as she placed the pillow under his neck. "You've been drinking, haven't you?" she asked, smelling the liquor on his breath.

"A little," he admitted. "That's why I didn't want to drive home. Thanks for putting me up and putting up with me."

Anytime, she thought sarcastically. *Anytime you're too drunk to drive home, anytime your date doesn't work out, feel free to drop in at Casa Riesman. I'm always here, I'm always available. You don't have to make small talk or be charming. Just walk all over me anytime you feel like it.*

"You're welcome," she said out loud, as she ascended the stairs.

She knew he was using her, but she was still glad to have him sleeping under her roof again. This time she *did* lock her bedroom door, and checked the latch twice before trudging around to her side of the bed.

Six months after Mike's death, Susan still slept only on her accustomed half of the king-sized mattress. Thirty years of habit wouldn't permit her to move over into the space his body had once filled; even an inch over the boundary seemed like trespassing.

Usually Susan took comfort in the empty half of the bed; it protected her from thoughts and feelings she didn't want to think and feel. But tonight a restlessness pervaded her body. It was a special kind of restlessness that she hadn't experienced in quite a long time, but the symptoms of which she recognized immediately. Her skin tingled with the pleasure of remembered sensations. There was a fullness in her breasts and a stiffness in her nipples. She couldn't help touching herself.

Susan buried her head in her pillow and sobbed silently. She had thought these feelings had been buried with Mike. Even before that, seven years ago. But now as she clutched the king-sized pillow tightly against her body, she imagined her arms were circling a large, broad back. And as she rocked herself soothingly against the comforting form, she pretended that she was pressing her bare breasts against a smooth chest and wrapping her legs around a pair of strong thighs.

Five

It was afternoon before the sun streaming through her bedroom window finally roused Susan from a state of semiconsciousness. She plodded quietly downstairs. Dale was still asleep on the couch, the blanket tucked up under his chin, his face turned slightly toward her. She leaned over him quietly, studying the smooth contours and well-shaped features of his face. He looked so peaceful, relaxed in a state of deep repose. Jeff had had the same innocent expression about him when he slept. It was the only time the tension had ever completely left his face. Susan shuddered. It couldn't be true. It just couldn't be. The strong resemblance had to be merely coincidental. She refused to believe it could be anything else.

She made up a pot of coffee in the kitchen. After gulping her first cup, she poured another for her houseguest. She set cup and saucer on the end table next to the couch and watched Dale sleep. The blanket had slipped down to his waist, exposing a tan, almost hairless chest. Susan leaned against the back of the couch and watched Dale's smooth, muscular chest rise and fall, feeling a sweet maternal affection for him.

Who are you kidding, Susan? sneered her tell-it-like-it-is self. You don't feel the least bit maternal toward him. You are very attracted to this man.

Dale had a tattoo on his left shoulder with the name "Paula" emblazoned on it. Susan also noticed a small scar just below his right breast, about half an inch long, consisting of several small stitches. As she reached out curiously to touch his flesh, Dale's eyelids flickered open. "G'morning," he said with a contented smile.

"Good morning," Susan said. "Actually, it's already afternoon. I thought you were an early riser."

"Six days a week," he yawned, stretching his arms above his head. Susan's eyes darted involuntarily from the thick muscles of his biceps to the golden brown tufts of hair protruding from his armpits. "Sunday's the only day I get to sleep in." Gratefully he sipped the cup of coffee she handed him. "I hope I haven't interfered with your plans."

"No, I just got up myself. Who's Paula?" she asked curiously, staring at his shoulder. "Your ex-wife?"

He followed her eyes to the tattoo. "No, my mother."

Susan looked at him in surprise, wondering if he was joking. "Were they all out of 'Mom' tattoos?"

"No, I've just always called my mother by her first name. She always seemed more like a big sister than a mother to me." He sat up and turned his right shoulder toward her. "This one's of my ex-wife." The name "Diane" screamed up in bold letters from a colorful tattoo.

"First or second?"

"First. The second didn't stick around long enough to etch a place on my body."

Susan smiled and pointed to the scar. "How did you get that?"

"You're playing Twenty Questions again, aren't you?" Dale teased. He touched the scar with his finger. "Somebody took a shot at me one night when I was trying to repossess a car."

Susan was horrified. "You do that, too? Repossess cars?"

"No, not now. That was just a job I had

85

when I was younger." He reached for his pants, which lay folded across the back of the couch. "Would you please leave the room or at least turn around so I can put my pants on?"

Susan was amused by his modesty. "Dale, I was married for thirty years and I have a twenty-four-year-old son. Believe me, you haven't got anything I haven't seen before."

"Is that so? Well, you haven't seen it on *my* body before. I won't even undress in front of my own mother." He grabbed the thin blanket and tucked it in carefully around his waist.

Susan smiled in the most motherly fashion she could manage and turned her back while Dale scrambled into his pants. When she turned back around, he was just zipping them up. Her eyes couldn't help but stare at the way the material stretched snugly over his body, especially where the zipper was. She forced her eyes away, only to have them settle on his broad bare chest. "Would you like to take a shower?" she blurted out.

He grinned. "Do I smell that bad?"

She blushed. "No, of course not. I just thought . . ."

Dale grinned again, as if he knew he was making her self-conscious and was enjoying doing it. "I *would* like to, if you don't mind." He grabbed the rest of his clothes and sauntered casually up the stairs as if he knew exactly where he was going and was used to going there.

When Dale came downstairs after his shower, he looked vibrant and healthy and well-scrubbed, as fresh as the sky after a rain. His wet hair glistened gold under the fluorescent lighting. He was wearing a shirt now, but it was not the same one he had worn last night. Clinging to his body, without benefit of undershirt, was a short-sleeved dress shirt with pencil-thin blue stripes running vertically through the white cotton blend.

"I hope you don't mind my borrowing Mike's shirt," he said apologetically. He wrinkled his nose at the balled-up black T-shirt in his right hand. "This one smells pretty bad."

She shook her head dumbly, unable to speak. There were very few items of Mike's clothing left in her closet, and the shirt he had picked was not one of them. It had been stashed in the back of the closet, unworn for seven years. It had been Jeff's shirt.

"You didn't have to do this," Dale smiled, as his eyes fell on the plates of pancakes, eggs, toast, and fried potatoes waiting on the small kitchen table. "You're going to spoil me, Lady."

Susan shrugged helplessly. "I'm a Jewish mother; what do you expect? Eat, eat," she said encouragingly, as he waited expectantly. "A young man needs to eat a good breakfast to keep up his strength."

The smile fell away from his face and was replaced by an intent, serious expression. "I'm not such a young man, Susan," he informed her dryly.

Susan shivered as his eyes stripped away her defensive shield. He knew. He knew she had made those statements to distance herself from him, to protect herself against feelings that she deemed inappropriate for a woman her age. At least as regarded a man of his age. Strangely, Dale seemed annoyed rather than relieved by her careful line-drawing exercise. He didn't seem to be at all discomfited by the possibility of a more intimate kind of relationship developing between them.

It had been a long time since she had breakfasted with a man at her small kitchen table. In some ways, it felt positively sinful. Yet, in other ways, perfectly normal. As if she were having breakfast with a man she'd known for years and with whom she felt perfectly comfortable. As if she were having breakfast with Mike.

"How long were you married, Dale?"

He stabbed his knife into the butter and smeared some on his toast. "The first time? Twelve years. Diane and I were high school sweethearts. We got married when I was nineteen. We struggled through some tough times, but all in all, they were good years."

"You still love her, don't you?"

Dale hesitated only a second. "No," he said slowly. "Not anymore. We got married very young, Susan. We were in love, but we grew up, and when we did, we grew apart."

"Do you still keep in contact with her?"

"Of course. She's the mother of my children. She lives in San Diego. I go down there pretty often to visit my son."

"What about your daughter? Where is she?"

"Here. She's a senior at U.C.L.A."

"So is my daughter," Susan said in surprise.

Dale smiled. "You see? I told you we had more in common than you think." He rose to pour himself another cup of coffee. "You ready for more coffee, Susan?" She held her empty cup out to him. "Cream and sugar?"

She nodded. "It does my heart good to see a man serve coffee."

"But I don't type, and I don't pick up dry cleaning." He returned to sit beside her.

"What about your second wife, Dale? You sound so bitter about her."

"I am bitter. But it was my own fault for thinking with my dick instead of my head." He glanced at Susan, concerned that his frank language might have offended her, but her eyes told him to continue.

"I married Judy, in all honesty, because I was hot for her body. I should have just lived with her until the infatuation cooled down, but I was stupid. After we'd been married only a few months, I realized I'd made a mistake. Judy was selfish and an inveterate shopper, and she really didn't give a damn about me or my needs. She was also pretty hollow from the neck up, which I really didn't notice in the beginning because I was so obsessed with the other parts of her anatomy."

"And when you did notice, it bothered you?"

He glared at her. "I may not have gone to a fancy college like you did, Susan, but I'm not quite as dumb as I look. I like intelligent women."

She hadn't intended her remark to be insulting, but Dale had apparently taken it that way. He was so sensitive about his lack of education.

"Thanks for the bed and breakfast," he said, wiping his mustache with a napkin.

"You're leaving?" Susan asked with poorly concealed disappointment. Of course he's leaving, Susan, she chided herself. So he spent the night on your couch, used your shower, and generally made himself at home. Did you expect him to move in?

Dale nodded. "I've taken up enough of your

Sunday. If I leave now, I can get in a few holes of golf while it's still light out."

He scooped up his dishes and carried them to the sink. "How long has this been like this?" he asked, noticing the dripping faucet.

"A couple of days. It'll stop if you turn it tightly, but it's not worth the effort."

He wiped his hands on a towel. "Got any tools?"

Dale fixed her leaky faucet and the broken spring in the toaster. He replaced the light bulb over the stove that she'd been meaning to change for weeks. "What else?" he said.

"Dale, you shouldn't have to work on your day off," Susan protested. "I can pay someone to do these things."

"You could, but you won't. And you can't or won't do them yourself. You need a man around here to help you take care of things. What else?"

She wanted to take umbrage at his chauvinistic remark, but its truth was irrefutable. She *did* need a man around the house. And not just to fix the wiring and plumbing. Sheepishly she handed him her "To Do" list of minor repairs that had been waiting much too long for attention.

Feeling helpless and ineffectual just standing around watching him work, she retreated to the kitchen to put on a pot of spaghetti sauce. Cooking was her way of dealing with minor stresses and anxieties, and spaghetti was one of her favorite comfort foods. She stood for a long time in front of the stove, numbly stirring the sauce, enjoying the sounds of Dale working in the other room. A sense of inner peace began to envelop her. It felt like a comfortable Sunday afternoon from the not-so-distant past, with Mike working on blueprints in the study and the kids playing outside or watching TV in the upstairs bedrooms.

She was startled out of her serenity when Dale came in to wash his hands after his chores. "Good luck on your golf game," she smiled, determined not to be clinging, resolving not to say or do anything else to try to make him stay longer.

"Too late for that now," he mumbled, eyeing the darkening skies that signified an early sunset. "I guess I'll just grab a hamburger somewhere and head home."

"I've got some spaghetti sauce cooking on the stove."

So much for her intentions. She couldn't believe she was being so transparent. But Dale didn't notice or, if he did notice, didn't care. He was apparently one of those men whose stomach was, if not the way to his heart, at least the direction in which the rest of his body happily followed.

"This was delicious," he said after eagerly lapping up three helpings of spaghetti and meatballs and dredging his French bread thoroughly through the remaining sauce. "You're a great cook, Lady." He stood and stretched his arms above his head. "I really should be going now." But he didn't head toward the door. Instead he wandered into the living room and seated himself in front of the TV, stretching his long legs under the coffee table.

"That section reclines," Susan said, showing him how to pull the footrest up.

"Thanks," he said. He didn't say much more. He didn't mention leaving again, and Susan didn't remind him.

The program he was watching was a PBS documentary about the Mayan Indians of Mexico. Susan found it only marginally interesting herself. But Dale seemed to be engrossed in the program. Susan sat down silently at the other end of the sofa and propped up her feet. She watched the TV intermittently, soothed by the droning monotone of the narrator's voice and the easy companionship of the man sitting at the opposite end of the couch.

It felt nice to spend the evening doing nothing special, just deriving comfort from another's presence. Susan hadn't realized till just now how edgy she had been these past few months. She had never felt relaxed when she was alone in the house at night. Every sound made her jittery; every few minutes found her eyes trained warily on the front door. Tonight, for the first time in a long time, she wasn't afraid. She had to admit she was comforted by having a man in the house again.

Not that Dale was paying that much attention to her. Except to acknowledge her bringing him food or drink, he seemed to be barely aware of her presence. But when she leaned back her head and half-closed her eyes in contentment, he patted his knee and held his arm out for her, urging her to move over and rest her head in his lap. Susan hesitated a moment, then slowly scooted close to him. Dale folded her in the wing of his arm and stroked her hair absentmindedly as his eyes returned to the screen.

She could easily have been with Mike, sharing the subtle pleasure of just being together usually appreciated only by couples who have lived together for years. She thought about what Dale had said the night before, about wanting to be with a woman that he felt comfortable with. He certainly seemed comfortable now. Dale's head angled itself against Susan's shoulder. He was half-dozing as the TV program ended, the evening's carnage report flashed on and off, and the opening credits of the late movie began to roll across the screen.

"I didn't realize it was so late," he said, returning his chair to its upright position. "I'm on my way home."

"You can stay if you like," Susan offered, before she could stop the words from coming out.

He shook his head but seemed neither shocked nor titillated by her proposal. "No, this time I'm really going," he smiled. "I don't even have a clean uniform for work tomorrow. I haven't been home since Friday morning."

Susan watched the taillights of the retreating pickup long after it had disappeared from sight, pondering his departing words. He had spent Saturday night and most of Sunday on her living-room couch. She wondered with just a tinge of jealousy on whose couch, or more likely, in whose bed, he had spent Friday night.

Dale began to drop over after work once or twice a week, sometimes bringing a six-pack of beer with him and a pizza. Usually, however, he took advantage of Susan's hospitality and cooking ability and allowed himself to be invited for dinner. Susan didn't *really* mind. It was nice to have somebody to cook for again, but it would have been nicer if he had called first.

Sometimes he only stayed for dinner, hurrying off afterward to what was presumably a date with a young lady. Susan never questioned him for details. He apparently thought of her as a substitute mother and her home as a convenient place to relax between his work and his social life.

Susan's evenings took on an interesting, unpredictable color. She never knew if Dale was going to come over, or, if he did, if he would stay awhile. She told herself that she was foolish to make his visits the highlight of her days. He was obviously using her, choosing to be in her company only when he had nothing more exciting going on. But she couldn't stop herself from beginning to care for him.

She was cleaning off her desk at five-thirty one afternoon when Ron Davis came into her office.

"I see you've got everything under control," he said approvingly. He flicked an imaginary piece of lint off his suit jacket and cleared his throat. "You want to go out and get a bite to eat with me tonight?"

Susan hesitated. Dale had said he might drop over this evening. "I don't think so, Ron," she said slowly. "I'm really pretty tired tonight. I'll probably just make a can of soup and fall into bed."

Visible disappointment washed over Ron's face, and Susan knew immediately she had done the wrong thing. In the fifteen years she'd worked for him, her boss had never before asked her out to dinner. Probably he had something on his mind that he wanted to discuss with her, maybe even a new project. Susan had been wanting for years to do a criminal case. This could have been a good opportunity for her to sell herself to her boss. It might have meant a raise or a promotion or at least a favorable attitude from the man who made those decisions. But she had blown it because of her crazy obsession with a youthful, handsome car mechanic.

Dale started coming over almost every night, and he wasn't always in a hurry to leave right after dinner. Sometimes he lingered until nine or ten or later, staying to watch TV or listen to music or play the piano while Susan did needlepoint or worked on legal briefs. He didn't ask her out to dinner again, or out anywhere, but he seemed quite comfortable in her company. Occasionally they talked until late into the night. Susan never asked him to stay over. When she saw that tired look come into his eyes, she just got up and fetched some linens, placing them beside him on the couch.

She didn't tell any of her friends about Dale, and when her children called and asked what was new, she never mentioned him. It wasn't that she was ashamed of him. It was just that they had such a strange relationship. She knew that he dated, almost every weekend, but whenever he wasn't on a date, he seemed to be at her house, and he seemed to take it for granted that she would always be there for him whenever he appeared. And she always was.

Although she tried to keep her time with Dale separate and secluded from her "real life," eventually, inevitably, his compelling presence spilled over into her daytime life as well. She was working on the computer at her office when her secretary informed her that she had a call.

"Susan, this is Dale," he said, as she came on the line.

"I know who it is," she said curtly. He had never called her at the office before. Was she annoyed at him, she wondered, for invading the sanctity of her professional identity? Or was she angry at herself for the way her fingers trembled at the sound of his voice?

He had a car to deliver to someone in her building and asked if she would be able to join him for lunch. "I'll just wait for you in your lobby, if that's all right."

She couldn't help thinking how handsome Dale looked, even in his grease-stained mechanic's uniform. "Your car is in the lot on the second floor, Mrs. Riesman," he said, keeping his eyes lowered as if in respect, as if a serviceman would not be so bold as to look directly into the eyes of the customer. The receptionist at the information desk looked up with interest for a brief second, then resumed filing her nails.

"Why did you do that?" she asked him as they walked outside the glass doors of the law firm and stood waiting for the elevator. "Why did you pretend that you were delivering my car?"

"I didn't want to embarrass you in front of anyone you knew. I wouldn't want them to think that a well-bred, professional woman like you would have lunch with a lowlife mechanic."

"Stop it, Dale," she said, unsure how much of his tone was sincere and how much was sarcasm. "I'm tired of this class-consciousness crap. You're not a lowlife, and I'm not ashamed to be seen with you, if that's what you're implying.

"Susan!" One of a group of well-dressed women called to her as they were about to enter the tunnel to the parking lot.

"Excuse me for a minute," Susan said to Dale, and walked over to them. "How are you, Deanna?"

Deanna's face was pointed at Susan as she answered, but her eyes lingered over the man who stood waiting a few feet away. "I was going to ask you to join us for lunch, but it looks like you already have a date."

"Don't be silly," Susan said, a little too quickly. "The man is my mechanic. I'm just taking him back to his shop. But I can't join you today. We'll do it another time."

Her face flushed crimson as she walked back the few feet that seemed suddenly an interminable distance. She knew that Dale had heard her. "I'm sorry, Dale," she said, when he didn't speak. "You were right about me. But you're not a lowlife: I am, for acting like I'm better than you. You're the one who should be ashamed to be with me."

He didn't say anything for a few minutes, and she knew she had hurt him deeply. "I'll forgive you because you admitted it," he said finally. "I guess, in a way, I'm glad it happened. It proves something to me that I didn't want to see."

Proves what? Susan thought, but she was afraid to ask.

It proves that I have no chance with you, Dale thought to himself. You're out of my league. I'm good enough to fix your car and your sink, but not to walk with you in public. There is no future for us.

He was silent throughout most of the meal. Dale's silence could be as punishing as another

100

person's outburst, so Susan was relieved when a page on his beeper took him away from the table for a few minutes.

"I've got to get back to the garage," he said, when he came back from using the phone. "I've got to go out to pick up a Porsche. Damn!" he exclaimed, bouncing his fist on the table. "I'm already three cars behind today and now I've got to spend an hour or so drinking tea with Mrs. Oliver."

"Can't you send Jose or somebody else to pick up her car?" Susan suggested.

"No. She wants me. She always wants me."

"Well, she's got good taste, anyway," Susan smiled. "I guess all the women want you."

"Except one," he said dryly, without looking at her. "The worst of it is, I'll have to spring another man loose to take me over there."

He was still annoyed with her, but not angry enough to refuse her offer to drive him to his customer's house. "So where are we going?" she asked, as they pulled out onto the freeway.

"Beverly Hills."

"Hoo-hah," Susan said, pretending to be impressed. "You have a high-class clientele."

"Yes, I do," he agreed. "Most of my customers live in Beverly Hills."

"Yes, and you charge accordingly. Your prices are higher than the Dow Jones average the day the Gulf War ended."

Dale was not offended. "I *have* to charge a lot," he explained. "My customers feel that they get what they pay for. I sell service, Susan. I do everything for my customers. I pick up and deliver their cars; I drive them to work; I rescue them if they're stranded on the highway; I drink tea with them and hold their hand and listen to their troubles. I've even driven school carpools."

Susan smiled. "You're a good businessman, Dale. You understand what product you're really selling."

The noonhour traffic was worse than usual. There seemed to be twice as many vehicles out on the streets, and all of their drivers were impatient to get where they were going. "Watch it!" Dale screamed, as a car entering the intersection from a side street tried to make a left turn directly in front of them.

Susan slammed on the brakes, but not before Dale had grabbed the wheel and wrested it away from her, swerving the car into an unoccupied lane. Although it was his fault, the driver who had caused the near accident offered an obscene hand signal as he drove around them. Dale returned the gesture.

"What the hell is wrong with you, Susan?" Dale directed his anger at her now. "Can't you drive *any* car? This one has an automatic transmission; all you have to memorize is which is the accelerator and which is the brake!" He went on and on.

Susan remained silent. It had not been her fault that they had encountered a crazy California driver. And she *had* had the situation under control. It hadn't been necessary for Dale to grab the wheel like that. He had just been trying to show her up. His action, as well as his anger, was probably a response, not to the driving incident, but to the insult he had suffered from her earlier. He was trying to make her feel as incompetent and inferior as she had made him feel.

"Turn right," Dale said calmly, after his fury was spent. "Turn left at the stop sign. This is it," he said, as she turned into a wide, residential boulevard of three-story homes, well-manicured lawns, and long, circular driveways. "The one at the end." He got out of the car without looking at her. "Thanks for the ride." He started to walk up the drive.

"Dale," Susan said hesitantly. He stopped walking but didn't turn around. "I'm sorry about what I did earlier. About the way I treated you. I won't do it again, I promise." She swallowed hard. "Are we still friends?"

He turned back to look at her now, but it was a long time before he spoke. "Friends? Is that what we've been? Yes, of course, we're still friends. What else could we be?" he asked, with just a touch of bitterness.

Susan was surprised by the intensity of the relief that she felt. She smiled hesitantly. "I'm glad. I'm glad you're not mad anymore."

Dale sighed in resignation. "What's the point of being mad? You are what you are. I am what I am, which is poor white trash. It's oil and water. We just don't mix."

Six

"It's starting to be irritating," Susan confided to her best friend, Barbara Strauss, in the ladies' room of the Chinese restaurant where she and several friends had met for dinner. She hadn't told Barbara, or anybody, about her friendship with Dale Clemens, and had not planned to, but she was beginning to feel taken for granted, especially after this evening's episode.

She had been dressed and on her way out to meet the girls when Dale knocked at the back door—as usual, without calling first. He'd sauntered in as casually as if he were at home, strode directly to the refrigerator, and peered inside.

"Hi, Suse," he had said without even looking at her. "You got a beer?"

He was already removing one and popping the tab before she could answer. He took a long swig, turned, and only then noticed she was dressed to go out.

"I guess I should have called first," he smiled sheepishly. "You got a date?"

Susan was tempted to say yes, just to see his reaction. "What about you?" she asked pointedly. "Don't *you* have a date tonight?"

"Yeah, but I'm early." He guzzled the beer hurriedly, raising the can almost upside down to receive the last drops. "Can I use your phone?"

Susan had heard snippets of his conversation as she made sure her purse was in order. She had a mental picture of a young girl dashing to put on makeup to be ready earlier than she had expected.

We women are so easy, Susan thought to herself. We're not liberated. We plan our days, and then a man comes along and tells us to change our plans, and we jump at the chance to please him. Especially a man like Dale.

"It's not that I mind him coming over," she explained over the rattle of teacups to four curious pairs of eyes. The private conversation between two friends in the ladies' room had turned into a full-scale, round-table discussion, with five women deliberating and picking apart what had up till now been her carefully guarded secret. "He's actually a very nice young man. But he just drops in like he owns the place and expects me to be available to cook for him and keep him company until he has to be someplace else. I'm surprised he hasn't started bringing me his dirty laundry." She didn't mention, of course, the nights that Dale had availed himself of her living-room couch.

"It sounds like you're getting a raw deal, Susan," Gloria Ross said, smearing her egg rolls with Chinese mustard. "He's getting all the comforts of home, but what are you getting out of it? He probably won't even send you flowers on Mother's Day. How old is this young man, anyhow?"

"I'm not sure," Susan lied. "I think about thirty." She told them she had met him in the waiting room of a car repair place, that he was a young widower who had recently lost his wife in a car accident. She was amazed at how quickly she could fabricate a story, an almost complete lie.

"What car repair place?" Ellen Landman asked curiously.

"The one just outside of Beverly Hills. Where Mike always used to take his Jaguar."

"Oh, *that* place," Ellen said knowingly. Then she looked at Susan suspiciously. "You're not talking about the owner of the place, are you? The good-looking guy with the mustache and the great body? I wouldn't mind a little extra-marital tumble in the hay with *that* man, I tell you."

Everybody but Susan laughed. "No, it was a customer, I told you," she said, a little irritably. She was going to have to remember the exact wording of everything that she had said so they wouldn't catch her in a lie.

"You know," Ellen mused, "he might not think of you as a mother. After all, this is the nineties. Age differences don't matter anymore. Did you know," she confided in a loud whisper, "Emily Weinman is going out with a younger man?"

"Can you believe it?" Barbara clucked. "Abe just keeled over a few months ago and she's already got herself a little party on the side."

Gloria rolled her eyes disparagingly. "I just can't see why a woman in her position would lower herself like that. I mean, the sex can't be that great."

"How would you know, Gloria?" Ellen attacked at the opening. "Sleeping with Stanley Ross can't be the thrill of the century. Living with him has got to be bad enough. If you weren't such a naive little virgin when you got married, maybe you would know better."

Susan edged back slightly from the table with her chair, withdrawing physically as well as mentally. In a way, she was relieved to no longer be the primary subject of the feline free-for-all. On the other hand, she felt a little hurt that her private revelations had been dealt with and dismissed so summarily.

"Maybe she loves him." It was the first comment from Beverly Werner, spoken softly and a little timidly. "Emily Weinman. Maybe she's in love with her new man." All the women turned simultaneously to stare at her, then turned away again in unison as if she hadn't spoken. At thirty-five, Beverly was the youngest member of their group, grudgingly admitted and barely tolerated only because she was the second wife of Arthur Werner, a long-standing member of their social circle and every woman's favorite plastic surgeon. Arthur's first wife, Sylvia, had been a well-loved member of their little group. Sylvia Werner had been a constant friend, always upbeat, never complaining about anything in her life. Nobody could understand it when she was found dead in bed from a fatal mixture of booze and pills.

"Maybe you should have an affair, Susan," Ellen suggested. "Take a young lover. Maybe that'll get you out of your doldrums, get your juices flowing again."

"Ellen!" Barbara and Gloria each gave her a withering glance. The women usually tolerated, and were often amused by, Ellen's earthy comments, but this time she had breached an unmarked boundary of propriety.

"I'm not going to take a lover, Ellen." Susan's response was firm and controlled. "This young man is just a friend. We are both lonely, and we fill a need for each other, that's all. I don't mean to complain about his visits. I enjoy the company. I'm just tired of being taken advantage of."

"Well, you *should* be," Gloria Ross agreed. "You shouldn't be a doormat, Susan. You've got to stand up for yourself. When my oldest son Elliot began using the house as a place to eat, sleep, and bring his girlfriends, and didn't pay one penny toward rent or groceries, despite the fact that he has a good-paying job, Stan and I got tough. We threw him out and made him get his own place. This young fellow isn't even related to you. I say, throw the bum out."

"Throw the bum out. Throw the bum out," the other women chanted in good-natured solidarity, like a chorus of fans at a baseball park.

The chorus was still ringing in Susan's ears when the doorbell rang late that night.

"I didn't expect to see you back tonight," she said in surprise as Dale walked into the living room. "I thought you had a date."

"I did," he said.

"It didn't work out?"

"It worked out fine." He sank down into the soft pillows of the couch and made himself comfortable. "I had a nice time. How was your evening?"

"Fine," she said, not allowing herself to be diverted from the subject. "If you had such a nice time, then why are you here at midnight, instead of playing Run-Around-The-Bedroom at your date's house?"

"Give me a break, Susan," he said wearily. "It was my first date with this woman."

"So?" she persisted. "Does that make a difference?"

He shot her an annoyed glance. "Of course it makes a difference. Do you go to bed with men on your first date?"

"It's been over thirty years since I had a date, Dale," she reminded him. "Of course *I* wouldn't. But I thought today's young women had much more casual attitudes about sex. It's good to know there's at least one woman who doesn't roll over on a first date just because a handsome guy asks her."

"She probably would have rolled over if I'd asked her," Dale confided quietly. "But I didn't ask."

Susan's eyes widened in surprise. "How come?"

His annoyed glance turned into an almost angry glare. "I just met this woman, Susan. I don't know her well enough yet to know if I want to sleep with her."

111

Susan thought she understood. "Fear of AIDS?"

"Partly, yes. But that's not the whole story. Susan, you've made several not-so-subtle insinuations about my love life. I may be poor white trash, but I'm not the sleaze you think I am. Now, don't misunderstand me," he said as she opened her mouth to protest. "I've had my share of women, probably more than my share, between marriages and even a few during my marriages. But I don't try to make every girl that I see; I only date one lady at a time; and I don't screw around on a woman I'm involved with when I care about her. Why do you have such a hard time believing that?"

"I don't know," she said quietly. But she did know. When Jeff was young and handsome, women had been attracted to him like bees to honey, and he had taken advantage of every opportunity his looks had afforded him. "I'm sorry," Susan said. "Jeff was like that. It's not fair, but I guess I just naturally assumed that you were the same way."

"Well, I'm not," Dale said emphatically. His penetrating green eyes turned full force on her for an instant, then lowered. At first Susan thought he was angry. Dale usually tried to mask his anger with silence. Apparently he wasn't aware that his eyes announced his emotions louder than words. But Dale's eyes were pensive now, not angry, as if he had something on his mind and was struggling to put it into words. He stroked his mustache thoughtfully. "Susan," he said finally, "if you're not busy Sunday, why don't you come and spend the day at my house? We can go swimming, and I'll throw a couple of steaks on the barbecue for dinner."

It was the first time since the day he'd bought the Jaguar that he had invited her anywhere. "It sounds nice, Dale," she said politely, "but I don't think so."

"Why not?" he persisted. "We've been not-dating for almost two months now and you've never even been to my house."

"I don't even know your phone number," Susan admitted. "I thought that was intentional. What do you mean by 'not-dating'?"

"You know what I mean," said Dale. "We've been practically living together!"

"You're the one always coming over here to get a free meal or a place to sleep!" she retorted.

"I hope you don't think that's the real reason I come over here so much. If that's all I was after, I could certainly get better accommodations and meals somewhere else. Well, maybe not better meals," he added, grinning. "You really are a damn good cook, Lady."

"Thank you," said Susan. "But flattery

won't get you off the hook. So why *do* you come over here so much?"

"You know why. I just like being with you. I enjoy the talks and the company."

"You don't act like it," she said. "Half the time when you're here you don't even talk to me. You just sit and watch TV like I'm not even here."

"I'm sorry if it seems like that," he apologized. "I guess I just sort of make myself at home. I have to smile and be charming to the customers at the shop all day, and when I go out at night, I have to do the same. It's nice to be with someone that I feel comfortable with, that I don't have to entertain every minute. I guess I overdid it a little. But I do notice you're here, Susan, very much so." He grinned contritely. "I'll be a better host on Sunday, I promise. Will you come?"

"I can't, Dale. My daughter's coming over this weekend."

"Great!" he said. "Bring her. I'll have my daughter come over Sunday, too. Tell Andrea to bring her swimsuit."

She guessed she shouldn't have been surprised that he knew her daughter's name. She was rarely surprised anymore by what Dale seemed to know about her. Some of the things he had undoubtedly learned from Mike, but some things he seemed to know instinctively, as if he could see inside her. Even Mike had never been able to read her that well. Only Jeff had.

She was secretly looking forward to seeing Dale's house but she tried to contain her excitement, especially with her daughter looking over her shoulder. A swarm of butterflies danced lightly in her stomach as she packed swimsuits and towels into a nylon beach bag.

"Mom, do we have to do this?" Andrea whined. "I look really fat in this swimsuit."

"How do you think *I* look?" said Susan. "I'll have to keep my cover-up on the whole time. Yes, we have to do this. I already told him we were coming."

"Who *is* this guy, anyway? Where do you know him from?"

"I told you. He was your father's mechanic. He's the owner of the garage, actually. I sold him Daddy's Jaguar, and he wanted to have us over to thank me. His daughter's in your class. You're sure you don't know her?"

"It's a big school, Mom. I don't think so. Why did you have to go and sell the Jag?" she grumbled. "You knew I wanted it. If Joel had wanted it, you would have saved it for him, I'm sure of that. But you don't care what *I* want. You never have. If Daddy were still alive, I'll bet I'd be driving that car right now."

"If your father were still alive, *he'd* be driving

115

it," Susan snapped. She bit her tongue to prevent herself from saying anything further. She was not about to tarnish the revered memory of a hero. Mike had been a wonderful man—in some ways, extraordinary—but he had not been without faults. In Andrea's eyes, however, he had always been the good guy who never refused anything his daughter asked while her mother had always been the one who said no.

Dale lived a good way out in the country. They drove over an hour before they reached the exit. When they turned off the highway, they were followed by a yellow Corvette convertible. The long blond hair of the girl driving it fluttered about her. She pulled up behind them at the first light and was still behind them a stop sign later. As Susan stopped to read over the handwritten directions, the yellow convertible whipped around them and peeled off ahead, leaving clouds of dust in its wake. When they turned into a gravel road off the main highway, however, they spotted the Corvette again just ahead of them.

"That girl looks familiar," Andrea mused.

"Of course she does," Susan said suddenly. "That must be Jennifer. We probably could have brought her with us." What a beautiful girl, she thought to herself. She's got to be Dale's daughter.

They followed the Corvette the rest of the

way. Jennifer must have realized who they were as well, because she paused and waited for them before turning into the driveway.

As Susan gathered their supplies, Andrea jumped up and ran to the other car. "Hi, I'm Andrea," she said, in a much friendlier tone than Susan would have anticipated from the way she'd behaved earlier.

"I remember you," the girl said coolly, but courteously. "I think we had a class together once. I'm Jennifer." The two girls strode together up to the front door of the small frame house.

"Hi, Dale!" Jennifer exclaimed as he opened the door, hugging him affectionately around the shoulders and giving him a perfunctory kiss on the cheek.

"Hi, Jen!" Dale responded in kind. "How's school?"

"Nearly over, thank God. I can't wait for graduation. This is Andrea," she said, indicating the girl next to her.

"So I gathered." Dale smiled. "Welcome, Andrea. I'm Dale. Where's your mother?"

Andrea pointed to Susan, still struggling at the car with the beach bags.

"I'll go help her. Jenny, why don't you take Andrea inside?"

"He's not bad," Andrea whispered to Jennifer as Dale walked down the steps, but it was more like a stage whisper, loud enough for even Susan to hear. "Is that your brother?"

"My *brother?*" Jennifer sounded appalled. "That's my *father!*"

Susan cringed. Just what she needed: Andrea smitten with Dale. Mercifully he was wearing a shirt and jeans. She'd had visions of him appearing at the front door wearing nothing but swim trunks. *That* really might have piqued Andrea's interest. Not to mention charging a few sparks in her own battery. Susan wondered if Dale had overheard the exchange between the two girls. Undoubtedly he had. He looked mildly amused as he sauntered to the car to greet her.

"How are you doing, Lady?" he asked, hoisting one of her bags over his shoulder. "What did you bring all this stuff for? Don't you think I have towels?"

"I didn't want to impose too much," she said politely.

"Impose all you like," he said. "I want you to feel at home here." He took the second bag out of her hands and led her up the drive to the house. "Did you have any trouble finding the place?"

"Nope. I just followed Jennifer. Dale, this is nice," she said, looking around as he placed her bags inside the front door. The living room was small but impeccably furnished. It held an antique sofa with antimacassars on the thick, rolled arms; a secretary desk; and two curio cabinets. In the corner stood a spinet piano. Susan touched the ivory keys reverently. "Was this your grandmother's?"

"Yes. Most of the stuff in this room was my grandmother's. Come on into the den. It's a little more my taste."

It certainly was a different style. The den was huge, the size of the rest of the house combined, and looked as if it had been added on fairly recently. It had a high, vaulted ceiling and paneling along three walls. The fourth wall was a full-length picture window which afforded a view of an L-shaped swimming pool and a spacious backyard. On the cream-colored leather sofa, which curved in front of the window, sat a man and woman who looked to be in their early sixties. A very beautiful woman of about thirty-five sat on a barstool, sipping a tall drink. She was wearing a black, one-piece, low-cut bathing suit. The terry robe she wore as a cover-up was unfastened, thus failing to cover up anything. At the other end of the built-in bar, which extended half the length of the wall, sat a boy of about sixteen. Jennifer and Andrea were stretched out on the floor in front of a big-screen TV.

Dale introduced the older couple as his next-door neighbors, Harold and Louise Curtis.

"This is Elizabeth Freeman," he continued, indicating the bathing beauty with the overripe bosom, "and her son Kenny. Liz lives down the street and she teaches at the high school here. I guess you met Jennifer. I'm going to fix a pitcher of Margaritas," he said after introducing Susan and Andrea to the group. "Suse, want to help?"

It was more of an invitation than a request for help. An invitation to be with him. "I really like your house, Dale," Susan said as she salted the rims of the half-dozen glasses he handed her and placed them on a silver tray.

"It's not what you expected, is it?" he grinned.

"Nothing is like what I expected. I didn't expect all these people. This is like a party. I must admit, when you first asked me here, I thought you were trying to lure me off alone into your bachelor's Den of Iniquity."

"Are you disappointed that I didn't?" he smiled, stirring the ice in the pitcher.

"I decline to answer that question. At least until I've had a few of these," she added, sampling her Margarita. She peered out the serving window at the company in the den. "Your friend Elizabeth is very pretty. Does she have a husband?"

"No," Dale answered guardedly. "She's divorced."

"I take it that you and she are an item?" Susan asked, sipping her drink casually in an effort to portray a pose of indifference.

"You take it wrong. We used to go out, but that was some time ago."

"*You* broke up with *her*, didn't you?" she asked.

"What makes you assume that?"

"Because she's still interested in you. I can see it in the way she looks at you."

Dale shrugged off her analysis. "Circumstantial evidence. Stop acting like a lawyer." He handed her the tray of drinks to carry into the den. Although there was plenty of room on the couch, he sat quite close to her, close enough to put his arm around her if he'd wished. Susan wondered if he was trying to give his former girlfriend a message.

The background mumble of television noise was abruptly shut off, and Jennifer bounced over to sit on the other side of Dale. "I think I'll go change," she said pertly. "I'm ready to swim."

Dale caressed his daughter's long, blond hair. "You and Andrea go ahead. Come on, Susan," he said, helping her off the couch as the rest of the party began to drift out the glass doors to the backyard. "I'll show you where you can change."

His bedroom was small but orderly and, like

the living room, not what she expected. She thought he would have dark massive furniture and a king-sized bed, maybe even a waterbed. She expected to see a comforter on the bed in a bright, geometric print or maybe broad, masculine stripes, and under it, black satin sheets. Instead, Dale had a regular double bed with a delicate brass headboard. A low nightstand stood next to it, and opposite the small window was a matching, narrow bureau. Several bottles of cologne lined a crocheted strip that traversed the length of the top of the dresser. It matched the delicate handwork bedspread.

"Your grandmother's?" she asked respectfully, touching the faded patterns of the antique spread.

Dale nodded. "There's a bathroom right inside that door if you want to wash up. I'll see you in a few minutes." He closed the bedroom door quietly behind him.

Susan sat down gingerly on the crocheted spread and ran her fingers over it the length of the bed. So this was the place where he slept when he wasn't curled up on her couch or in the arms of some young lady. She wondered if he ever brought his dates here to this bedroom. It didn't seem likely. The room was very romantic in an old-fashioned way, but it didn't seem to be, well . . . sexy. She couldn't visualize Dale's large virile body churning on these squeaky springs. She couldn't even imagine him sleeping alone in this room. It didn't seem very masculine at all.

Nor did the prim austerity of the living room. Both rooms contrasted sharply with the airy, modern style of the den, a room which suggested wild, boisterous parties as well as more intimate liaisons. Now there was the "swinging bachelor pad" Susan had expected. The den did seem like Dale, at least like the part of him she had seen, or assumed she had seen. But it was the softer, more cerebral atmosphere of his bedroom that spoke to Susan. It said that he was a man of strong, traditional values, a man who lived within his means. He had apparently bought this modest house before he'd owned the garage. When he could afford it, he'd built on, instead of risking the success of a young, fledgling business by committing himself to a large mortgage payment. The place of honor he'd given his grandmother's furnishings in his home showed an unusual reverence for her memory. He had obviously loved his grandmother very much.

The man was the salt of the earth. His house and the contrasts within it revealed a facet of him that Susan never would have guessed. It showed that Dale didn't embrace change only for the sake of change or dispose of things just because they were old and no longer fashionable. Maybe, she thought hopefully, he was the same way about people.

She pulled herself up from his bed and went into the bathroom to change into her swimsuit. The bathroom was very small, with barely enough room to turn around, but she felt awkward about undressing in Dale's bedroom. There was a full-length mirror attached to the back of the bathroom door. Susan stripped off her clothes and posed in front of the mirror, cupping her hands under her breasts and inspecting her nakedness with a critical eye. She wasn't bad for a woman her age, but she was no competition for what was out there at that pool right now. She sighed and reluctantly squeezed her middle-aged body into her jade green one-piece suit. Then she pulled a long, silk-screened T-shirt over her head, tugging at it until it hung almost to her knees.

Susan was about to rejoin the others when her eyes fell on the small bookcase opposite the bed. Somehow she never would have figured Dale for an avid reader, but there must have been thirty or forty books crammed into the two narrow shelves. Most of them were thin paperbacks, detective novels and the like, but some of the titles surprised her. There was a large hardcover volume about the theater and another about ancient Greek and Roman architecture. There was a book about the life of the Buddha, as well as a series of books on the ancient civilizations of Egypt, China, and Mesopotamia.

She sat down cross-legged on the floor in order to take a closer look at a couple of books on the second shelf. One was entitled *The Religion of the Jews* and the other was about Jewish customs and life-cycle events. Her curious fingers reached to pull that one out.

"Looking for something?"

Susan jerked her fingers back guiltily. It was only a bookshelf, but she felt as if she had been prying into his private business. That didn't restrain her from asking questions, however. She fingered the large, heavy tomes. "Dale, have you read all these books?"

He entered the room and sat at the foot of the bed. "No. I just use them to press specimens for my insect collection."

Susan wheeled around sharply to peer into his face. Dale had Jeff's infuriating ability to purge all emotion from his voice, making it next to impossible to tell if he was serious, joking, or sarcastic.

"I do know how to read, Susan," he said acerbically. "Even the rinky-dink school I went to taught 'readin', 'ritin', and 'cipherin'.'"

Sarcastic, definitely. "I'm sorry," she said. "I didn't mean to insult you. I'm just surprised that you have such eclectic tastes. You seem to be interested in so many different subjects."

"I know what *eclectic* means, Susan."

She couldn't seem to say anything without offending him. Not on this subject.

"Susan, I may be ignorant, but I'm not stupid. I'm very aware of how much I don't know. I know that what little knowledge I've been able to acquire by reading is no match for the education you've had, but I don't appreciate your patronizing me. I don't like being made fun of."

Within his determined gaze, she saw the face of another man, a young man with an eighth grade education who had read Shakespeare and Dostoevsky and the Bible in the original Hebrew.

"I wasn't making fun of you, Dale. I know you're not stupid. I think you're very intelligent. You've just never had the chance to prove it to yourself." His eyes flashed in surprise as if she'd guessed a secret he didn't know he had. Susan touched his hand tentatively. "You're good at what you do, but if you'd been given a chance, you might have been just as good at something else. You never even thought about going to college, did you?"

He stretched his arms out in front of him and cracked his knuckles. "As a matter of fact, I did. I had pretty good grades in high school.

I even applied for a scholarship at Southern Illinois U. But my grandparents couldn't afford for me to go away to school. I had to get out and get a job."

"I'm sorry," Susan said.

Dale shrugged his shoulders. "It was no big deal." But his eyes revealed otherwise.

"You know, it's not too late if you still want to go to college. I was a teacher for seven years before I decided to go back to school and get my law degree. What were you planning on studying?"

He sighed and threw back his head. "Engineering, probably. But it *is* too late. The shop can't run without me, and I can't afford to give up four years of income. And even after I got my degree, it would take years of working before I could begin to make anywhere near the money I'm making now."

"You have a point," Susan said thoughtfully. "Given your situation, I don't think that an engineering degree would be the best course for you right now."

"You sound like you have another suggestion."

"I do. Business. You run a good business from the technical end, but now that it's growing so much, I'll bet you're feeling a little inadequate about the management aspects."

"Well, I have an accountant audit the books,

127

and Terry's pretty good about keeping the invoices straight."

"You can have good people, Dale, but there's no substitute for knowing at least a little about the business end yourself so you won't get ripped off. Someday you may want to expand or diversify into another type of business. Business skills are transferable. I think you should check into taking a few accounting and marketing courses at night. They have classes that start as late as eight-thirty. Surely you can get away from the garage by then. You can ask your daughter to get you the information and application forms."

He stroked his chin thoughtfully. "What you say makes sense. I could handle a course or two at night. You're a pretty smart lady, Susan."

"You're a smart man. And," she added, admiration filling her eyes, "very special."

He shook his head. "There's nothing special about me, Susan. I'm just an ordinary guy who goes to work every morning and busts his ass all day to make a living. It's just that every once in a while, I look around me and wonder why the hell I'm doing it. Don't you ever wonder why we're here, Susan? Do you think about the people who came before us, and how we got to be where we are now, and what direction we're going to and why?" He looked at her impassive face. "No, I guess you don't. I guess you know all the answers to those questions already." Dale stood up. "I'd better get back to my guests. You coming?"

"In a second. And, no, I don't know all the answers. I ask the same questions you do."

She dashed into the bathroom to retrieve her bag. There was more to Dale Clemens, she thought, than first met the eye. Besides being attractive, he was perceptive, intelligent, and quite introspective. One thing was certain: he was *not* ordinary.

Before following Dale down the hallway, Susan glanced at the bed once again and was suddenly seized by an overpowering itch of curiosity. She tiptoed toward it and delicately pulled the spread back all the way to reveal the sheets and pillowcases beneath. They were black satin.

$\mathcal{S}\varepsilon\upsilon\varepsilon n$

When she emerged from the house, everyone else was already in the pool except Louise Curtis. Susan set her tote bag down on an empty chair between Louise's and another lounge chair which held Dale's shirt and jeans.

"Hey, Susan!" Dale yelled from the pool. "Come in and join us. I think the ladies need some help."

They were playing water volleyball. A low net was strung across the shallow end of the L-shaped pool. The teams were evenly divided, with Dale, Hal, and Kenny playing against Jennifer, Andrea, and Elizabeth.

"No, thanks, not yet," Susan declined. "It always takes me a while to get psyched to go in."

Elizabeth's figure was as sensational as Susan had known it would be. The curves of her breasts and hips undulated in smooth rhythm as she reared back to serve the volleyball. What did you expect, Susan? she taunted herself. The woman is twenty years younger than you are. Susan felt a perverse sense of satisfaction in noting that Elizabeth's figure, nice as it was, was not even worth noticing next to the youthful figure of Dale's daughter. Jennifer was shapely and agile, her hair cascading almost to her slim hips, and bouncing when she jumped for a high volley. She was a "ten," that was for sure. Susan was certain Andrea had noticed. She looked at her daughter. Andrea looked very nice in her two-piece suit, not as nice as Jennifer, granted, but very appealing, and certainly not fat.

Having given all the women the hypercritical once-over, she turned her eyes to the men's side. Hal Curtis had a pretty fair body for a man of his age. He had a masterful serve and played every bit as well as Liz Freeman's teenage son. That's the age of man you should be looking at, Susan, she told herself. But her eyes kept turning to Dale's athletic body.

It was impossible not to stare at him. He was just too gorgeous: tanned, muscular, looking like he'd been carved in the image of a god. His swim trunks, thankfully, reached midthigh. Susan hated seeing men over the age of twenty-five wearing those skimpy bikini suits that revealed everything they had. What Dale had was revealed enough, and it looked wonderful. He had strong, athletic thighs, the muscles of which rippled with tension as he leaped in the air to return a volley. His chest was as solid as a plate of armor. He had a bit of a paunch around the midriff, not surprising for a man of his age who drank as much beer as he did. But even his beer belly was tight and controlled, allowing no flab to hang over the waist of his swim trunks. Susan admired Dale's smooth back and the rhythmic flexion and expansion of his shoulder blades as he leaned back to serve the ball.

"That's enough for me," Harold Curtis puffed laboriously, retreating to the steps of the pool.

"Me, too," said Andrea, scrambling out the side.

"What are you guys, a bunch of wimps?" Dale teased. "Come on, I'll play you all. Kenny, you go help your mother and Jenny."

Andrea took the lounger next to Susan and dropped her body onto it, dripping cold water as she shook out her long brown hair.

"Be careful!" Susan rescued Dale's clothes from Andrea's mini-shower and placed them on her lap. Unconsciously she began to caress his shirt.

Andrea bent her knees and leaned her chin on her legs, watching the pool action. "Quit drooling," Susan said, as she noticed her daughter's eyes fixated on Dale's sturdy physique. "He's twice your age. What would Mark think?"

Mark had been Andrea's boyfriend since sophomore year of college. It was assumed by everyone, Susan included, that they would soon be getting married.

"So what?" Andrea said defensively. "I'm just looking. What about you? He's half *your* age. You're not even entitled to look."

Susan's eyes flashed indignantly. "I beg your pardon," she bristled with controlled anger. "Your father was a wonderful man, and I will always love him, but I don't think he would have wanted me to crawl into the grave with him. I *am* entitled to look at attractive men. I'm entitled to do more than look if I want to."

Andrea contemplated her mother oddly. "Sorry," she said. "You don't have to have a fit about it."

Susan relaxed, regretting her edginess. Andrea always knew just what to say to get her dander up, and she always fell for the bait. "So, are you having a good time? You seem to be getting along well with Jennifer. You did know her after all?"

"I know *of* her," Andrea emphasized. "Jennifer Clemens is one of the most popular girls on the entire campus. I've seen her around, but I've never talked to her. She's usually surrounded by at least half a dozen guys." She turned her head, abruptly terminating the conversation with her mother, then turned back again, deigning to share additional information with her. "You should see her closet. She has the most beautiful designer clothes."

The volleyball game was just breaking up. Dale came out of the water, rubbing a towel across his broad shoulders, and strode over to the lounge chairs where Susan and Andrea were sitting. Casually he moved Andrea's legs so that he could sit beside her at the end of the chaise.

"You shouldn't have deserted your team," he teased. "I beat them twenty-one to six."

Andrea smiled politely, but her eyes were following the motions of the towel caressing his chest. "Do you work out?" she asked Dale bluntly.

He grinned. "No. I just work. Crawling under cars all day gives you plenty of exercise."

"Oh," Andrea said, a little embarrassed. "I thought you might lift weights."

"You mean like this?" He picked up the girl by placing an arm beneath her shoulders and another under her knees, and dumped her unceremoniously into the pool. Andrea squealed with indignant pleasure.

Dale leaned back in the chair she had vacated, pulling it closer to Susan's. "You don't have to hold those," he said, pointing to the clothes she still had in her lap. "Just put 'em on the ground."

Susan abruptly dropped the jeans and shirt she had been fondling, nudging them with her toe under Dale's chair. Dale's eyes followed the movement of the clothes and darted back to the smooth, silky legs their removal had uncovered. Then they traveled subtly up to her torso.

"When are you coming in, Lady?" he whispered. "That's a very nice shirt you're wearing, but I'm looking forward to seeing a little more of you."

Susan blushed. "You've seen about all I care to expose. The rest is not worth seeing."

"Why don't you let me be the judge of that?" he smiled.

Susan shook her head. "Maybe later, Dale. I'm just a little self-conscious with all these beautiful bodies around." Mainly yours, she almost added. She leaned back in her chair and watched Andrea and Jennifer half-swimming, half-talking in the water. "Jennifer's a beautiful girl, Dale," she commented.

His face lit up with a father's pride. "Thanks."

"I understand she has a closetful of great

clothes and I notice she drives a Corvette convertible. Can I assume that she has a very generous father?"

Dale smiled. "I didn't buy the Vette new. I bought it from a customer about two years ago, and I fixed it up and painted it for her. Yellow is Jen's favorite color. As for the clothes, Jenny designs and makes her own. She's an Art major. Fashion Design."

Susan scratched a mosquito bite on her leg. "I think it says something about you that you bought your daughter a chic convertible two years before you bought one for yourself."

"Yeah?" He gave her a curious glance. "What does it say?"

"Maybe that you're a good father. Or maybe that you're a guilty father. Do you feel bad about not being there for your children when they were growing up?" Susan bit her lip and wished she could take the words back. This was the kind of hard-hitting "lawyer's" question that Dale tended to resent. And rightly so, she realized.

"I *was* there," he answered emphatically. "Jennifer was twelve and Randy was ten when Diane and I split up. Even after the divorce, I saw them two or three times a week, at least. They used to live a few blocks from here. Diane only moved to San Diego a few years ago when she married Bill. Jenny lived here with me, in fact, the first year of their marriage. She was in her senior year in high school and didn't want to move."

"I didn't know your ex-wife was remarried," Susan said.

"She's not anymore. She and Bill split up two years ago. I warned her not to marry that guy. I told her he was a worthless deadbeat, but she wouldn't listen."

The look that Susan fastened on him held not jealousy but admiration. "You really care for your ex-wife, don't you?"

"Yes, I do," Dale answered without apology. "I don't love her anymore, but I still care for her."

Susan touched his fingers in a semicaress. "I think I know why Diane's second marriage didn't work out," she said softly. "I think that Diane is still in love with you."

He waved off her comment, a little embarrassed by it. "You think everybody's still in love with me." Dale stood and threw down his towel. Susan watched the smooth curve of his back glisten in the sun as he returned to the pool and dived into the deep end. He began swimming laps.

After about his tenth one, Susan found the courage to wade into the shallow end of the pool. She waited until Dale was swimming away from her, and all the others were busy swimming or engaged in conversation, before she shyly stripped off the T-shirt and plunged into the water. It was nice, not too cold, just clear and refreshing. She paddled around for a few minutes in the four-foot water. She was turning to see if Dale had noticed her entrance into the pool when she felt a body squeezing between her legs, almost thrusting her over backward.

"Jeez, Dale, you scared me," she exclaimed. "I thought I was being attacked by a shark."

"Lucky shark," he grinned. "Come on, I'll take you out in the deep end, where the grown-ups go. You can swim, can't you?"

"Barely," she said, as he took her hand. "Not like you. How many laps did you just do?"

"Twenty. I do twenty every day."

She had to admit that it was pleasurable feeling his arms around her, holding her up in the buoyancy of the water. She was aware, however, of everyone's eyes on them, especially Andrea's. She was relieved when he got out to tend to the barbecue and bring out a fresh round of drinks.

"When is dinner going to be ready, Dale?" Jennifer asked.

"In about five minutes. You can tell everybody to get out and get dried off now."

"Why do you call your father 'Dale'?" Andrea asked as she slipped onto the bench next to Jennifer.

"Why not?" Jennifer answered casually. "That's his name."

"Your father tells me you're in fashion design," Susan said to Jennifer with a friendly smile, as they ate barbecued chicken and steak at the redwood table on the pool deck. "Have you decided yet what you want to do when you graduate?"

"Jenny's already got a job with a fashion house in New York," Dale informed her proudly. "She starts work in September."

"That's wonderful," Susan exclaimed. She turned back to Jennifer. "So now you get to spend the summer looking for a place to live."

"I've already got a place to live," Jennifer said. "A studio apartment in Greenwich Village."

"You found an apartment in the Village? And they're going to hold it for you till September? That's incredible, Jennifer. How did you manage that?"

"Well," Jennifer answered, a little bit uncomfortably, "a friend of mine, an artist, is already living there. He's offered to let me share the place." The girl looked to her father for support. Susan turned to Dale also, her eyes questioning.

Dale turned away from Susan's glare and

jumped in to steer the conversation in another direction. "What about you, Andrea? You're graduating, aren't you? What are your plans?"

"Teaching," Andrea answered. "In a school for the deaf."

"Oh," said Dale approvingly. He raised his right hand above the table and extended his fingers. "That's . . . very . . . interesting," he said slowly, signing the words as he spoke them. Susan glanced up in surprise.

"That's very good," Andrea signed back. "How did you learn to sign?"

"One of my mechanics is deaf," Dale explained. "He taught me."

Dale and Andrea continued a silent conversation as the others watched in fascination. Not good with languages, my foot, Susan thought. She was beginning to get the distinct impression that Dale Clemens was good at absolutely anything he tried.

They had just finished their dinner when two young men appeared at the back gate looking for Jennifer.

"Dale, I'm going to go over to their place and ride for a little while," Jennifer announced to her father. Dale nodded toward Andrea, reminding his daughter of her manners, but Jennifer didn't need reminding. "Andrea, do you want to come and ride with us?"

"Horses? I'd love to. But I'm not very good."

"I'll put you on Missy. She's too old to give you any trouble."

"Be back before dark, please," Dale cautioned. "I don't like you driving back to L.A. alone at night."

"I'm going to take off now, too, Dale," said Elizabeth, tugging at his elbow.

"You're not staying for dessert?" he asked, surprised.

"No, thanks. I've got a date. And it'll take me the next two hours to paint my face and put my body together."

Dale put his arm around her and said, "Your face and your body look put together just fine to me."

"Yes, well. You never did have such great taste. Bye, hon," she said, stretching up on her toes to reach his face. "See you soon." Elizabeth planted a kiss on his cheek. Dale pulled her toward him in a friendly but, to Susan's mind, totally unnecessary embrace.

"Take care, Liz," he waved, as she and her son walked out the gate.

The Curtises said their goodbyes, too, and ambled out the side gate to their own yard. As the sun dipped closer to the horizon, Dale took a beer from the cooler and flopped down into

141

a lounge chair. "I thought they'd never leave," he confided.

Susan eased into the lounger beside him. "I thought you were enjoying the company."

"I was. But I wanted to have some time to be alone with you."

His tone made her nervous. "Do you ride, too, Dale?" she asked. Growing up on a farm, of course he must.

"Used to. I haven't been on a horse in a year. If I had more time and I was home more, I'd buy my own and stable it right there." He pointed to a wooden building two hundred feet to the side of the pool area.

"That's not part of your property, is it?"

Dale nodded. "This is all my property. It goes just past that grove of trees over there. Come on, I'll take you for a walk."

His eyes followed the length of her body as she stood and slipped on her shoes. Self-consciously, she grabbed her shirt and pulled it over her. Dale smiled in amusement. "You don't need to be ashamed of your body, Susan. It's a very nice one."

She blushed, despite a vain attempt not to. "I didn't know you'd noticed."

"Of course I noticed. I noticed as soon as you got into the pool. Don't you think I've been watching you all afternoon?"

She didn't know what to reply. She let him

take her hand and lead her across the yard. "I can see now why you don't want to sell your place, Dale. The house is beautiful and you have so much land."

He nodded and led her toward the grove of trees. The waning sunlight glinted through the branches, creating interesting patterns of light against his chest. She could feel the warmth of his body, although he wasn't touching her.

"My daughter seems to have developed quite a crush on you," Susan said nervously. "I guess you noticed."

Dale smiled. "Yes, I did."

"Does it bother you?" she asked uncomfortably.

"No, I'm used to it. Lots of Jenny's friends have been attracted to me. Don't worry. They forget the attraction ten minutes after they've left the house."

They had reached the cover of the cluster of trees. "I'm not interested in any of Jennifer's friends, Susan," Dale said, guessing her next question. "I'm certainly not interested in Andrea." He stopped walking and drew Susan close to him. "I am, however, very interested in her mother." Holding her head firmly with his hand, he leaned over and kissed Susan on the mouth.

She shrank back from his embrace, disturbed by her own feelings as well as nervous about his intentions. "Dale!" she said, in a shocked tone. "I thought we were friends."

He moved away a little and dropped his hands to his sides. "We *are* friends," he assured her. "I've really enjoyed the time we've spent together. But I want more."

A tiny wave of panic surged in her stomach. "What—wh-what do you want?"

Dale looked at her almost with pity as if she were a naive young girl who had to have everything spelled out for her. He breathed in slowly and fixed his serious green eyes on hers. "I want to make love to you, Susan."

Inadvertently, she gasped. Her palms began to shake and she felt sweat forming on her upper lip.

Dale put his arm around her to steady her. "Don't panic; I don't mean now. I know that you're still in mourning for Mike. I know you probably haven't even thought about being with a man again. You can take all the time you need to think about it. I just wanted to be honest with you about the way I feel."

Susan closed her eyes and tried to think what she could say to him. She knew what she felt. She didn't want to feel what she was feeling, but she knew it was there just the same. And he undoubtedly knew it, too. Dale was probably used to getting whatever he wanted. Just looking at his beautiful, majestic body made her quiver inside and out, but she knew if she gave him what he wanted, she could never respect herself again.

"Dale," she said at last. "I'm very flattered by your proposition, and I appreciate your honesty. I'll be honest with you, too. I do like you very much, and I am attracted to you. But," she added firmly, "I'm a recent widow with an established lifestyle. I was married practically forever to one man, and I've only loved two men in my entire life." She blinked her eyes and looked at him sadly. "I just don't think I could handle a casual affair."

His words took her breath away and left her heart shunting about aimlessly in her rib cage. "I'm not interested in a casual affair," he said.

Eight

"Susan, you can't be serious!" Barbara Strauss exclaimed the next time they had lunch. "You're not actually considering going to bed with this guy? This *is* the same one you told me about—the thirty-year-old widower?"

"Actually, he's a little bit older than that," Susan mumbled, but Barbara didn't hear.

"You said it was a mother-son relationship! How long have you been dating him?"

"About three weeks." She coughed nervously. "And he's always been a perfect gentleman."

Her friend snorted. "Gentle*boy* is more like it. Where does he take you when you go out, a playground?"

Susan winced. "Barbara, he's not that young. He's forty-one years old. I lied about that." She took a deep breath. "In fact, I lied about everything."

Barbara stared. "He's not a widower? You didn't meet him at Ellen Landman's car repair place?"

"I did meet him at that car repair place. That's the only thing I *didn't* lie about. But he wasn't a customer. He was . . . he is . . . the owner of the place." She caught her breath and sucked it in.

"Susan!" Her friend's face registered shock and a touch of contempt. "How could you? A garage mechanic?"

"What's wrong with that?" she said defensively. "It's an honest living. And you heard what Ellen said. She was drooling just at the thought of being with him."

"The thought was *all* she was drooling about! Susan, Ellen is all talk. She would never cheat on Charlie. If this guy, or any guy, ever came on to her, she probably wouldn't even know what he was doing!" She shook her head incredulously. "I can't believe you would actually date a man like that!"

Susan's back arched. "What do you mean—'a man like that'?"

"You know what I mean. You two couldn't possibly have anything in common. Where *do* you go on dates, drag races? Or does he just sit around your place drinking beer and watching sports on TV in his undershirt?"

Susan flinched at the crack which struck a

little too close to home. Dale had taken her just that Sunday to watch drag racing. "All right," she admitted. "He does drink beer and watch sports on TV. But he watches documentaries, too. After ESPN, I think his favorite channel is PBS."

Barbara looked amused. "That's only when you're around. He's just trying to impress you, Susan. Don't you see what he's up to?"

Susan frowned. She had never been one to make decisions easily, especially not unpopular decisions. She was having enough trouble rationalizing her own feelings about dating 'a man like that'; she had hoped for more support from her best friend.

"Barbara," she said now, "you've got to promise me you won't say a word about this to anybody else. Ellen and her crew would have a field day with this gossip."

"I promise," Barbara said solemnly. "I swear as your best friend. But I hope you understand what you're getting yourself into."

"Dale's a good man," Susan said petulantly. "I enjoy being with him. Why can't you be happy for me?"

"I *know* what you enjoy," Barbara said crudely. "I remember Ellen's description. Susan," she said earnestly, "I know that you're lonely. It's been almost nine months since Mike died, and when you've been married as long as you two were, it's hard to be without a man. I'm sure that this man is attractive, and he probably stirs strong feelings in you, but you're very vulnerable right now. I'm afraid you're going to be hurt."

"You think that he's using me."

Barbara bit her lip. "It's not out of the question," she said, in a voice that indicated that it was precisely the question.

"So why shouldn't I use him as well?"

Barbara sighed. "Susan, we've been friends for a long time. I still remember like it was yesterday pushing Andrea and Stephanie in baby carriages to the park and watching Joel and Jonathan on the playground. You know I want the best for you. If I thought that a good roll in the hay would make you happy, I'd say go for it. But I know you. You're not going to be able to enjoy sex for its own sake and let it go at that. You're going to fall in love with this man."

Susan sighed a long, slow sigh. "Well, Barbara," she said at last, "if that's what your concern is, I'm afraid you're already too late."

"Susan, Mr. Davis wants to see you. In his office."

"Thanks, Mary Ann." Susan took the stack of messages her secretary held out to her and flipped through them all without reading one. A summons to Ron's office was unusual. He tended toward a much more casual management style, preferring to discuss business at the water cooler or by dropping into employees' offices. Susan combed her hair and checked her lipstick before making her way down the hall to the partners' area, feeling like a third grader being sent to the principal's office for cheating.

"Come in, Susan." Ron's tone was more formal than usual, and he did not ask her to sit down. Susan's attention was drawn to a tall, regal-looking man with slightly graying hair and a confident smile. The visitor stood quietly in a corner but filled up the entire room with his imposing presence. "Susan Riesman, this is Ted Samuelson."

Susan shook the man's hand cordially but reticently. She had heard of Ted Samuelson. He was Bridges and White's star attorney, and his name appeared frequently on the pages of the daily newspapers below headlines like "Heiress Accused of Killing Billionaire Husband" and "Wife's Lover Found Murdered in Husband's Mistress's Bed." Ted Samuelson was the defense attorney of record for the Gentleman Rapist, who had accosted twelve women and murdered one before he had been apprehended two weeks ago. Susan wondered what Mr. Superstar was doing here.

She didn't have to wait long to find out. "Susan, Ted is going to be joining us here. I'm sure you'll want to let him know how glad we are to have him and join with me in welcoming him." He nodded at the newcomer, and as if it were a prearranged signal, Ted excused himself to get a cup of coffee.

"Quite a coup, isn't it?" Susan remarked as Ron closed the door behind him and returned to stand behind his desk.

"Yes, it is." He couldn't help smiling proudly as he sat down, and indicated that Susan was to do the same. "Susan, I'm going to give him your office. It's larger than most, it's got a good view, and it's convenient to the conference room and other facilities." He looked down at his paperweight as he spoke. "It wasn't easy to coax Ted over here as you can well imagine, and we need to do everything we can to keep him happy."

Susan gulped inwardly, hoping her reaction wasn't noticeable from the outside. She was used to Ron's frank, no-nonsense approach, but this information put her at a loss for words. Where was he planning to move her, out the front door?

"I guess you're wondering where I'm going

to put you." Ron smiled in understatement. "I'm giving you the office next to mine."

"Steve's office?" Susan gasped inadvertently. That office had been empty almost two years since the last junior partner left. Susan was one of the few who knew the reason it had been vacant so long. Ron had been hoping that his son, a recent law school graduate, would join his father's practice. But Steve Davis had thumbed his nose at the high-pressured, materialistic world of corporate law, preferring to use his talents in legal aid to the underprivileged. This decision of Ron's was an apparent concession of the hope that his son would change his mind.

Ron raked his fingernails over the soft felt of his desk blotter. "I'd like you to help me out on a couple of projects I'm working on, Susan. We're a little understaffed in the research department now, and I'm reluctant to bring in summer interns on a project of this sensitive nature. It'll involve working closely with me as well as fairly frequent travel. I trust that won't be a problem."

"Of course not. You know I've always been willing to do whatever the job requires."

As she walked back to her office to box up her files, Susan felt more confused than enlightened. This was apparently what Ron had wanted to discuss that night over dinner. But why hadn't he mentioned it at another time, instead of just dropping the bombshell on her after the fact? Was this a punishment for something she'd done, or hadn't done? Perhaps for not having dinner with him? Or was it a kind of promotion? The work he'd described sounded routine and clerical, but it *was* an opportunity to work closely with the boss. It could be the route to an eventual partnership.

Susan sighed as she loaded a box of computer printouts onto a rolling cart. It was definitely going to mean a greater time commitment. Six months ago she would have welcomed an assignment like this, a chance to get outside herself and smother her grief through work. Now that her life was starting to turn in a new direction, she wasn't so sure she welcomed the additional responsibilities.

Or the traveling. She wondered how much Ron had in mind. Now that she and Dale were officially dating, she didn't want to be away from him for long periods of time. She was sure that Dale would have no trouble at all, if she were not available, replacing her companionship.

Going out with Dale was an adventure, an introduction to a side of life Susan had rarely, if ever, experienced. Barbara would have been chagrined at the kinds of places he took her to. Roadside barbecue stands and dirt-bike races and high-school football games. And bowling alleys. When Dale told her they were going to the Palace, she assumed they would be dining in an upscale restaurant and dressed in what she felt was appropriate attire: a knee-length red cocktail dress, two-inch heels, and a solid gold necklace.

"Susan, you look great!" Dale exclaimed when he saw her. "But a little overdressed for my bowling league."

"Bowling?" Acutely embarrassed, Susan rushed upstairs to change into jeans and a rayon shirt.

Dale was obviously proud to show off his new girlfriend to his friends. Lenny and Chuck and Jerry and Chuck's wife, Felicia, treated her respectfully, almost with awe, as if she were royalty or a movie star. It had been twenty years since she'd been bowling, and although Dale asked her if she wanted to rent some shoes and play with them, she declined in favor of sitting at the scoring table with Felicia, munching on a hot dog and chips. Felicia was sweet and the men were good guys. Jerry was recently divorced, and when he found out what she did for a living, he bombarded her for the rest of the evening with questions about child support payments, penalties, tax planning, and the like.

"I'm sorry about tonight," Dale said, when he walked her to her door that evening. "You were a really good sport, but I know you were uncomfortable all night."

Susan frowned apologetically. "Was it that obvious?"

"No. It wasn't obvious at all. Nobody but me noticed. Jerry thinks you're the greatest thing since sliced bread. He asked me if I was serious about you, and if I wasn't, if I'd mind if he asked you out."

Susan smiled, not sure if Dale was joking or not, but she was pleased that she hadn't embarrassed him too badly in front of his buddies. She didn't want to act like a snobby suburban socialite, but she really didn't have much in common with Dale's friends. The funny thing was, he didn't seem to have much in common with them either. He didn't laugh at their jokes the way he did at hers, and he always seemed to be at the edge of the conversation, not really involved in it. She wondered if he realized that he looked quite uncomfortable himself.

"I tried, Dale. I know I didn't fit in, but I tried my best. I hope I was good enough for you."

"You were wonderful. In fact, you were a smash hit. It all goes to prove, a woman with class can get along with anybody and fit in anywhere." He leaned over her and kissed her lightly on the mouth, then drew back. "I'll call you tomorrow."

Susan watched his back as he loped to the Jaguar, her fingers itching to caress its broad expanse. Although it had been six weeks since they started going out, six weeks since his lustful declaration, Dale had hardly touched her. His kisses were brief and innocent, and usually offered only at her doorway at the end of an evening. She knew it was out of respect. She was, after all, a widow still in mourning. Susan appreciated Dale's sensitivity and was grateful not to be rushed into a physical relationship she knew she wasn't ready to handle. But although her heart and mind said "wait," the urges of her body grew more and more demanding. She wondered if he was feeling the same urges and, if he was, how he managed not to show it.

Dale didn't only enjoy what Susan's friends would consider low-rent entertainment. He took her to some pretty high-life things, too. The theater and nice restaurants and concerts. Susan was taken aback, however, when Dale suggested that they go to the opera.

"I didn't know you were an opera buff," she said in surprise.

"To tell you the truth, I've never been to an opera," he admitted. "But I've always wanted to try it. This is the first time I've ever dated

156

a woman who had the class to understand it and enjoy it."

"I think you're overestimating my classiness by quite a bit," Susan protested. "I've only been to three operas in my whole life. One I enjoyed very much, but at the other two, I was bored to tears."

"Which one did you like?" he asked curiously.

"*Carmen.*"

"That's the one we're going to see."

They made plans for dinner and the opera on Wednesday, but when Susan got home from work that day, there was a message to call Dale on her answering machine.

"Susan, I'm sorry," he began, as soon as he heard her voice. "I know you've heard this before, but this time it can't be helped. I promised Dr. Berger I'd have his car first thing in the morning. I've been waiting all day for the parts, and they just came in an hour ago."

"So you want to cancel our date," she said dryly. This was not the first time that Dale had changed their plans because of work.

"No! No way. We're still going to the opera. But we'll have to skip early dinner. I'll take you out for a late supper afterward. You'd better grab a snack now, though. Otherwise I know your stomach will be singing louder than the baritone."

Susan laughed. She couldn't stay mad at

him. "Do you want me to bring you something to eat?"

"No, I'm okay. But I'd appreciate it if you would come and meet me here. It'll save time."

When she got to the garage at seven, the main gate was open. The service doors were up and the bays lit, but Susan saw no one around. Finally she saw a foot sticking out from under a gray BMW.

She tiptoed into the service area and stood beside the car, wondering how long it would take him to notice her. "Wow!" a voice exclaimed, after about thirty seconds. "What great legs! I sure am glad my baby's out of town tonight. Maybe you and me can get something going here. I am hot for a woman who wears black lace panties."

Susan gasped and drew her legs together quickly. "Could you really see my underwear?" she asked as Dale emerged, grinning, from under the car.

"No," he admitted. "It was just a guess. But I guessed right, didn't I?"

She ignored the question. "You did know it was me, though, didn't you?"

Dale just smiled.

"You shouldn't leave the gate open when you're working here at night by yourself. Especially when you're under a car."

"I usually don't," he said seriously. "I left it open for you. I'll lock it now."

She handed him a sandwich when he got back. "Thanks, Suse." He gobbled it in four bites. "You look gorgeous," he exclaimed, looking over her black-sequined dress.

"Well, *you* are a mess." She laughed at the sweat and dirt on his face and in his hair. "You'd better start cleaning up. Are you almost finished?"

"Not even close. I'll have to come back later tonight. I just want to finish up one thing before I leave. It'll only take a few minutes."

"Anything I can do to help?"

"Just stand here and talk to me. And keep your legs a little apart. Maybe I *can* see up your dress if I try."

She frowned with mock disapproval as he disappeared under the car again. It took more than a few minutes, as Susan had known it would. She tried to be patient, but she couldn't help tapping her high heels against the grease-stained pavement. The rhythm of the heel-clicking matched the movements of the second hand of the large clock on the wall like a metronome.

Suddenly a spasm of terror gripped her throat so hard it almost knocked her down. "Dale!" she screamed. The shriek tore out of her mouth of its own accord before she ever heard the creaking noise or saw the jack collapse.

159

Nine

Dale scrambled out from under the BMW in a fraction of a second, clearing by inches the 3000-pound car as it crashed to the concrete.

"Oh my God!" Susan exclaimed, as debris clattered all around. She dropped to her knees to assure herself he was all right, her eyes wildly swooping about, inspecting his body for injuries. When she was satisfied that he was unhurt, she fell on top of him, covering his face with kisses, not just on his lips, but on his cheeks, his eyes, his forehead, totally unmindful of the grease and dirt on his face that was transferring itself to hers. She grabbed his neck and clung to him desperately, weeping into his shirt, her tears mixing with the oil stains on his uniform.

Dale lay on his back placidly and quietly, in sharp contrast to Susan's hysteria. "I'm okay," he said calmly. And then, in a purposely low-key, almost bemused voice, "I didn't know you cared so much."

"Yes, you did," she blubbered, sobbing more tears onto his shirt. "Oh, yes, you did."

Finally she rolled off of him and raised herself to her knees. Dale didn't get up. "Dale?" she said fearfully. "Can you move?"

"In a minute," he said quietly. "Susan, go over to that toolbox and get a scissor." She did as he said. "Now cut my shirt," he directed.

Susan gasped in horror as she looked where he pointed. Dale's shirttail was still pinned beneath the BMW.

When he was free, she helped him pull himself up to a standing position. He tottered, dazed and unstable, holding on to Susan for support. Ignoring the dirt on his face and on hers, he pressed her close to him and kissed her fervently on the mouth. They held each other for several minutes in an embrace so tight that it was painful, but neither one wanted to break the lock.

"Thank God you got out in time," Susan said, when at last they released each other. "I can't believe you moved so fast. Did you know something was wrong before I screamed?"

"I heard a weird noise a few seconds before," said Dale. "I was thinking about coming out to check on it, but I never would have made it out if you hadn't screamed." His lip quivered and a single tear slid down his left cheek. "You saved my life, babe."

They embraced again. Finally they broke apart, trying to regain their composure, but still shaking from fright. Dale turned around to survey the BMW.

"Jesus Christ!" he exclaimed. "Dr. Berger is going to have my ass for lunch. I may have to buy him a new car!"

Susan looked down at the strewn pieces of broken tailpipe and the fenders mashed like an accordion. "Surely it's not totaled. Can't you fix it?"

"I don't know. Definitely not by eight o'clock tomorrow morning." He wiped his forehead with a grimy sleeve. "I could lose my business over this!"

Susan frowned. "Dale, it wasn't your fault. Don't you have insurance?"

"Sure, I do, but it'll take months before insurance comes through with anything. Meanwhile, I'm responsible. Susan, do you have any idea how much a new BMW costs? At least fifty thousand dollars. I don't have fifty thousand dollars."

"You have twenty thousand dollars," she said calmly. He looked at her blankly, not comprehending. "The money you gave me for the Jaguar. It's still in liquid assets. If he does sue you, we can use it to make a deal. Dale, please don't worry about business now," Susan begged. "Everything will work out. The important thing is, you're all right."

He rubbed his head with his hand. "I've got to talk to Dr. Berger," he said. He put his arm around Susan and slowly walked her toward his office, but it was unclear about who was using whom for support. "But first," he said, unlocking the door marked "Private," "I need a drink."

It took three drinks before he got up the courage to make the call. Susan sat quietly on the sofa, sipping a straight scotch, watching Dale's face screw up in consternation and worry as he talked, but mostly listened, to the furious customer. She couldn't make out Dr. Berger's specific words, but his angry tone poured through the receiver loud and clear. She felt sorry for Dale and was embarrassed to listen to his humiliation. He apologized, he tried to assuage the man's anger, he even offered him the Jaguar to use until his own car could be replaced. Susan had never seen Dale act so subservient, so conciliatory. He was scared and he was begging, begging for his livelihood.

Finally she could stand it no longer. She went out into the waiting room and picked up the telephone at the cashier's desk. "Dr. Berger," she interrupted brashly, "this is Susan Riesman, Mr. Clemens's attorney. Mr. Clemens is not at fault for what happened to your car. On the contrary, he has made every effort to reasonably accommodate you, even to the point of offering you his own personal vehicle. I'm advising him not to speak to you anymore without an attorney present as he is under considerable strain right now. I don't believe you understand what happened. Mr. Clemens was under your car when it fell. He was very nearly killed."

There was a gasp from the other end of the line. Susan felt a stab of satisfaction at having secured this reaction from Dale's antagonist, while at the same time she shivered at the truth of the words she had just spoken. "Mr. Clemens will be filing a suit against the company that manufactured the faulty machinery," she continued, "as well as filing with his insurance company for the damage to your car. I'm sure that you and he can come to some interim solution until those claims are settled. However, if you persist in harassing Mr. Clemens with threats of a negligence suit, I will be only too happy to file a countersuit charging that your car was the immediate instrument that endangered his life and caused him physical injury, not to mention mental anguish."

There was a short silence. "You tell Dale I'll

be in at eight in the morning," Dr. Berger said. "We'll talk then."

"Are you crazy?" Dale asked as she came back into his office. His cheeks were flushed with anger, but his expression held unmistakable admiration. "You practically invited this guy to sue me."

"He's not going to sue you," Susan said wearily. "He was just baring his fangs. He'll calm down by morning."

"And if he doesn't? I don't *have* an attorney. Are you going to represent me as you said? Not to put down your talents, Susan—you did a great job of tough talking just now—but you're a divorce lawyer. You don't know beans about these kind of suits, do you?"

"No," she admitted cheerfully. "But I know people who do. And if it comes to that, I'll see that you get the best."

"I can't afford the best," he mumbled.

"You can't afford anything less. Don't worry, Dale, I won't let you lose your business. Have another drink." She poured another jigger of scotch and held it out to him.

"Drinking won't solve this problem," he muttered, but he downed it in one swallow, anyway. Susan poured herself one and tried to copy him. But she couldn't swallow the whole thing in one gulp. Liquor trickled down her chin and over the black-sequined dress.

"Damn!" she said. "Now I've ruined my dress."

Dale looked at her and began to laugh. "It's too late for that. That dress was ruined twenty minutes ago." Susan looked down in anguish at the great blobs of grease patterning her dress in tie-dye fashion. Dale continued to laugh hysterically. "You should see your face," he said. "You look like Santa Claus after going down the chimney."

Susan went into the bathroom. When she saw her face and her dress, she didn't know whether to laugh or cry. After only a few seconds of debate, she cried. But it wasn't over her face or even her expensive dress. She was suddenly shaking convulsively upon realizing how close she had come to losing Dale.

She washed her face as best she could. To hell with the dress, she decided, not even trying to blot the stains. She wet a clean washcloth and came back out to sit beside Dale on the couch, gently cleaning his face with the rag. When it was wiped, she put her arms around him and kissed him passionately on the lips and on the cheeks.

Dale returned her kisses. Between embraces they drank. Susan didn't even know what she was drinking or how much. She only wanted to be lulled and numbed, to forget about the terrors of the evening, and to try to ignore the

166

yearnings of her body that she was feeling right now.

"I guess I lied, Susan," Dale said as he nuzzled her cheek. "I don't think we're going to make it to the opera tonight after all."

Susan smiled. As drunk as he was already, Dale wouldn't have been able to walk to the theater, much less drive. She relaxed again in his arms. They continued drinking and kissing, chugging scotch as if there were a prize at the bottom of the bottle, and making out like teenagers at a 1950s drive-in movie. They were innocent clinches, for the most part. At first.

"Dale, don't," she said as he started to unzip her dress. Susan felt cool air on her back and then warm hands as the dress slowly slid over her shoulders. She tried to hold it up from the front. "I mean it."

Dale's lips were on her throat and descending lower, oblivious to her protests. He pulled the damaged dress away from her body, exposing her from the waist up, her full breasts protected by only a thin black lace bra.

Suddenly Susan was cold sober and very frightened. The reality of her situation slapped her in the face like ice water. She was alone in a locked-up business, isolated from the other businesses on the street and set at least one hundred feet back from the road, with a man who was a foot taller and a hundred pounds heavier than she was. And very drunk. If she screamed, nobody would hear her. If anything sinister happened to her, nobody would even find out about it until morning.

"Dale, please!" she begged. "I'm not ready for this. Not this way. Please, please stop!"

He looked up at her. Susan gasped when she saw the expression in his eyes. She had seen that look before in eyes that looked just like these. She watched, transfixed in fear, as the gray sparks of his eyes flashed and then settled again into their liquid green pools. Dale stared at her intently, breathing rapidly.

"Don't play with me, Lady," he warned. "I told you I'd wait, and I will. Only please do not tease me." Then he abruptly stood up and stomped into the bathroom.

Susan breathed a slow sigh of relief. She tried to get dressed, but the thought of pressing her body back into the greasy garment filled her with disgust. She was looking around for something else to cover herself with when Dale emerged from the bathroom.

He had washed his face and splashed his hair, and his eyes looked clear and rational. He had pulled his own greasy shirt away from his body, but it was still partly tucked into his waist and hung over his belt like an apron. He sat down beside her on the couch, not leering at her, not even seeming to notice her exposed state. The fear she'd felt of him only a few minutes ago had completely evaporated, replaced by a pensive, plaintive longing.

"I didn't mean to tease you," she apologized. "I didn't mean for anything that happened tonight to happen. I was just so scared. Dale, it's not that I don't want to. It's just—"

"I know," he interrupted. "It's still too soon." He sat silently for a minute, then rose to his feet. "Get up," he said.

Susan reluctantly complied, holding the dress around herself. Dale motioned her out of the way as he tossed the cushions off the couch and started to pull the mattress out for the sofa bed.

"What are you doing?" Susan asked cautiously, although his actions were obvious.

"Going to bed. I've got to be up at six tomorrow, and I don't like the way my head feels already. You're staying here tonight," he said as she looked at him questioningly. "Don't worry, I won't bother you. I gave you my word. But I'm in no condition to drive you home tonight, and you're not in any better condition yourself."

He went to the closet next to the bathroom and took out some linens. "Here," he said, tossing a shirt at her. "You can sleep in this.

Put that dress in the garbage. I don't want grease all over my sheets."

She didn't have to do as he said. She was a mature, independent woman; she could go to the phone, call a taxi, and be home in half an hour. The cab driver might raise his eyebrows a bit at her unkempt, half-dressed state, but so what? It was still better than staying here all night and sneaking out in shame and embarrassment in the morning. Dale might appear harmless and subdued at the moment, but could she really trust him to keep his word? And what made him think she would just meekly follow his orders? Just because she had followed the dictates of a man all her life? Dale just seemed to assume that she would do exactly as he said, just because he had said it.

Susan took the shirt and went into the bathroom.

When she came out again, buttoned up from her neck to her thighs, Dale was lying in the sofa bed at the extreme edge, facing away from her, apparently asleep. Susan tiptoed forward and slipped in under the covers, hugging the opposite side of the bed. But something compelled her to move closer. She edged in gradually until her body was almost touching Dale's smooth, broad back. Gingerly she touched her fingers to his skin. It was cool but electrifying. She moved her fingers lovingly across his back, expressing with her fingertips the feelings she couldn't allow herself to speak out loud.

Dale didn't open his eyes, and his breathing never changed its pattern. But as Susan's lips gently touched his back, he turned around to face her and reached for her, wrapping his arms around her and folding her into the warm recesses of his body.

She awoke the next morning to the steady pounding of a hammer inside her head. She had consumed more alcohol in the few months since meeting Dale than she had in all her previous years, and she was beginning to get used to the hangovers that followed an evening with him, but this one was totally different. The hammering seemed to be coming not just from inside, but outside her eardrums as well.

She opened her eyes and sat up. When she realized where she was, she understood the hammering noises. She was relieved to know that they were coming from the garage and not her tortured head. The shop was obviously open and Dale was already working. The wall clock confirmed her assumption. It was nine-thirty. Fortunately she didn't have to meet with any clients until this afternoon.

Susan prodded herself out of the bed and into the bathroom to wash. She unbuttoned

171

Dale's shirt and was about to remove it when the sickening realization hit her that she didn't have any clothes to put on.

She padded over to the door which led to the reception area, intending to try to peek out and see if Dale was anywhere about. It was locked from the outside. Susan started breathing slowly and evenly in an effort to override the incipient panic that was settling into her stomach. She was a prisoner here. She was naked and locked into a room for which only one person held the key. Dale might return at any minute or he might not return for hours.

She was about to pound on the door and scream for help when she noticed the piece of paper on the floor. The note had a piece of cellophane tape attached and had apparently fallen off the door where she was supposedly to have seen it when she got up.

"Dear Susan," it read. "I locked you in so that some bozo wouldn't try to open the door and walk in on you by mistake. When you get up, dial the main number from the private line on the desk and ask for me."

She smiled in relief. She really had been paranoid this morning. This excessive drinking had to stop.

"Did you find your clothes?" Dale asked when she got him on the phone.

Clothes? She then found them in the closet,

a blue suit and ivory blouse, her navy heels, even clean underwear and panty hose. She showered and was dressed by the time Dale came in.

"I took your keys and went over to your house this morning," he explained. "I hope I got the right stuff."

"You did fine," she thanked him. "I hope you had a good time in my underwear drawer. Why didn't you wake me up?"

"I checked your appointment book when I was at your house. You didn't have anything listed for this morning, so I figured I'd let you sleep. You feel all right?"

"I've been better," she admitted. "Dale," she said, in a sudden flash of memory, "what about Dr. Berger?"

"He was here this morning. He apologized for last night, even asked if I wanted him to get me a good doctor. I told him I was fine, and I arranged a rental car for him. I've already called the insurance company, and they're sending an investigator out today. I looked up the manufacturer of that jack that collapsed, but I haven't contacted them yet. I figured I'd let an attorney do that."

"Good move," Susan affirmed. "I'll talk to Jack Halvorsen today. He's the best. I'm glad it worked out with Dr. Berger. Was I a help or did I make it worse?"

"I think you were a help," he smiled. "Good cop, bad cop, you know? I think he was only too eager just to deal with me."

"I thought so," she smiled proudly.

Dale pulled the sheets off the mattress and then folded the bed back up into a sofa. "A friend of yours was in here this morning. Mrs. Landman. She asked me if I knew you."

"Ellen?" She opened her mouth in consternation. "What did you tell her?"

"I told her you were asleep in my bed at that very moment."

"Dale!"

"I'm kidding," he said smiling. "I told her that I knew your husband, and that I had met you once or twice. Was that okay?"

"That was wonderful. Thanks, Dale. I am *not* ashamed of you," she said emphatically. "I just don't want everybody to know just yet that I've been . . . dating. Dale," she said, dropping her voice to a whisper, "are you still mad at me about what happened last night? Or, rather, about what didn't happen?"

He took her in his arms. "I wasn't mad at you. I was just worried and frustrated and very drunk. I'm sorry if I got a little carried away. You were right to stop me. I'll wait till it's right for you, Susan. What is the proper mourning period, anyway?"

"Mourning period? What are you talking about?"

"Your religion. Don't you have to wait a set time before you're allowed to . . . go out? Is it a year?"

She stared at him curiously, remembering the books she had seen in his bedroom. "It's not exactly a set time," she said awkwardly. "It's eleven months for a parent, and that's the longest." She looked down at her fingertips as if a more satisfying answer could be found there.

"So it's strictly up to you, then?"

"I guess so," she said uncomfortably.

Dale stroked her hair and rubbed his nose against her cheek. "Susan, am I wasting my time with you? I'm not trying to rush you: I understand you still need time to work out your feelings. I just want to know if there's a chance that you could ever feel about me the way that I feel about you. And I'm not just talking about sex. I know that you want me that way."

Susan was about to protest but realized there was no point. He was right about that and they both knew it.

"I mean," he continued, "I don't want to get my hopes up if there's no chance that you and me could ever happen. If you're unsure, I understand, but if you're just slumming—if you

175

know right now that there is absolutely no way that a woman like you could ever love a guy like me, I wish you'd save us both some heartache and tell me now." He dropped his hands to his sides and turned his face away.

There was nothing but silence for several minutes. "Susan?" Dale said finally, as if reminding her that he was still there. "You haven't said anything."

"You're right," she said, smiling shyly as she reached for him. "I haven't."

Dale continued to come by Susan's house almost every night after work, and they went out two or three times a week, but he didn't repeat the aggressive affections of that evening. If anything, he seemed more cautious and aloof than he ever had. He rarely came inside when he brought her home at night, and when he did, he didn't stay long. He never slept at her house anymore, even when Susan asked him to, no matter how late it was when they got in or how early he had to be at work in the morning. Susan lay in bed alone every night, recalling how his arms had felt around her waist when they had slept together at his office, wondering what it would be like to feel his hands all over her body.

Dale didn't forget his promise to take her to

the opera. He got tickets for *La Traviata* for a Saturday evening. "Do you realize," Susan said as she put the finishing touches on her makeup, "that this is the third Saturday night in a row that we've spent together?"

"I realize it," Dale said quietly.

"And we've been together every single night for the last two weeks." She looked at him coyly. "You haven't been dating anyone else, have you?"

"I haven't been out with anyone else in three weeks," he affirmed. "And if you want to know how long it's been since I've made love to a woman, it's been almost two months."

"Really?" Her feigned coyness was replaced by honest surprise. "How come?"

"I should think," he said wryly, as he fastened the catch of her necklace for her, "that the answer to that question would be obvious."

The theater was full, and they stepped gingerly over the toes of the other patrons as they made their way to their center-section seats.

"What do you think of it?" Dale asked at intermission.

Susan tried to think of a diplomatic response. The truth was, she'd been bored, but Dale was so eager to embrace and appreciate "culture" that she didn't want to dampen his enthusiasm. "Weren't the costumes brilliant?" she said at last.

Dale grinned, not at all fooled by her verbal sidestep. "I was bored, too. What do you say we get the hell out of here?"

They went to a club that played music from the fifties. She didn't know how he'd found that place, but for Susan it was a blissful trip down memory lane. She nursed her watered-down drink, inhaling the atmosphere. Dale, surprisingly, had only one drink himself. He spoke little but stared at her constantly, his eyes glistening with an expression that looked like pride. When he stood and spread his jacket over the back of his chair, Susan couldn't keep her eyes from staring at his chest. Dale's blue silk shirt was long-sleeved and not at all transparent, yet she felt as though she were seeing not only his body, but the muscles beneath the fabric.

He took her hand and led her slowly to the dance floor. Susan hadn't danced with Dale since waltzing to Natalie Cole at her house. He held her much closer this time, grazing her cheek with his lips and pressing her tightly against his body. She felt herself flow into his warmth. Although he was a head taller, they fit together perfectly in the dance position as she knew they must fit together in bed. She was soothed at first by the romantic music, but after a while she didn't even hear the band, only the beating of Dale's heart.

When he brought her home that night, he didn't give her his usual perfunctory peck. He pressed his lips against hers with an urgency that was as sweet as it was compelling. When his tongue plunged into her mouth, Susan felt the moisture between her legs. Dale leaned her over backward until she was almost horizontal, supporting her only with the weight of one broad palm. Although she realized, somewhere in the back of her mind, that she could break her neck if he dropped her, Susan drank the honey of his lips in total trust.

As he pulled her upright, their lips still sealed together, her body still enveloped in his strong arms, she felt his hardness pressing against her thighs. "Can I come in?" he whispered.

Dale had never asked permission to enter her house before. And she knew that wasn't what he was seeking admission to now. She wanted to say yes; she wanted to feel that hardness within her; she wanted to drown herself in the ocean of his body and the tide of his encompassing arms. And then she saw Jeff's face in Dale's eyes.

She pulled back as if she'd been shot. "I don't think so, Dale," she gasped, barely able to speak. "Not tonight. I . . . I don't feel very well."

She waited for the flash of anger in his eyes. But there was none. There was, in fact, almost a bemused twinkle and the hint of a smile playing about his lips. It was the smile of a general who has lost the battle but knows he has won the war. The smile of someone who knew that he would soon be sleeping once again in her house and that the next time he did, it wouldn't be on the living-room couch.

Susan couldn't sleep at all that night. Each time she tried to relive Dale's embrace, she was haunted by that earlier memory and that fear. What if he was who she thought he was? Was it fair to fall in love with him? Should she tell him the truth or should she keep silent? She didn't want to hurt him. And she certainly didn't want to risk losing him. She wanted his embrace, wanted it so intensely she was shocked and immobilized by the extent of her passion.

It was wrong to feel that way. Not so soon after her husband's death. How could she let lust override thirty years of love, respect, and affection? How could a middle-aged widow, a respectable woman with children, allow herself to express the pent-up yearnings that had cried out within her all her life?

* * *

"Susan, are you okay?" Dale's anxious voice crackled over the phone wire as the midmorning sun smacked her in the face. "I thought you would call by now. Are you feeling any better?"

"What time is it?" she asked in confusion.

"Eleven o'clock."

"At night or in the morning?"

Dale chuckled. "Susan, did I just wake you up?"

"No," she mumbled incoherently. "I just went to sleep."

She wasn't making any sense of his words, but his voice sounded so soothing. "Go back to sleep," he said. "Call me when you get up."

When she finally did get up, it was five o'clock. Susan dragged herself down to the kitchen and made herself a pot of strong coffee. It probably was a very pretty Sunday, she thought as she watched the last rays of the sun flashing off her neighbor's fence. Too bad she'd missed it. She helped herself to a slightly stale cherry danish. Then another. She was still in her nightgown and robe when Dale called again.

She let her answering machine pick up. She didn't want to talk to anybody right now, least of all Dale. She propped her feet against the rolled arm of the living-room sofa and closed her eyes for a few minutes.

When the phone rang again, it sounded strange and distant. Susan reached out blindly for the portable princess, patting the sofa all over until she found it. As she picked up the receiver, Susan heard only a dial tone. Then she realized that the ringing was coming from the front doorbell.

"What is with you?" Dale asked as she finally let him in the door. "I must have rung the bell ten times." Critically he looked over her night-gown-and-robe attire. "You haven't been out all day, have you?"

Susan shook her head wordlessly.

"Go get dressed," he ordered. "I'm taking you out for a ride. I think you could use some fresh air."

Susan did begin to feel better as the cool evening breezes caressed her face and her hair. It was a beautiful night to be in a convertible. Dale put his arm around her and hugged her close to him as they drove out near the beach. It seemed to help drive the demons away.

"Susan, have you eaten anything today?" he asked suddenly.

"Two cherry danish."

Dale pulled off the highway. "Let's get some food in you," he said. "No wonder you're acting like a zombie."

They went to a drive-up hamburger place and Dale ordered two supersupreme burgers, fries, and sodas. Susan felt like a cheerleader out on a date with the captain of the high-school football team. He probably *was* the captain of his high-school football team, she thought, gazing at Dale's broad shoulders.

"You're too good to me," she said, as they unwrapped their food. "You take good care of me, Dale."

"I like taking care of you," he said. "I'll always take care of you, Susan."

Susan caught her breath sharply. Something in his voice hadn't sounded quite like Dale. And it didn't sound like Jeff, either. She stared into the green eyes, and behind them she saw warm brown ones, eyes that promised fidelity and comfort and security. They were Mike's eyes.

When they got back to her house that evening, Dale pulled the Jaguar into the garage and reached into the back seat. "Are you spending the night?" Susan asked as he pulled out a freshly laundered uniform on a dry-cleaner's hanger and carried it in with him.

"Yes," he answered succinctly.

When Susan got into bed that night, she felt her eyelids close willingly with exhaustion and relief. It was comforting to know that Dale was downstairs. It had been a long time since his presence had filled her house like this, and she had missed that feeling.

She was just drifting off to sleep when she heard a rustling beside her elbow. Dale was sitting at the edge of her bed, pulling off his boots. Susan pretended to be asleep. Squinting out of the corner of one eye, she watched him remove his pants and peel off his shirt. As he crawled under the covers and lay down beside her, she slowly opened her eyes. Her eyes widened even farther as Dale gently slid his hands under her nightgown and pulled it up over her head. "It's time, Susan," he said.

A shiver rippled through her body as each inch of flesh was exposed. She knew her nipples must be tense with anticipation. Dale didn't touch her with his body but hovered over her, supporting himself on his knees and elbows as he kissed her softly, gently. Then he pulled back to look at her face. His eyes were warm seafoam green.

Dale kissed her again, this time plunging his tongue deeply into her mouth. Susan sought his mouth as well, grasping his neck to pull him closer. As his chest lowered to touch her breasts, she gasped.

"Am I too heavy?" he whispered.

She wouldn't have cared if he was. She delighted in the feel of his flesh against hers, in the honey-almond odor of his skin. "No. Hold me tighter. Touch me."

His hands were larger than she remembered, his chest broader. But the feel and smell of his body was unmistakable, imprinted on every pore of her skin.

She had waited so long to hold him like this. He'd been away for such a long time. She had wanted to make love to him that last morning, but there had't been an opportunity. He had looked at her with those somber green eyes as if he knew it was their last time together, as if he knew his plane was going to crash.

Susan stretched her arms around him, walking her fingers along the length of his back, slipping them inside his briefs to caress his firm buttocks. Dale groaned at her touch. Quickly he shed his undershorts, dropping them to the plush beige carpet. Then he pulled a slim package from the pocket of his jeans.

Dale entered her slowly the first time, then withdrew, as if giving her a chance to change her mind. Susan grabbed his shoulders and kissed his chest, then drew him to her again. He was warm and hard inside her, filling her up with a wholeness she had not felt in years. Susan wrapped her legs around him and held him close, forgetting her age and situation, forgetting everything except her own desire and the wonderful passionate fire of Jeff's body.

Ten

When Susan came downstairs the next morning, Dale was already in the kitchen, sipping a cup of black coffee. Tiptoeing up behind him, she flung her arms around his neck.

"Are you as good as I think you are," she asked coquettishly, "or has it just been a long time since I had sex?"

Dale raised his head but didn't return her hug. "It's been a long time since you had sex," he replied modestly. "Hell," he added, stroking his mustache, "it's been a long time since *I* had sex."

Susan smiled and waited to see if he would offer a compliment or at least a comment. He didn't. He didn't even look at her.

"Would you like some eggs?" she asked, walking to the refrigerator and opening it.

"No, thanks," Dale said tersely. "Coffee is fine." He kept his eyes focused on his cup.

Susan stared into the refrigerator without seeing anything inside it. He's disappointed, she thought. I wasn't good enough for him. He was expecting much more, especially since I made him wait so long. He's too disgusted to even look at me.

Eventually she removed a carton from the open refrigerator and poured herself a glass of orange juice. She wrapped her bathrobe tightly around her, suddenly very self-conscious about her body. It was probably her body that had disgusted him. Dale was used to dating young women whose slick, flawless bodies rolled effortlessly between his satin sheets. What must he have thought of the breasts that had nursed two babies, the stomach that was no longer flat, the thighs that screamed of cellulite? A lone tear slid down her cheek, but she dabbed it away with a dish towel.

Susan sidled into the seat opposite him, but Dale still didn't look up. "You're sorry we did it, aren't you?" she asked bravely. "I wasn't good enough."

At last he looked up, but his face was devoid of expression. "You were good enough," he said dully. "You were more than good enough."

She wanted to feel relieved, but somehow his remark didn't sound at all like a compliment. She felt compelled to humiliate herself still further. "Were you . . . disappointed," she asked, "in my . . . body?"

Dale shook his head. "I wasn't disappointed, Susan. You have a nice body. And not just 'for a woman your age.' For a woman of any age."

"Then *what?*" She nearly screamed it at him. "Why won't you talk to me?"

He slammed his cup onto the kitchen table, bouncing what little coffee was left in it over the sides. His chair scraped against the floor as he drew himself up to his full six feet two and glowered at her without speaking. Then he grabbed the chair with one hand, flung it toward the table, and stalked out of the room.

Susan listened nervously to the pounding of Dale's boots against the parquet floor as he paced agitated circles around the living room, wondering if she should follow him or stay where she was. She waited. After a few minutes he returned to the kitchen, picked up the chair he had tossed, and plopped down opposite her, staring at her with cold eyes.

Dale scrutinized Susan's face for long minutes. She tried not to blink under his glare, but that was impossible, and every time she did, she felt like she was flinching in guilt. "You lied to me, Susan," he said finally. "Jeff wasn't just your best friend. He was the love of your life, wasn't he?"

Susan felt her face pale. "Wh-what . . . what makes you think that?"

His face screwed up in distaste as he spat out, "Because you kept calling his name all night."

"Oh my god!" Susan clamped her eyes shut and reared back in her chair, hoping some theatrical mechanism would swoop down from the ceiling and carry her away. "Dale, I'm sorry. I didn't reali—I didn't . . . I'm sorry," she finished lamely.

"Sorry doesn't mean shit," he said curtly. "You don't love me. You don't feel anything at all for me. It's Jeff you were in love with all your life, and you still are. You wanted me because I remind you of him, because I look like him. You wanted to make me over into the image of your great lover. Jesus!" He laughed bitterly, running his fingers through his light brown hair. "I thought I was going to have a hard time competing with Mike. What a joke! Mike wasn't even in the running, was he?"

"It's not true!" she cried. "I loved Mike. And I never tried to make you over to be like Jeff. The part I like best about you, Dale, is the part that *isn't* like Jeff. Sure, you remind me of him. But that's not the only reason I was attracted to you. I do . . . care for you, Dale, very much."

His eyes went wild with anger. "You *care* for

189

me? You *care* for a dog or a cat. Susan, I wanted to love you with all my heart and soul. I wanted to spend the rest of my life with you. And you—you *care* for me?"

She broke down then, anguished tears churning out of her aching soul. Dale did not put his arm around her to comfort her. He just kept staring hate at her.

"All right," she said weakly, when the worst of the crying spasm had passed. "Jeff *was* the love of my life. I fell in love with him when I was twelve years old, the first time I ever saw him. And there hasn't been a day since that I haven't thought about him. But it wasn't a sexual relationship, not primarily. Yes, I *did* go to bed with him," she admitted, as Dale eyed her distrustfully. "But it wasn't until after we'd been friends for years and years."

Dale got up and went to the window, staring outside aimlessly for several minutes. When he sat down again, his voice sounded calmer. "Did Mike know about your relationship with Jeff? The sexual part?"

"He did at the end. Actually I think he knew about it all along. Jeff always said he did, anyway. He just didn't want to show it." She pounded her fists on the table. "Dale, I can't help the way I felt about Jeff. You can't choose who you love. I didn't want to love him, not that way, not after I met Mike. But I couldn't stop. I couldn't shut off my feelings."

"Damn you, Jeff!" Susan yelled in frustration at the ceiling. "Why did I ever have to meet you? Why did I have to fall in love with you? You have ruined every single relationship I ever tried to have. And you're still doing it!" She collapsed, sobbing, against the table, the rage and frustration of forty years spilling out of her gut.

This time Dale stood up and walked around to her. He knelt beside her and patted her head. "I loved him so much, Dale," she wept. "And he loved me, too, as much as he was able to love anybody. But he couldn't give me what you want to give me. And I could never give to anybody else what I wanted to give him." Until now, she thought. And now it's too late.

She buried her face in Dale's bare chest. He shivered slightly as the trickle of tears tickled his breastbone. "Take it easy, Susan," he said gently. "Maybe we can work this out. It can't be as bad as all that."

"Yes, it can," she sobbed. "It's worse." She cried for several more minutes before she was able to speak again. "I haven't told you everything, Dale. And I can't. I've hurt you enough already. If I'm right about what I'm thinking, it could devastate you."

"Now *there's* a good way to divert my interest," he said sarcastically. "I would never want to know what you're talking about with a lead-in like that."

"I don't know what I'm talking about," Susan said. "I have no proof. It's just a guess, a hunch, woman's intuition. Chances are my theory is totally and completely off base."

"Goddammit, Susan!" Dale cried, grabbing her by the collar of her robe. "You know damn well you have to tell me now. Just spit it out. Now."

Susan took a deep breath. Then another. Finally she decided it was best to do it the way he had suggested. Just spit it out.

"You do remind me very much of Jeff, Dale," she said, watching his eyes for any sudden manic change. "I don't believe that's just a coincidence. I think . . . I believe . . . he was your father."

Dale's face turned as white as the paint on the kitchen walls. His knuckles clenched and dug into the table. He opened his mouth to speak but no sound came out. When he finally was able to get words out, they were the same two words over and over. "Jesus Christ!" he kept repeating. "Jesus Christ!"

"I didn't want to tell you," Susan said miserably. "Maybe it's not even true, and I've upset you for nothing."

Dale had stopped shouting and was trying

desperately to regain his composure. He paced around the kitchen several times, quickening his steps each time as if the faster he walked, the faster this nightmare would be over. At last he stopped and leaned his back against the sink, his legs no longer able to support his own weight. "Jeff told you that he had an illegitimate son?"

"Oh, no," she said, eager to correct the misunderstanding. "If you are his son, Dale, he didn't know about it."

"What makes you so sure?" Dale asked acidly.

"He would have told me," she replied. "If not at the time, then . . . later." Jeff had always regretted not being able to have children. It had been a bitter pill for him to swallow, especially considering how active he had been, sexually in his youth. No, if Jeff had had any inkling that he had a child somewhere, he would have been out looking for him. He had wanted a son so much.

Dale spat out his words venomously. "Then why do you think he had one? And why me? There must be thousands of guys with my general physical description."

Susan took a deep breath in an effort to keep her voice even. "I'm twelve years older than you are, Dale. I met Jeff the same year you were born."

"So?" His sneer was triumphant. "I was born in Illinois. You grew up in Houston. That proves your stupid theory is a bunch of bull. He couldn't have been in two places at the same time."

Susan sighed. Dale did not have an open mind about this; he was going to fight her at every step. He obviously did not want to find out who his father was, at least not if it was *this* father. "Dale," she said carefully, "Jeff was *from* East St. Louis. He had just moved to Houston when I met him. And any third grader can tell you that it takes nine months to make a baby. So not only could he have been your father, but most probably, he didn't know anything about it. He probably moved away before your mother even knew she was pregnant."

Dale shook his head vehemently from side to side. "Lady, you're crazy. You're the lawyer, not me, but I'd say your case is based on a lot of circumstantial evidence. All you've told me is that I look like him and that he was in the same city at the time that my mother got pregnant. There were thousands of babies born in East St. Louis that year. And half of them were probably illegitimate. What makes you think that of all the shit-assed bastards who fathered little bastard boys that your friend was responsible for me?"

"Your eyes," Susan said promptly, gazing into them soulfully. "You have his eyes, Dale. I've never seen eyes like that before or since, and I'd know them anywhere. And I'll tell you another reason I think so, although you're going to tell me I'm crazy. I was psychic about Jeff. I used to get these strange premonitions, sometimes even sharp pains inside me almost every time he was hurt or in trouble." She swallowed hard. "I knew as soon as I saw his plane go up that it was going to crash."

Dale was looking at her curiously, but his green eyes were no longer scoffing. They were intent on her next words.

"I'm the same way about you, Dale. That night in the shop, when the jack collapsed—I didn't see it fall or even hear it move. I was facing the other way. The scream that came out of me came from someplace else."

Dale's body flinched. The skeptical expression remained on his face, but Susan could see the change in his eyes. He believed.

She wrapped her arms around him as if her fragile limbs could shield him from the hurt she had cast at him, but the heart-piercing arrow had already delivered its poison. "I'm sorry, Dale," she wept, wishing with all her heart that she could suffer his pain for him. "I've been praying and hoping that it's not true, but I think it is."

Dale's body quivered in her arms, but he didn't break down. He was as strong and as tough, on the outside at least, as the metal frame of the sturdy cars he worked on every day. When he finally raised his head, his eyes were wounded but completely dry. "Susan," he said slowly, "you were only twelve years old at the time this is supposed to have happened. How the hell old was he?"

"Fifteen."

Dale stared in shock. "My father was only fifteen years old?"

It was the first time he had used those words, the first time that he had allowed that Jeff might actually be his father.

"He might have been sixteen by the time you were born. Your birthday is in July, isn't it? What day?"

"The tenth."

Susan caught her breath and, despite the seriousness of the moment, began to shake with involuntary, hysterical laughter.

Dale didn't ask her what she was laughing about. He didn't need to. "He had the same birthday, didn't he?" he asked with the prescience of the damned.

She nodded. "I know that's just a silly coincidence. I know it doesn't prove that you're any relation to him. But it is eerie, isn't it?"

"It's *all* eerie," Dale responded. "And it's all coincidence. You have no proof, Susan."

"No," she admitted, "I don't. You're the only one who can provide the proof, Dale."

"Me? How?"

"You know how. Ask your mother."

Finally his composure dissolved. He turned around and slumped over the kitchen counter, his head in his hands. "Dale?" Susan asked anxiously. "Are you all right?"

"Oh, I'm just fine," came the muffled reply. "As fine as anyone would be who found out that the woman he thought he loved was really the lover of the father he never knew."

She let him cry silently, assuming that was what he was doing. Jeff had cried like that, not once, but many times, hiding his painful sorrow from even those who loved him. The clock over the stove ticked loudly, the only sound in the room. Susan wondered if Dale realized that it was Monday morning and almost seven o'clock.

"Jose will open up if I don't show," he said, when she got up the courage to mention it. "I don't think I can go to work this morning. If it's all right with you, I'm going back to bed."

Susan *did* have to go to work that morning. She had a courtroom appearance to make, a divorce case. The husband was claiming that his wife, Susan's client, deserved only a modest settlement because she had had an affair with his partner three years before. Susan was arguing that the affair was irrelevant; that the husband's real concerns were strictly monetary; and that an affair of three years ago that he'd only recently found out about was obviously in the past and therefore had no bearing on the present condition of the marriage.

Susan felt like a lying hypocrite in the courtroom. She knew only too well how relevant a past affair could be. She could have testified for the other side about the strength of a love that could persist for seven years after the lover's death. She knew she still had feelings for Jeff. But it wasn't true that she saw Dale as his reincarnation. She saw Dale as himself. At least she thought she did.

Not surprisingly, the settlement she was able to obtain for her client was far less than what she'd hoped for. As soon as her court appearance was over, Susan couldn't drive home fast enough. Much to her relief, the Jaguar was still parked in the garage. Thank you, God, she prayed silently. She had been sure that when she got home, Dale would be gone. If not to work, then just gone, gone for good. Maybe there was still a chance, then. Hadn't he almost said so? "Maybe we can work this out." Susan clung to the thin hope in those words.

She was worried when she went upstairs and found Dale still asleep, though it was midafternoon. Susan clattered her briefcase noisily against the bed, but he didn't stir. Stepping over his jeans and shirt, which lay in a crumpled pile on the floor, she removed her jacket and hung it over the back of the vanity chair. She sat down beside him, touching his cheek. "Dale?" she said, but there was no response. She leaned over him nervously, pressing her ear to his chest to make sure he was breathing. He was. He was just sleeping deeply.

Susan sighed in relief and kicked off her shoes. She turned back to watch him sleep. He really *is* beautiful, she thought. She touched the taut skin of his chest with delicate fingers. Mike had always worn his undershirt to bed. Dale apparently preferred to sleep bare, at least from the waist up. Jeff had been the same way, she thought wryly. Susan pressed her lips to Dale's smooth, muscular chest. He smelled like honey.

She slipped out of her skirt and blouse and lay down beside him. She was suddenly very tired. The gravity of the morning's anguish pressed her body into the mattress like a heavy stone.

When she woke up, the place beside her on

the bed was empty and the pile of clothes was missing from the floor. Susan kicked her way out of the covers and dashed to the second-floor landing. She couldn't see Dale, but she could hear him moving about downstairs. She wanted to call out to him but couldn't make the sounds come out of her throat. She retreated to the bedroom.

"I love you, Dale," she whimpered out loud. "I don't know why I haven't been able to tell you that. I didn't think I could love anybody again, not the way I loved him, but I do. You're the best thing to come into my life in a long time. Please, God," she begged, "let us work things out!"

"I'm willing," said a cool voice at the door of the bedroom. "If you meant what you just said."

She turned to see Dale's imposing figure framed in the doorway. "I do," she whispered. "I do love you." He held out his arms and she rushed into them. "I love you, Dale," she repeated. "I love you. I love you. I'm so sorry I hurt you."

His fingers caressed her back, but his eyes were focused on some imaginary object beyond her shoulder. "I was very upset this morning. I still am. You hit me with a double whammy, Lady. That's tough to bounce back from. I was ready to pack it in. I tried to leave, but I couldn't. I'm already in too deep." He pressed her to him. When he kissed her, Susan felt in his embrace if not forgiveness, then at least a thawing of his anger.

She suddenly realized that she was wearing only her bra and slip, but she felt no pang of modesty. Dale sat down on the bed and settled her beside him.

"I owe you for a long-distance phone call," he said. "I talked to my mother today." Susan felt her eyes jump out of her face. "I don't know what the charges are going to be. You can tell me when you get your bill."

"Will you forget the damn long-distance charges?" Susan cried impatiently. "What did she say?"

"I didn't ask her. It's not the kind of thing you can talk about on the phone. I'm going to go out there and see her next month." He looked Susan squarely in the eyes. "Suse, I want you to tell me about Jeff."

"Okay," she said guardedly. "What do you want to know?"

"Everything," he said firmly. "You can leave out the intimate parts; I'll spare you that. But I want you to tell me everything else you know, every detail you can remember."

"Dale, I'll be glad to tell you anything and everything, including the intimate parts," she offered. "But don't you think it's a little pre-

201

mature? Don't you want to wait until you've talked with your mother?"

"No," he answered. "If he *was* my father and Paula admits it to me, she'll be curious about him. She'd probably like to know what happened to him in his later life."

"But what if he wasn't your father?" Susan asked gently.

"Even if he wasn't, he was a very big part of your life for many years. I want to be a part of your life now. I need to know about him."

Susan stretched back on the bed with her head on the pillow, easing herself into a comfortable position. Dale lay beside her, resting his head on her stomach as Susan stroked his hair.

"Once upon a time," she began, "there was a boy with the face of an angel and the body of a god. He had so much love inside him that he wanted desperately to share, but he had so much pain and hurt in his life that he just didn't know how."

Eleven

"Susan, you look good!" exclaimed Gloria Ross as the women lined up in their usual places at aerobics class. "You've lost weight, haven't you?"

"A little," Susan smiled, stretching her leotard over her buttocks.

"What's your secret, a new diet?"

"Not really," Susan answered cryptically, glancing over at Barbara Strauss in the front row. "I guess I've just been getting more exercise." Barbara caught her glance and returned it with a wink. Susan was relieved to hear the instructor call for toe touches. The blood rushing to her cheeks as she bent over disguised the flush of embarrassment.

"It's not just the weight," Ellen Landman asserted as they were jogging in place. "You look happier than I've seen you in a long time. You know what I think, Susan? I think you're ready to start dating."

"Dating?" Susan gulped.

"Why not? You're still young. There's no reason to shrivel up and die. Charlie knows a couple of doctors from the hospital who are looking to meet someone nice. Would you like him to try to fix you up?"

Susan grimaced involuntarily at the unwelcome vision of a balding, sixtyish man wearing a hot pink shirt and a paisley tie. "No, thanks, Ellen," she puffed as she raised alternating knees to her chest. "I don't think I'm quite ready for that."

"Not ready for that?" Barbara teased as they showered and changed in the locker room later. "From the looks of that blush in your cheeks, Susan, I'd say you were already way beyond that." Susan blushed again. "So how *is* Mr. Super-Stud?" Barbara asked, as she adjusted the nozzle of her hair dryer.

"He's wonderful," Susan bubbled. "And not just in bed. He's really a terrific guy."

"Well, I am glad you think so," Barbara said. "Although you'll have to forgive me if I don't share your wide-eyed innocent enthusiasm."

"You still think he's using me, don't you?"

"What else?" Barbara shrugged. "He's already gotten into your panties. Has he gotten into your bank account yet?"

Susan flinched, although she wasn't quite sure why she did so. Barbara's implication was completely unjustified. Dale had never asked her for money. He always took her to nice places when they went out, and he always paid. But it was impossible not to raise at least the question that a May-September relationship like this one begged.

"Frankly, I'm surprised at you, Susan." Now that Barbara had found a vein, she proceeded to draw the blood out of it. "You've spent half your life counseling naive women who've gotten themselves hooked up with conniving, unscrupulous men. I would have thought that you of all people would know better."

Susan placed a cotton kerchief over her wet hair, tying it at the back and pulling the front down over her forehead. "Maybe I do know better," she snapped. "Maybe I've had enough experience in these matters to be able to tell the con artist from the genuine article."

The empathetic gaze Barbara fastened on Susan held just a sliver of pity. "Maybe there's a difference," she said softly, "between seeing someone else's situation with a clear head and seeing your own with a clouded heart."

She was a cornered rat who couldn't run; she had to fight. "You think I'm such a loser, Barbara?" Susan stuck her chin out aggressively. "You think it's totally out of the realm of possibility that a man could actually love me for myself?"

Barbara dropped her hairbrush and embraced her friend. "Of course not," she said reassuringly. "Of course a man could love you for yourself. A man closer to your own age and your own class. And your own religion," she added. She turned to Susan earnestly. "Have fun with this one, hon, but don't be too disappointed when your fairy-tale bubble bursts. And meanwhile," she cautioned, "hold on to your purse."

Susan dismissed Barbara's warning airily, but a sickening feeling grabbed hold of her stomach wall and settled in. Why *would* a man of Dale's age, who could probably have any woman he wanted, be interested in a woman like her? Why would a man with the face and body of a Greek athlete be attracted to a middle-aged widow with the face and body of a middle-aged widow? The answer was too obvious and too painful to acknowledge.

It didn't help that that week Oprah had on "Men Who Are Attracted to Older Women" and Sally Jessy had "Women Who Married Con Men." Susan watched Dale's face every time they were together, trying to glean some indication of any covert motivation, but she saw in his visage only loving tenderness. He *did* love her; he must. But she was afraid to look too deeply or too closely.

She vowed not to let emotion compromise

her judgment. She enjoined herself not to confuse lust with intimacy. But each time Dale wrapped his arms around her and smothered her face with kisses, she forgot her resolve. His eyes and his body made her trust him. In bed with him she lost all inhibition, seeking fleshly delights with a spontaneity she had not expressed in thirty years of marriage. He drew out her hidden desires and made her whole.

"You're magnificent," she murmured appreciatively, shivering with pleasure after a satisfying encounter.

Dale smiled. "We aim to please, Lady." He doffed an imaginary cap, a rather humorous image to contemplate as he lay on his back in her king-sized bed, completely naked. "Service is my business, you know."

"Well," Susan grinned, luxuriating in his arms, "you certainly know your business."

He drew absentminded circles with his finger around her nipple. "You're pretty damn magnificent yourself, Lady."

Susan blushed. "I haven't always been like this. I mean this . . . responsive. You think that maybe I'm only just now reaching my sexual peak? In the 'autumn of my years'?"

Dale smiled. "Could be. Could be you've got a lot of passionate years left in you. Don't think of yourself as autumn, Susan. I think you're just beginning your second spring."

She certainly did feel younger, prettier, more desirable, and her bliss, like the glow that marks an expectant mother, apparently showed on the outside as well. Her colleagues at work now accompanied their cheery morning greetings with knowing smiles. Susan wondered if they had guessed her secret. She had brought Dale to the office once, to see Jack Halvorsen about his suit against the jack manufacturer, but she had behaved very professionally and Dale had been more than discreet. In fact, he had acted like he barely knew her. Yet whenever she wandered down to the coffee room for a fix of caffeine, Susan felt eyes boring into her back and imagined she heard whispers and giggles. Especially when she was coming from Ron's office. Perhaps she was oversensitive. But the gigglers definitely clammed up whenever Ron showed up, and she knew she wasn't imagining that. Maybe, Susan thought with amusement, they thought she was having an affair with the boss.

Probably they were all resentful of the time she was spending with Ron. She spent the better part of each morning in his office, working with him on his special project, and often they took lunch together as well, either in the coffee room or at the bustling deli down the street. The traveling Ron had described was frequent, but required very few overnight stays. Most of their trips were to neighboring counties to conduct interviews or acquire depositions, and allowed them to return to L.A. by late evening. If Ron wondered, when he brought Susan home those nights, why her house was completely lit up and why the front door often opened seemingly by itself, he never asked about it.

Dale and Susan had already been asleep for hours one night when the phone rang. Susan pounced on it anxiously. Lois Webster had called three nights out of the last five at odd hours of the morning, reporting threatening phone calls and attempted visits from her abusive husband. The last time, Simon Webster had been thrown into a holding cell by police, but Susan had learned that by morning he'd been released on his own recognizance by a judge sympathetic to the well-heeled doctor's political connections. She feared that this time the telephone call was about more than verbal threats.

It wasn't Lois Webster. The woman's voice was vaguely familiar, but one she didn't recognize. "Is Dale there?" the voice asked brusquely. Susan's eyebrows furrowed in suspicion, but she wordlessly handed him the phone. Dale stirred himself awake and pressed the receiver to his ear. Susan went downstairs for a glass of water.

When she returned, Dale was putting on his pants. "Jennifer's car died on the highway," he explained. "I'm going to try and get her started."

"Jennifer? What is she doing out alone at two o'clock in the morning?"

Dale shot her a sideways glance as if to determine whether the intent of her question was concern or criticism. "She was coming home from a boyfriend's house." He tied his shoes and stood up, kissing Susan briefly on the cheek. "I won't be too long. Keep the bed warm for me."

She walked him downstairs. "You sure she'll still be there when you get there? A girl who looks like Jennifer is bound to have some guy stop to help her."

"She's had three guys stop already. That's why she called me."

Susan thought about how difficult it must be to look like Jennifer, so beautiful that you couldn't help attracting attention even when it was unwelcome. She had never felt sorry for a beautiful woman before, but she was beginning to grasp some understanding of what Jeff had always told her, that physical attractiveness could be a curse as well a blessing. If it was true for a man, it must be even more so for a woman. Susan wondered how many boyfriends the young woman had. And what about the man in New York that Jennifer was supposedly going to live with? There seemed to be a lot of unanswered questions about Jennifer Clemens. But the question that bothered Susan the most was: how had she known where to reach her father?

"Dale," she asked bluntly when he returned a few hours later, "how did Jennifer know to call you here in the middle of the night?"

He sipped the cup of decaffeinated coffee Susan had made for him. "She knows I've been dating you, Susan. If she couldn't reach me at home or at the garage, this was the next likely place to try."

"She knows we've been sleeping together? You discuss your sex life with your daughter?"

"It's not a secret, Susan. It's a reasonable assumption to make about two grown-ups who care for each other. Is it supposed to be a secret? You mean to tell me that your daughter doesn't know about us?"

"Of course she doesn't. At least I never told her. I don't discuss with my children what goes on in the privacy of my bedroom."

"Susan, maybe your daughter is that naive, but I think *you* are the naive one. What's the big deal, anyway? Are you afraid for people to find out that you're a sexual person with human needs and desires? Or are you just ashamed because it's me?"

"Of course I'm not ashamed of you," she said uncomfortably.

"The hell you're not. If you were screwing a doctor or a lawyer, you probably couldn't wait to spread the word to all your lunch buddies. *And* your children."

Susan sulked into her coffee cup. "That's not true. It's not because it's you. It's just that I have a reputation to uphold."

The pompous words grated on him, but she sounded so pathetically serious that Dale almost felt sorry for her. "Susan," he said kindly, "are your parents still alive?"

She looked up at him, bewildered by the question. "My mother is. Why do you ask?"

"Because you're acting like a twenty-year-old kid who needs her parents' approval for everything. So if it's not your parents, it's your children. Or your friends. You are so worried about pleasing everybody. Everybody but yourself. Screw everybody else, Susan. What do *you* want?"

I want you, Dale, she thought to herself, but she couldn't say it. She wasn't used to answering questions like that. She wasn't even used to asking herself questions like that. She had always defined herself by what others expected of her. She had played the good girl role all her life, eager to please her parents, her teachers, her friends. When she'd married, she had, of course, attempted to please her husband. And her children. Somebody else always had first call on her emotions. Even when she'd made a conscious effort to please herself, she hadn't always been sure what she wanted. Mike had been the one to see that she had been unhappy as a teacher. Mike had been the one to suggest she go to law school.

"Why not, Susan?" he had asked when she had protested, more out of fear of the unknown than anything else. Mike couldn't understand her reluctance. He had never known fear himself, not of that kind. Mike had always known what he wanted and how to get it. He had always forged boldly ahead after his goals, not stopping until he had achieved them. Susan only felt comfortable in a well-defined situation. She had been petrified of starting over again after years as a teacher, of sitting in classes where the students were several years younger than herself. Of watching them leave campus after their last class in groups of threes and fours to repair to the local bars for happy hour cocktails while she drove home to take care of a husband and baby.

But Mike had been supportive and helpful. When Joel had screamed his head off at three o'clock in the morning as she studied for semester exams, Mike had taken the infant for a two-hour ride in the car to calm him down and give Susan some peace. Mike had insisted on hiring a full-time housekeeper so that Susan wouldn't have to worry about household chores. When she'd finally walked up on that stage to receive her law degree, Mike had clapped the loudest and smiled the broadest of anyone in the audience.

Mike had been her rock, her manager. He had helped her find meaning in her life. They had grown together, fighting windmills together. In thirty years she had never made a decision without him.

It wasn't that she wasn't capable of managing by herself. After his death she had capably and efficiently put her husband's affairs in order, saving her sorrow and stark terror of being left alone for private moments. Her work had provided stability and continuity in her life, a twig to hold on to as the oceans swirled beneath her feet. Susan knew she owed her reputation as a competent, well-respected attorney to her own hard work and resourcefulness, not Mike's aggressive protection. Yet a big part of her life was missing without him. She had been one-half of a pair of oars; now she was a boat adrift without a rudder. As long as she stayed in charted waters, she was all right. But to start now, at her age, to redefine her needs and desires, this wasn't something she thought she could do. She had her life. Maybe it was only half a life, but it was predictable and well-ordered. She knew what to expect. She knew what was expected of her. Did it really matter whether or not it was what she really wanted?

"How come you're never home on Sundays anymore, Mom?" Andrea asked when Susan returned her call late one Sunday evening. "Every time I call you lately, I get your machine."

"Oh, I don't know," Susan said evasively. "Sometimes I go to flea markets or to visit friends. Sometimes I go in to work for a while. Today," she lied, "I just took a drive up the coast. It was such a beautiful day for a drive, don't you think?"

How could she tell her daughter the truth, that she had spent the day at Dale's house, lazing away the afternoon in the sun, enjoying the company of the man she loved? She just didn't know what Andrea's reaction would be. She might feel it was too soon after her father's death for her mother to be taking up with another man. She might feel it was out of character that Susan, for once in her life, should be satisfying her own needs and desires. Joel might be more understanding, but even he would be shocked if he knew to what extent Dale had taken over her life.

She wasn't ready to tell her children about Dale just yet. How could she? "I'm working on an interesting case now, and Grandma sends her best wishes, and, oh, by the way, I'm having an affair."

No way. There was no way she could tell them that their mother had taken a lover. She was uncomfortable even talking to Joel or Andrea on the phone when Dale was around. Although he was always quiet and unobtrusive during her conversations, just his presence in the house made her uneasy. Even if he were doing nothing more suggestive than lying on the couch reading a newspaper, Susan felt his sexuality and was sure that her children could accurately read what was going through her mind as she talked to them on the phone.

So she avoided talking to her children when Dale was in the house, and she didn't ask Andrea to come over except on those weekends when he went to San Diego to visit his son. She knew Dale had to be aware of what she was doing, but he was always cooperative and rarely seemed offended by the circuitous arrangements Susan made to elude being "discovered." Yet he was confident, too, as if he understood that he had her on a rope with a long let-out, a rope that he would eventually reel in when she got too tired, or too scared, of floundering alone.

Only to Barbara Strauss did she confide her secrets. The two women giggled like teenagers over Susan's romantic adventure, enjoying the rush of excitement it brought to both their lives, but Susan was constantly aware that beneath her friend's sympathetic interest lay a healthy layer of skepticism.

"Marty's working late tonight," Barbara announced in the shower room after exercise class the next week "You want to grab a bite and maybe catch a movie?"

"I can't tonight," Susan replied, toweling dry. "I'm picking Dale up at the airport and then I'm taking him out to dinner for his birthday. Barbara," she said suddenly, "why don't you come? It'll give you a chance to meet Dale."

"Oh, I couldn't, Susan," she demurred. "I don't want to interfere with your big welcome-home scene."

"It's no big deal," Susan assured her. "He's only been gone a few days. Join us. Dale won't mind. Maybe if you get to know him, you'll change your mind about him."

Ten minutes after they met the plane from Kansas City, Susan was sorry that she had urged Barbara to come. She was dying to know what Dale had learned from his mother, but she hadn't had five seconds alone with him since he arrived. Barbara was always right there at her elbow.

She didn't know what she would say when she *was* alone with him. She hadn't mentioned Jeff in weeks, not since that first time they'd made love. Dale hadn't said anything either, but she knew it must have been on his mind almost constantly. They were both afraid to talk about it. They were like defendants in a lengthy trial, their lives hanging in abeyance while they waited for the jury's verdict, those few simple words that could change the complexion of their relationship forever.

"He *is* gorgeous, Susan," Barbara admitted when Dale went to claim and identify his luggage. "And," she said reticently, "he seems very nice." Susan smiled distractedly.

Dale put his arm around Susan as they rode up the escalator. "Yes," he said, patting her shoulder affectionately. Susan coughed uncomfortably, mindful of Barbara standing just a step behind them.

"So you had a good flight?" she asked nervously.

"Yes."

"You saw your mother?"

"Yes," he said.

"She's doing okay?"

"Yes."

They walked out into the parking lot. "I'll bet your mom was excited to see you. It's been a long time since you went out to visit her, hasn't it?"

"Yes," Dale replied.

Susan nervously fit the car key into the trunk. How could she ask him what she wanted to ask him? Could she use some kind of code that he and not Barbara would understand? Finally she cried in frustration, "Dale, don't you have anything to say to me? Don't you have something to tell me?"

He smiled wanly as he hoisted his garment bag into the trunk of her car. "I've been trying to tell you for twenty minutes, Susan. The answer to your question is yes."

Twelve

"It's a hell of a birthday present, isn't it?" Dale commented wryly when they finally were alone in bed that night. "After all these years, to finally find out who my father was. And the bastard had to die before I ever got a chance to meet him."

"I don't even have a picture of him," Susan lamented.

"You don't?" Dale sat up curiously. "Why not?"

Susan bit her lip hesitantly. "Jeff was . . . Jeff was . . . well, extremely good-looking. And he knew it. And he used it, too. But he was always insecure about it. He always felt that people, especially women, liked him only because of his looks. He got so mad about it one day, he destroyed all the pictures he ever had of himself. He said he felt like a prisoner inside his own skin."

Dale smiled, but it was a sad smile. A smile of understanding.

"I wish you could have known him, Dale. I know he would have wanted to know you. Of course," she said sadly, "with the small age difference between you, I don't think he would have been much of a father for you, but I do think you could have been good friends. How did your mother react?"

"She was shocked. She couldn't believe that I actually found out on my own. At first she didn't want to talk about it. Like denying it would make it untrue. I had always thought that she hated my father, that he was some sleaze who practically raped her and that was why she never wanted to tell me anything about him. But I found out this week that the opposite was true. She was in love with him. But he apparently didn't feel the same way. She was embarrassed and ashamed that she'd given herself and gotten nothing back."

"She has nothing to feel embarrassed about. She may have been the first, but she certainly wasn't the last. All women felt that way about Jeff. I don't think he ever intentionally tried to hurt anybody. In fact, I think he did all he could *not* to lead women on, but he couldn't help it. He was just so damn sexy."

She spoke those words without noticing the despondency in Dale's eyes. He had turned them away because he didn't want to show her his pain, but it was obvious to Dale that Susan was no exception to Jeff's rule. She was still in love with the man, even though he had been dead seven years. Dale shuddered. It was difficult enough to compete with a ghost, but how could he contend with the memory of his own father? When Susan looked in his eyes, whose eyes did she see? When he held her in his arms, whose arms did she feel? When they made love . . . He tossed the painful image out of his brain. This had to be one for the tabloids. It was about the most perverted thing he had ever been involved in.

He buried his face in the down pillow. Susan's fingers stroked his back lovingly as doubts of her own flooded her consciousness. What am I doing? she asked herself in shocked disgust. I'm making love to my lover's son. Jeff's child. The product of his loins. If Dale were a little younger, he could almost have been *my* child. The product of our love together.

Her eyes caressed the naked body of Jeff's son, the child neither of them had known he had. This was crazy. Dale wasn't a child; certainly he had never been Jeff's child in any sense but the biological one. He was a man. He was the man she had fallen in love with, the man who created and satisfied her desires.

Her love for Dale was totally separate and without bearing on the love she'd felt for Jeff. Or so she told herself.

At the end of the summer, Barbara and Marty Strauss held their annual Labor Day bash at their Malibu beach house. "Come one, come all," Barbara announced, handing out computer-written invitations at exercise class to their circle of friends. "Bring your spouse, bring your lover, bring your spouse *and* your lover, bring your dog. *Don't* bring your children." This last was not-so-subtly directed toward Beverly Werner, whose three not-very-adorable stepchildren had practically wrecked Barbara and Marty's beach house last year.

"You can bring Dale, Susan, if you like," Barbara whispered, as they dressed at their lockers, out of earshot of the others. "You *are* coming, aren't you?"

"I don't know. I mean, yes, I am coming—that is, if you don't think I'll look like the poor pitiful widow who doesn't know enough to stop hanging around her married friends after her husband dies. I don't know about Dale. He'll probably have to work. Saturday is his busiest day."

Not that she gave him the chance to make that call himself. Susan never even asked him if he wanted to go to the party with her. Dale would be out of his social element, she rationalized as she parked her dark gray Cutlass beside a grassy embankment and walked past the dozen or so cars already stretched in a line toward the beach house. What would he talk about, car engines?

As she joined the scene on the beach, Susan felt somewhat justified in her autocratic decision. Marty Strauss, an accountant, was lamenting the demise of the tax shelters that had kept his clients' money away from the government's coffers and funneled deep into his own pockets. This complaint was said to Ellen's husband, Charlie Landman, who in turn bewailed the high cost of malpractice insurance. Susan poured herself a drink from a pitcher on one of the round glass tables and went in search of her hostess.

"Glad you finally made it, Susan," Barbara beamed. Her eyes took in Susan's singular situation, but she made no comment. "Ron was here earlier, but he left. He asked about you."

"Ron Davis? My boss?" Marty Strauss's CPA firm was the accountant for Davis, Dobbs and Engels, and the Strausses and the Davises had been friends for many years. "He probably wanted to know if I had the Adams file. I took it home with me to work on this weekend."

Barbara's eyes indicated that Ron's interest had not been in any file, but she didn't pursue the subject. "Well, help yourself to some chips and vegetables. The hamburgers will be ready soon. Ellen's out there somewhere, supposedly setting out plates."

Ellen Landman was flitting about coquettishly, tasting sips of everyone's drinks and hors d'oeuvres, pretending to be far drunker than anyone could possibly be on twelve sips of watered-down liquor. Ellen. Mrs. Landman. Dale called her Mrs. Landman, even when he spoke of her to Susan in private. Ellen might think he was good-looking in a wild and dirty sort of way, fun to fantasize about from her own lofty perspective, but she would definitely be *très* ticked off if *her* car mechanic—Ellen thought of service people as her personal servants—were to see her in a bikini. And Dale would be embarrassed as well at being placed in that awkward position, a position which might even cost him a good customer.

It was possible there might even be others at the party who would recognize Dale and know what he did for a living. Everybody in southern California seemed to be driving foreign cars these days. She had definitely made the right decision.

"Susie! Good to see you!" A robust, middle-aged man waltzed over and clapped Susan on the back. Stan Ross, Gloria's husband, owned a men's clothing store in a less-than-affluent Los Angeles neighborhood, and he was forever bragging about how he swindled and cheated his unsuspecting customers. "Those goyim are so stupid," he crowed proudly. "I just sold a suit for $599 by telling 'em it was a deep-discounted $900 designer label with the label cut out, when it was really a piece of schlock I picked up for $149 at a warehouse close-out."

Susan cringed and tried to escape politely before Stan bent her ear with another horror story. She was *very* glad that Dale would not be meeting Stanley Ross.

And then there was Beverly and Arthur Werner. Beverly and Dr. Arthur Werner, the noted plastic surgeon. Art had a face that looked like he'd designed it himself.

Beverly Werner was adoringly and rapturously in love with her catch of a husband. She even wore a solicitous, caring face, in public, for his three irascible, incorrigible children. At home, of course, the little brats were taken care of by a housekeeper, and Beverly never even went near their second-floor bedrooms.

Beverly doted on Arthur and never tired of bringing him drinks and listening to his stories, sitting submissively at his feet or leaning in over his words like a wide-eyed doe. "Isn't he cute," she chirped, when Arthur flashed his teeth at practically every woman in attendance at a party, eyeing more than a few breasts and squeezing more than a few bottoms with the flirtatious pretense of measuring the posteriors for a fanny tuck. "Arthur just loves to flirt, but it's all just a joke."

The joke was on Beverly, of course. Everyone but his wife knew that Art Werner had been fooling around with his office nurse for three years and probably half the nurses on three floors of Cedars Sinai Hospital as well.

Susan looked around her at the people who had made up her small social circle for the past twenty-five years. Dale would never fit in with her "sophisticated, cultured" friends. He was a man who dealt honestly and fairly with his customers, and treated every person with whom he came in contact with the respect he'd accorded his grandmother. He just wouldn't fit in at all.

She filled a plastic cup with piña colada punch and sat alone at a glass-topped table, scanning the darkening skies as thick clouds began to gather over the Pacific. A tear skirted the inside corner of her eye and trickled slowly down her nose. She didn't even bother to wipe it away. She had been afraid for Dale to meet her friends. She had thought she was ashamed to introduce him to people who might think themselves his "betters." She should have been ashamed for him to see the shallowness of the people with whom she'd spent a large portion of her existence. What a fool she had been, a

fool commanded by vanity. She had a rare, un-
polished diamond, and she had traded it for
a shimmering handful of worthless rhine-
stones.

The crowd was thinning out as the skies grew
more threatening and a few sprinkles of rain
fell on the picnic tables. "Not to worry," Barbara called as the few remaining guests
reached for their car keys. "It's a southern
California shower. It'll be over in a few minutes."

But the drizzle turned into a downpour. The
guests scooped up the plates and serving
bowls, and scurried into the house to take ref-
uge from the storm. A glass of red wine and
flickering flames of glowing firewood helped
restore the warmth to Susan's drenched body
and chilled soul.

When at last the rain subsided, the last couples departed. Barbara and Marty walked
Susan to her car.

It wasn't where she had left it. Not exactly.
The assault of water against the too-dry
ground had turned the sparsely grassed embankment to mud, and the loose dirt had
sloshed over the sides, carrying the two front
tires of Susan's car with it into the shallow
ditch.

"Wow!" Marty exclaimed. "You're going to
need a tow truck to get that out. And lots of

luck getting one at this hour on a Saturday night."

Susan looked at her watch. It was only a little after seven. "I think I just may be able to find someone to help me."

"This is Dale Clemens," the answering machine announced when she phoned the garage from the Strausses' kitchen. "Service hours are from seven to six. If this is an emergency . . ."

Susan waited for the message to finish. "Dale," she entreated, "if you're still there, please pick up. My car is stuck—"

He answered before she finished her sentence. "What happened, Suse? Where are you?"

She told him, and in twenty minutes Dale's maroon and white pickup pulled up to the knoll near Barbara and Marty's house.

"Looks like you've got yourself in pretty deep," he remarked with a half-smile as he hooked the winch from his truck to the back bumper of the gray Oldsmobile. When it was securely fastened, he stepped into the cab of the pickup, leaving the door open, and gunned the motor. The truck lurched forward suddenly and jerked backward. The Cutlass's wheels spun against the ground, furiously spitting mud, but the car did not move. Dale tried again. This time the car moved inches, but only inches, up the embankment. After another almost futile attempt, Dale jumped out of the truck.

"You try it, Marty," he commanded in a voice that was polite but authoritative. "Just rev it slowly and keep the wheels straight."

As Marty got in the truck, Dale climbed up the embankment and step-slid carefully into the ditch, coating his boots with a thin veneer of brown mud. He braced his arms against the front of the Oldsmobile and gave Marty the signal to pull. The car groaned and whined, sputtered a last complaint, and with a powerful boost from Dale, heaved its front wheels out of their entrenchment and climbed in one great gasp to the top of the embankment.

Susan and Barbara clapped and whistled. When Susan caught sight of Dale, she broke out in hysterical laughter. His face, arms, and clothes were splattered with brown sludge. His mustache was two shades darker than it had been, and even his forehead was dotted with dirt. Dale's eyes sparked with anger at Susan's reaction, but as he looked himself over, he began to laugh as well.

"Come on inside, Dale," Barbara offered, her eyes twinkling, "and get cleaned up. You can borrow some of Marty's clothes to wear home."

As they removed their shoes and scraped the bottoms against the braided rubber mat inside the doorway, Dale's ever-observant eyes took in the plastic plates and utensils, the half-eaten dips and leftover snacks. "Looks like you had quite a party here," he remarked without emotion.

Uh-oh, Susan thought.

"Oh, yes," Barbara chirped. "It was one of our best, till the storm hit. I'm so sorry you couldn't make it, Dale. I'm sure everyone would have been delighted to meet you."

Marty was six inches shorter than Dale but about twenty pounds heavier. When Dale emerged after a quick shower wearing Marty's slacks and shirt, the loose pants bagged about his waist but only reached mid-shin. The flannel shirt reached his waist, but the sleeves were nowhere close to his wrists. He joined the others in front of the fireplace and gratefully accepted a snifter of brandy.

"I understand you're the world's best car mechanic," Marty said as they drank a toast. "At least Ellen Landman thinks so. Do you work on Porsches much?"

Dale grinned. "Only five or six a day."

They made an appointment for Marty to bring his car in the following week. They continued to talk about sports and politics and business. Dale seemed completely comfortable, not at all self-conscious, and certainly not angry. He even wrapped his arm around Susan and cuddled her close to him on the floor in front of the fireplace, engendering knowing nods between Barbara and her husband.

As the hour grew late, Dale raised himself up and helped Susan to her feet. "If it's all right with you, folks, I'd like to leave Susan's car here overnight. The engine's probably flooded—I wouldn't want to try to start it up now, and that winch on my truck's not strong enough to tow it clear across town. It'll probably dry out enough to drive by morning. We'll come back to pick it up then."

He put his arm around Susan's waist to guide her through the darkness, waving good-bye with a bright smile to their host and hostess. Gently he helped Susan climb into the cab of the truck, then walked around and hoisted himself into the driver's seat. Then the bright smile faded.

Uh-oh, Susan thought again.

When they reached the main road out of the beach community, Dale scratched his head thoughtfully and remarked, as if it had just occurred to him, "You know, Susan, I must be getting old and forgetful. This party today completely slipped my mind. In fact, I don't even remember your inviting me."

Nobody could do sarcasm the way Dale could. The more innocent his tone, the more accusing it seemed. She waited for the rest of it.

"I'm sorry, Dale," she mumbled finally. "I did it to you again, didn't I?"

His answer was almost cheerful. "Yeah, babe, you did." He leaned his arms over the steering wheel and pretended to stare intently at the traffic. He said no more about the incident. He said nothing more about anything.

Susan didn't say anything either. There was nothing she *could* say. She had denied him for the third time, and there was no excuse for her actions. No excuse except her own gutlessness.

It was a long, silent drive home. Susan hated Dale's silent treatment worse than anything. It was maddening to see him act so calm when she knew he had to be seething inside. When at last he pulled the truck up into her driveway, he didn't turn the motor off but remained sitting for a long time behind the wheel. Susan waited expectantly, biting her lip to avoid asking "Aren't you coming in?" Finally, resignedly, she climbed down from the truck and closed the door. After another minute, Dale switched off the engine and followed her inside.

Susan breathed a small sigh of relief. Apparently Dale's sense of duty was stronger than his feelings of anger. He had made a commitment to bring Susan back to pick up her car the next morning, and he was going to honor it.

When he crawled into bed beside her, she almost wished he hadn't stayed. His body faced pointedly away from her, discouraging any attempt at reconciliation.

Susan tried to turn over and go to sleep, but her body kept turning to face his. She wanted to caress his body with her hot fingers, to kiss him all over in penitence. Who was she kidding? Her body ached not with repentance, but with desire. She yearned for him to turn over and embrace her. She craved the satisfying feeling of his flesh against hers; her body felt open and exposed without him. This torture was the worst punishment he could have inflicted on her: to lie so close, to smell him and feel his warmth, and not be able to hold him.

"Dale?" she whispered, but he didn't hear her. She turned away quickly in shame. She had almost begged. She couldn't believe she had sunk so low, to need a man that much. She buried her face in her pillow and whimpered.

At 3:16 Dale turned to face her. He held out his arms for her and Susan quickly settled into them. He held her tightly, closely, in a tense lock. His fingers were rougher than usual and his caresses fewer. His body was urgent and hard, and penetrated hers much sooner than usual. It was almost too soon for Susan. She bit her tongue but refused to cry out. She knew the tightness inside her would be better for him, and tonight she wasn't concerned about her own gratification. She wanted only to yield to him whatever pleasures she could give him.

Afterward, he didn't roll away immediately but lay on top of her for several minutes, stroking her breasts with the tenderness that had been virtually absent in his lovemaking. His fingers on her body played a concert of apology for his earlier roughness. He buried his face in her neck. His hair was matted and sweaty, and his eyes pressed wet salt into her skin.

Susan held him with an aching tenderness. She needed him so much. She was addicted to this man, both in and out of bed. But she was flirting with danger. Dale wasn't from her world. He was good and kind and decent, but he was foreign to the life she lived. She shared no common memories with him as she did with her friends. So maybe her friends weren't the most morally upright and charitable people in the world, but they were still her friends. They had shared the same rites of passage together. They had been through childbirth and diapers and potty training. They had attended Passover Seders in one another's houses. They had watched their children toddle off to school on their first day with hopefulness and trepidation. They had drunk innumerable cups of coffee together, dishing out dirt about whoever was not present at the time. They had seen their children become friends, carpooled them to Hebrew school, compared notes and aggravations about Bar Mitzvah celebrations. They had held one another's hands in times of marital discord, suffered each other's pain, and shared one another's joy. They had watched their children grow up and leave the nest. They had seen husbands die.

She had to be crazy at her age to want to challenge the way of the world. It was her duty, her fate, to accept the image she had developed over decades. To break away from that mold would be a reckless and immature act. She was a respectable widow. A respectable widow, she thought wryly, whose loins went wet at the touch of the man who now lay beside her.

She fitted her body against his and let Dale's arms encompass her like a protective tent. They slept until the sun's rays squeezed through the tiny slits between the miniblinds.

Dale woke first, kissing her softly and waiting patiently for her sleepy response. When Susan opened her eyes, she saw immeasurable sadness in his. "It's not going to work, is it?" he said.

Susan gulped as the warmth which had enveloped her body dissipated like the early morning mist. "What isn't?"

"You and me. No matter what I do, I'll always be poor white trash. I could go to school for ten years and get a Ph.D. in Nuclear Physics and I still wouldn't be smart enough for you. I'll never be rich enough for you or classy enough." His voice became barely audible. "You'll never love me."

"You don't understand, Dale," she said, as tears brimmed in her eyes. "I do love you. I never thought I could ever feel this way about anyone again. But people don't exist in a vacuum. It's not just you and me. I bring a lot of baggage to this relationship. I've lived the same kind of life for thirty years. Anything new that I add to it has to fit in."

"And I don't." It was a statement, not a question.

"No," she said sadly, "you don't. But it's not just because you're not a doctor or a lawyer. It's because you're not what I'm used to. It's because you're not from the same factory that all my friends and relatives are from. It's because you're not . . . Jewish."

There it was. She couldn't believe she'd said it just like that. She had just blurted it out.

Dale looked at her like she had uttered a totally incomprehensible statement. After a minute he said, "You mean because I'm not circumcised?"

She blushed bright red. "No, that's not why. It has nothing to do with your physical attributes, Dale." Which are pretty impressive, she couldn't help thinking as her eyes focused on his body.

"Then what?"

He didn't have a clue. His background was so different from hers that he couldn't even see how different they were from each other. "It's culture," she tried to explain. "It's the way I was brought up. My religion is important to me."

"Since when?" he asked acerbically. "Susan, I've been here an awful lot of Friday nights and Saturday mornings, and I've never seen you go to synagogue once."

She was surprised and a little bit pleased that he knew when services were held. This was not knowledge drawn from the general wellspring of Dale's background. He had obviously been reading up. "Well, of course I haven't," she replied. "It's because you were here."

"Bullshit. I never stopped you from going anywhere. Saturday mornings, I'm usually gone before you even get up. If you don't go to synagogue, it's because you'd rather sleep, not because of me."

"Well," she conceded lamely, "I might have gone Friday nights."

Dale stared at her. "You never told me you wanted to go to services. I wouldn't have minded if you had. Hell, if you'd wanted me to, I would have gone with you."

"You would?" Genuine surprise lit her face.

"Sure, why not? I've never been to a synagogue before. I wouldn't mind seeing what it's like."

She smiled like a child. "If you'd really like to, I'll take you with me sometime. Maybe at Rosh Hashanah. And," she added in a spirit of fairness, "I'll go to church some Sunday with you if you'd like."

Dale laughed. "It'll probably be a cold Sunday in July. I haven't been inside a church since my wedding day."

It was a relief to have finally given voice to the concerns that churned within her and to have received such a favorable response from Dale, but Susan knew that the issue had only been opened, not resolved. Dale just didn't understand. It wasn't about going to church or synagogue; it wasn't about worship. It was about being who you are. It was understanding how others saw you.

"Never marry a *goy*, Susan," her mother had warned her as a child. "No matter how nice he is, no matter how liberal he seems, the first time you have an argument, he's going to call you a dirty Jew."

Dale wouldn't understand about that. He couldn't see why the difference in their religions was suddenly so important to her. It hadn't been, she had to admit, when they were just friends or even just dating. It certainly didn't matter in the bedroom. But when you were considering spending the rest of your life with someone . . . She shook her head sadly. He just didn't understand.

Thirteen

The Indian summer days of late September heralded the approach of Rosh Hashanah and Yom Kippur, the Jewish High Holy Days. Susan's children usually spent the holidays in Los Angeles with her, attending the synagogue that she and Mike had belonged to since Joel was a baby. This year, however, Andrea was going to be spending the holidays in Philadelphia with her boyfriend and his parents. Susan had met Mr. and Mrs. Berman just once, at Mark's college graduation, and they seemed very nice, although a little on the formal side. Mark's father, a scion of a wealthy Philadelphia banking family, was a graduate of an ivy league college and business school. Mark himself was a very bright boy, a chemist at a major petroleum company subsidiary, and he seemed to have a promising career ahead of him. Susan's eyes glistened as she saw wedding bells in the near future.

Joel was planning to drive in from San Francisco on the Friday afternoon before Rosh Hashanah for an extended weekend. It had been several months since Susan had seen her son, and she was excited about his visit. She was a little nervous about what to do about Dale, however. She couldn't very well make up four or five excuses to keep him away from the house every night. Besides, she had practically promised to take him to Rosh Hashanah services. After some deliberation, she decided that *not* to invite him to meet her son would not only be socially awkward, but a grievous insult to him. She asked him to come for Friday night dinner.

"Are you sure that's what you want?" Dale teased. "Aren't you afraid he might guess that we sleep together?"

"I'm only asking you for dinner. You'll have to go home afterward, if you don't mind." She felt suddenly rude and uneasy. "You *don't* mind, do you, Dale? I mean, Joel is not Andrea—I think he's mature enough to handle it—but still, I don't want to flaunt it."

Dale smiled. "I don't mind. I know you want to spend some time alone with your son. I *do* know how to be discreet."

On Friday afternoon Susan left work early

so that she could prepare chicken soup and appetizers. She had promised her son a traditional Friday night dinner with all the trimmings, and she wanted everything to be just right. As if serving a good dinner would guarantee Joel's liking Dale. She knew she shouldn't need his approval. But Joel had always had a good head on his shoulders, and she trusted his judgment. As long as it concurred with her own judgment, she thought wryly.

She was just setting out the wine glasses when Dale called to say he wouldn't be able to come. Jennifer's car had broken down on her again. She had planned to drive it to San Diego that night to visit her mother, but now, he explained, he'd have to drive her there himself.

"Your daughter's still in town? I thought she was moving to New York."

"Next week. She wanted to spend her last few days in California with Diane and Randy."

"But it's only a couple hours drive to San Diego," Susan protested. "Why don't you bring Jenny here with you tonight? You can leave right after dinner."

After some persuasion, he agreed. He and Jennifer were having drinks in the living room when Joel arrived.

"I thought you said you sold Daddy's Jaguar," he remarked, after hugging Susan and

243

bussing her on the cheek. He cast an eye out the window at the red convertible sitting in the driveway.

"I did. I'd like you to meet the new owner." She introduced him to Dale as he entered the kitchen.

Dale and Joel shook hands warmly and said the polite things. Susan noticed Joel's eyes take in Dale's face, body, and demeanor in one three-second glance. He had apparently already formed an impression.

"You look sort of familiar," Joel said as Dale helped him push his suitcase out of the kitchen. "Have we ever met before?"

Oh my god, Susan thought, Joel notices it, too. He sees the resemblance to Jeff. A vague panic settled in her stomach. She hadn't considered this eventuality, that Joel might figure out who Dale really was. She didn't know what she would do or say if he did. Her main concern right now, however, was for Dale. What must be going on *his* mind? Was he fearing the same thing?

But Dale was smiling. "We have met actually, although I wouldn't have expected you to remember. It was a long time ago. Your dad brought you into my shop a few times when you were first learning to drive. He wanted me to teach you how to take care of a car and do routine maintenance."

"I remember!" Joel said. "You made me take the carburetor apart and put it back together. That was at that place over on Hill Street. You still work there?"

"No, I have my own shop now. Speaking of which, your mom tells me you're a computer genius. Maybe you could advise me what software to use for my financial system."

"Sure thing." Joel was smiling, not just a polite smile now but a sincere one. Susan felt hopeful.

Joel's smile got broader and his eyes lit up when he was introduced to Jennifer. Susan was a little surprised. Joel didn't usually get bowled over by a pretty face. He had always had the capacity for insight, the ability to see with his heart, even as a child. His keen eyes had never let fine trimmings or elegant manner obstruct his view of the person underneath. That was why she'd always respected his judgment. That was why she was so anxious to know his opinion of Dale.

At the moment, though, Joel seemed much more interested in Jennifer, and Dale's daughter was apparently as impressed with Joel as he was with her. Susan left her guests to talk while she put the last touches on dinner, worrying what Dale and his daughter would think of the unfamiliar foods and customs.

Dale and Jennifer listened politely as Susan

and Joel did the Friday night blessings. They sipped their wine at the right places, and Dale helped slice the large loaf of challah bread. Susan felt somewhat relieved. Maybe these ceremonies didn't seem as alien to him as she had feared.

She looked around the table at the three faces. Dale sat at the head, enjoying his soup, looking very much like the master of the house. She sat at the foot, closest to the kitchen, the eternal mom. Susan sighed with longing at the scene playing around the table. It was very much like a family scene.

Memories flooded Susan's consciousness. She could almost envision Mike sitting where Dale was now and Andrea sitting in Jennifer's seat. She had lived this family holiday dinner so many times. Now Mike would be clinking his spoon against the wine glass to say a few words, and Andrea would be shoving her gefilte fish, which she detested, onto Joel's plate while he stole her chopped liver and hid it under the table.

Susan blinked her eyes and returned to the present. It was Dale sitting across from her now, and tousle-headed, nine-year-old Andrea had turned back into sophisticated, blond-haired Jennifer. Dale's daughter seemed much more animated than she had at their first meeting at Dale's house. She and Joel sat opposite each other at the dinner table, conversing as if there were two screens separating them from the ends of the table, barely aware of the presence of the others. Dale smiled at Susan knowingly over the heads of the young people. Apparently he was used to this.

After dinner Joel and Jennifer retired to the living room to continue their conversation while Dale helped Susan with the dishes. She was pleased that the kids were getting along so well and grateful to be alone with Dale for a few minutes. It had been difficult for her to spend the whole evening without touching him. Since they had become intimate, she found it hard to keep her hands off him whenever they were together. Now, after making sure that they could not be seen from the living room, she linked her arms around his neck and pressed her body against his. Dale leaned over her and kissed her sensuously, massaging her buttocks with his hands as he pulled her in even closer.

After a few minutes, Susan reluctantly pulled away. "We'd better not start something we can't finish," she whispered. "I'm going to miss you tonight."

"Me, too," he said, smoothing her rumpled hair with his fingers.

"Will you call me tonight when you get back in town?"

Dale shook his head. "I'm not coming back tonight." Susan's eyebrows jumped up involuntarily. "As long as I'm going, I might as well stay for the weekend." He spoke to her surprised expression. "You're going to want the time to spend with Joel, and it's been a while since I've seen my own son."

"The garage?" she asked in disbelief. "You're going to take a Saturday off?"

Dale laughed. "Jose knows where to find me if he needs me."

Susan rubbed his back, already missing him. "Where do you stay when you go down there?" she asked, slightly fearful of the answer.

"At the house. Usually in Jen's room if she's not with me. Or on the couch."

He waited expectantly for the question that he seemed to sense was coming. Susan hesitated to ask it. Dale, like Jeff, rarely compromised truth for the sake of tact. You didn't want to ever ask him a question unless you were prepared to a hear an honest answer. "Do you—do you ever sleep with your ex-wife?" she stammered finally.

"Yes," he answered candidly, as Susan had known he would. "Sometimes I do, when Diane isn't involved with anybody." He looked at Susan significantly. "I'm not going to do it tonight."

"Oh?" She tried to make her voice sound casual. "She's involved with somebody now?"

"No." He watched her eyes as he spoke, completely aware of how keenly she was awaiting his next words. "But I am."

Until she felt her breath expire with relief, she was unaware that she had been holding it. She still wasn't convinced, however. "But what if she asks you to?" she pressed.

Dale smiled at her insecurity. "I know how to say no, Susan. That prerogative is not just reserved for women." He brushed her ear with his lips. "I told you, I don't mess around on the woman I love."

They finished loading the dishwasher in silence. Susan's heart was too full with love to speak.

"I'd better get going," Dale said reluctantly, as Susan wiped off the counter. "Jen," he called out, "are you ready?"

Jennifer was staring into Joel's eyes, looking like the last thing she wanted to do was leave. "You don't have to go, Mr. Clemens, if you don't want to," Joel said suddenly. "I'll be glad to drive Jenny to San Diego."

"Joel, are you crazy?" Susan butted in. "You just drove eight hours from San Francisco. Aren't you exhausted?"

"Not anymore," he replied, his eyes gazing

dreamily into Jennifer's. He looked at Dale again. "Is that okay with you?"

Dale smiled resignedly. He didn't answer, but he put down the bag he'd been holding, his own, and picked up Jennifer's. "Let's take a look at your car," he said at last.

Susan felt almost amused as Dale opened the hood of the Toyota and slowly inspected it for worn belts and loose hoses. Most fathers would be cross-examining the boy about his intentions, protective of their daughter's honor. Dale had to check out his car.

"You take good care of my baby," he said, as Joel and Jennifer got in the car. "I don't have to give you the speech, do I?"

"No, sir," Joel grinned. "I'll behave myself, Mr. Clemens."

Dale extended his hand. "The name is Dale," he said.

"So how come you didn't give him the speech?" Susan teased, as she and Dale walked back inside after the kids had left.

"He didn't need it. Besides, I'm giving him the benefit of the doubt because he's your son. If he messes with my daughter, I'm going to come after you, Lady."

"Oh, yeah?" Susan smiled coquettishly. "Just what are you going to do to me?"

Dale rolled his eyes lasciviously. "Things too terrible to say out loud." He leaned her over the living-room couch and nuzzled her neck with his lips.

"I'm surprised to hear that you even *have* a speech like that," she said carelessly. "I thought you practically encouraged your daughter to be promiscuous."

Dale straightened up abruptly and let Susan's body drop unceremoniously onto the couch. He sucked in his breath slowly and deliberately. "Now what the hell do you mean by that?"

She knew she had said the wrong thing, probably the absolute worst thing she could have possibly said, but it was too late to back out now. "How could you let your daughter go off and live with a man in New York?" she asked accusingly. "You tell *my* son to behave himself, but your daughter hardly qualifies as a Vestal Virgin. You know that she sleeps around with a whole army of boyfriends, and you don't do a damn thing about it!"

Dale's cheeks puffed out like two red tomatoes. His eyes turned into hard steel. His fingers were clenched into two tight balls. Susan had never seen him this angry before. He didn't say a word, didn't make a move toward her, but for a long, terrifying moment, she was afraid he was going to hit her.

"I didn't mean that," she said quickly, as Dale stared at her with a dangerous, frightening expression. His breathing was slow and heavy. "I'm sorry I said it."

There was no response. Just more tortured breathing. And daggers shooting from glazed, narrow eyes. Finally he turned away from her and strode toward the back door.

"Dale, don't." She ran after him breathlessly. "Don't run away. I know you're mad. Go ahead and yell at me. Call me names. Insult *my* children if you have to. Only don't walk out mad like this. Please!" she screamed as he turned the doorknob. "Don't."

He stood there a long time. After an eternity he let go of the doorknob. After another eternity he turned around and looked at her. His face bore an expression of not only anger but extreme pain.

"All right," he hissed. "You wanted it; you've got it." He kicked the door with his foot. "You don't know what the hell you're talking about, Susan. You never do. You just always shoot from the hip without thinking about what you're saying, without thinking about who you're going to hurt. It's pretty damn selfish of you, if you want to know the truth. Everything has come easy to you; everything has always gone your way. You sit here in your big house with your goddamned superior airs looking down on everybody else. Well, you may have had the best education and the best professional training, but when it comes to understanding people, caring about people, you don't know a goddamned thing. You don't cut anybody any slack. You're a spoiled, selfish, rich bitch who cares more about pretenses than about real feelings. Anybody whose lifestyle doesn't fit into your narrow little view of how things should be is automatically wrong!"

Well, Mom, Susan thought wryly, he didn't call me a dirty Jew. But I don't think he left out anything else. Susan seethed with anger and hurt, but she kept silent. She *had* asked for it. And Dale had every right to be angry with her. She had practically called Jennifer a slut. She had insulted his only daughter, his beautiful daughter that he loved, the daughter who was obviously the light of his life.

She stood shaking silently in front of him, praying that his verbal attack would not turn physical. Dale was shaking as well, as if he were unused to giving vent to his angry feelings. After a long silence, he stalked into the living room. Susan followed at a respectful distance.

Dale sat down on the couch, staring at some invisible shadow on the wall. Susan edged her body into the loveseat opposite him, afraid to get too close. The suspense of wondering what he was going to do next was worse than the agony of waiting for a jury's verdict. It must have been fifteen minutes before Dale spoke again. When he did, his voice was calm and controlled.

"I've tried very hard to be a good father to my children, Susan. It hasn't always been easy. Maybe if their mother and I hadn't gotten divorced, things would have been different, but I honestly don't think so." He leaned back and propped a foot on the coffee table. His anger seemed spent now; he was starting to breathe normally again.

"My son was always a difficult child. I had always dreamed that both of my children would go to college. We were lucky to get Randy through high school. With Diane pulling and me pushing, he managed to squeak by with a D average. You wouldn't know anything about that, I don't suppose. Probably Joel and Andrea were both straight A students from kindergarten on. I guess I should be grateful," he sighed, "that Randy's never been in jail, and he does work—occasionally. At a motorcycle repair shop." Dale frowned. "I had hoped that my son could do better than his father.

"Jennifer was the exact opposite. From the day she was born, she was a joy. Smart and beautiful and talented. Got A's all through school without even trying. Won drama contests and cheerleading contests." His chest swelled with pride.

"And she was always Daddy's girl." They

were the first words Susan had spoken since Dale's wrathful explosion.

"Yes," he admitted, with a slight smile. He reached his hand out to her, his fingers beckoning in forgiveness. Susan came to him and sat beside him on the couch. But she didn't touch him.

"Jennifer's always been a popular girl, Susan. Ever since she was twelve, there have always been boys hanging around her house. And around my house, too, whenever she was around. I used to joke with her about beating them away from the door with a baseball bat. But after she got to be about fifteen, it wasn't a joke anymore. Jenny has always had a mind of her own. She was going to do what she wanted no matter what her mother or I said about it. I knew that Diane could never tolerate the idea of Jenny being sexually active, and I was afraid of what might happen to Jennifer if she sneaked out with boys to go to motels, or worse places. So I let them come to my house."

Susan gasped. "You let your daughter and her boyfriends sleep together in your house?"

Dale nodded. "What's the point of being hypocritical about it? They're going to do it anyway. At least this way I know where she is, and I can protect her from bodily harm. And she comes home more often."

Susan was stunned by his attitude. "I can't believe you're so complacent about it. Don't you ever worry about AIDS?"

"Of course I do. Constantly. But I can't stop her from having sex, Susan. She's a grown woman. All I can do is make sure she carries protection and then pray that she uses it." He fastened his eyes on Susan's face. "Your daughter is the same age as Jennifer. Surely you don't believe she's still a virgin?"

Susan lay her head back against the sofa cushion and closed her eyes. "No," she said softly. "I know she's not. Not that she's ever told me," she added, almost to herself.

"Did you expect her to?"

"No," she murmured. "Not really. I never talked to my mother about those things, either. It's just that somehow, with my own daughter, I thought things would be different."

"Some children can talk to their parents about sex, and some can't. Jennifer never talks to her mother about it, either. Diane always complains that Jenny talks to me and not her, but secretly, I think she's relieved. Diane never was comfortable talking about sex. Certainly not with the lights on."

Susan looked at Dale respectfully. She no longer felt older or more mature than he was. In fact, she felt slightly in awe of him. "Jennifer talks to you about . . . stuff?"

He smiled at her reluctance to even use the word. "Yes. Both my kids do. That's why I don't act like a turkey and try to lay down the law to them. They're not going to listen to me anyway. At least if they trust me, they'll let me know if they get in trouble. My home is always open to my kids and their friends, Susan."

Her heart ached for him. He obviously loved his children very much and resented having to defend them to unsympathetic strangers. In his own way, he was trying to protect his daughter.

"I see now why Jennifer calls you 'Dale' instead of 'Dad,'" Susan said almost wistfully. "She thinks of you as a friend instead of a father."

"She thinks of me as a father," Dale rebutted. "I know you think that I'm a pushover, trying to buy my children's love with presents and easy discipline, but it's not true. I've always been hard-line with my kids. When they were kids. But they're not anymore. It's time to let them grow up. And for your information," he added, "Jenny always used to call me 'Daddy.' It's only in the past year or two that she started this first-name business."

Susan touched his fingers. "Dale," she asked softly, "how are you going to protect her in New York?"

He shrugged his shoulders. "I can't. She's

twenty-one and an adult. She can live with whoever she likes. But I don't think she even sleeps with that guy in New York. I think he's gay. They're probably just going to share the rent."

Maybe he really thought that, or maybe he only hoped it was the case. In any event, Susan regretted having criticized him. He was doing the best that he could, probably considerably better than she could have done under the same circumstances. What would she and Mike have done if Andrea had been as stunningly beautiful as Jenny was and had attracted boys like moths to a flame?

"Dale, I owe you an apology. I should never have said what I did, not without understanding the situation."

He looked at her intently for a minute, then kissed her gently on the cheek. "Apology accepted. I'm sorry for what I said, too. At least about being unfeeling and uncaring. I know that's not true." He put his hand on her back and hugged her briefly. "And I'm glad you said what you did."

"You are?"

He nodded. "It was pretty insensitive the way you did it, but at least you said what you were thinking. And I'm glad you made me stay and let my anger out. A relationship is more than sweet talking and making love. If this relationship is going to work between us, I need to learn how to fight with you. It's something I never learned with Diane."

She looked at him in surprise. "No?"

He shook his head. "I never once got angry at the woman. Not directly. Whenever I felt anger coming on, I walked out of the house. Just as I tried to do tonight."

She pulled him down beside her and put her hand in his. "Well, once you got the hang of it, you certainly managed to get angry enough with me. I was afraid you were going to hit me."

He grinned sheepishly, thinking that her words were a poetic exaggeration; then he realized that she was not joking. His eyes became very serious. "I've never hit a woman in my life, Susan." He stared straight ahead for a minute. "I haven't hit anybody in over twenty years."

She threw her arms around him and hugged him. Dale responded tentatively, uncomfortable in her embrace. He moved back and looked at her strangely. "Did you really think I could hit you, Susan?"

She lowered her eyes. "I didn't know what to think. I've never dated anybody who was 'poor white trash' before. Your phrase," she said defensively, as he glanced sharply at her, "not mine."

259

"Have you ever known me to get violent?"

"No." Susan buried her face in his neck. "Why did you become a pacifist?"

"I'm not a pacifist. I served my stint in the Navy. I never saw action, but if asked to, I would have been glad to fight for my country."

She looked up at him expectantly, knowing there was more than he was saying. His eyes like Jeff's, always gave away his secrets. Or at least the fact that he had a secret. Dale pressed his lips to her forehead, twirling away a stray lock of hair with his fingers. "All right, I'll tell you about it. When I was twenty, I got into a fight with a buddy in a pool hall. I don't even remember what it was about, but I know it was something stupid and unimportant. I didn't know I hit him that hard. He crashed down on one of the tables and practically split his head open. The emergency-room doctors thought he was going to die. At the very least, they thought he'd have permanent brain damage." He paused.

"What happened?"

"He was very, very lucky. He wound up with an ugly scar as a souvenir but no brain damage. At least," he chuckled wryly, "no more than before. Eventually he even forgave me. But I never forgave myself."

"So you never got in a fight again."

"Nope. I've been called 'chicken' so many

times I thought it was my middle name. And that's one of the nicer things I've been called." He wrapped his arms around Susan and clutched her tightly for support. "Maybe that was just a fluke or something—maybe I'm not really that strong—but I'm afraid to find out."

Susan hugged him warmly. So that was why he had never gotten angry at his wife. He was afraid to express anger, afraid of repeating that horrible near-tragedy. It was why his anger at her had always been so tentative, expressed in subtle sarcasm rather than as a direct hit. It was why he went cold and emotionless on the outside when by rights he should be spitting out fury.

After a few minutes she released him and raised her head to look into his face. "Dale," she said curiously, "what *is* your middle name? Do you even have one?"

He smiled mysteriously. "Yep."

"Well?" she prodded, when he didn't say anything more. "Come on, it can't be that bad. You can tell me. Even if it is that bad, I promise not to laugh."

"It's not that bad," he assured her. "And you already know my middle name." Susan looked confused. "Dale is my middle name."

"So?"

"So what?"

"Don't be coy. So what's your first name?"

261

He paused for several seconds, then lowered his head with a sheepish smile. "Jeffrey."

Susan gasped. "Then you knew! You knew before I did that he was your father."

"I didn't; I swear it. When you first talked about him, I never made the connection. But when you told me why you thought he was my father, I had one more reason than you did to believe that your crazy intuition might be correct. That's why I fought you so hard on it, Suse."

He stood up and took his car keys out of his pants. Susan grabbed his hand and put them back in his pocket. "Dale, you might as well stay."

He looked at her questioningly, cocking his head toward the driveway as if he expected to hear Joel's blue Toyota drive up at any minute.

"He won't be home for at least a couple more hours, and he'll still be asleep when you leave in the morning. He'll never even know you were here. Please stay."

Fourteen

Susan was dozing on the living-room couch when she heard the back door creak open.

"What are you doing down here?" Joel asked in surprise.

"Waiting for you. I didn't know if you had your key." She sat up and rubbed her eyes. "How was San Diego?"

"Hot and humid. So much for perfect southern California weather. And my air conditioner is for shit. I think I need freon." He sat down tentatively on the arm of the couch.

"Ask Dale to put some in for you tomorrow. You don't want to be driving around L.A. without air conditioning."

Joel smiled knowingly. "It must be nice to have your own private mechanic. How long have you been dating him?"

"Dating? I—" She tried to think of a convincing denial, then gave up. "A couple of months." She looked for the censure in his eyes, but there was none. "I invited him here tonight so you could meet him. It's too bad you two didn't get a chance to talk."

"We did talk. When you were in the kitchen." Susan looked at him expectantly. "He's nice. Not that you need my approval, Mom, but if that's what you're asking for, I like him."

Susan smiled. "I'm glad. He's . . . a good friend."

Joel chuckled. "He's a lot more than that, isn't he?"

Susan paled. "Why do you say that?"

"Mom, I'm not a kid. And I have eyes. Eyes which just happened to notice that the Jaguar is parked in the garage. He's upstairs in your bed right now, isn't he?"

She started to sputter indignantly, then relaxed. In a way, it was a relief to have it out in the open. "Does it bother you?" she asked softly.

"Me? No. It shouldn't matter to you if it did. Daddy's not coming back. You deserve to have a life."

Joel was a good kid. A good man. Sometimes Susan thought that he had been born with the maturity of an adult.

"Of course I'm glad to hear you say that.

But it does matter to me what you think. My family's feelings are important to me."

Joel slid down the arm and settled in beside her on the couch. "Are you serious about him, Mom?"

It was difficult to answer truthfully. "No. Not yet. But sometimes I think I could be. He's not Daddy, of course, but he's a good man. Good to me, anyway. Yes," she said, almost to herself. "I could be serious about him. Except . . ." Her voice trailed off.

"Except what? What bothers you?"

"Surely you must know what bothers me. He's not Jewish."

"So what?

Susan blinked. Joel's reaction to her concern was almost exactly the same as Dale's had been. Where had she failed? She had considered it her duty as a Jewish mother to imbue in her children a sense of Jewish identity, a love for Jewish culture. It was true that she and Mike had never been especially observant, not in the religious sense, but they had discussed Jewish books and subscribed to Jewish magazines, seeking to bring the best parts of their heritage into their home. They had sent the children to Hebrew school, attended services occasionally, seized the opportunities to introduce them to Jewish art, plays, music. They had emphasized the importance of tradition, particularly in carrying on the faith to their own children.

Susan had always encouraged her children—yes, maybe even brainwashed them—to date within the faith. It was a tenet that the kids had initially rebelled against, but later had come to accept, even embrace. Andrea had dated a few non-Jewish boys in college. Susan had held her breath patiently and kept silent, knowing that her interference would only propel her daughter even faster into the arms of the forbidden stranger. When she had started dating Mark, though, Susan had breathed a sigh of relief that had probably been heard in Nevada.

Joel had dated Gentile girls when he was in college, too, and Susan knew that he often did still, but she also knew that he would never get serious about any of them. Since the summer of his Bar Mitzvah, the summer he had spent with Jeff in Israel, he had been an ardent Zionist, philosophically, at least, committed to his religion and his people. Of all of her friends' children, Joel, she had always thought, would be the last one to discard his heritage. Especially in light of the education she'd given him, she would have expected him to be more disturbed, maybe even scandalized, by her relationship with Dale. At the very least, she'd expected to be treated to a very severe lecture on hypocrisy. But his response had been a mere "So what?" Where had she gone wrong?

Susan raised her eyebrows. "That's all you're going to say? You're not going to give me a hard time about all the speeches I've given you on the subject now that the tables are turned?"

Joel smiled. "Nope. In fact, I'm kind of pleased that you're dating him. Because now you won't be able to give *me* a hard time about dating Jennifer."

Jennifer? In her preoccupation with her own love life, Susan had almost forgotten about Joel's instant infatuation with Dale's daughter. "You mean you're going to see her again?"

"First chance I get."

Susan opened her mouth in shocked surprise. It just wasn't like Joel to be so impetuous. He had always been like his father, slow to make a decision, weighing all the angles, but rarely changing his mind once the decision had been made. Especially when it came to women.

She looked at her son protectively. "You just met this girl," she said guardedly. "You spent a few hours with her. You don't know anything about her."

"I know enough," Joel said firmly. "I know that she's beautiful and intelligent, and I know that I want to see her again."

Susan bit her lip. She didn't want to hurt

him, but she felt that, for his own good, she had to speak up. "Do you also know," she said slowly, "that she's going to New York next week to live with another man?"

He was unfazed. "Nick? The artist? Yeah, she told me about him. He's not her boyfriend, Mom. *He* has a boyfriend."

So Dale had been right in his assumption. "I guess you two did a lot of talking tonight."

Joel grinned. "Well, going seventy miles an hour on the freeway, it's a little difficult to make out."

She smiled and pretended to punch him in the ribs. "I'm not going to preach to you about Jennifer, Joel. As you pointed out, I'm living in a glass house. But it looks like you're contemplating a long-distance relationship here. Coast to coast is not a commuter trip. Do you have any idea if she feels the same way about you as you do about her?"

He nodded solemnly. "I'm sure of it. I know this doesn't sound like me, Mom, but something just clicked tonight. I've never felt this way about any girl before. It's like I can't wait to see her again, but in another way, I can. I know she'll still be there for me."

Susan put her arm around her son's shoulders. If the feelings he described were real and mutual, then she was happy for him. She knew what it was like to be helplessly attracted to someone the instant that you saw him, and bound forever after by a mystical magnetism. She feared for Joel's well-being, though, should Jennifer turn out to be not as committed in love as he apparently was.

The phone rang at eight o'clock the next day. "Good morning, Mrs. Riesman," said a friendly voice at her ear. "This is Jennifer."

"Hello, Jennifer." It always made Susan feel so old to be called Mrs. Riesman. "Your dad's not here. He should be at the garage."

"I know. I didn't call for him. I called to talk to Joel. Is he up?"

"I've got it, Mom," said her son's sleepy voice from another extension.

Susan hung up the phone. Two hours later, after she had breakfasted, showered, and dressed, the red button on line one of her bedroom phone was still lit.

"Well, I'm glad that wasn't on *my* phone bill," she said teasingly, as Joel finally emerged from his bedroom. His face was flushed and crimson-happy as if he were arising from bed after sex instead of a telephone conversation.

They spent a pleasant Saturday afternoon together, mother and son catching up on the details of each other's lives, reminiscing about the past and speculating about the future. Andrea called from Philadelphia to wish them a good year. Susan felt like the honored matron of a beautiful dynasty. But even as she basked in the glowing warmth of her loving family, a sense of loneliness pervaded her. As the evening skies began to grow dark, her ears perked up unconsciously, listening for the sound of a late-model Jaguar or a five-year-old pickup truck. It felt strange to spend a Saturday night without Dale, although it had been her request that he stay away. Even though Joel knew about her relationship with Dale, she didn't want to be brazen about it.

Dale did come over on Sunday afternoon, wearing jeans and a cut-off sweatshirt, but carrying a suit, shirt, and tie to wear to Rosh Hashanah services that night. Susan worried about what the three of them would talk about together. Would Dale and Joel have any interests in common, or would the entire afternoon consist of painful, embarrassing small talk and awkward pauses in conversation?

She needn't have worried. There was a football game on television. The two men sat transfixed for three hours in front of the screen, occasionally punctuating particularly good performances by gleeful shouts.

Susan smiled to herself. *Déjà vu.* She could remember countless Sunday afternoons when Joel was a boy, with him and Jeff sitting in front of a TV football game just like this. Jeff had never even been a football fan when he was younger. He was thirty-five years old before he ever began to follow the game. Sometimes Susan thought that he had done it because of Joel, so the two of them would have something to do together and talk about. Jeff had loved Joel so much. He was the son he never had. Susan's eyes filled with tears. Here, sitting in her living room watching the game with Joel instead of Jeff, was the real son that he had never known.

"Did you play in high school?" Joel was asking Dale.

"Dale played quarterback," Susan informed him rather proudly, as she handed Joel a bowl of popcorn. "He was the captain of his high-school football team."

"I was the captain of the football team," Dale said, turning to look at her. "And I did play quarterback. But I never told you that. How did you know?"

She smiled. "Lucky guess. You know," she said, leaning over Dale and curving her fingers around his neck, "it's a good thing I met you in March. If we had met in football season, I'm not sure this relationship would have ever made it this far."

"Quiet, woman," Dale growled playfully, turning his eyes back to the screen. "The kicker is getting ready for a field goal." Although his tone was gruff, his fingers caressed hers lightly. He raised her hands to his lips and kissed them from heel to fingertips. Without taking his eyes off the screen. "Damn!" he exclaimed, as the kicker missed the play. "You're a jinx, Lady," he complained, although there was not a whit of seriousness in his voice. "Get out of here and go do some needlepoint or something."

As she showered before getting dressed for services that evening, Susan felt a slight sense of trepidation. Dale had never been inside a synagogue before; she was worried about what he would think and how he would act. Would he be put off or bored by the foreign sounds of Hebrew chanting? What if he tried to put his arm around her or hold her hand during services?

You're being silly, Susan, she told herself. Dale was always a model of decorum in any public place; he would know how to handle himself. Still, she wished she hadn't been so hasty about inviting Dale to join them on this particular night. Practically everyone she knew would be there, and she could already feel the eyes boring into her as she strolled in with her son and . . . and . . . her lover?? Susan shuddered. She was *not* ashamed of Dale, she assured herself, but this was not the time or place to bring their relationship "out of the closet." Not at this most holy time of the year, at this service of serious prayer, when a "guest" from outside the faith would most likely feel uncomfortable and unwelcome. Not in this place where she had come every year with her family, where her children had grown up, where her husband had served as president of the synagogue. It was not just her own position about which she was circumspect, she told herself, but Dale's as well. He was bound to feel embarrassed if people were cool to him, and he wouldn't understand the reasons why. Susan wished she had chosen some other time, some less important occasion, to introduce Dale to synagogue services. But she had made a promise, and she wasn't about to go back on it. She would just have to make the best of the situation.

"You're not dressed!" she exclaimed as she stepped out of the bathroom to find Dale sitting on her bed, still in jeans and sweatshirt. "You'd better hurry—services start in half an hour."

His eyes scanned her winter-white dress, scant makeup, and mid-height heels. "I'm not going," he said quietly.

"What? Why not?"

Dale scratched his mustache. "Susan, I've been thinking about it. I don't belong there tonight. This is a time for you to be with your family and your people. I know you meant well by inviting me, and I *would* like to see what your services are like, but I'd be just a curious onlooker, not a real participant. I *am* a stranger. I think I'm beginning to understand now what you mean about that. I'd be out of place, and you would feel out of place and uncomfortable with me being there. I think I'd better sit this one out, Susan. I don't want you to feel like a stranger in your own home."

The man was first-class all the way. Susan dropped to her knees beside him and hugged him gratefully, hoping her relief didn't light up her face too much. "I *will* take you sometime, Dale. I want to. But tonight . . . it just . . . I mean, I . . ." She couldn't express herself. The word that finally came out was "Thanks."

B'nai Israel Synagogue was just a few blocks from Susan's house, a medium-sized, Conservative-Reform congregation that she and Mike had always felt comfortable in. "Such a handsome boy!" gushed one of the matrons over Joel, as if he were still wearing the baby curls and denim overalls he had when the Riesmans had first moved to that neighborhood. "Look how nice he's grown up."

Joel endured the invasive gestures and sticky-sweet comments with patience and courtesy, smiling graciously at all the older ladies who had known him since childhood and had not seen him in one or more years. When they encountered Lara Aviv and her daughter Rachel, Susan felt hopeful. Joel and Rachel had dated a number of times when they were in high school, even after he went to college. Susan had not been especially eager for that match at the time, but in light of the most recent developments in Joel's love life, she suddenly found herself remembering many of Rachel's good points. She steered her son in the Avivs' direction. Joel was friendly to Rachel, and the girl certainly seemed happy to see him, but after only a few minutes of distracted conversation, he was ready to move on.

"I'm going to drive down to San Diego tomorrow after services," he informed Susan as they walked home after synagogue Monday afternoon.

"Oh?" She hated that interjection. It was an old person's response, but she didn't know what else she could say without knowing what he was going to say next. The less she said now, the less she could regret later.

"I'm going to pick up Jenny and bring her

back here. Then she can drive back to San Francisco with me and spend a few days before she has to catch a plane to New York."

Susan coughed politely. "I thought she was planning to spend this whole week with her family."

He grinned sheepishly. "Well, she's sort of had a change in plans."

"I'll pick her up," Dale offered when she told him about Joel's intention. "I need to go down there, anyway. We'll come back early Wednesday morning before rush hour and then the kids can leave whenever they want."

Susan was relieved by his suggestion. It didn't even bother her that he would be spending the night in San Diego in the same house as his ex-wife. Not as much as it bothered her to think of what she would have done with Joel and Jennifer if they had arrived together at her house on Tuesday night. She knew they were dying to sleep together, but she couldn't allow that, not in her house. She wasn't anywhere near as liberal as Dale was in these matters. But how could she *not* let them sleep together when they both knew that their parents were doing the same thing? How could she be so hypocritical? And if she *were* to allow that, which of course she wouldn't, then what of Dale? She'd been keeping him away from her bed the last several days for propriety's sake.

If Jennifer and Joel spent the night together at her house, then of course, so should she and Dale, and wouldn't that all turn into a hell of a three-ring circus?

"It's for the best," Susan explained to her son when he protested about the change in arrangements. "Dale would like to have a little time alone with his daughter, too, you know. He's not going to see her for a long time, either."

"It's really funny, isn't it?" Joel mused.

"What is?"

"You and Dale. Me and Jenny. Wouldn't it be something if we all had a double wedding?"

"Don't go buying your engagement rings before they're hatched," she warned him. "And don't be making any assumptions about me and Dale, either."

"Why not? He's obviously crazy about you. You're obviously crazy about him. You're a perfect match."

He was head-over-heels, poor kid, and he was speaking from the viewpoint of an unabashed romantic who has discovered love for the first time. "Joel, I'm probably wasting my breath talking to you because you just met a girl who you think is the love of your life and you're looking at everything through rose-colored glasses. But there's more to a relationship than sex. When passion cools down you have to have something else: background, interests in common. Dale and I don't. He's just not my type."

Joel chortled. "Not your type? Mom, I think you're kidding yourself. Dale is exactly your type."

She was confused and a little offended. "I don't know what you mean. Your father was my type. Dale is nothing like Daddy."

"He is, a little bit, but that's not what I meant. I wasn't referring to Daddy."

Susan raised her eyebrows. "Then what?"

"Mom, I'd have to be blind in both eyes not to notice that Dale is a dead ringer for Uncle Jeff."

She gasped. So he *had* noticed. "Do you really think so?" she asked innocently, as if she were considering the resemblance for the first time. "I'm surprised you even remember what Uncle Jeff looked like. You were only seventeen when he died. I sometimes have trouble remembering him myself. It's not like I have a picture," she said bitterly. "God, I wish I had those photographs that he destroyed. The bastard didn't leave me a one. I am so mad at him for that. If he wasn't already dead, I could kill him!"

"I have one," Joel said quietly.

"What?" She had heard him, but the message wasn't sinking in.

"I have one," he repeated. "A photograph. He gave it to me at my Bar Mitzvah. He told me he had rescued it when he destroyed all the others. He said he just couldn't bear to tear that one up. He wanted me to have it, in case he ever got the urge to destroy it, too."

"And you still have it?" Her tone was reverent, as if they were speaking about the shroud of Jesus or a Torah rescued from the Holocaust. "Where is it?"

"In my wallet."

She couldn't wait until his fingers produced it. It was a picture of Joel as a baby. Jeff was holding him in his arms, looking deep into the infant's eyes. The beauty of that captured moment assailed Susan deep in the gut. The expression in the faces haunted her. She knew she had seen those expressions somewhere before, maybe in a work of art. That was it. Looking at the picture of Jeff holding his beloved "nephew" in his arms, she saw the Madonna and Child.

"Can I have it?" she whispered. "I'll make a copy. I'll give it back to you."

"Sure. Keep it as long as you like."

She fingered the faded portrait lovingly, gingerly caressing the pinked border of the frame.

"You still love him, don't you?" It was not a twenty-four-year-old boy talking. It was a man with depth and wisdom.

"Of course I do. He was my best friend. He was like my brother."

"I don't mean as a friend. Or a brother. Look, I know Uncle Jeff wasn't really my uncle. And I know that he meant more to you than either a brother or a friend. You don't have to keep your secret anymore, Mom. I understand."

Susan stared at him stonily, not emitting a word.

"All right, be that way. You don't have to admit it if you don't want to. But I know you loved him. And I know that he loved *you*. He loved you till the day he died."

Her voice was cold and her eyes were narrow slits. "He told you that?"

"He didn't tell me anything. He didn't have to. I spent part of every summer with him since I was eleven. Uncle Jeff was good at hiding his emotions, but he wasn't completely opaque. I could see through him. I probably understood him better than anybody else did, except you."

Susan stared at her son. If anybody had ever loved Jeff as much as she had, it was Joel. The boy and the man had been devoted to each other since Joel was the age in the photograph. Jeff had fastened on her son a breadth of emotions he had been unable or unwilling to share with a life partner, and Joel had been deeply bonded to Jeff as well. She hadn't realized till now, though, just how much her son missed his "uncle." Probably more than he missed his own father.

Joel was not intimidated by her gaze. "No," he said, returning her stare, "Uncle Jeff never told me anything. But I could tell by the way he looked at you. Especially when he thought no one noticed. He was aching for you inside, Mom."

Susan was silent for long moments, breaking eye contact to stare at the floor. Finally she raised her head. "You're still too young to understand, Joel. You think that all love is romantic love, the way you feel about Jennifer. There are many more kinds of love than that. The way I felt about Uncle Jeff was probably different from any other kind I could describe. It was different from the way I feel about you, different from the way I felt about Daddy."

"Different from the way you feel about Dale?"

She sighed a long, hard sigh. "Maybe not."

When Dale and Jennifer arrived from San Diego Wednesday morning, there was no mistaking the delight that filled the two young people's eyes at their reunion. Dale unloaded Jennifer's baggage from his truck and transferred it to Joel's car. He looks tired, Susan thought, as she watched him stretched over the truck body. He'd probably been up most of the night talking and then gotten up very early this morning to drive back. And now he had to go to work.

"You might as well wait for the rush-hour traffic to die down," Dale cautioned, as they all ate pancakes in Susan's kitchen. "If you leave now or leave an hour from now, you'll probably get out of the city the same time."

"How about you, Dale?" Susan asked. "Do you have to go yet or have you got time for another pancake?" It was after seven o'clock.

"I'll wait until the kids get off." He helped himself to another whole stack of pancakes.

He looked so natural sitting at her kitchen table, stuffing his face with pancakes. He belonged here. It had been only five days since she had slept in his strong arms, but Susan couldn't believe that she'd missed him so much. She missed warming her nose in the curve of his back in the middle of the night. She missed hearing his voice suddenly whisper in her ear when she'd thought he was asleep. She missed the power of his lovemaking and the tenderness of his caresses.

At last they stood together with their arms locked around each other's waists, each waving with their free hand as Joel's Toyota backed down the driveway. "What do you think about that?" Susan asked as they watched Joel and Jennifer drive away.

"I don't know what to think," Dale answered. "It seems pretty heavy from Jennifer's side of the fence. Joel's?"

"Um hum." She nodded.

They turned to face each other. She knew he wasn't thinking about the kids any longer. Susan certainly wasn't. Her body bristled with desire as they stared at each other for a full minute.

"Well," he said at last, "I guess I'll hit the road, too."

"Now?"

He took his car keys out of his pocket. "I'm already an hour late for work, Susan."

So as long as he was already late, what difference would it make if he was a little later? "But do you have to leave right now?"

He jingled the keys in his hand, passing them rhythmically from one palm to the other. "Is there something you want me to do before I leave?"

Damn him, he knew what she wanted, and he must want it, too. He was playing with her and loving every minute of it. "What do you want me to do, beg you?"

Dale smiled. "Yes. Or at least ask me. I want to hear you say the words out loud."

They were outside in the side yard. Susan's nosy neighbor, Lena Kessler, was lingering about the hedges that divided their properties, ostensibly picking up her newspaper, but probably seeking news of a juicier content than could be found in the front section of the *Los Angeles Times*. Susan folded her arms around Dale's neck and pulled herself up on tiptoe so that her lips were next to his ear. "I want you to make love to me, Dale. Don't you want to?"

He grinned a slow and mischievous grin. "Try and stop me, Lady."

Susan squealed like a teenager and ran into the house with Dale following in hot pursuit.

Susan attended Yom Kippur services alone that year. Joel was back in San Francisco, and Dale was taking a night class at U.C.L.A. Following her advice, he had signed up for an accounting course in the continuing education department.

She didn't really mind going alone. Rosh Hashanah, New Year services, were meant to be attended with friends and family. It was a day for wishing everyone one knew a good year to come, with the Hebrew greeting, *"Chatima Tova"*—"May you be inscribed in the Book of Life." The Day of Atonement, ten days later, marked the end of a period of repentance and self-examination. It was the last chance to review one's life and to ask for forgiveness for one's sins before the Book was permanently sealed.

Susan knew she had a lot of sins to atone for this year. They jumped up at her as soon as she opened her Machsor, the High Holy Day prayer book. "For the sin we committed in thy sight by evil impulse. For the sin which we committed in thy sight by lustful behavior. For the sin which we committed against thee by wanton glances." She symbolically beat her breast as she said the words out loud. Fortunately everyone in the congregation was required to say the words as well. It was only her heart that heard her private condemnation.

Dutifully she made her way through the recitation of fifty-four sins, guiltily seizing eagerly all that applied to her. But something was strange. They were the same sins that she had asked forgiveness for every year. Nowhere in the litany of guilt was there the atonement "For the sin of loving a Gentile." God had neglected to add that one this year for the special purpose of castigating Susan Riesman. But God was all-knowing and all powerful. If that was indeed a sin, why had He not included it?

Nowhere in the prayers, nowhere in the chants, could she find an injunction to forswear the love of a man who was kind and loving, hard-working and responsible, patient and sensitive. Not one paragraph stated, "We have strayed from the ways of our country club and our social status. We have embarrassed our friends and family by choosing someone who does not meet our preconceived notions of a gentleman." She found nothing for which to ask her friends' and family's forgiveness.

But she found a great deal for which she should be asking Dale's forgiveness. "We have acted treasonably, aggressively, and slanderously. We have acted brazenly, viciously, and fraudulently. We have acted perniciously, disdainfully, and erratically."

Susan's head was spinning. Perhaps from the fasting. Yom Kippur observance required an entire day of fasting and prayer, from evening of one day to nightfall of the next. As the lengthening afternoon shadows signalled the approach of Neelah, the Concluding service, she knew there was little time left to make amends. At the end of that service the Book of Life would be sealed, sealing the fates as well of the people in the Congregation.

She had not felt such religious fervor since she was a young teenager just beginning to comprehend the meaning of Yom Kippur. This year she felt a sense of urgency, a need to right the wrongs before that irrevocable moment.

As she walked home at the break before the Concluding Service was to begin, Susan knew what she had to do. Even though he would think she was crazy. She called Dale at the garage.

"Dale," she began in a voice that was breathless and importunate. "I'm sorry that I didn't know how to introduce you to Betsy and Greg. I'm sorry that I told my friends at work that you were my mechanic instead of my date. I'm sorry that I didn't tell my friends the truth about you. I'm sorry that I was ashamed and embarrassed to tell my children that the greatest joy of my life is when you are making love to me. I'm sorry for all the times I took you for granted or insulted you or acted like I was better than you. I'm sorry for anything and everything I ever said or did that hurt you or gave you the impression that I felt any way except grateful to God for the day I met you." She paused, finally, briefly, for breath, and then hurried on. "For all of those things I ask your forgiveness, Dale. Please, please forgive me."

Fifteen

She had forgotten what it was like to be in love. Susan began to leave work at five for the first time in years, eager to hasten the evenings. She lived for the moment that Dale would drive up in the red convertible, greet her with a cheery "Hi, Suse," and scoop her up in his arms. She could hardly wait to feel his breath in her face, to smell his distinctive scent, and to hear his seductive growl in her ear. She was becoming more and more dependent on Dale's presence in her life and in her bed. The warmth of his body next to hers at night gave her the comforting security she had always known with Mike. The sensuality of that body aroused passions in her that she had not felt since Jeff.

"When did you fall in love with me?" Susan asked coquettishly, as she nestled against Dale's chest one night. "Was it love at first sight?"

Dale eyed her circumspectly as he folded her into the wing of his arm. "No," he said candidly. "To be honest, I wasn't even attracted to you at first sight. But I did feel something—not chemistry, exactly, not in the sexual sense—it was more like some kind of a psychic bond between us. At first I thought it was because I knew Mike, and, through him, I felt as though I knew you. But later I realized it had nothing to do with Mike. It was you. There was something connecting us. I felt like I'd already known you, and known you well, for a long time."

"Like you'd known me in another lifetime?"

He started. "Exactly. How did you know?"

"Because that's the way I always felt about Jeff."

She saw the flicker of pain in his eyes but pretended she didn't. She knew that Dale was still jealous of Jeff. Why shouldn't he be? Any man would be curious about how he compared to a former lover, but how did you deal with it when it was your own father? Susan tried to keep Jeff's name out of the bedroom, but even when she mentioned him in casual conversation, Dale's eyes flinched with pain. Yet sometimes he brought the subject up himself, eager for details about the man whose genes he had. She couldn't help hurting him. Dale seemed to feel cheated in two ways: he was jealous of his father for what he'd been to Susan, and he was jealous of Susan because she'd known his father and he hadn't.

Fearful of hurting him even more, Susan waited a long time before showing Dale the photograph. And then she didn't have the nerve to do it directly. When they were at his house one Sunday, Susan slyly drew out from her purse the picture of Jeff that Joel had given her, the beloved, treasured photo that she had not missed looking at every day since. She placed it on Dale's dresser, propped it against the mirror, and waited.

When he noticed it, Dale's reaction was not what she would have anticipated. "Susan, where did you get this picture?" he demanded sharply. "Have you been pulling things out of my photo albums?"

She was confused. "No, of course not."

"Then how did this get out? It's supposed to be right here."

He pulled a slim volume out of a bookshelf in the hallway and set it on the bed, searching carefully through the pages. When he found what he was looking for, he scratched his head. "That's funny."

Susan leaned over the bed and looked over his shoulder. It was a picture of a handsome young man, blond and burly, holding a beautiful baby. "Is that you?" she asked softly.

He nodded. "With my son. That's Randy at his baptism." He walked over to the dresser and retrieved the other picture, holding it next to the one in the album. The two photographs were almost identical. Dale turned to Susan with a quizzical look in his eyes.

"That's not you, Dale," she said softly, pointing to the picture she had brought. "It's your father. With *my* son, Joel."

Dale's eyes widened, then returned to normal. "Son of a gun," he said incredulously, "I really do look like him, don't I?" He kept staring at the picture, moving his eyes from that one to the other in his album, shaking his head in disbelief. "It's really amazing. No wonder you were so sure."

Finally he tore his eyes away and sat down in the big rocking chair next to his bed. He rocked pensively, his eyes slightly dazed. Susan leaned curiously over the open pages of the photograph album, cocking her head toward Dale to ask his permission to look through it. He didn't respond, but as he didn't seem to object, she began to turn the pages gingerly.

It was the first time she had ever seen pictures of his ex-wife. Diane was a pretty woman, with blond, medium-length hair and dimples. Pretty, but not knock-out striking. Jennifer's unusually good looks apparently came from her father. Susan flipped back toward the beginning of the book. There were some earlier pictures of Diane, wearing much longer hair and dressed in a cheerleading uniform. "I knew it!" Susan exclaimed triumphantly. "The captain of the football team and the head cheerleader. The perfect high-school romance."

Dale smiled and slid out of the chair to sit quietly beside her on the floor. "You think you know everything, don't you? All right, Miss Lawyer, what else do you think you know? Let's see how good your deductive skills are."

Susan warmed to the challenge. "You were the most popular couple in your high school. You went everywhere together, school dances and county fairs and parking in secluded lovers' lanes. Especially lovers' lanes. You were young and fun-loving and optimistic, and you thought you had life by the tail. And then you had to get married."

Dale's face darkened. The game wasn't fun anymore. "Why do you say that?"

"You're hardly twenty years older than your daughter, Dale. You said you got married when you were nineteen."

He leaned back against the foot of the bed and stretched his legs out. They reached to the opposite wall. "You're pretty smart, Lady. Yes, I *did* have to get married. But we were going to get married anyway after Diane graduated high school and I got out of the service. Diane's getting pregnant just speeded things up a little."

Susan had always been grateful that Mike had been just a little too old for the Vietnam War. She touched Dale's arm sympathetically. "You were drafted?"

"No, I enlisted."

Susan raised her eyebrows slightly. She and Mike had demonstrated against the war and considered that an act of patriotism. It had not occurred to her that Dale had grown up with a different value system. But she wasn't inclined to provoke a confrontational political argument. Vietnam had been over for a long time. "So you believed in the war," she said gently.

"Actually, I didn't. I didn't think we should have been in Vietnam, but it wasn't my place to question the morality of the war. I leave that to the politicians. I joined up because I felt it was my duty to serve my country. Not that I had much choice. I wasn't eligible for a student deferment and I didn't have a rich daddy with connections to get me in the National Guard. I was just plain 1-A. But I probably would have joined the Navy even in peacetime. I wanted to see the world. I was a farm boy who'd never seen the ocean. Well, I got to see the ocean, but just the edge of it. We were stationed in San Diego my whole tour."

"How come?"

"They needed mechanics to work in the Navy yard. I was lucky to pull shore duty, I guess. I was a married man with a baby. Diane didn't want me to be away on a ship for months at a time, even years. And of course she was scared to death that I wouldn't come back. I knew a lot of guys that didn't. So I guess I was really lucky."

He didn't look like he felt lucky. He looked disappointed. He had wanted to see the world, but his aspirations had been denied him.

Dale looked into Susan's judgmental eyes. "I've never regretted getting married then, Susan. I have two beautiful children to show for it. Randy may never be a rocket scientist, but he's a good kid. He has a good heart. Diane and I were a little young to start a family, but sometimes you just have to take what life throws at you."

"You do what you have to do," she said in a faraway voice. Dale looked at her questioningly. "It's just something that Jeff used to say. You really *are* like him in a lot of little ways." She closed the photo album. "Dale, why did you divorce Diane? It was you that wanted the divorce, wasn't it?"

Dale sighed. "You *do* know everything, don't you? Yes, it was me. How did you guess that?"

Susan scooted beside him and rested her head against his chest. "It wasn't hard to figure out. I don't think any woman in her right mind would let you go if she had a choice, Dale."

He waved off her remark, embarrassed by the tribute. Folding his arms around his knees, he lay his head back on the bed, deep in thought. He was silent for several minutes.

"You don't have to tell me if it's too personal or too painful," Susan said finally. "I'm sure it's difficult to explain."

"It's not too personal. And it's actually not that difficult to explain. I could say it in just a few words, but you'd think I was the most selfish, boorish bastard who ever lived."

"Try me."

He emitted a long sigh. "I was bored, Susan. That's the plain and simple truth. Diane was a good wife. We had good kids. I couldn't complain about my sex life. I had everything going for me; I should have been a happy man, but I wasn't. There was no excitement in my life. Everything was so predictable. I worked hard all day, and then I'd come home to a predictable dinner, and in the evenings, if we went out, it was to Little League games and church suppers and bowling leagues. Always the same people, always the same places. There was nothing wrong with that, I suppose; Diane seemed to be contented with that life, but I wanted more. I just felt there had to be something else."

"So you just walked out."

"I wasn't quite that crass. I thought about it for a long time before I did it. I tried to talk to Diane about it, but she just didn't understand. I know you think I'm crazy when I talk about 'class,' Susan, but you don't understand what I mean. I'm not sure what I mean myself. But I *don't* mean belonging to a country club or knowing which fork to use. It's culture, it's education, it's having a worldview of things instead of seeing everything through the tiny peephole of one's own personal experience. It's just something you have and take for granted, something that I know I lack. But I wanted to know what I was missing. I didn't want to be poor white trash all my life. I didn't desert my family. I left Diane money and I kept close to the kids. But I just had to get out. I had to see what else was out there."

Susan nuzzled his cheek and played with his mustache. "So what did you find?"

He grinned. "The cold, cruel world. Hollywood tinsel. The bright lights and the big city."

"Wasn't that what you wanted?"

"I *thought* it was what I wanted, Susan. I

thought that what was missing from my life was excitement, sensual thrills. So I lived in the fast lane for awhile. I hung out at expensive clubs that I couldn't afford, and I got involved with some of the beautiful people, whom I certainly couldn't afford. I married a Hollywood movie starlet."

"Your second wife was a movie star?"

"Star*let*. She had a few small parts in some poorly received B movies. She never had a starring role in her life, unless you want to count some runner-up billings in a few porno flicks."

Susan stared. "You were married to a porno queen?"

Dale smiled at her surprised look. "I told you Judy had a great body."

Susan was fascinated. She tried to sound clinical instead of jealous. "I'll bet she was great in bed."

He grinned salaciously. "She could be, when she wasn't worrying about getting her hair mussed up."

Susan patted his hand and shook her head from side to side. "Dale, most men would give their eyeteeth to have what you had. How come you gave it up?"

He shrugged. "There's more to life than sex, Susan."

She stared into his wise, mature eyes. Sometimes she had to force herself to remember that Dale was twelve years younger than she, not older. He had already experienced two life-styles and had had the courage to reject them both. Susan had never even dared question her own style of life, let alone change it. What if she made a mistake? What if she took a risk and it didn't work out, and she lost what she had?

"Why didn't you just go back to Diane after that?" she asked curiously. "Was she already remarried?"

"Nope. She probably would have even taken me back. She does still love me, Susan. You were right about that, too. But I couldn't go back. It wasn't like Dorothy in Oz searching for her heart's desire and finding it in her own backyard. I knew where I'd been. I knew it wasn't there."

"So you've kept searching. And now you think you've found it in me, this indefinable 'class' that you're so bent on having."

"Susan, I'm not that big of a jerk. It's not like I think a little will rub off if I stand next to you. I know it's something I have to earn myself. But I never had any encouragement for my efforts. All the women I've ever gone out with have been low-rent like me. If I had ever suggested to one of them that we go to the opera or a ballet or a museum, they would have laughed at me. You don't. You're comfortable with these things and you enjoy them or at least understand them. And despite what I said when we first met, I don't feel like you look down on me."

Quite the opposite. She admired his willingness to admit his weaknesses and mistakes, and respected his courage to try again. Unlike Mike, who had always known what he wanted, Dale was still trying to find meaning in his life. Mike had always taken the direct route to his goals; Dale followed a circuitous path, ambling around and backtracking at times. But like her late husband, Dale didn't give up easily. He was determined to find what he needed. And Susan thought she knew what that was.

"Of course I don't look down on you, Dale, even though I may have acted like it sometimes. That was my ignorance, not yours. It's not class that you lack; I think you are one hell of a class act. But I think I know what it is that you've been missing all your life: intellectual stimulation."

He looked at her blankly. "Obviously I have, because I don't even know what that means."

"Yes, you do. You're an intelligent man, Dale; you've got your father's genes. He dropped out of school in eighth grade, but he went on to finish and go to college and law school. You may not be a genius, but you're probably a lot smarter than most of the people you grew up with. But you were afraid to show it because you didn't want the people you hung around with to think you were some sort of egghead or weirdo."

"You're right about that. Where I came from, higher education wasn't expected, it wasn't even valued. It was considered more important to be the captain of the football team. It was different for you. Love of learning is your birthright. I know that Jewish people put a lot of value on education. You probably knew you were going to college since you were six years old."

"I did, and your life was programmed in another direction. But that's why you were bored and unhappy: you were never intellectually challenged. I don't think it's sensory stimulation that you need; you need food for your mind."

He pursed his lips together. "Maybe you're right. You know, I was really nervous about taking a class in college. I was afraid I'd look like an idiot in front of the teacher, in front of the other students. Accounting is almost like another language, and you know how I am with languages."

"Yes: very good. You've gotten A's on all your tests so far."

"Well, I've had to spend a lot of time studying. Time that I've felt guilty about not spending with you. But I haven't minded the studying, I've actually enjoyed it. And I really appreciate the support you've given me, Suse." He took her in his arms and clenched his fists across her back. "You've never complained that I'm neglecting you. You've been understanding, helpful, and loving. Diane would have never understood why I wanted to do this." He bit his lip nervously, hesitant about his next words. "Susan, I'm going to enroll as a regular student next semester, if they'll take me. I'm going to sign up for freshman courses and go for a diploma. I know it'll take me a long time to get anywhere, taking one or two classes at night each semester. I know I may never get a chance to complete my degree. I don't care. This is just something I want to do for myself." His voice was choked a little with tears, but it resonated in determination.

They lay on the floor and held each other, their hearts beating against each other's breasts. Dale had shared his dreams and his hungers with her, the crying out of his soul. Although they were both fully clothed, Susan couldn't have felt closer to him now if they were naked and inside each other.

Dale began to spend almost every night at her house now, often dropping by for a quick bite after he'd closed up the garage and then darting out again to his class. It was usually after ten before he returned, but Susan didn't mind the wait. The nights with Dale were worth it.

At first he arrived each evening bearing a clean uniform for work the next day; then he started bringing two or three at a time, hanging them in her bedroom closet. "This is getting ridiculous," Susan laughed, as he checked the closet one night to make sure he had a clean uniform. "Why don't you just bring all your clothes here, Dale? Move in with me."

"I don't want to move in with you."

His voice was too somber for Susan's comfort. "Why not?"

"You don't have a swimming pool."

"You and your damn swimming pool." She laughed in relief, thinking he was teasing her as usual. "You hardly ever swim in it anyway. You're never home. You're always here."

"You're right about that," he admitted. "But that is about to change. Starting tonight."

She knew he wasn't teasing now. An uneasy feeling began to simmer in the pit of her stomach.

"I need to go home, Susan," Dale explained. "I'm starting to feel like a damn gypsy. You have a lovely house, and I do feel comfortable here, but it is *your* house. I feel like a guest. I want to spend some time in my own place, surrounded by my own stuff. I miss my pool and my routine. I miss sleeping in my own bed."

She winced. The uneasy feeling suddenly grew larger, bumping around the walls of her stomach like a rubber ball. He was tiring of her. He wanted out of the relationship. This was just the first step. First it would be going home to sleep at night, then would come the nights he would be too tired to come over for dinner, until finally would come the day that he wouldn't come at all. Susan held her sides to keep them from splitting open with pain. She should have been prepared for this. She knew it had to happen one day. She could feel the tears rising through her throat, but she held them back. Don't make a scene, Susan, she warned herself. Don't be a baby. Try to act with the class he's always given you credit for.

"I understand, Dale," she said bravely. "You need your space."

The look he gave her convinced her that he could see inside not only her mind but her entire body. He was looking right at those bubbles of insecurity. "You *don't* understand," he said. "I don't need my space. You give me all the space I need. But I need my *place*. I need to feel the comfort of home. I do want to sleep in my own bed, but I don't want to sleep there alone. I want you to come with me tonight,

Susan. And every night. I don't want to be away from you. I don't want us ever to be apart."

She blinked back the tears just in time, but she couldn't keep her body from shaking as she folded her arms around his neck and hugged him until her arms were sore. He stroked her back gently. "Unless," he added, with a twinkle in his eye that she couldn't see but knew was there, "my bed is too small for you."

Susan pressed her body against his so tightly that she was sure the ruffles on her blouse were making indentations in his shirt. "I love you, Dale," she whispered. "I'd sleep in a peanut shell with you."

They ended up sleeping together at his place two or three nights a week, the rest of the time at Susan's. The commute to Dale's house seemed shorter each night. In fact Susan came to treasure the moments of relative privacy they had while stuck in traffic in the Los Angeles area freeway system. And it was nice to wake up to the sound of birds chirping through the open window, and the smell of fresh air instead of the pervasive Los Angeles smog.

It was difficult, however, to get used to waking up before dawn. Dale rose every morning before it was light and padded outside, stark naked, to swim his twenty laps. Some days Susan tiptoed out quietly after him and watched him surreptitiously from the picture window in the den, following his strokes as the moonlight bounced off his back and buttocks. Most days she stayed in bed and waited for him to wake her up with a wet kiss from cold lips and a drizzle of water on her forehead from his dripping hair.

Susan had never been very enthusiastic about morning sex, preferring sleep to sunrise gymnastics. But when she saw Dale standing before her in his nakedness, beads of water glistening on his body, she never failed to hold out her arms for him.

She almost came to prefer sleeping in Dale's narrow bed. It mitigated the guilt she had been feeling about sleeping with another man so soon after she had lost her husband, and cavorting so shamelessly with him in Mike's bed.

"It's natural that you should feel uncomfortable," Dale said when she confided her feelings to him. "You slept in the same bed with the same man for thirty years. I'm the one who should feel guilty." He grinned sheepishly. "Mike is giving me hell about you."

"Mike? He talks to you?" She assumed he was joking, but with Dale, sometimes it was hard to tell for sure. "What does he say?"

"He says 'Dale, you son-of-a-bitch, I wanted

you to have my car. I did not invite you to fuck my woman.' "

Susan giggled. "And what do you say to that?"

"I try to explain to him that it's not like that, that I have deep feelings for you and I want to take care of you now that he can't anymore."

"I see. And what does he say to that?"

"He says, 'You'd better, you bastard, because if you don't take good care of her, I'm going to come after you and beat you up with a nine iron."

Susan smiled seductively and kicked off the sheet which covered her nude body, stretching out provocatively in front of him. "I guess you'd better take care of me, then."

"Again?" Dale pretended to be shocked. "Woman, you are insatiable. You're going to wear me out." But he didn't have a bit of trouble obliging her.

Dale watched Susan's eyelids droop and close as she lay back on her pillow in exhausted satisfaction. He loved to look at her face. It was a beautiful face in a very simple, uncluttered sort of way. When Dale looked at Susan, he saw youthful innocence. It wasn't that he didn't see the wrinkles and creases in the aging skin or the silver-gray strands of hair woven in among the brown. They were plainly there, and Dale had never been one to romanticize away things he didn't want to see. But under the face of the mature woman Dale saw the face of a little girl, a little girl who needed love and protection. He wondered what she had been like when she was younger. He wondered what would have happened if he had met her before she married Mike. Absolutely nothing, he reflected wryly. The year Susan and Mike got married he was only eleven years old.

He spread his fingers over Susan's well-shaped breasts. His large hands completely covered her chest like two protective ferns. Susan purred contentedly as his fingers kneaded gently into her stomach, lulling her to sleep. Dale understood very well what she liked and how to give it to her. And it hadn't taken him very long to learn. Sometimes he felt as though he had always known the secrets of her body, as though the knowledge of how to please this woman had always been on file deep in the recesses of his mind, waiting for a chance to be used.

It's probably in my genes, he thought bitterly. I'm probably making the same moves my father used to make on her.

Dale knew he couldn't compete with Mike; he had never suggested to Susan that he even thought he could do that. But he also knew he didn't have to compete with Mike. It was Jeff he was in competition with, and always had been.

Did she really love him? he wondered for the hundred and fiftieth time as the pain welled up once again in his gut. Or was she still in love with his father? Could she, would she, ever let go of the ghost she held in her heart and begin to love him the way he wanted her to? Or was he doomed forever to be a second-rate substitute?

Dale clenched his fingers into a tight ball and pushed his fist into his mouth to stop that scream that wanted to fly out. Susan was what he needed, what he had always needed. An independent woman, professionally and financially strong, yet emotionally vulnerable. But did she need him?

Dale lay down beside Susan, folding his hurt back up inside his heart. He didn't think he wanted to know the answer.

"Springsteen is coming to town next week," Dale remarked a few days later. "How would you like to go to the concert?"

Susan's eyes wanted to sparkle with delight, but she dulled them on purpose. "Not possible," she said practically. "Those tickets have been sold out for months."

Dale grinned. "I know somebody who knows somebody who knows somebody. I'll see what I can do."

Susan knew what that meant. "That's going to be awfully expensive," she warned. "At least let me pay for it."

"No!" he countered sharply. "I said I was taking you."

She had hoped not to be the only representative of her generation attending the rock concert, but Susan felt like the matriarch of the crowd. Everywhere she looked she saw teenagers, including thirty- and forty-year-old teenagers, garishly dressed or half-undressed.

"I must have been living in a cave the past ten years," she remarked. "Is that what the girls in your classes look like?" She pointed to a dark-maned beauty wearing a Band-Aid halter top and the briefest of brief shorts.

Dale followed her gaze. "More or less," he said disinterestedly. "More clothes. Less hair."

"And that one? What do you think of that one?" she asked, as a girl with no stomach and no bra, only a head of long pearl blond hair, wiggled past them. The snap on her tight black jeans threatened to pop if she breathed, and the see-through top was more of an invitation than a garment.

"Not interested," he said. "She's not my type."

"Not your type? Oh, come off it, Dale," she teased, "she's everybody's type."

He grinned. "Okay, I'll admit I wouldn't kick her out of bed. She'd be good for one night. But that's it." He squeezed her hand. "I don't like girls, Susan. I like women."

As they weaved their way to the parking lot after the concert, breaking free from the swarm of arms and shoulders, a couple of boys in their late teens or early twenties, with punk hairdos and dangling earrings pushed past them, almost knocking Susan over. A third sidled up casually beside them and brushed his hand roughly against her breast, accidentally-on-purpose, Susan thought. They looked her up and down thoroughly, undressing her with their eyes.

"You must be pretty hard up, man," one of them said to Dale, "to be making it with your mama."

"Yeah, man," the other one giggled in a falsetto voice, "when this dude does it to his old lady, he really does it to an old lady."

Dale grabbed her arm roughly and pushed her ahead of him. "Let's go," he said. He didn't say anything else until after they'd reached his truck and inched their way slowly out the exit gate. "I'm sorry, Susan," he said. "I know you're disappointed in me; I know you feel like I should have defended your honor back there. But you know why I didn't."

"Never mind," she said soothingly. "What do I care about what a couple of lowlife punks think of me? And I can think of a lot worse things to be called than your mother. I would have been proud to have you for a son." A faint smile parted her lips as the truck cruised easily through the streets. "Hell, I almost could have been your mother, if things had turned out differently."

There was a screeching of brakes as Dale pulled the truck over to a curb and stopped. "Don't say that!" he said angrily. "Don't ever say that. You're not my mother. You're not anything like my mother." He pulled Susan close to him. His arms around her shoulders felt rough and aggressive at first, but as her body submitted willingly, he relaxed. "I'm glad things didn't turn out that way," he whispered. He was calm and loving again. "I'm glad they turned out just the way they did."

Susan hugged him warmly, reassuringly, but the incident had disturbed her more than she cared to admit. Rationally she knew that Dale had done the right thing. She hadn't been in any danger; the boys were just small-time roughnecks looking to get their kicks from provoking a fight. It was just a case of infantile name-calling.

But Dale hadn't even talked back to them, hadn't even spoken up at all. Sure, there were three of them, but he was three inches taller and fifty pounds heavier than the biggest of them. Why hadn't he at least postured or snarled or shot them a threatening glance?

She didn't like what she was feeling and thinking. She was beginning to wonder if Dale had made up that story about almost killing a man. She thought about the fact that he had sat out the Vietnam War in a safe American port while others had risked their lives in combat. Maybe he really was . . . chicken.

This is childish, Susan, she told herself. You're vilifying the man because he didn't act like a junior high-school bully with fists for brains? Dale had acted prudently. It wasn't necessary for him to prove anything to anybody. What did she want from him, anyway?

What did any woman want from a man? Susan wondered philosophically. We *say* we want a man who is sensitive and caring. But deep down, do we really want a Tarzan-type he-man, a man who will defend us and fight our battles for us, risking physical harm or even death? No wonder men are so confused.

Sixteen

"Mother!" Andrea's voice rang out in hurt surprise as she burst into the kitchen one evening. "Why didn't you tell me?"

"Tell you what?" Susan barely looked up as she spread cream cheese on one side of a cut bagel. Dale had rushed off to class without any dinner, so she was preparing a late-night snack for him.

"That you've been dating somebody. That you've been—" Andrea lowered her voice to a whisper although they were alone in the house "—*sleeping* with somebody. As often as I've been here, as often as we've talked on the phone, you've never said one word to me. I had to hear it from a stranger."

Susan put down the spreading knife and took a deep breath. Her lips tightened and her mouth drew up into a little bow. "Who?"

"Mrs. Kessler, your next-door neighbor. She

313

just asked me how I liked my new stepfather. Well, you can imagine my shock and amazement. I didn't know what to say. Here I thought you were adjusting so well, finally, to Daddy's death. And now I find out you have a man living here in Daddy's house, in *my* house, and I've never even met him."

Susan pursed her lips together even tighter. She wiped her hands on a dishtowel. "He doesn't live here, not all the time. He has his own house. And you *have* met him. You were in his house."

Andrea's eyes bugged out of her head. "Jennifer Clemens's father? Mother, how could you? How could you do this to me?"

Susan put down the towel and stared at her daughter. Andrea's reaction was the same one as her standard reply during her teenaged years when Susan had embarrassed her by wearing her skirt too long or too short, or by wearing boots when they weren't in fashion or by not wearing boots when they *were* in fashion. Andrea's trademark indignation. A minute ago Susan had felt humble and conciliatory under her daughter's accusation. Now she felt angry.

"Do this to you?" she repeated. "What have I done to you?"

"Mom, you've embarrassed me in front of the whole neighborhood, the whole community. My mother, who's supposed to be a respectable widow, running around with a man half her age. Mark will be so upset if I tell him about this. And his parents? Oh my god, if his parents find out, I'll be just devastated, I'll be ruined forever!"

"Dale is not half my age," Susan said with practiced calm. "And I'm not 'running around' with him. You make me sound like the town tramp or the mother character out of a Cher movie."

"Well? He's not exactly the type of man to get serious with someone . . . like you." Susan surmised that she had been going to say "someone of your age," but had refrained. "Where is he tonight anyway? Hiding under the bed?"

To say that Susan didn't like her daughter's tone or her attitude would have been a great understatement. "He's in class," she said quietly. "He goes to night school."

"I can just imagine what he's studying," Andrea said cynically. "'The Mating Habits of Freshman Girls.' Mom, I can't believe you could actually go out with a guy like that. When we were at his house that day, he even tried to make a pass at me."

"He *what?!*" Susan's attempt at retaining a calm demeanor failed her now. "What did he say? What did he do to you?"

"He told me I had a nice smile. And later

he told me that I had pretty hair, a nice color, and he said he could see where I got it from."

Susan's breath, which had stopped in her throat as if a large stone had lodged there, gradually let itself out. "That's it? He didn't touch you or anything?"

"Of course not."

Susan sat down in the kitchen chair, feeling a sudden need to take a heavy load off her feet. "I thought you liked Jennifer. What do you have against her father?"

"I don't have anything against him. Not as Jennifer's father. But as my mother's lover? My god, Mom, don't you have any shame? Can't you see that people are talking about you? You've already had a husband. You're over fifty years old. You should act your age!"

She had just pushed every one of Susan's buttons, and red lights were flashing. "I'm not supposed to have a life, is that it? I'm supposed to stay home and knit socks and live on my memories. Well, I've got news for you, young lady. God willing, I've got maybe twenty-five years left to live, and I don't intend to spend them with needlepoint and television as my only companions. And I don't intend to sleep alone the rest of my life, either. That's what's really bugging you, isn't it? Mothers aren't supposed to have *sex*." she spat out the word, which she'd once found too embarrassing to utter aloud, in stark defiance as Andrea stared, open-mouthed. "Grow up, darling. Yours was not an Immaculate Conception. And my life is not over. I have every right to the same pleasures that you enjoy with your boyfriend. You don't think I know that you're at Mark's apartment more than you are at your own?"

"That's different," Andrea said huffily.

"Oh, yeah? What's different about it?"

"Mark and I are in love. And we're going to be married—if you and that lowlife greaser don't mess it up for me with Mark's parents. They're coming into town next week, and I was going to ask you if you would invite them over here for dinner, so you could all get to know each other. But I certainly wouldn't dare bring them over here now. You and your 'boyfriend' might be going at it right in the middle of the living room!"

Susan didn't know where the slap came from. She had never struck her daughter in her life, except for light taps on the bottom when she was a small child. But there it was, five uncontrolled fingers lined up against the young girl's cheek. Her gasp was louder than Andrea's when she realized what she had done.

Andrea held her cheek and looked at her mother in shock.

"I love Dale," Susan said slowly and deliberately. "And he loves me. And you're just going to have to get used to that."

"No, I don't," Andrea retorted. "I don't have to get used to anything. Because I'm never coming back here again."

The door slamming behind her was louder than a sonic boom.

She didn't tell Dale about her estrangement from Andrea. There was no point in embroiling him in a family argument which only indirectly involved him. Susan and her daughter had had these types of clashes before. Andrea was becoming a bit of a prig, in Susan's estimation, selfish and intolerant. Maybe she and Mike had spoiled her too much. Susan wasn't about to give up Dale even temporarily for the sake of impressing Andrea's boyfriend's self-righteous parents. This particular altercation had been much more intense and heated than their usual arguments, but it would surely be as short-lived as the others. In a few weeks, Susan reasoned, she and Andrea would be reconciled. She hoped.

"How's it going, Susan?" Ron Davis asked in his typically upbeat style. "Are you snowed under or do you think you can handle one more?"

Susan threw a cursory glance at the sheaf of papers Ron spread over her desk. "A murder case?" she asked incredulously. "Isn't that Samuelson's department?"

"Attempted murder. I expect you to plead it down to simple assault. Ted can't do it. He's got the Williams trial to prepare for." Leonard Williams was the Gentleman Rapist. The case had gotten a lot of pretrial publicity for Ted and, likewise, for the firm. "He'd hoped to get a continuance, but the judge won't grant it. Anyway, it's your client."

Susan's eyes darted back again to the documents. The name Lois Webster jumped out at her. She barely noticed Ron leave the room as she focused on the papers in front of her.

Lois's husband, Dr. Simon Webster, had once again violated the restraining order against him. He had appeared at his former household at midnight, threatening to break every window and take a baseball bat to Lois's car if she didn't let him in. When she did, he assaulted her with his fists and forced her into the bedroom for further aggression. But this time Lois was ready for him. She reached under the bed and retrieved a loaded pistol. The beleaguered wife missed her mark and shot her estranged husband in the leg.

Susan couldn't wait to get started on the case. It had been a long time since she had been able to sink her teeth into one this meaty. It wasn't that she minded doing the routine cases, divorces, adoptions, etc. Somebody had to do them, and Susan felt that she did them well, with her unique perspective as the only woman in an office of six men. But she felt that her talents had been underutilized and underestimated. This was her opportunity to shine just like superstar Ted Samuelson.

She was deep into the brief, pondering her angle, when she noticed, out of the corner of her eye, two shiny black shoes in the doorway. Thinking that Ron had forgotten to tell her something, she raised her eyes slowly from the shoes up the pant legs past the tight, athletic thighs and broad, robust chest.

"Hi!" she said with cheerful surprise as her eyes reached Dale's handsome face. "How'd you get in here? Mary Ann didn't buzz me."

"I just came from Mr. Halvorsen's office."

"Oh?" She turned her chair to face him. "Anything new on your case?"

For an answer, he held up the large yellow settlement check. Even from a distance, the word *thousand* jumped out at her. "That's terrific!" She jumped up and hugged him, then hastily closed the door behind him. "Does the cost of Dr. Berger's car come out of this?"

"Nope. He's already been taken care of. This is all mine." He seated himself in the visitor's chair as Susan resumed her place at her desk.

"Congratulations, Dale. What are you going to do with it?"

"Well, first I'm going to treat myself to a much-needed vacation. How does Mexico strike you?"

"It's nice. Mike and I went to Puerta Vallarta a few times."

"Then I'd rather go someplace else. How about the Caribbean?"

"Dale, are you asking me to go on vacation with you?"

"Well, I guess I *could* ask Mr. Halvorsen, since he's the one that really got me this check. All *you* did was save my life. But I think you'd be much more fun. Can you get away next week?"

It sounded wonderful. "I'm sorry, Dale," Susan said in disappointment. "I'd love to go. But I've just accepted a case that goes to trial week after next. I probably won't even have time to sleep until it's over, let alone go on vacation. Maybe you'd like to take your son?" she suggested halfheartedly.

"Are you crazy? I'd rather take Mr. Halvorsen. I'll wait till you can get away, Lady. How about over Thanksgiving? That way I won't have to miss too many classes. Or were you planning to fix a big Thanksgiving dinner for your family?"

She always had. She bought the biggest turkey in the supermarket and the kids would dress it, and Mike would carve it, and her mother would fly up from Houston. . . . She choked back a tear. Not anymore. Her husband was dead, her mother was too ill to fly, and the kids were grown up and living their own lives.

"No," she said courageously. "Joel is planning to go up to New York for Thanksgiving. I can't imagine why," she teased playfully, knowing that Dale was well-aware of the reason for Joel's interest in visiting New York. "And Andrea . . ."

She frowned. The truth was, she didn't know *where* Andrea was planning to spend Thanksgiving. It had been two weeks since the big blow-up, and she and Andrea were still not speaking to each other. Susan forced a smile onto her face so as not to arouse Dale's suspicion. "Andrea might go out of town, too." She pretended to check her desk calendar. "Thanksgiving should be fine," she said crisply. "I'll just have to check with my boss and see if he can spare me then."

"Is he that thin guy with the gray hair and mustache? The one who was leaving your office just before I came in?" Susan nodded. "There shouldn't be any problem then."

She looked at him quizzically. "Why not?"

"Because he has the hots for you. He'll let you do anything you want." Dale grinned. "Just don't tell him who you're going with."

Susan laughed, certain that he was kidding. "Are you sure you don't mind waiting, Dale? I know you really need a vacation now."

He kissed her on the cheek. "Some things are worth waiting for. It's settled, then. You pick the island, and I'll make the arrangements."

"You pick it, Dale. It's your settlement money. Besides, my idea of a vacation is to not have to do anything in the planning. Just pick me up that day and tell me where we're going."

Susan was delighted to have an important case to work on and pleased that Dale had agreed to postpone his plans for her. Mike would have never done that. As rarely as he'd taken vacations, when he had been able to get away, he'd expected Susan to arrange her schedule to match his.

"Way to go, Mom!" Joel affirmed when Susan told him of her vacation plans, but she was not exceedingly cheered by his response.

She knew exactly what was going on in her son's head. He was taking note of the parallels in the relationships between the members of the Riesman and Clemens families. If it was okay for her to vacation in the Caribbean with Dale, then she was tacitly approving Joel's trip to New York to visit Jennifer. Susan wasn't so sure she wanted to give blanket approval to that relationship. But she couldn't see how she could stop it without setting herself up as the biggest hypocrite to ever draw breath.

"I wouldn't worry about Andrea's tantrums if I were you," Joel said breezily, after Susan had reluctantly told him about their latest tiff. "Andy's always been like that. Remember when she threw a fit because you bought her a five-speed instead of a ten-speed bicycle?"

"She was eight years old then," Susan said wryly.

"She was twenty-one when she complained about your buying her a Buick instead of that Firebird she wanted."

"The Buick was your father's idea. I agreed with him, of course, but Andrea only addressed her anger to me, as usual."

"You agreed with him?" Even over the telephone, Joel couldn't hide his smirk. "Would it have made any difference if you hadn't agreed with him?"

"Stop it, Joel," Susan said curtly, well-aware

of what he was implying. It was a familiar song with a monotonous refrain. "Your father and I discussed everything and always reached our decisions democratically. It just so happened that I always agreed with him."

When Susan told Barbara Strauss about her vacation plans, her friend temporarily shelved her disapproval of Susan's romance, and eagerly accompanied her on shopping quests for everything from swimwear to negligees.

"Barbara," Susan asked warily as she tried on bathing suits in the fifteenth dressing room of the fifteenth store in the mall, "has Ron Davis ever said anything about me . . . personally? I mean—do you think he . . . likes me?" She wasn't about to use Dale's words.

Barbara smiled. "Yes, I do. I think he's been trying to tell you that for a long time. He's just not very aggressive."

"Not aggressive? He stole Ted Samuelson away from Bridges and White at the height of his career. He's brought more business into the firm in the last five years than Marshall Dobbs did in the twenty years before it."

"I don't mean professionally. I mean personally. Ron never was very good at social skills. He always relied on Peggy to handle those things for him. I wondered if he was ever going to get your attention. How did you finally notice it?"

"I didn't. Dale did."

Barbara seemed surprised that Dale was that perceptive, and not at all pleased. Her smile turned off like a light switch. "I don't like it," she said, as they carried Susan's selections to the cash register. "Having an affair with a dumb, good-looking mechanic is one thing, but this man is not dumb. He's slick and he's smooth and he knows you too well. I don't like it," she repeated.

Susan was not going to be brought down by Barbara's gloomy cynicism today. "Quit worrying," she smiled. "What's wrong with his knowing me well? Dale treats me wonderfully."

"Well," Barbara said reluctantly, as the cashier rang up the purchases. "Have fun on your trip. But I'm warning you, be careful."

Susan laughed out loud. "Barbara, I'm not going to get pregnant."

"That's not what I meant. I meant—"

"I know. Hold on to my purse."

Susan saw very little of Dale for the next few weeks. She worked seven days a week on the Webster case, grabbing a sandwich at the office and working until eleven or twelve at night. Many nights she came home to a cold and dark house, Dale having gone without her to his own home. More often she found him studying in the downstairs den. On several occasions, she trudged upstairs late at night to collapse into what she assumed would be an empty bed to find a warm and willing body waiting for her. No matter how exhausted she was, Dale could always cajole her into his arms for a brief sweet bout of passion.

Her diligent professional efforts were well worth the sacrifice. After only two and a half hours of deliberation, the jury voted Lois Webster not guilty of assault with a deadly weapon. Susan knew the exact moment she had swayed them. She had seen it in the eyes of every juror in the front row. The feelings of euphoria she felt as she packed up her briefcase were incomparable to any other case she had tried. Her victory was even sweeter in the knowledge that in the courtroom across the hall, Ted Samuelson had lost the Leonard Williams case. Susan was relieved, of course, that the Gentleman Rapist would remain safely behind bars instead of out on the streets to rape and kill again. But more than a part of her pleasure was a feeling that she had succeeded where the firm's new darling had failed.

The only thing missing was someone to share her triumph with. Mike would have basked in her excitement, deriving pride from its warm glow. Jeff would have understood what she was feeling without her saying a word. She wasn't sure that Dale would know what the victory meant to her. Nevertheless, she drove directly from the courtroom to the garage, flush with anticipation, only to find he wasn't there.

"This calls for a celebration," he said, when she finally got him on the phone. "Dinner tonight at any restaurant you choose. Where would you like to go?"

"It doesn't matter, Dale," she demurred quietly. "Wherever you want to eat."

"I told you where I want to eat. At the restaurant of your choice. Why can't you ever make a decision? You always leave these things up to me."

Because I always left them up to Mike, she thought silently. Perhaps there was more truth to Joel's implications than she had been willing to admit. Mike had made all the decisions in their family. Even about where to go for dinner. But it hadn't always been that way. When they were first married, Mike had sought her suggestions, eager to please her. But whatever suggestions Susan had made had met with subtle disapproval. This restaurant was too far away; at this one the food was too spicy; at a third the service was poor. They always ended up going to the restaurant that Mike had probably preferred all along. Susan couldn't remember when it was that she had stopped making suggestions.

"Well?"

Susan smiled. Dale was not manipulative like Mike, but he could be pretty insistent when he wanted to be. If she stayed with this man long enough, he might actually force her to reach for what she wanted out of life. If she ever decided what those desires might be.

She blurted out the name of a very upscale, very popular restaurant. Dale didn't blink at her choice. He even ordered the most expensive bottle of champagne on the menu. "Congratulations, Lady," he said, reaching across the table and cupping her small white hand with his. "You really did a sensational job in that courtroom. It was very impressive."

She beamed. "Thanks. But how would you know what I did in the courtroom?"

"I was there."

She looked askance at him. "You were not. I didn't see you."

"I wore a disguise. I didn't want to make you nervous if you recognized me."

She hated when he did that, emitted some outlandish statement with a perfectly straight face. This time she really didn't know if he was kidding or not. "Why would you? You've never been interested in watching me work before."

Dale was not intrigued by courtroom drama, as Susan was, not even in the movies; he preferred science fiction or action films.

"It's not that I wasn't interested. I didn't feel it was my place. You've never tried to tell me how to fix cars; I didn't want to interfere with your area of expertise. But this trial was so important to you and you worked so hard on it."

"So you wanted to see what it was all about."

"I wanted to see what *you* were all about. I don't know anything about the law, and to tell you the truth, I don't much care to, anymore than you care about what I do all day. Admit it," he challenged, "you don't know a piston from a pump, and you don't care if you ever do."

She grinned guiltily. "I guess I should."

"Why should you? You don't have to like what I like, Susan. I don't have to like everything about your world, either. We have our own lives. We don't have to be joined at the hip."

She stroked his hand with her fingers. "You don't think it's important to have interests in common?"

"It's nice. But it's not everything. If it was, I'd be sleeping with Jose every night."

Susan smiled. "Were you really in the courtroom today?"

"Yes, I was. I may not care about the same

330

things you care about, but I do care about you. I have to tell you, you were great. I really enjoyed watching you work."

"Well," Susan said, squeezing his hand affectionately, "I wish I could say the same for you. But it makes me nervous to watch you work. Especially when you're on the floor under a car. Didn't you learn anything from your close call? Why don't you use a lift?"

"I only have two lifts," Dale said practically. "With that restriction, I could only finish half the cars that I do now. Besides," he grinned mischievously, "we have this Caribbean vacation to show for my experience. The next time a car nearly kills me, maybe we can try the Far East."

"The next time I might not be around to save you," she said, not at all amused.

"I hope you will," he whispered seriously. "I hope you'll always be around to save me, Lady."

The waiter brought their champagne and a chilled bucket. Dale raised his glass to hers. "Lechayim," he said with perfect pronunciation. "Mazel tov, Lady."

Susan smiled and felt very warm inside. Dale might not think common interests were important, but he was certainly making a conscious effort to understand her world. "Dale," she asked tentatively, "why do you have all those

331

books about Judaism in your bedroom? Because of me?"

"Sure," he admitted readily. "I never dated a Jewish woman before. I wanted to know if there were any special customs or observances I should know about. I didn't want to do or say something embarrassing.

She had seen those books before they had ever started dating. For whatever reason, he had obviously been interested enough in her even then to be willing to research things about her. Susan pushed her glass aside as the waiter brought their appetizers. "What religion are you?" she asked curiously.

Dale laughed. "That's a good question. I'm not sure what my grandparents were. Church of Christ, I think. They used to drag me to church every Sunday, and to Sunday school, until I got too old for my grandpa to take his belt to me when I refused. Diane was Congregationalist. She had the kids baptized and took them to church a lot on Sundays, generally without me. Church is not my thing."

"Why not? What didn't you like about it?"

"Bunch of damn hypocrites. The respected elders of the church would cheat people in their stores in the town all week, and then on Sunday they'd come and teach us kids about loving your neighbor."

Susan chuckled. "Yeah, we have some of

them in our religion, too. What else did they teach you in Sunday school?"

"The usual garbage. Hell and damnation, virgin birth, resurrection, all that."

"You didn't believe that?"

"Of course I believed it. Along with Santa Claus and the Easter Bunny. I chucked them all about the same time."

"When was that?"

"As soon as I was old enough to read the Bible and think for myself."

Susan smiled, amused by Dale's irreverent style, but impressed by his thinking. She watched him spear a shrimp with his fork and purposely waited till his mouth was full. "Is Jennifer religious?"

She posed the question casually, but Dale could always detect a serious intent behind her words. "Why do you ask?" he said warily, when he'd swallowed his bite.

He knew why she'd asked. He had to know she was concerned about the attraction between Joel and Jennifer, and, like any mother, felt not only justified, but obligated, to butt in. "Dale, don't you think they're getting awfully serious awfully soon?"

He blotted his lips with his napkin. "You don't think my daughter is good enough for your son?"

"I didn't say that. I'm only concerned that they might be rushing things a little."

"You can't put a timetable on love, Susan. If it's right, it'll happen."

She sighed, feeling helpless and out of control. This wasn't what she had foreseen happening in her life. This wasn't the future she would have picked out for herself and her son. What if Joel was right; what if they ended up having a double wedding?

"Dale," she asked hesitantly, as he undressed and got into bed beside her that night, "would you ever consider converting to Judaism?"

"No," he said flatly.

His peremptory answer surprised her. He had always seemed so open to her religion and so interested in the synagogue services he'd attended with her on several occasions. And he certainly didn't seem to care very much about his own religion. "Why not?"

He stretched out on his back with his elbows behind his head. "Because I'm too old a dog to learn new tricks. I've been a lousy Christian all my life, and I'd be, at best, a lukewarm Jew. I'm interested in your religion, but conversion requires more than just an academic interest. It requires a very strong commitment. A commitment which I'm not willing to make. Certainly not just for the dubious advantage of humoring your family and friends. Just to relieve you of the stigma of dating a *shegetz*."

Susan blinked. She wondered where he had picked up that Yiddish word. She also wondered how he had comprehended her real motive in asking him that question. She hadn't even been aware of it herself.

"I don't believe in doing things halfway," Dale said. "If I were to make such a commitment, it would have to be because I really, truly believed in it. Otherwise it cheapens the whole thing."

He had obviously thought this out before. Susan was pleased that he had even considered it. And she admired his reasons for rejecting it. Barbara was right about one thing. This man was not dumb.

Dale sat up and stared at her with his penetrating, soul-searching green eyes. "I think I know what this is about, Susan. It's not just about you and me. It's also about Jennifer and Joel. That's why you're so nervous and unhappy about their relationship. You feel like you're losing your whole family to the 'uncircumcised heathen.'"

The reference was Biblical, but in his case, also literal. Susan blushed in embarrassment as her eyes turned to his nude body and fixed helplessly on the organ in question.

"You've never dated anybody from outside

your religion, have you? Your parents wouldn't let you."

"That's not true. I dated non-Jewish boys in college. My first boyfriend was not Jewish. But I didn't marry him. I could never marry anybody who wasn't Jewish."

She gulped and swallowed, regretting instantly that she had said that. But Dale didn't seem to be the least bit perturbed. What he said next, however, perturbed the hell out of her.

"Then we have no problem. Because I'm not marrying you."

Seventeen

Susan was shaken. Rationally she knew that she shouldn't be. Dale had told her practically on the day they met that he never intended to get married again. But somehow she had assumed, once they became lovers, that his sentiments had changed. You know what happens when you assume, Susan, she thought bitterly.

She felt hurt and betrayed. She had fought this relationship so much in the beginning, all too aware of the dangers of becoming involved with a man so much younger than herself, so different in so many ways. But Dale had overruled most of her apprehensions with patience, logic, and just plain sexual magnetism. She had let her guard slip, allowing herself to fall in love with him. Only to be stabbed in the heart. Not only had he not proposed marriage to her; he had continually refused, despite Susan's urgings, to sell his house and move in with her. And if that were not humiliating enough, she realized with an anguished pang, he had never even told her, in so many words, that he loved her.

What am I doing here? she thought as she waited in the crowded airport terminal for Dale to process their tickets to Jamaica. All around her were people in love: young newlyweds, thirtyish couples on vacation from their children, older retired people on their second honeymoon. Why was she about to embark on a romantic vacation with a man who was not her husband, a man who had no intention of becoming her husband?

She scanned the scraggly line of passengers waiting to check in their luggage at the airline counter. There were a dozen people in the queue, but her eyes lit on Dale immediately. He seemed to have an aura that glowed about him, an aura of sunshine bursting through clouds. Damn! but the man was handsome. A couple of young yuppie girls stood just ahead of him at the ticket counter, struggling with too many items of luggage. Dale helped them get their suitcases on the weigh machine and engaged them, as was his style, in friendly conversation. Susan could overhear most of it. The girls were apparently going to be staying at the same hotel that they were.

Susan usually didn't mind Dale's friendly

flirtations. That was just his way, as well as his bread and butter. But when she heard one of the girls ask, "Are you traveling alone?" she perked up her ears.

"No, I'm traveling with my mother. I'm giving her this vacation for her sixty-fifth birthday," he said, jerking his head toward Susan.

"I heard that," Susan said icily, when he returned to sit beside her.

"Well, I certainly hope so," he grinned. "I said it loud enough."

He had intended for her to hear it, then. Obviously he thought he was being funny. But Susan didn't find the joke amusing. She found just a hint of meanness in his humor. Dale's barb seemed to be a subtle retaliation for the times she'd made him feel uncomfortable and out of his social element. Now he held the upper hand in their relationship, and he seemed to sense his advantage. She wondered what he planned to do with it.

Well, at least he wasn't after her money, she thought wryly. If he were, like any normal acquisitive man, he would be anxious to marry her. Under California's community property laws, marriage would give him legal claim to half of Susan's assets. Those assets, the holdings that Mike had worked so hard all his life to amass, were considerable, and Dale undoubtedly knew it. So why *didn't* he want to marry her? What *was* his game plan?

"How are you doing, Mama?" Dale smiled at her and squeezed her hand as the plane ascended over the Los Angeles metropolitan area. His smile could melt harder hearts than Susan's. She entwined her fingers through his and stroked his hand fondly.

Susan loved Dale's hands. They were big and capable and comforting. And his eyes. Translucent green pools of deep understanding that a woman could get lost in. And his shoulders, strong and sturdy to cry on. She sighed in resignation. She knew why she was here. She was a woman in love, and she would go to the ends of the earth with this man if he asked her. This vacation was a much-needed opportunity for the two of them to be alone together. Twenty-four hours a day for seven days. Susan was looking forward to it. But she couldn't help thinking that if Dale did have ulterior motives, it was a long time to keep up a facade, a long time with no place to hide. Eventually he would have to reveal his true colors.

Their hotel room was more like a cottage: roomy, comfortable, and detached. It was segregated from the other rooms by a walkway of lush greenery. Like a private love nest, Susan thought.

"Know what I'd like to do right now?" Dale

said, as he unlocked the suitcases and flipped them onto the king-size bed.

Susan fumbled in her suitcase for her new black lace negligee, anticipating his answer. "What?"

"Well, first, I'd like to jump in and have a dip in that gorgeous Caribbean water."

"Oh." She took her hand off the negligee and folded it back inside, smoothing some other clothes over it so he wouldn't notice. Dale had found his swim trunks and was stripping off his clothes. Susan admired out of the corner of her eye the bronze back and the well-shaped buttocks.

"And then," he said, unbuttoning the back buttons of Susan's blouse for her, "I'd like to come back here and make love to you all afternoon until my bones ache, until I'm too tired to lift my head to the pillow." He kissed her lightly on the back of the neck, and Susan reached around behind her and stroked his stomach. "And then let's take a nap, and when we wake up, I want to take you out for dinner to the nicest restaurant on the island."

Susan turned around and kissed him right in the middle of his chest, happy tears shining in her eyes. "Whatever you say, son."

After dinner they joined a beach party. It was a setup for tourists, really, with drinks and dancing and probably even artificial sand. But the reggae beat was good, and after three rum cokes, Susan felt like dancing. She was swirling in Dale's arms when she noticed the two girls from the airport at a table near the bamboo-and-board stage.

They smiled and waved at Dale. He didn't let go of Susan, but he reached his arm down for the two of them to get up and join in. They danced on Dale's periphery, floating singly in the crowd, but every so often he left Susan's side to twirl one or the other of them under his arm. The shorter one was a pretty good dancer, but Susan didn't feel upstaged. Maybe her confidence came out of a bottle, but she felt like no slouch herself on the dance floor tonight.

"That woman is not sixty-five years old," she overheard one of the girls saying suspiciously to Dale. "And she's not your mother either, is she?"

"No," he admitted, beckoning them in closer to meet Susan. "Pam and Jackie, this is my wife."

"I wonder what lie you're going to tell them the next time," Susan mumbled, as she cuddled under the cool sheets and against Dale's warm body that night.

"Tell who?"

"Pam and Jackie. You've lied to them twice already. First you told them I was your mother, and then you told them I was your wife."

"I only lied to them once." Susan looked at him quizzically. "You *are* my wife, Susan. Not legally, but in every other sense. At least that's how I feel. I want to share my life with you. I want to share my body with you. From now until forever."

It was a beautifully romantic thing to say. And maybe he really meant it. But Susan couldn't leave it alone. "Why not legally, Dale? If you feel that way, why don't you want to marry me?"

He seemed surprised at her even posing the question. "You know why. I've told you how I feel about that. Marriage to me was a cage of responsibility. Financial responsibility and responsibility for children. I want my life with you to be different. Our children are grown; we can do what we want. I want this relationship to be for me. For me and you as two individuals. No strings. No cages. Built on nothing but love and respect for one another. I've had the other shit, and I don't want it anymore. And frankly," he laughed wryly, "I would think that legal marriage would be the last thing that *you* would want."

She leaned away from him and moved her

eyes slowly over his face and body. "Why would you think that?"

He stopped laughing when he saw the seriousness of her expression. "My god," he whispered, "that *is* what you want, isn't it? You want me to make an honest woman out of you. Jesus, Susan, I can't believe I was so dumb not to realize it. I never even guessed."

"Well, I didn't say anything about it because you made it clear that wasn't what you wanted. But why would you assume that I didn't want it?"

"Because you'd have the most to lose. You're the one sitting on a million dollar inheritance, not me. Especially with your being a lawyer, a divorce lawyer, at that, I never would have considered even suggesting marriage to you. I figured you'd have me signing so many prenuptial papers I'd have writer's cramp for two months!"

She couldn't help smiling. He *was* in pretty much of a no-win situation. She moved next to him again and caressed the few stray hairs on his chest. "Dale, will you answer a question? Honestly?"

He sat up and leaned his back against the headboard. "Of course."

"Do you love me?"

He laughed heartily, as if in relief. "I thought you were going to ask me something hard. Of course I do. Haven't I told you that a million times?"

"No. You've never said it at all, except . . . in bed."

Dale ran his fingers gently over her lips. "Do you think I would have said it then if I didn't mean it?"

"I don't know."

"Well, I do."

"Do what?"

"Mean it."

"Mean what?"

"What you said." It was a game now, with Dale pushing to see how long he could keep the conversation going without saying the words. He smiled sheepishly as he ran out of turns. "I love you, Susan. I've loved you since almost the first time I met you. You didn't believe it then, but I hope you believe it now."

"I believe it, Dale." At least she wanted to believe it. She wanted to believe it so much. But nagging doubts still tortured her mind. As he wrapped himself around her, Susan clutched his shoulders helplessly, needing his warmth and wanting him close to her but hating herself for her weakness. Would you still love me if I didn't have money? her heart raged even as she surrendered herself to his magic embrace.

The cool voice of reason was muffled by the

hot urgency of passion. I don't care, Susan thought, as her body reverberated with the pleasure of his touch. I don't care if you want my money. You can have it, all of it, anything you want. Only just don't ever stop doing this. Don't ever let this wonderful dream end.

Susan *did* feel like they were husband and wife. She felt like they were on their honeymoon. As they strolled the streets of Montego Bay together, shopping and exploring, Susan noticed more than once the encouraging smiles of the tourists and locals, beaming at the happy lovebirds. Here they were not lawyer and mechanic, nor Jew and Gentile. They were just two people in love.

She never wanted to leave. Everything was so simple here. Dale was her man and she was his woman. There were no excuses to make, no criticisms from friends or relatives, nothing to hide. They spent their days on the beach and their nights in each other's arms. Sometimes they spent the days that way, too. It rained for three days straight in the middle of their stay and they hardly even noticed.

"Why can't it be like this all the time?" she lamented, as they lay next to each other in bed, each reading a book. "It's so different here. You're different here."

346

"No, Susan," he said, turning to her with a serious expression. "I'm not different. I'm the same as I've always been. You're the one who's different."

"How do you mean?" she asked, although she thought she knew the answer.

"You're yourself. In L.A. you try to be what everybody else expects you to be. You have all these external influences pressuring you. Work, children, social responsibilities. Here it's just you and me. And I have to tell you, Susan, this is the first time since I met you that I've ever felt that you belonged to me."

She wanted him that night as much as she ever had. But they had been making love almost constantly for the past week, and her body was beginning to show the signs of wear. When he entered her that evening, she felt no pleasure, only discomfort. And eventually pain.

"Ow," she winced, when their coupling became unbearable.

Dale withdrew immediately. "I'm sorry. I didn't realize I was hurting you."

"It's not your fault," she gasped when she could breathe freely again. "It's just . . . well . . . at my age, women sometimes have . . . a bit of a," she blushed, "lubrication problem."

Dale grinned a slow, lascivious grin. He winked at her seductively and licked his lips with his tongue. Then he extended his tongue even farther, stretching it out and curling it up until it just barely brushed the tip of his nose. "That's not a problem, Lady. Lube jobs are my specialty."

Their last night in Jamaica, Dale suggested that they sleep out on the beach. A week ago Susan would have answered, "Are you crazy?" but now she willingly dragged her blanket out to the deserted shoreline and stretched out comfortably next to Dale as he pointed out some of the stars and constellations.

"This is beautiful," she murmured. "You can't even see the stars from L.A. at night. Too much smog, too many lights."

"You can see them from my house," Dale said pointedly.

"Is that what you do?" she asked curiously, realizing the answer now to something she had often wondered about. When they slept at Dale's house, he often got out of bed in the middle of the night and disappeared for an hour or more before returning. "Is that where you go in the middle of the night? To look at the stars?"

"Yes," he answered. "It relaxes me. Sometimes I do my best thinking in the middle of the night."

Susan leaned in toward him and slid her

hand under his shirt. "Do you ever think about what you want out of life, about what things are most important to you?"

"Yes. I've always had two goals, one of which I've already achieved."

"What's that?"

"I've always wanted to be my own boss. I never liked taking orders from anyone. Owning my own business was my dream come true. That's why I work so hard at it, Susan. This is the first real vacation I've taken in five years."

Her fingers caressed his chest and lightly scratched his stomach. "You should be very proud of yourself, Dale. You're a self-made man."

He laughed. "Nobody is. Nobody ever does it alone. We all need somebody to give us that little push to get over the hurdle. Mike did it for me. I wouldn't have been able to buy my business if it wasn't for him." He looked at her surprised face. "You didn't know that? He never told you?"

"Told me what?"

He sat up and folded his arms across his knees. "When I wanted to go out on my own, I couldn't find a bank willing to lend me the money. I was just a dumb, hard-working mechanic with no assets and no collateral. Mike guaranteed the loan for me so I could buy my business. He stuck his neck out for a relative stranger." A drop of moisture touched the corner of his eye. "He was a super guy."

Susan patted his hand. "Yes, he was. But he was also a very good businessman and a very conservative one. Mike didn't take long-shot risks. If he backed you, he must have had a lot of faith that you would succeed."

"Well, I have, but it's not because I knew what I was doing. I made a lot of mistakes in the beginning, but I worked hard to build the business up to where it is today, and I paid off my loan two months before it was due." He beamed proudly. "When I made arrangements to finance the Jaguar, I didn't have a bit of trouble finding a bank to lend me the money."

"You deserve everything you have, Dale." Susan touched his lips with her finger. "What about your other goal?"

He smiled. "I'm still working on that one. To find a good woman who loves me and trusts me as much as I love her, and to settle down and spend the rest of my life with her."

"And you haven't achieved that?"

"Not completely. I know that you love me, Susan. I think I knew it before you did. I can feel it in your body when we make love. But I don't feel like you trust me yet. It's beautiful being alone together on this island, and it seems like nothing could ever spoil the feelings we have now, but tomorrow we'll be back in

L.A. again and I'm afraid that everything will be just as it was before."

"Then let's not go. Let's stay here forever and never go back."

He smiled as he rocked her in his arms. "I wish, Susan. But I have to work to live. And I think you know you have to go back, too. It's your world."

A world that would no longer be the same without him. "Dale," she asked bluntly, "why do you want me? Why me? You could probably have just about any woman you want."

"I probably could," he said immodestly. "But I've *had* all the women I want." He leaned on his elbow and stared at her earnestly. "Susan, I've been looking for someone special all my life. When I met you, I knew that you were that woman. You are intelligent and beautiful, you've got a great sense of humor, and you're easy to talk to. I feel comfortable with you. What I want at this point in my life is comfort, sharing, and mutual trust. I wasn't looking for fireworks. To be honest with you," he said, gazing into her brown eyes with his own disarming green ones, "I wasn't expecting anything more than a mediocre sex life. That part of our relationship has turned out to be a very pleasant surprise."

She blushed. "Am I too much for you?"

He pushed her down flat on the blanket and

covered her body with his. "Are you kidding? The day that I can't handle it, Lady, they ought to put me out to pasture."

As if to prove his point, he pulled up her T-shirt and began to caress her breasts with his lips. "Dale, this is a public beach," she reminded him.

"A deserted beach," he emphasized. "Nobody can see us but God. And He already knows how we feel about each other."

She would have made love to him in the main plaza of Montego Bay at high noon. His presence was so compelling, his body so alluring. She abandoned herself to the pleasure of his talents.

The concept of making love on the beach was the quintessence of romance, but the reality was much less enjoyable. "Yuck!" Susan exclaimed as they sat up again, wiping the soft gritty sand from her body. "I think I've got sand inside places where I didn't even know I had places."

Dale grinned. "Let's go wash off," he suggested, pulling her to her feet.

"Inside?" she asked hopefully. Never an outdoor person, right now Susan would more than willingly have traded earthy romance for civilized clean sheets.

But Dale was standing facing the ocean. "Innocent that you are, I'll bet you've never been skinny-dipping before," he remarked.

She had been, just once, many years ago. Ironically it had been with Dale's father. But then she had been a shy, innocent, fourteen-year-old. She had held her body away from Jeff's, afraid to touch him, modestly hiding her shame under the fickle churnings of the Galveston waves.

But with Dale she felt no such shame. Susan walked proudly beside him toward the silver waves of the ocean as the tropical breezes caressed her bare breasts. She felt like Eve to Dale's Adam, surveying the territory of their own private garden of Eden.

The warm Gulf Stream waters tickled her feet then her legs, then her thighs as she stepped gingerly into the sea. She didn't know which was more seducing, the feel of the waves against her back or the slickness of Dale's body as he pressed against her, proffering warm, salty kisses on her lips and cheeks. Susan closed her eyes and surrendered her body to the swirling waters and to Dale's loving presence. In the passions of ecstasy with him, she felt as though she could give up everything else in her life and live on this island with him forever.

When they emerged from the water, their bodies slick, they made love again on the cool, deserted beach. This time Dale pulled Susan on top of him to protect her from the rough sand. Susan was exhausted when they finished, not only from the physical activity but from the wind and water. "You don't really want to sleep out here tonight, do you?" she asked, as Dale rolled her off him and turned on his side. "Dale?"

There was no answer. Susan blew in his ear and tried to shake him into consciousness, but she knew it was a useless effort. When Dale wanted to sleep, nothing could arouse him. Reluctantly she pulled the sandy sheet over her and cuddled against his back.

The next thing she was aware of was Dale's voice in her ear. "Susan, wake up. It's almost light out."

Her eyelids felt too heavy to open. She moved away from his lips and fell back into inanimate slumber. She didn't stir again until she felt a hand inside her thighs, struggling with her underpants.

"Dale, stop it," she whined. "Not now. I want to go back to sleep."

But sleep was out of the question. Persistent fingers kept moving about her flesh. Susan slapped the hands away in annoyance. She really resented this. It was not like she wasn't usually acquiescent to, even eager for, Dale's morning desires. When she was awake. But she resented like hell being nudged into awareness before she was ready, just because *he* was in the mood. She sat up and opened her eyes, ready to give him a piece of her mind. Then she realized that Dale was struggling, not to yank her panties off her, but to pull them on.

"Susan, you've got to get dressed," he insisted. "There's likely to be people out here any minute. We could get arrested for vagrancy or indecent exposure. Do you want to spend the rest of your life in a Jamaican jail?"

She was dressed in thirty seconds.

"It's a good thing we're leaving today," Dale commented as he shook out the sheet and blanket, and rolled them up. "The maid is going to be pissed as hell when she sees this."

They scrambled up to some boulders overlooking the beach to watch the sunrise. Susan felt tired, gritty, and badly in need of a shower. But as they watched the sunrise together on that quiet Caribbean morning, she also felt blissful and serene. The dawn was breaking not only over the ocean, but on a new chapter in her life.

Eighteen

Susan tried to hold on to the warm contentment she had felt in Jamaica with Dale, but it didn't take long for life's cruel realities to shatter the memories of those idyllic moments, strewing them to the winds like the sands of the Caribbean beach. The first blow was struck within twenty-four hours of her return to Los Angeles. When she walked into her office on her first day back, she found an unsmiling Ron Davis waiting for her. "Lois Webster is dead," he said.

She had been found in her bedroom with her throat slit, three days after her acquittal of the attempted murder of her husband. The first-floor windows had been smashed in the manner of a burglary, but nothing seemed to be missing. Dr. Simon Webster was charged with his wife's murder.

"I wouldn't leave town again if I were you,

Susan," Ron said coldly. "The Grand Jury is going to want to take your statement."

"Mine?" She was incredulous. "Why?"

"Because according to telephone company records, your home phone was the last number Lois Webster called before she died."

Susan swayed against her desk, grateful its hard surface kept her from fainting. Her client was dead and it was her fault. Lois Webster had known she was in trouble and had called her lawyer for help, but instead of being there for her client, Susan had been cavorting on an island beach thousands of miles away, frolicking like a teenager discovering sex for the first time. When Lois Webster had needed her, she had been oblivious to her cry, oblivious to everything but her own passions for a man almost young enough to be her son.

"Rotten bastard," Dale mumbled when she told him. "I'd like to give him a good punch in the jaw."

Susan raised her eyebrows. Any suggestion of violence, coming from Dale, was unusual, but weighed against the offense of murder it seemed a rather mild vengeance.

"That's all?" she asked. "I'd like to see Simon Webster hung by his you-know-what."

"I didn't mean Webster. I was talking about your boss, Mr. Davis. He just couldn't wait to tell you the bad news. He should have known you would take it to heart, that you'd beat yourself up with guilt."

"Why would he? How was he to know how I would take it?"

"He's known you for fifteen years, Susan. I've only known you eight months, but I knew as soon as I walked in the door that you were upset about something. Davis could have waited till later to tell you your testimony would be needed. He *wants* you to feel guilty. He's trying to punish you for going on vacation with another man."

Susan shook her head in disbelief. "Dale, don't you think you're being a little ridiculous?"

"Am I?"

She thought so, but after three days of the cold-shoulder treatment from Ron, she wasn't so sure. She was no longer invited into his office to collaborate on projects; in fact, her boss barely spoke to her beyond a frosty "Good Morning." His few direct comments were in reference to Lois Webster's death and carried the implication that Susan was somehow responsible for the tragedy. Susan's colleagues seemed to take note of the fact that she was no longer an Honored and Respected Person. Following the boss's lead, they avoided her in the coffee room and at lunch. Susan was hurt and confused.

A measure of relief came, at last, from an unexpected source. She was unlocking her office door at six-thirty one morning when she heard footsteps behind her. "I'll bet you haven't had breakfast yet," boomed Ted Samuelson's oratorical voice.

She hadn't. She'd had to drive Dale to work because both his car and his truck were at the garage. Ted grabbed his overcoat and walked her to the diner a few blocks away, taking her arm as they crossed streets as if they were old friends.

"So," he began as they sipped their coffee, "how does it feel to be a handsome prince at a convention of ugly frogs?"

Susan pulled a wisp of hair away from her face. "I'm afraid I don't understand."

He smiled wryly. "You will." Ted snapped his breakfast menu shut and gave his order to the waitress. "Congratulations on winning the Lois Webster case," he said after Susan had made her selection. "I heard from objective observers that you did a damn fine job for your client."

"A lot of good it did her," Susan muttered bitterly. "If I'd lost the case, at least she'd be safe now in jail."

Ted shrugged philosophically. "Susan, we're attorneys, not psychiatrists. And even psychiatrists aren't on call twenty-four hours a day.

What would you have done if you had been there to answer the phone? Chances are, you couldn't have saved her."

Susan looked up in surprise. This was a side of Ted Samuelson she had never seen before. A warm and distinctly human side. Perhaps she had misjudged him. "That's not the way Ron feels about it," she sighed. "As well as everyone else in the office."

"Some people can't stand to see somebody else succeed. They begrudge other people's talents because of their own lack of ability. Davis gave you the Webster case because he didn't have anybody else to handle it. He didn't have the guts to try it himself. He knew he'd probably screw it up. But you won the case and now he's jealous as hell."

"Oh, no," Susan protested. "Ron is an excellent trial lawyer. And I'm sure he's not jealous of my success. He's just . . . upset about something else, probably."

"He's an ugly frog, Susan. They all are. They kept you down for a long time. Doing little cases, being a 'women's' lawyer. Now suddenly you're in another category and everybody wants to pull you down." He grimaced in satisfaction. "Now you know how it feels."

Everybody seemed to have his own theory to explain her ostracism. Dale thought it was personal jealousy; Ted, professional jealousy. She

360

suddenly realized the meaning behind the words Ted had just spoken. "That's how you feel, isn't it?" she said softly. "Since you came here we've all seen you as the hot-shot lawyer who never loses a case, and we couldn't wait to see you fail. Myself especially. I'm ashamed to admit that I felt even better about winning my case because you lost yours." She swallowed hard. "I'm sorry, Ted. I was wrong about you. You really are a caring person."

He frowned. "You're not going to think that after I say what else I have to tell you. I'm going to defend Simon Webster."

She gasped in shock. "Ted! How could you? The man is guilty as the snake in Eden."

"Maybe. Maybe not. The 'maybe not' is why we're here, Susan. Simon Webster has the right to a fair trial like everybody else. Anybody can take the easy cases. Even your friends at Davis and Dobbs. I didn't make my mark representing sweet old ladies and white-collar criminals. I did it defending the scum of the earth. And I'm good at it. Damn good." He pushed his breakfast plate away and wadded up his napkin. "I'll tell you one more thing, Susan. In confidence. This is my last case with Davis, Dobbs and Engels. After this, I'm hanging out my own shingle."

Susan gulped uncomfortably. She knew the sacrifices Ron had made to entice Ted Samuelson to the firm; she was almost certain there had been a lot of up-front money offered to sweeten the deal. This news would not be taken kindly. "Why are you telling me this?" she asked.

"Because I want you to come with me. I think you're a better attorney than you have a chance to be here. I'm not offering a partnership, you understand, but if you produce, you'll see rewards. Well?" he asked as Susan tapped an empty spoon against her teeth.

"I don't know what to say, Ted. Of course I'm flattered. But I've been with Ron a long time. I don't make changes in my life easily."

Ted scooped up the breakfast check and slid out of the booth. "I kind of thought you'd say that. Let's leave it open for a few weeks in case you change your mind. Meanwhile, do me a professional favor and keep what I just told you under your hat."

"Well, are you going to tell him?" Dale asked when she related the incident to him that night.

"Ron? I can't. I gave Ted my word."

"So you're going to take the job he offered."

"I don't know. Do you think I should?"

"How should I know? I know cars, not law-firm politics."

She didn't tell him how to fix cars; he didn't tell her how to win cases—that was Dale's attitude. Dale had no experience in these matters, and even if he had, Susan believed that he wouldn't offer any recommendation. Mike would have sat down with her and advised her, leading her gently until she came to the right decision. For the first time in her life, she was forced to rely solely on her own resources.

She felt so lonely sometimes, even when she wasn't alone. The endless hours of ecstatic passion which had marked the beginning of their romance had become brief moments, shunted aside by the demanding pressures of daily life. Dale was still kind and loving, and faithful as far as Susan could tell. But the fireworks of an illicit love affair had fizzled into the flickering candle of a staid marriage. Many evenings Dale didn't come home from work or school until after ten, and Susan was working a lot of late nights as well. When they were together, they were short with each other and grated too easily on each other's nerves. The loving feelings Susan had thought eternal slid too quickly into the background under the stresses of modern existence. Many nights they went to sleep without even making love.

"You drink too much, Dale," Susan said as he popped the tab on his fourth beer of the evening. "I wish you'd try to cut down a little."

Dale shot her a warning glance out of the

corner of his eye. "I know what I'm doing. I know exactly how much I can drink."

"I'm not so sure. And I'm not so sure you can control it, either." She paused dramatically. "Dale, your grandfather was an alcoholic."

He glared at her silently at first, as if she were casting unwarranted aspersions on the family that he loved. "Oh," he said finally. "You mean Jeff's father. Well, then I've got it from both sides. My other grandfather was also pretty good at putting away the booze. And Paula's no slouch with a bottle, either. So," he said, sipping his beer defiantly, "I guess biology is destiny. I guess I was born to die of cirrhosis of the liver."

Susan yanked the can out of his hand and put it behind her, beyond his reach. "That's not funny, Dale. I was widowed once by a man who didn't know when to stop working. I don't want it to happen again because of a man who doesn't know when to stop drinking."

He stood up slowly to his full height. "Don't tell me what to do, Susan. I know how to control my body. It's always been there for you when you wanted it, hasn't it?" He walked over to the beer can and grabbed it up righteously. "You're starting to act just like a nagging wife. And that's a good way to become an ex-wife."

Nothing seemed the way it was in Jamaica

when she and Dale had comprised the whole universe. Gone were the uncomplicated days of love and romance. Besides hassles at the office and squabbles at home, there were the inevitable interferences of well-meaning friends.

"I really have got a guy for you this time," Ellen Landman said, as they sipped their drinks and poked at their salads after exercise class one evening. It was not the first time Ellen had suggested getting a blind date for Susan, but tonight she seemed especially adamant about it. "He's a radiologist. Regular hours—I wouldn't want to fix you up with an Ob-Gyn, they're never home at night. David is divorced, two years, but he's only now just starting to get back in circulation. You'd better grab him quick. I promise you he won't last long. Good personality, good sense of humor, and, oh, yes—dare I mention it—good-looking. He has a lovely house; Charlie and I were there a few years ago for his fiftieth birthday party. He'd be perfect for you, Susan. I'll call him this week."

It was after eleven when Susan returned from the "girl's night out," and the house was dark. "Dale?" she called warily as she unlocked the back door.

"In here," he replied. He was in the downstairs den, studying, as usual. He looked up and smiled as she entered the room. "Hi, how was exercise class?"

"Fine. We all went out for drinks and dinner afterward, that's why I'm so late. Did you fix yourself something to eat?"

He nodded. With the brown tortoise shell glasses that he wore for reading and studying, he looked even more handsome, Susan thought, than usual. The eyeglasses credited his face with the intelligence that it deserved. He took them off now and motioned for her to come to him. Susan sat on his lap and wound her arms around his neck, kissing him softly on the cheek.

"Did you see your friend Mrs. Landman? I need to call her and tell her it's time for her fifteen-thousand-mile checkup."

"Oh, I don't think she needs a checkup," Susan said cryptically. "She's working on all cylinders. She's trying to fix me up again," she explained, as Dale looked at her quizzically. "Says she has 'the perfect guy' for me."

Dale pushed her gently off his lap and shook his head despairingly. "You still haven't told your friends about us, have you?"

"I tried, I really did, but she wouldn't let me get a word in edgewise."

"So you agreed to go out with her friend."

"Of course not. I just didn't say I wouldn't, that's all. If he calls, I'll just tell him I'm busy.

I'll tell him I'm involved with somebody." She turned her head and body and started to walk toward the kitchen, unable to look at him.

"Tell him you'll go out with him."

Susan whirled back around. "What?"

"Tell him you'll go out with him," Dale repeated. "I want you to."

"But why?"

"Because you're obviously not sure enough of your feelings for me to say no to anybody else. I don't want to win you by default, Susan. If you're feeling that you might do better with somebody else, then go for it. What's this guy's name, anyway?"

"David Cohen. Dr. David Cohen," she couldn't resist adding. Dale raised his eyebrows. "Why, do you think you know him?"

"Maybe." He shrugged his shoulders. "The name sounds sort of familiar."

"It probably does. Dale, every tenth Jewish man over the age of thirty-five is named David Cohen. But it doesn't matter anyway because I'm not going out with him."

"Yes, you are."

Susan stared at his eyes. They were deadly serious.

"Susan, I'm tired of pretending I'm not with you whenever we run into one of your friends. If you can't accept me the way I am, you'd better find somebody else who fits into the storybook picture you want. No, I mean it," he said as she began to protest. "You go out with this Dr. Cohen. Give it your best shot. I don't want to hold you back. I don't want you to be with me unless you really want to be."

Dr. David Cohen was not a disappointment. He was indeed everything that Ellen had promised. He had a full head of hair and wore it combed in the usual way, not hanging long and swept over one side of the head which was the typical way of hiding a receding hairline. His hair was mostly black, with only a few patches of gray, and very curly, almost like Mike's had been. He had white, even teeth and a very nice smile. He was *very* good-looking.

And very nice. He was courteous and polite, and ever eager to cover up any embarrassing lapses in the conversation with small talk. He was an educated professional, had gone to the same college she had as an undergraduate, and knew many of the same people Susan did. David was absolutely everything that she could want. Or everything she thought she *should* want.

He was also a perfect gentleman. In a moment of frivolous fancy Susan almost wished that he wasn't. She had this romantic fantasy of Dr. Cohen driving her to a lonely country road overlooking a cliff, pulling her out of the car, and suddenly becoming boldly and forcefully aggressive with her. There would be no-body to hear her screams, she thought, and then, suddenly, a red Jaguar would appear on the road out of a cloud of dust. Dale would emerge with flashing eyes but a cool expression, would grab David by the shoulder, and knock him out with one punch. Then he would sweep Susan into his arms and they would . . .

Who was she kidding? Dale would never punch out anybody; she had seen that first-hand now. Certainly not in a fit of jealous frenzy. Dale wasn't the jealous type. He not only didn't care that she was out with another man; he had encouraged it. Why *should* he be jealous? He wasn't going to have to stay home and watch reruns of "The Golden Girls" on TV; he could call up any woman within a fifty-mile radius and have a date in five minutes.

"Susan? Chocolate mousse or strawberry shortcake?"

"I'm sorry," she apologized. "My mind must have been wandering. Mousse, please," she said, pointing to the selection on the dessert tray.

After dinner, David suggested dancing. As they got back in his car, Susan reached auto-matically to flip down the visor to fix her hair and check her makeup as she was used to do-ing in the mirror of the Jaguar. There *was* a mirror there. With lipstick smeared all over it. It was dark, but the headlights of the car behind them revealed in stark clarity the lipstick-printed words: *I love you, Susan.*

Susan slammed the mirror back into its normal position and settled back into her seat as if she had never touched it. When she had attained a relaxed, normal-looking pose, she stole a look at David. He didn't seem to have noticed her actions or be at all aware of anything unusual about his passenger visor mirror.

Susan did not usually pay attention to car makes and models, but suddenly she was very interested in what kind of vehicle her date was driving. She looked at the insignia on the dashboard. It was a BMW.

"David," she asked casually, "have you had your car worked on recently?"

"Why, yes," he said. "Today, in fact. How did you guess?"

"Oh, I don't know. I guess it just has that new car smell."

"Yeah, they always clean it up for me real nice. I take it to that repair place just outside of Beverly Hills."

After that, she couldn't wait for the evening to end. She danced and smiled politely for two long arduous hours, but when David finally brought her home, the sigh of relief that was hiding in her stomach almost made its way to her throat. When he leaned over to kiss her good night, Susan didn't protest. Not because she was eager for his kiss, but because she was anxious to say goodbye and send him on his way. "I had a very nice time tonight," she said courteously but with finality.

She let herself in the door, and as soon as she heard the BMW back down the driveway, dashed out of it again with her own car keys in her hand, not even pausing to change her shoes or go to the bathroom. She drove seventy miles without stopping. When she finally pulled up in front of Dale's house, she turned off the engine and heard, for the first time, the chirping of the crickets in the blackened night.

The house was dark, and Susan knocked on the front door timorously. After a long wait, it finally creaked open, just a crack. "Susan?" He opened the door all the way. "Are you all right?"

The moonlight shone on Dale's bare chest like a searchlight. He was barefoot and wore only his pants, which were unbelted and only halfway zipped. She had apparently woken him up.

"Can I come in?"

Dale closed the door behind her, but still

371

stood like a colossus facing her, blocking her path. "Are you alone?" she asked.

The sleepiness began to fall away slowly from his eyes. "Except for the three Chinese acrobats I picked up at the Moscow circus. Boy, have those girls got moves. I swear they must be triple-jointed."

"Dale." She glared at him until he stood aside. Sometimes he could sound so serious, even when she knew he was joking, that she was afraid to ever assume he *was* joking.

"Of course I'm alone," he said seriously. "Didn't you think I would be?"

"I *hoped* you would be," she said.

He moved aside all the way now as if finally welcoming her into his home. "So," he said coolly, "how was your date? Did he give you a rough time?"

"No," she said, easing her body into the kitchen and onto a chair. "He was very nice. *And* good-looking. In fact," she said, scouring his face for some crack in that chilly facade, "he was perfect in every way except one."

Dale moved into the room with her and leaned against the kitchen sink expectantly, in a pose that said, "Okay, I'll bite." "What's that?" he said out loud.

Susan rose and moved to stand opposite him. "He wasn't you, Dale," she said softly. She threw herself into his arms, pressing herself against a body that was impassive at first but gradually yielded to the sincere, determined pleadings of her flesh. He locked his fingers around her and lifted her in his arms. "No more games, Dale," she promised. "No more indecision. I don't know why in the world you want me, but if you still do, I'm yours. I want you. Only you."

He didn't say anything in response.

"Dale?" she asked nervously. "You still do want me, don't you?"

After another moment of silence, he answered in that cool, unemotional manner he loved to employ when he wanted to make her squirm. "Well," he said indifferently, cocking his head toward the back of the house, "I guess I could make some room for you."

Susan didn't know how she could ever have thought his bed was small. As tightly pressed together as they were that night, there would have been room for two more people to sleep on either side of them. When at last their flesh separated, Susan lay silently for a few minutes and watched Dale sleep. Then she tiptoed out to the kitchen and found her purse. Returning to his bedroom, she quietly and surreptitiously slid the covers off him. Then, with deft and patient strokes, she wrote "I love you, Dale" in lipstick down the length of his nude body.

Nineteen

"Dale," Susan asked at breakfast one morning, "can you tell if my car needs a tune-up?"

"Nope," he said flatly, taking a big bite out of his muffin. "Not without driving it."

She shook her head in exasperation. "Smartass. Well, will you drive it for me and tell me?"

"Now?"

"Would you like me to make an appointment for a week from Father's Day? Of course, now."

He took a gulp of his coffee and grabbed her keys from the kitchen counter. "Lady," he said when he returned, "when's the last time you had your oil changed?"

"I don't know." She thought about it. "Not since Mike died. Maybe never." She looked at his forbidding face. "I need a tune-up, huh?"

"You need *everything*," Dale said emphatically. "It's a wonder that thing hasn't just fallen apart on you. I'll take you to work in it this morning and take it into the shop."

Susan frowned. "Today's not a good day, Dale."

"Why not? You need the car during the day?"

"No, but I have exercise class tonight after work. Let's do it tomorrow, instead."

He shook his head. "We're doing it *today*."

Her eyes flashed. "And just who the hell do you think you are to give me orders?"

"I'm the guy that loves you and doesn't want to see you die on the freeway when your car collapses in the fast lane. I'll pick you up at work tonight and take you to exercise class. What time?"

"Five-thirty class and you'll never make it. You couldn't leave the garage before six if your life depended on it. Look, I can probably get a ride from work to class. Do you think you can meet me at the Health Club at six-thirty?"

"Yes, ma'am. Service is my business. I go out of my way for my customers, especially those that are getting their cars completely overhauled for free."

She threw a dried-out muffin at him, but she was smiling. She liked Dale's way of handling her, of overriding her protests. It wasn't Mike's way at all. Mike had been a benevolent dictator, she realized now. He had never raised his voice, never abused her or openly dominated her, but through kindly coercion and subtle manipulation he had always held his way over her.

Dale, on the other hand, rarely even asserted himself. Most of the time he just let Susan have her way about everything. Except when he felt it was important and when he knew he was right. Then he gave no quarter. At those times Susan cheerfully conceded to him, because when Dale did take a stand, he almost always *was* right.

She thoroughly expected him to be late, so she didn't actually notice his arrival at the Health Club during the next-to-the-last set of stretching exercises.

"Ellen!" someone in the front row called. "Your car is here. Isn't that your mechanic that just came in?"

Ellen Landman peered out at the sidelines. "Yes, but I've got my car today. Susan is the one without a car tonight. Susan," she asked, rolling over on her mat to speak to her, "is he here for you?"

Susan nodded mysteriously, hiding a Cheshire-cat grin.

"I'm surprised. I didn't think Dale worked on American cars."

The music ended, the instructor folded her mat, and Susan stood and folded a towel around her neck. "He doesn't, usually," she said sweetly. Then she simultaneously raised and lowered her voice so that it sounded like a stage whisper: deliciously secretive, but loud enough for everyone in the entire exercise room to hear. "He's not really my mechanic. He's my LOVER."

She turned and walked calmly over to where Dale was standing. His expression never changed, but she knew by his eyes that he had heard every word. And was pleased.

"Nice going, Suse," he said as they walked outside together. "You said that so daringly, *so* blatantly, that nobody would ever believe you in a million years."

"You don't think so?" She stopped and gestured toward a group of women behind them. "Look at them. They can't stop talking about us." Ellen Landman was whispering to Gloria Ross, who looked quizzically at Beverly Werner. Barbara Strauss just stood there knowingly, enjoying the spectacle.

Dale turned to Susan. "Well, should we give them something to talk about?" He folded her in his arms, and planted an enthusiastic kiss on her lips. Susan returned it with dramatic embellishment, swooning histrionically for effect. She started out playing for the audience, but as the passionate kiss extended past the thirty-second mark, she forgot the people that were watching and lost herself with true ardent fervor in the sensuality of Dale's embrace. When they finally came up for air, her friends were nowhere to be seen.

"I love you, Dale," she shouted, as they ran like children to the car. "I don't care who knows it. I'll tell everyone in the world about it. I'll even take out a full-page ad in the *Los Angeles Times* if you like."

"That won't be necessary," he smiled, tears of happiness in his eyes. "What you just did is proof enough for me."

Over the next few days, Susan's phone rang off its cradle. All of her friends were fascinated by her brazen announcement; all wanted to know all the dirty details. Susan was tempted to program her answering machine with the message: "Yes, he is wonderful in bed. In fact, the reason I can't come to the phone right now is that I am in the middle of experiencing multiple orgasms in numerous G-spots."

Prurient curiosity overcame any snobbish reservations her friends may have had about the nature of Dale's employment. Everyone wanted to meet Susan's handsome new boyfriend. Susan and Dale were inundated with dinner invitations and requests for their company. It got to the point, in fact, that they rarely had an evening to themselves.

"Don't start dinner," Dale said as he bounced in the door quite a bit earlier than usual one evening. "And I hope you haven't accepted any dog-and-pony-show command engagements. I'm cooking tonight. At my place."

A sweet-smelling fir tree was loaded in the back of his truck. "You chop that yourself?" Susan teased.

"Yeah, I've been out in the forest all day. The one right next to the K mart parking lot."

"It's nice, Dale," she said after he'd struggled with the snapping branches and planted the tree in a stand in his den. "But it does look kind of naked. Don't you have any ornaments?"

"Ornaments are for sissies," he said stoutly. "The Clemens men use natural decorations."

They popped popcorn and were about to string it with cranberries and other fruit to hang from the tree needles when the doorbell rang.

Susan looked up in surprise. "You expecting company?"

"As a matter-of-fact, I am. I guess I forgot to mention it." Dale grinned. "Why don't you get the door, Suse?"

"Joel!" she squealed, as she opened the screen door and embraced her son. "Hi, Jennifer," she added, bestowing a more moderate

379

hug on Dale's daughter. "How come nobody told me you were coming?"

"Dale's idea of a Christmas surprise," Joel said, pulling off his gloves. "I told him you didn't celebrate Christmas, but he wouldn't listen to me."

Dale was beaming from ear to ear as she pulled the guests into the den. He offered the kids some hot wassail and put them to work trimming the tree. It was fun, Susan had to admit. It was like being part of a family.

"Come here." Dale beckoned Susan and the others into the small living room. She gasped; she wasn't sure why. On a wooden table next to the window was a small brass menorah. Five thin white candles and one larger blue one were placed in the holders, and a box of matches stood nearby.

"How did you know it was the fifth night of Chanukah?" Susan whispered, as Joel lit the match to the *Shamos*, the tallest candle.

Dale smiled and shrugged his shoulders. Susan grabbed those broad shoulders and hugged him. "Thank you," she mouthed, when all the candles were lit.

"Jenny and I are going to drive down to San Diego tomorrow," Dale explained, as they all ate a late dinner on the floor in front of the Christmas tree. "Spend Christmas with the family. Joel can drive you home, Susan. I figured you wouldn't mind a little company over the long weekend even if it isn't your holiday."

He had thought of everything. Except one thing. "Dale," Susan whispered when the kids were out of earshot, "where are they going to sleep tonight?"

Dale stroked his mustache thoughtfully as if it were the first time he had considered that question. "I only have two bedrooms," he said innocently. "I suppose you could bunk with Jennifer. And Joel and I could share a room."

"Very funny," she frowned. "Dale, why are you doing this to me?"

"What?" he asked coyly. "What am I doing?"

"Don't play games. You know what I'm talking about. You know how I feel about this situation. I'm well-aware of what goes on when they're in San Francisco and New York, and I close my eyes and mind my own business. I have no control over what they do there. But this is here. There are two unmarried couples in this house right now. You and I not only set a bad example, we're encouraging our children to flout morality. If I let my son sleep with his girlfriend while I sleep with my lover in the same house, I'm condoning premarital sex."

Dale's eyes turned hard, ejecting their innocent look. *"You're* not condoning anything, Susan. This is *my* house."

There wasn't anything more to say. Susan

undressed quietly when they went to bed that night, pulling the robe she kept at Dale's house from his closet and hanging it conveniently from the headboard.

"You're really mad at me, aren't you?" Dale asked, as he slipped into bed beside her. "You're not going to make love to me for six weeks and you want me to go sleep on the couch tonight."

"I'm not going to make love to you tonight, that's for damn sure," she said. "Not with my son and your daughter sleeping just across the hall. But," she added, as he reached to the floor for his pants, "I don't want you to sleep on the couch. I want you to sleep right here beside me where you belong."

It was nice to have her son home for Christmas. Even though it wasn't their holiday, it *was* a long weekend, and it could be a very lonely one if you had to spend it by yourself. Having Joel with her helped Susan refrain from dwelling so much on what might be going on in San Diego. A cozy family Christmas. Dale reunited with his daughter. And his son. And his ex-wife.

Something was definitely wrong with that picture. It was a family-album picture, a one-frame shot of the Clemens family all together for the holidays, almost as if Dale and Diane were still married.

It was silly to be jealous, Susan told herself. She could trust Dale. He was only doing it for the children, so they wouldn't have to stretch themselves to be in two places to see their parents at Christmas.

Joel returned to San Francisco the day after Christmas, and Dale came home a day later. For New Year's Eve he reluctantly agreed to go with her to a dance at Susan's country club, the club to which she and Mike had belonged for years. Susan knew Dale didn't feel comfortable around doctors and "professional types," although she really didn't see why. He cleaned up pretty damn good when he wore a suit, and he didn't lack for social graces. He was easily the best-looking man at the party and the best dancer. Susan felt proud to show him off.

"You're uncomfortable being at a Jewish country club, aren't you?" Susan asked, before Dale had a chance to make that comment himself. "But, you see," she assured him as they danced away the hours before midnight, "it's just like any other country club."

"Oh, I've been here before," Dale said, surprising her. "I've played on this golf course several times. I guess they didn't realize a *goy* had sneaked in. Luckily," he grinned, his eyes twinkling, "I never had to take my pants off."

Susan was working on her third rum coke when she saw David Cohen across the room. She tried to shrink herself into near-invisibility, but it was too late. He had already seen her.

"Hello, David," she said as he approached. He grasped her hand warmly as if they were old and dear friends, all the while scrutinizing Dale with polite curiosity. Dale was wearing his usual poker expression, but when David's eyes met his, his body stiffened and his eyes filled with apprehension. Susan was about to introduce them, when all of a sudden David's face lit up like a jack-o-lantern with a flashlight inside it.

"Oh, I get it," he said in wry amusement. "All this time I've been wondering about that lipstick message on my car mirror. Now I think I understand."

Dale cringed in embarrassment. "I'm sorry about that," he said. "I'll make it up to you. Your next checkup for the BMW is on me."

David laughed. "I get the free checkup, and you get the girl, right? It's okay, Dale," he said, patting him affectionately on the shoulder, "if it helped things work out for you, I'm glad my car could be of service." He bowed and leaned over Susan. *"Mazel Tov,"* he whispered with a wink.

"Having a good time, Dale?" Barbara Strauss asked as she and Marty waltzed by.

"It's not as much fun as a toothache," he grinned, "but I think I can handle it." He grabbed Susan's arm and escorted her to the dance floor beside them.

"Is it really that bad for you?" she asked with concern.

Dale smiled. "No. In fact, I really am having a good time. I'd have a good time anywhere with you."

When Susan grew tired and limped off to talk to Barbara, Dale invited one of the hostesses to dance. Susan smiled as she watched him charm his partner. She couldn't believe she had once been ashamed to bring him to a place like this.

"Have you seen Ron yet?" Barbara asked conspiratorially.

"No, I haven't. He doesn't usually come to these things, does he?"

"Well," Barbara smiled, "he's here tonight with bells on. And he's not alone."

She saw him a minute later, talking with a bright-eyed, silver-haired woman who looked to be in her late fifties. "Susan," Ron said stiffly, "I'd like you to meet Helen Weissman. Soon to be Helen Davis."

Helen Weissman shook her hand graciously, her bright eyes twinkling with mirth and intelligence. Susan looked at Ron in surprise but recovered quickly and murmured her congratulations. "Well, I guess I missed my chance," she said to Barbara with fake lightness.

"I guess you did," Barbara answered somberly. She drew Susan away from the crowd. "Are you sorry?"

Susan's face became solemn as her eyes turned to the man she loved. "No," she said seriously, "I'm not. Not at all."

After midnight Dale and Susan wandered outside in the gardens. "Want to take a walk?" Dale suggested. "It's such a nice night."

It *was* a nice night, clear and unusually warm for that time of the year, even in southern California. Susan linked her arm through Dale's as they strolled through the streets of the affluent neighborhood. "Have you made all your New Year's resolutions yet?"

Dale smiled wryly. "Well, there is one I'm having a little bit of trouble with." He stopped at the iron gate of one of the driveways and leaned against it. "You remember on your Day of Atonement, when you told me you had to ask my forgiveness for your sins before God would forgive you?" Susan nodded. "Well, I need to do the same thing. Ask your forgiveness. Susan, I have a confession to make."

She waited expectantly. Despite the warmth of the night, Dale shivered and wrapped his arms across his chest. "When the kids and I were in San Diego last week for Christmas . . . I slept with my ex-wife."

Suddenly it seemed very cold to Susan, too. Her wool cocktail dress felt very thin and her teeth began to chatter slightly.

"I'm sorry, Susan. I didn't intend for it to happen. It's just that it was Christmas, and we were all together, and Diane seemed so very sad. Being Jewish, you don't understand how it is. Christmas is supposed to be the happiest day of the year. It's supposed to meet or exceed every expectation you ever had of family bliss, only it never does. If you're not feeling absolutely ecstatic at Christmas, you feel miserable, feeling like life has passed you by. Well, Diane was feeling pretty miserable. She's been so lonely, Suse."

"You're trying to tell me you went to bed with her because you felt sorry for her."

"No. I wouldn't try to sell you that old line. I went to bed with her because I wanted to. We were married for twelve years, Susan, and we were together in a very familiar situation, and suddenly it seemed like the most natural thing in the world. It's not that I wasn't thinking about you; I did. But you and I have our whole lives and this was just one night. I know it doesn't make it right. But it seemed right." He hung his head miserably. "I'm sorry. Please forgive me."

She was ready for the tears to come out now, but her eyes were absolutely dry. What was wrong with her? She wanted to be angry at him, incensed, even. She wanted to threaten to kill him, or at least, leave him. But she just felt very cold and hurt. And as she looked into his sincere, plaintive eyes, she knew that she had already forgiven him.

But how could she trust him? She was shivering so much now, she tucked her arms inside his jacket and wrapped them around his back. Dale massaged her shoulders, then took off his jacket and folded it around her. Her heart felt as open and exposed as the wool dress under his suit jacket.

"You can trust me, Susan," he assured her. "I didn't have to tell you this, you know."

"Why did you?

"Guilty conscience. Even so, I considered not telling you. It didn't seem fair to absolve my guilt by hurting you. But I wanted to be honest with you. My intentions are good, Susan, but I'm just not perfect." He covered her with his arms and bent her head into the crook of his neck as he stroked her hair. "Look, next time I go down to San Diego, I think you should go with me. Not because I don't trust myself: I promise you, I swear to you, that what happened last week won't happen again. But you're my wife now. You're part of my family, just as I am of yours."

Whether they like it or not, Susan thought wryly as she wrapped her arms around him. When she pressed her lips against his cold, hesitant mouth, he returned her kisses eagerly, pressing her tightly against him. Susan closed her eyes and just felt him, smelled him, tasted him, drinking in his skin and his pores.

Twenty

As Susan pushed open the glass door to the service area of Dale's garage and waded her way through stacks of tires and scattered tools, she was stopped by a long-haired mechanic she hadn't seen before.

"Hey, lady, you can't go back there," he said brusquely. "No customers allowed in the service area."

Jose looked up from a car he was working on and smiled at Susan. "It's okay, Randy," he informed the other mechanic. "She's not a customer. That's the boss's lady."

The boss's lady, Susan smiled silently to herself. It sounded good. It sounded very good.

"Hi, Suse," Dale grinned, suddenly appearing from under a white Volvo.

"Hi, boss," she grinned back. "Can you get away for lunch?"

"Sure, why not? Randy," he called brusquely

to the young mechanic who had tried to bar her entrance, "Front and center. In my office."

Susan was afraid Dale was going to bawl out the new man for being rude to her when actually he had only been doing his job. She was about to speak up in his defense when Dale announced, "Susan, I'd like you to meet my son. Randy, this is Susan."

Apparently Randy didn't need any further explanation about who she was. He lowered his eyes and shook her hand, mumbling some polite but almost incoherent words. "When did he get in town?" Susan asked, as she and Dale shared French fries at their favorite hamburger joint.

"Yesterday."

"You didn't waste any time putting him to work, did you? How long is he staying?"

"I don't know. Maybe permanently. Diane says she can't handle him anymore. He drifts from job to job, spending every paycheck as soon as he gets it. She's afraid he might be on drugs, but she hasn't seen any evidence. She says he's withdrawn, and he clams up whenever she tries to talk to him. Of course, he's always been like that, so I don't see anything unusual about it." He sipped his double-thick chocolate shake with a big gulp. "So I'll keep him here for a while. At least I'll get some work out of his butt."

They went out to dinner that night and although Randy was invited, he declined to join them. Susan was just as glad. Dale's son was certainly not the charmer his father was. He seemed as moody and morose as a character in a Gothic novel. Susan had felt ill at ease with him at their meeting that afternoon that had lasted only twenty seconds; she didn't know what she could say to him for an entire evening.

"I'm ordering a bottle of the most expensive wine on the menu tonight," Dale said magnanimously. "In honor of you and me. On the other hand," he said thoughtfully, "maybe half a bottle will be enough."

Susan looked up at him. She remembered a time, not so long ago, when Dale could have easily drunk a whole bottle, or two, by himself. "You don't drink as much as you used to, do you?" she asked him curiously.

He seemed surprised that she had only just noticed. "I hardly drink at all anymore," he said quietly. He stroked her hand tenderly. "I drink when I'm hassled or unhappy, Susan. I used to drink a lot to deaden my nerves, because I didn't want to face life cold sober. But lately I find my life is too sweet to miss half of it being drunk. I want to be sober to enjoy every minute of it."

Susan raised his hand to her lips and kissed

his fingers from the tips to the knuckles. "I love you, too," she said, as her eyes filled up with wistful tears.

There was no question that Dale had sweetened her own life, at least the part he played in it. But other facets of it were awash with bitterness. Ron Davis had remained cold and abrupt with her, making her days at Davis, Dobbs and Engels almost unbearable. A dozen times a day she vowed to accept Ted Samuelson's job offer, but something always kept her from following through on it. And although she had still not shared with Dale her anguish as a mother, her heart grew a little heavier with each day that passed without a word from her daughter.

Every time she had her hand on the phone, ready to call Andrea and apologize, Susan jerked it away in determination. Why should she be the one to make the call? She was the injured party. She would never have encouraged a client to accept a settlement in a case she knew could be won; why should she grovel for her daughter's forgiveness when she was the one in the right?

"Mom?" Susan's heart turned over as the familiar voice came over her telephone. It sounded so distant, as if five years had passed instead of five months. Without any preliminary pleasantries, Andrea informed her coldly that she and Mark were now Mr. and Mrs. Mark Berman. They had married in Philadelphia in a small ceremony in a rabbi's study, with Mark's parents as witnesses.

Susan felt like she'd been pounded in the face with a wet towel. Married. Without even a wedding. But they'd *had* a wedding, she reminded herself. They hadn't eloped. That would have been more palatable. But this was a direct slap in the face. They'd gotten married without inviting her. She had been specifically excluded.

"I wouldn't even be telling you now," Andrea said haughtily. "Mark insisted that I call you."

"Where are you, Andrea?" Susan asked through welled-up tears. "Here in L.A.? Are you living in Mark's apartment?"

"No, we've bought a house. Mark's parents made the down payment for it." She rattled off a house number and street address while Susan frantically grabbed her little black notebook. "Don't bother to ask for directions. *You* won't ever be invited here." She slammed down the phone.

The grating hum of the dial tone droned on and on as Susan collapsed, sobbing, on the couch. She was still crying when Dale came home.

"Susan, what's wrong?" he cried, rushing to

her. His eyes fell on the disconnected phone. He picked it up, looked at it, and placed it back on the receiver. "Is it bad news? Is it one of the kids?"

Still weeping, she told him what had happened. Dale knelt beside her and rocked her gently in his arms. "It's my fault," he muttered.

"It's not your fault," she protested, trying to will her tears to stop. "You didn't do anything. Andrea's just being a bitch."

"It's not just Andrea," he sighed. "I know you've been taking a lot of flak because of me, Susan, from all directions. At work. And at your club. I saw it that night at the New Year's Eve party. Those rich society bastards who've got their noses stuck up their own asses were looking at you like you were dirt. Dirt by association. I didn't mind them doing that to me, but when they looked at you that way, it hurt me, Suse."

"That's not true," she protested halfheartedly. "If anybody was looking at us, Dale, it was because you looked so damn good. Every woman in the place was jealous."

He dismissed her rebuttal. "I know what I saw." He laid his head in her lap to hide his face. "I'm so sorry, Suse. I wanted to make everything nice for you. I wanted to make your life easy and wonderful. Instead all I've done is hurt you."

She stroked his hair, comforting *him*. She wanted to say something to reassure him, to tell him he was wrong, but she couldn't.

When he lifted his head, there were moist dots in the corners of his eyes. "I think," he said slowly, "that maybe I should take a long vacation."

She didn't have to look in his eyes twice to understand what he meant by that. "No!" she shouted. "I'm not giving you up, Dale. Andrea is my daughter, and I love her, but she's not giving up her life for me. I'm not going to give up mine for her."

Dale moved to sit beside her on the couch and took her in his arms, kissing her briefly but significantly. "Then let's get married. Let me make an honest woman out of you."

She looked at him sharply. It was what she wanted, more than anything, but she knew he couldn't have changed his mind just like that. "No," she said.

"What do you mean, 'No'? I thought that was what you wanted."

"I've changed my mind."

His fingers kneaded the muscles of her neck as he drew her close to him. "No, you haven't."

"Well, neither have you. You can't tell me that after all these months you've suddenly had a change of heart. You still don't want to get married."

"No, I don't," he admitted. "Not really. But it's personal preference, not religious dogma. I don't want to be a stubborn asshole about it, not if my decision is causing you pain. Marry me, Susan," he said, warming to the idea. "We'll go down and get blood tests tomorrow, and we can get married this weekend. Or wait. We can have a small wedding, big wedding, courthouse wedding, anything that you want."

"No!" Susan repeated stubbornly. "This is a stupid reason to get married."

Dale smiled sheepishly. "It's as good as my reasons for *not* getting married."

"That's for damn sure," she said enthusiastically. "I never have understood why you're against it, Dale, outside of this vague fear you have of making the same mistakes over again. But your reasons, stupid as they might be, are still your reasons, and I'm not going to ask you to change your beliefs for the sake of these 'rich society bastards,' as you put it. I'm not going to dance at the end of anybody else's string, and neither are you. If we ever *do* get married, it'll be because you and I both want to and no other reason is good enough!"

Her diatribe over, she sank back on the couch. "I always said you had class, Lady," Dale observed, admiration flooding his face. "Now I know I was right." He picked her up in his arms and started to carry her up the stairs.

"I'm not in the mood now, Dale," she demurred. "Sex can't fix everything."

"I'm not suggesting that it can. And I'm not suggesting sex. I'm going to run you a bubble bath and scrub your back for you. And then I'm going to give you the best massage that you ever had in your life."

Nothing could alleviate the hurt she felt in her heart, but Dale's powerful hands rubbing and pounding her back did help to relieve the strain and exhaustion she felt in her body. "Why don't you take the day off tomorrow?" he suggested as his fingers kneaded circles in the tight muscles of her shoulders. "Maybe I can go in a little later, too. We'll have brunch and go for a walk in the park."

Susan raised her head. "Can't. I've got to drive to Sacramento tomorrow. On business. I'll be gone overnight. Maybe even a few days."

Dale nodded in understanding. "Well, if you're driving, be sure to take plenty of cash with you. A lot of the gas stations on that highway don't take credit cards."

"I will. I took a lot of money out of the bank this morning."

Susan slept fitfully that night, tossing and turning for hours before drifting into a deep sleep. When she finally did, Dale slipped quietly out of the bed and tiptoed downstairs.

Her purse was where she usually left it, lying invitingly on the couch where any prospective burglar could see it through the window. Dale reached into the mammoth pocketbook which could have doubled as an attache case. Susan's bulging, burgundy leather wallet jumped up at him, stuffed with crumpled bills.

Reaching into the huge, seemingly bottomless purse, he fumbled around until he found what he was looking for. He removed the small black notebook and laid it open on the coffee table. Pulling a pen and a piece of paper from the purse, he flipped to the address book section and jotted down an entry. Then he slipped quietly upstairs and shoved the paper into his pants pocket.

Twenty-one

The next Saturday morning, after Dale left for work, Susan pulled on her old gray sweats and drove to Malibu. She felt the need to do some serious running, and the beach behind Barbara and Marty's house seemed just the place do it.

Barbara greeted her at the door in her bathrobe. "Susan! What are you doing up so early?"

"I haven't run for a while. Do you mind if I use your beach?"

"Of course not. Would you like some company?"

"I think I'd rather run alone. I've got some thinking to do."

She ran for an hour. The soles of her Nikes dug into the soft sand. She saw and heard nothing but the sunrise flashing on the beach and the ocean rolling in against the shoreline. The wind blew sweet nothings into her ears.

After some time she stopped and turned around, leaning over her knees and breathing hard. She examined the myriad of footprints she had left in the virgin sand. She had come so far already. How could she go back? Yet how could she keep running ahead? She plodded on, more slowly this time, until she dropped from exhaustion onto the wet sand next to the shore. Little fingers of ocean caressed her weary feet. After a short rest, she forced herself to go on. She ran and ran as if the wind might catch her.

When she got back to the house, Barbara had a cup of tea waiting for her. Susan sipped it gratefully.

"Good morning for a run," Barbara began tentatively.

"Uh-huh. I think I'm run out." Susan held her cup like a welcome crutch, sipping at it every few minutes. She was down to the tea leaves before she spoke again. "I'm going to break it off with Dale," she said quietly.

Barbara Strauss had had years of experience at being a friend. She knew better than to speak unkindly of a girlfriend's man, not even if the friend spoke badly of him, *especially* if the friend spoke badly of him. In most of those cases, the couple eventually reconciled, and it was the sympathetic friend who was booted out into the cold. "Why?" she asked cautiously. "What did he do?"

"He didn't do anything, Barbara. He's the most wonderful man in the world, and I'm crazy about him. But my life is a shambles because of him. My daughter is not speaking to me, I've lost my son to the *goyim*, and all my friends think I've flipped out and gone middle-aged crazy." She told Barbara about her estrangement from Andrea which had culminated in the girl's hasty, spiteful marriage, and about Joel's involvement with Dale's daughter Jennifer.

Barbara clucked sympathetically. "I'm so sorry, Susan."

"No, you're not," Susan said bitterly. "You're gloating. So go ahead and enjoy it. Gloat. Say 'I told you so.' "

"All right, I told you so. I told you you were going to fall in love with him and you did. You made your bed, you slept in it, but as soon as it gets a little uncomfortable, you want to crawl out of it."

Susan stared at Barbara in confusion. "Well, don't you think I should? I thought you'd be rejoicing at my decision, as much as you hate Dale."

"I don't hate him. I just don't trust him. But I'm not the one who has to trust him, Susan.

You do. You love him. And he obviously loves you."

Susan raised her eyebrows skeptically. "What makes you, all of a sudden, so sure of that?"

Barbara sighed, reticent to concede any points to Dale's sincerity, but wanting to be honest and unbiased. "He doesn't have wandering eyes. I watched him very carefully at the New Year's Eve party at the club. There were a lot of young, beautiful women at that party, but Dale's eyes were always on you. Even when he was dancing with somebody else, he never looked away from you for more than a minute. That man loves you, Susan."

"And I love him. But there are so many obstacles. Not just the age difference, not just religion. We just don't have anything in common." She focused her eyes into her teacup, embarrassed to look in her friend's face as she uttered her next words. "He's a wonderful lover, Barbara. He makes me feel young and beautiful and sexy. But after we have sex, sometimes we just lie there together, and I feel like I don't have anything to say to him."

Barbara raised her eyebrows. "Are you sure you're not just using him, Susan? Is he just a stud service to you?"

Susan choked. "What do you mean?"

"I mean, is that all you want from him? After sex, do you feel uncomfortable with him there?

Do you wish he'd just go away and leave you alone? Do you feel stifled and crowded in your own bed?"

"Oh, no," she answered sincerely. "I never feel that way. I love sleeping with Dale. I just love lying quietly next to him, just being with him. But I don't always want to talk. I feel like we don't have to talk, like we communicate without words."

"You *don't* have to talk, Susan. Love isn't a conversational marathon. It's being comfortable together. Did you always talk to Mike after sex?"

She grinned sheepishly. "I did, a lot. And he didn't always appreciate it, either, now that I think about it."

Barbara smiled. "Every relationship is not made the same way. Look, Marty is no great shakes as a lover anymore, and his looks certainly don't compare to Dale's. But he still keeps me warm at night, and I'd miss him like hell if I were away from him. Don't let well-meaning friends cheat you out of that feeling, Susan. I include myself in that loathsome group. The women who might thumb their noses at you at the country club are secretly dying to have what you have. And those that aren't have a man at home that they love. Which you won't if you send Dale away. And

404

you might never find anybody again who warms you up as good as he does."

Barbara got up and poured some more tea into her cup. She stared inside it, as if seeking inspiration from the tea leaves. "Susan, Dale isn't Mike. He can't replace Mike; nobody can. But don't you understand, you don't *need* another Mike. You needed Mike, or someone like him, when you were young and hope-filled and thought that you could change the world. Mike was a wonderful father and a wonderful provider. He gave you the support you needed, financially and emotionally, when you decided to go to law school and fulfill your heart's desire. He gave you direction in life. I'm not sure Dale can do that for you or could have done that for you then, even if he were the same age you are. But you don't need that anymore. You've raised your children. You've found your direction. Now you just need someone to share your life with, someone to make you happy. Does he do that?"

"Oh, yes," Susan whispered, "he does that. But is that enough?"

"Sometimes it is, Susan," Barbara said philosophically. "Sometimes it is."

Susan's body began to shake as she wept silent tears into her tea. Barbara put her arms around her. "Don't let him go, Susan. Not if you love him. Andrea will come around."

405

"What if she doesn't? And what about Joel? He would never have met Jennifer if it weren't for me and Dale."

"You can't blame yourself for that. He might have met another beautiful *shiksa* and fallen for her. Your children have their own lives to lead, Susan. Let them. But don't let them tell you how to lead yours. You've got to let go of your children's lives and grab onto your own happiness."

Susan wanted so much to be convinced. She was grateful to Barbara for understanding. Of course she knew that Dale wasn't Mike; if anything, she had seen him as a reincarnation of Jeff. But suddenly she saw that he was like Mike in ways she hadn't noticed before. He was comforting and understanding and constant. Like a pair of old shoes. Maybe that was why she didn't feel they needed to talk all the time; she felt as comfortable with him as if they'd already been married for years.

She began to shake again, wanting to get out all of her hurts and fears, but afraid and embarrassed. "He doesn't want to marry me, Barbara." She forced the words out.

Barbara's eyebrows rose in concern. "You mean he wants to see other women?"

"Oh, no, nothing like that. He wants us to be together. He says he thinks of us as husband

and wife. He just has this hang-up about making it legal."

The eyebrows slowly settled into a smooth curved line again. "Well, that's not so terrible, is it? I mean, you and Dale are not kids. You've already raised your own kids, so you don't have to put up any kind of front for their sake. You're not going to have children together that need to have the legitimacy of a name. Financially you're much better off keeping your legal properties separate. Offhand, I'd have to say that I agree with Dale. If I were you, I'd just live with him and forget about signing any papers."

Susan was shocked. "You mean live in sin?"

Barbara chuckled. "Why not? You're not twenty years old anymore, Susan. You don't need the same things from a relationship now that you did then. Why do you need the piece of paper? Just to keep gossipy, sanctimonious tongues from wagging?"

Susan blinked her eyes. She had not expected this attitude from Barbara.

Barbara spoke very slowly now and expressively. "Susan, you're my best friend and I love you. But when I come in this house at night and go to bed with my husband, I'm not thinking about you. And I guarantee you that nobody else whose opinions you are so worried about thinks about you at that time, either. Nobody gives a good goddamn whether you have someone to sleep with or not. You're going to have to decide whether it's more important for you to put on a proper posture for the country club matrons of the world or whether it's more important to please the man you love."

"Barbara, I'm shocked at you," Susan said incredulously. "You've done nothing but hassle me about Dale since the first day I told you about him. Why are you all of a sudden taking his side?"

"I'm not taking his side, I'm taking *your* side. I want you to be happy. And I've never seen you as happy as I have since you've been dating Dale."

Susan was confused. "You mean you haven't seen me so happy since Mike died."

"No," Barbara said cautiously. "I mean I haven't seen you so happy *ever.*"

Susan tried to be cheerful as she laid out the dishes for the Passover Seder, but the large dining table seemed so lonely set for just three people. Her mother had decided not to make the trip from Houston this year, as her arthritis had been acting up a lot lately. Andrea, of course, would not be there. Susan was glad that at least Joel had been able to take a few days off and come down to share the celebration with her. Dale was a lot more enthusiastic, looking forward to his first Passover Seder. Susan had invited him to bring his son, but Randy was away visiting friends that week. It would have been a lie to say that Susan wasn't relieved. She had no reason to distrust the boy; she had never even spoken more than three or four sentences to him, but his manner and his dress just made her uncomfortable.

"I guess I don't even need to put the table leaf in," Susan said sadly.

"Put it in anyway," Dale suggested. "You cooked a lot of food. You'll need someplace to put it."

They were about to begin the Seder when the doorbell rang. "I'll get it," Susan said, slightly annoyed by the disturbance.

"Hi, Mom," Andrea said cheerfully at the door, bussing her mother on the cheek as if they had just seen each other last week. "I'm sorry we're a little late."

Susan blinked in surprise.

Andrea smiled sweetly and handed Susan a bouquet of flowers. "I know you like pink carnations; Mark wanted to get something more expensive, but I told him this is what you'd like."

Susan was completely speechless. She stood in frozen shock as Andrea strode brazenly toward the dining room as if she were an expected guest.

"Hello, Mark," Susan finally managed to say to Andrea's husband. It was the first time she had seen him since he had become her husband. *"Mazel Tov."* Mark smiled and kissed her lightly on the cheek, like a good son-in-law. They walked into the dining room together.

Susan was beginning to wonder if her eyesight as well as her memory was playing tricks on her. Mysteriously there were now two more chairs at the table and two more places had been set. Joel conducted the Seder, pointing to the appropriate items on the table at the specified times and delegating selected readings to the participants. Susan, in a daze, just read what she was told to read.

When it was time to begin the festive meal, Susan rose to bring the hot dishes from the kitchen. Andrea followed her. As the kitchen door swung closed behind them, they just stood and looked at each other helplessly.

"Well," Susan said finally, "what did Joel use to bribe you to come?"

Andrea leaned against the counter with her palms outstretched, as if in a gesture of surrender. "It wasn't Joel, Mom. It was Dale."

"Dale?"

Andrea had been about to go out shopping

410

that Saturday morning when the doorbell rang. At first she thought the man standing there was her neighbor from down the street. When she realized who it was, she was tempted to slam the door as easily as she had opened it, but it was too late. Instead, she stood silently with her hand on the doorknob and stared at the unwelcome visitor.

"Your mother doesn't know I'm here," Dale had said, in answer to the question she hadn't asked. "I'd like to talk to you, Andrea. May I come in?"

"Invite him in, Andy." Her husband's voice materialized suddenly behind her, soft-spoken but powerful as a volcano.

She'd had no choice but to introduce Mark to Dale. Mark had nodded pleasantly through the introductions, then tactfully disappeared.

Dale wasted no time getting to the point. "You're breaking your mother's heart, Andrea; you know that, don't you?"

Andrea drew up her nose disdainfully. "I'm not the one who's doing that. If you want to know who's hurting Mom, why don't you try looking in a mirror?"

Dale's sigh was long and pensive. Declining to sit in the chair she offered him, he leaned instead against the living-room wall and took a deep breath. "I know you think I'm after her money, Andrea. I'm not. I know you loved your father very much, and you don't think anybody else can take his place. I'm not trying to do that, either. I knew your father for many years. He was a wonderful man, and I know I don't come close to being anything like him. Except in one way."

He paused for breath. "I love your mother very much. But I know you don't believe that, and I'm not going to waste my breath defending myself or trying to convince you of that. So let's play it your way. If I *was* trying to take advantage of your mother, who is there to stop me? Certainly not your brother. As heavily involved as he is with my daughter right now, interfering with my relationship with your mother is the last thing he'd want to do. You're the only person who can talk her out of being with me, and you've voluntarily removed yourself from the situation."

Dale took his eyes off her for a second to glance at the paintings behind her head. "Andrea," he said softly, "if your mother had given you a hard time about a boy that you were dating, how would it make you react? Would you knuckle under to her disapproval or would you go out with him just to spite her?" He paused for a second to let his message sink in. "You're pushing her right into my arms."

He had touched her on the shoulder then,

a gesture she found somewhat disconcerting, but also calming. "Your mother misses you terribly," he'd said, in a voice that could melt ice cream, "but she's too stubborn to make the first move. You do it."

It had not been a plea, but an order. Andrea had resented his manner and had hated him for being right about everything he said. But she had liked him, too, for having the guts to be honest.

Andrea walked tentatively now over to Susan, whose arms had somehow become outstretched. "I'm sorry, Mom," she whispered. "I'm sorry for all the things I said. Especially about Dale. He's not a lowlife. He's really not a bad guy at all."

"No, he's not," Susan agreed. "He happens to be a very good guy. But that's beside the point. Even if he weren't, I'm still entitled to choose whoever I want to be in my life. I didn't hassle you about your choice."

Andrea looked up in surprise. It was almost the same message she had heard from Dale. Either he understood her mother very well, or else all parents thought exactly alike.

"Well," Susan smiled in forgiveness, "at least I'm finally getting to welcome Mark into the family. I'm glad you didn't decide to run off with a biker just to spite me."

"Mom," Andrea smiled, "Mark and I would

like you to come to dinner next week. You and Dale," she added.

It was the most wonderful Seder dinner Susan had experienced in a long time.

Twenty-two

Susan stared at the slip of paper in her hand. "Please see me in my office," the note read. There was no signature, only a large *R* scribbled with a flourish at the bottom of the page, but there was no mistaking the sender's identity. Well, at least he didn't write it on on a pink slip of paper, she thought dismally.

"Come in, Susan," Ron said stiffly when she knocked on his office door. She stood awkwardly near the door, the more convenient to make a quick exit if necessary. Ron cleared his throat and raised his eyes to the ceiling. "Helen was very impressed with you when she met you New Year's Eve. She asked me to invite you to our wedding. It's next Sunday."

Susan's jaw dropped open.

"I realize it's rather short notice. And I'm sorry for not sending you a formal invitation. But it's a small ceremony, and we decided to have it at the last minute. And Helen prefers personal invitations, anyway."

Susan put her jaw back where it belonged. "I'd be very honored to attend your wedding, Ron. Your fiancée seems like a very lovely lady." And very much like his first wife, she couldn't help thinking. Already she was taking charge of her future husband's social life, and Ron seemed very relieved about that.

Her boss looked at her directly for the first time. "That man you were with at the club—he seemed very nice, too. I've seen you with him before, haven't I?"

"Yes," Susan stammered. "I think so."

"You can bring him if you like," he offered.

"Thank you," she said. "But if the wedding is as small as you indicated, I'd probably better not."

Ron looked slightly relieved. "I'll tell Helen." He started to turn away, but as Susan remained facing him, he leaned against his desk and eyed her objectively. "Was there something you wanted to see me about, Susan?"

She sighed and took a deep breath. Then, without giving herself time to change her mind and back out, she told him quickly and briefly about Ted Samuelson's plans to leave the firm.

Ron's eyes turned very sober. He seemed

cool and in command, but Susan had known him long enough to know that he was quite upset and very angry. "This is quite interesting information. How did you happen to come by it?"

"He told me."

Ron Davis's eyebrows tilted slightly upward in a gesture very close to suspicion. "Ted doesn't strike me as the type to be so open about his private business. How is it that he happened to take you into his confidence?"

She took another deep breath. "He asked me to go with him."

He stroked his chin casually as if they were discussing plans for lunch and responded after missing only a few beats in the conversation. "I see. Are you going to?"

"No." It was not until she actually said the word that she was one hundred percent sure of what she was going to say. "Not unless you want me to."

Ron sank into his desk chair as if his body had suddenly become very heavy. "Of course I don't want you to, Susan. You've been very valuable to this firm, and to me, over the years. Perhaps I've taken you for granted, especially lately. I know you haven't been happy here for a little while. What can I do to make your job more satisfying? Do you want a raise? More management responsibility? Of course, you can have your old office back, after Ted leaves. Do you want to get away from family law and branch out into the more sensational cases?"

Susan was astonished. Five minutes ago she had been afraid she was going to be fired. Now she was being given a chance to write her own ticket. Ron was offering her money, authority, anything she wanted. But what *did* she want? It was a question she had had to contemplate more than once in the year and a half since Mike died.

She wet her lips and formed her words slowly and deliberately. "I don't mind staying with family law. It's what I'm best at, after all. But I would like an opportunity, now and again, to try other types of cases. If not alone, then with somebody else." She paused significantly. "I don't want to get into management. There are enough changes happening in my life right now, and I don't need any extra stress or responsibility. However," she smiled, "I will take that raise, thank you."

Ron smiled as well. It was the first smile she had seen from him in months. He held out his hand to her and shook hers warmly. "Welcome home, Susan."

A glow spread through her body, warming her with relief and satisfaction. "Susan," Ron called to her as she was turning to leave.

She turned back expectantly. Her boss was

no longer smiling, but his face held a concerned, wistful expression that she had seen at least once before. He shifted his weight from his right foot to his left. "Susan, are you in love with that guy?" he asked bluntly, using all his strength in the formation of the question.

She answered quietly but firmly. "Yes, Ron. I am."

She was very much in love with Dale and no longer ashamed or embarrassed about that fact. In fact, she was happy to admit it to anyone who asked, but the opportunities to say it to the object of her love were becoming fewer and further between. Since his son had come to live with him, Dale rarely stayed at Susan's house anymore. Of course, she was always welcome at his house, and she went home with him often, but it wasn't the same with Randy there as it had been when it was just the two of them in a romantic hideaway. Many nights she just felt the need to come home and relax in comfortable, familiar surroundings, and when she did, she slept alone.

Susan wasn't happy about that situation. When she drove to the garage to meet Dale for lunch one day, she had a plan sizzling in her head.

"Hi, Susan," Randy Clemens said cheerfully,

as she entered the waiting room. His long hair had been cut, in fact, shaved on one side, and he wore one long silver earring, but he seemed pleasanter than usual and actually smiled at her. "I'll tell Dad you're here."

Dale was too busy to leave the shop, so they had a picnic-style lunch in his office. "How's Randy working out?" she asked, as they popped the soda tabs and unwrapped the sandwiches.

"Pretty well, actually," Dale answered. "He's getting to be a damn good mechanic."

"Well, he has the world's best damn mechanic for a teacher," Susan smiled. She took a sip from her Coke and put it aside. "Do you think you can leave him alone for a few days? I want to take you away for a long weekend. There's a real nice place just a few hours drive from here with cabins and a lake and riding stables."

"*You* want to take *me* away?" Dale asked, earning a perfect three-pointer as he tossed the wadded-up wrapping paper from his sandwich into the wastebasket six feet away. "What am I, a kept man?"

It was the perfect opening for a discussion that Susan desperately did not want to open. In all the time they had been together, they had never, except for occasional oblique references, discussed the subject of Susan's money. Or Mike's money, to be more precise. She knew they had to talk about it sometime, but she didn't want to be the one to bring it up. It would look like she didn't trust him. Maybe she was afraid to bring it up because, deep inside, a minuscule part of her still *didn't* trust him.

"I won a free vacation," she told him. "Well, not exactly, it's one of these promotional things. You know, you get to spend three days for free in this cabin and in return they try to sell you property. So we'll have to spend a few hours one afternoon touring the grounds. That won't be so bad, will it?"

Dale shook his head. "I can't right now, Susan. It's not just Randy. I've got work to do here. Business is booming and one of my mechanics just quit."

"It's not really a full-fledged vacation," she pleaded. "Just a weekend. We can even go during the week if you don't want to miss a Saturday at the garage. Come on, Dale, we never have time together anymore. Let's just do it."

It was probably the riding that got him. Dale hadn't been on a horse in months, and when she saw the pleasure on his face as he mounted a beautiful black stallion, Susan was convinced she had done the right thing to urge him to come. He needed this atmosphere, this fresh, clean-smelling air of the great outdoors. Susan was neither an athlete nor an outdoor person herself, but Dale was. He bloomed in this kind of setting. It was what he was. It was why, after they had been together almost a year, he still refused to sell his house and move in with her.

Susan flushed guiltily at that thought, the thought that betrayed her ulterior motives. She didn't dread the hard-sell talk that the land salesman would give them tomorrow. She had every intention of buying property here. It was beautiful, loaded with recreational activities, and less than a four hours' drive from her house in Los Angeles. Easily made on any Friday night of a regular weekend. It was barely twice the commute that Dale made from his house to his shop almost every day. She wanted to buy this place for him. For him to retreat to, relax in, be alone with her away from the pressures of the city that always contrived to drive them apart. If he liked it here, if he felt at home here, then perhaps eventually he would be willing to sell his own house. Perhaps eventually he would move into Susan's home completely, if not as her husband, then at least as her permanent "significant other."

Susan was helped onto a smaller, slower horse that was more her speed. Dale walked his horse beside her for a while, but it was evident that both he and his horse were chomping at the bit, eager to run free in the cool, pungent countryside.

"Go ahead," she urged him. "You don't have to stay with me. Go enjoy yourself."

"Are you sure?" His voice was protective and considerate, but his eyes begged to be let loose.

"Go," she insisted. "I won't have any fun if I know I'm holding you back."

He galloped off into the distance like a knight in armor on his steed, jumping over low fences in eager delight. He was like a child discovering his freedom. Susan had never seen him like this before. She wished she could bottle up the happiness she saw in him now and take some of it back to refresh him every night.

Thankfully, horseback riding was not the only thing that excited and refreshed Dale. Although their lovemaking was good almost all of the time and outstanding on numerous occasions, it was on vacations like these that Susan felt they really enjoyed each other to the fullest. Dale had been right about the feelings being different when they were alone and away from social and familial influences. The cabin they stayed in that night was small and had only two single beds, but they didn't need any more than one twin bed to satisfy all of their yearnings and desires.

"I love you, Susan." Dale held out a steaming fresh cup of coffee made from the pot in the small kitchenette. The sun was only just stretching above the horizon, but he was already dressed in jeans, a flannel shirt, and boots, eager to be out and riding in the fresh country air. "It was a great idea to come here. This is a beautiful, wonderful place, and I'm glad you twisted my arm and made me come."

Susan yawned and stretched herself awake. "I'm glad you like it so much," she smiled happily, taking the coffee from his hand. "I've been talking to the people here about buying our own cabin."

Dale narrowed his eyebrows at her. "You made these arrangements without consulting me?"

"I *am* consulting you. I haven't signed anything yet. Oh, Dale," she effervesced, "we can get a place right by the lake. You can go swimming in the middle of the night if you like. And they have a private stable for the permanent landowners and a full-time staff to care for the horses. You can finally get your own horse! There's a caretaker living here all year round. And it's close enough to drive up any weekend!"

Dale's enthusiasm seemed appreciably dampened. "Susan, you shouldn't have done this without asking me first. You don't even know whether I can afford it."

"*I* can afford it. I want to buy this place for you. For us."

"No." The steel gray in his green eyes stood

out as hard, dark flecks. "I pay my own way here. I don't want to be Mr. Susan Riesman." He stormed out the doorway of the small cabin, slamming the screen door behind him.

Susan dressed in silence. Suddenly she understood why Dale didn't want to sell his house. It had nothing to do with the damn swimming pool. It didn't even have all that much to do with the country air or the acreage. He had told her what it was long ago, but she hadn't understood him. "I don't need my space, Susan; I need my place." *My* place. She had misread the emphasis. Dale needed his own identity. He was afraid of being swallowed up by her priorities and her social stature. He was his own man, and he was intent on *being* the man, not a pretty trinket obscured behind the skirts of a wealthy, controlling woman.

She creaked the cabin door tentatively open. Dale was sitting on the slatted wooden steps of the front porch. His arms were crossed in front of his chest to block out the harsh early morning wind. The mountain air could be quite crisp before the sun had fully risen.

Susan grabbed both their windbreaker jackets from a peg in the corner. Dale hardly looked at her as she sat down beside him. He slipped his arms into the sleeves of the jacket she handed him, staring straight ahead.

"Susan, we need to talk. About a lot of

things. But mainly money. We've been operating under the unwritten rule that you pay for groceries, and I pay for everything else. And it's beginning to wreck the hell out of my budget."

She glared at him. "Well, whose fault is that? I've offered to pay for things a million times. But you never let me. You always have to be the macho man. You just can't stand to let a woman pay for anything."

He shook his head, facing her now. "No, that's not true. I have no problem with letting a woman pay once in a while. With most of the women I dated, we often shared the bills equally or at least took turns now and again. It's only with you that I've been so insistent about always paying."

"Why?"

"Because I know you don't trust me. You think I'm after your money. If I'd ever let you pay one dime toward anything, I was afraid I'd get it thrown back in my face."

"What do you mean, I don't trust you? Have I ever once said anything to that effect?"

He smiled wryly. "You didn't have to. I know what your friend Barbara thinks of me. And probably all your other little country-club friends, too. And whatever your friends think, that's what you think. You don't have the guts to make your own decisions. Do you deny that it's at least crossed your mind that I'm using you to get your money?"

"No," she said quietly.

They sat in silence for several minutes, each looking at the pine needles scattered in angular patterns at their feet. "Well?" Susan said finally. "Are you? After my money?"

He looked up at her. The expression in his eyes now was fluid and ambiguous, very hard to read. "Yes." He reached down to scoop up a handful of pine needles and snapped them in half with his fists. "And no."

"What the hell kind of answer is that?"

"The kind of answer that question deserves. What the hell am I supposed to say? If I was after your money, do you think I'd admit it? And if you could actually ask me that question, it proves that you suspect me, and all the denying in the world wouldn't convince you otherwise."

He stood up and ambled slowly to a tree a few feet away. He broke off a piece of bark and began to scratch designs on the naked trunk with the chip he held in his hand. After a few minutes he turned and walked toward her again, tossing the sliver of bark in the air and letting it fall to the ground. "Susan," he said heavily, "if you didn't have money, it wouldn't matter to me. If you would be willing to sell your house, move in with me, and live on the money I make, you could retire tomorrow and I would be happy to support you for the rest of your life. But I don't think you could do that. You're too fond of eating out, taking vacations, buying expensive electronic toys, and generally doing whatever you want to do without thinking about the cost."

She resented that. "I could do it if I had to. I can live without my fancy, expensive toys. But what about you? What do you call the Jaguar if not an expensive, fancy toy? You already have a truck and you can only drive one vehicle at a time!"

"Susan, let's not start attacking each other. I admit that luxury sport cars are my weakness. I just want you to admit you have yours. You do have an expensive lifestyle, and my income alone won't pay for it. And there's no reason why it should have to. You're sitting on a small fortune, doing God knows what with it, and you expect to just let it lie and earn interest while you live off me. And since you brought it up, I have to tell you, the Jaguar is one thing that chaps the hell out of me. I'm paying a steep car note every month for the privilege of driving the car of my dreams. I don't really mind doing it. You have to give up something to get what you want. But you didn't give up anything. You've got the money *and* the car. You didn't lose a car; you just gained a driver!"

Of course he was right. The Jaguar had been of no use to her before Dale came along; she didn't even know how to drive it. "What do you want me to do," she asked curtly, "give you back your twenty thousand dollars?"

"Not me. Us. I think we should open a joint bank account. You put in the money I gave you for the Jag. I'll put in what's left of my settlement money. We can each add a certain amount from our income every month."

Susan eyed him warily. It sounded too pat. "And I suppose you wouldn't mind," she said caustically, "if I were to add some of Mike's money into the pot to fatten the nest egg a bit?"

"No," he said, surprising her by his candor, "I wouldn't. I'm not addicted to pride, Susan; I think money should be used. If you want to give it to your children or use it to buy them houses or something, that's fine with me. If not, why shouldn't you and I enjoy it?"

She felt like a snare drum being stretched on both sides. "Dale," she said slowly, "what if I were to do as you suggest? And then take the rest of the money, the bulk of Mike's money, and put it in accounts for Joel and Andrea? So that I wouldn't even have access to it? So that even if I got married again, my next husband would have no legal claim on that inheritance? Would that be all right with you?"

He stared at her as if he had been slapped. "It's your money, Susan. It's your decision to make. You can do whatever in the goddamn hell you want with it."

She wasn't sure if she was chopping off her hand or cutting out her heart, but she had to know. "And if I did do that, when I came home from work next week, would I still find you waiting for me?"

He rose to his feet slowly and deliberately like the freeze-frame of video photography. His words were clipped and controlled, and she couldn't read anything in his eyes. "That's my decision to make."

He turned away from her and walked with measured, unhurried steps into the woods. Susan stared at his back until it disappeared in the heavy overgrowth. She kept sitting and staring for a long time after that. Finally she noticed that the morning sun had risen to a ninety-degree angle with the earth. She slipped off her jacket and went inside.

It was over. She had forced the confrontation and in a matter of minutes, her life had gone from serene and fulfilled to ripped open and flagellated. He wasn't coming back. She had insulted his integrity, and he was too much of a man to tolerate that. Or perhaps his outrage was a smoke screen; perhaps he really *was* after her money and she had been correct in doubting his integrity. The fact that she may have been right to suspect Dale's motives did not assuage her misery in the least. As she sobbed into her pillow, she only wanted to feel his body by her side, hear his voice whispering comforting words into her ears. Even if they were lies.

When the sheets were saturated with her tears, she raised her head. She told herself she had to be practical. She had to figure out what to do next. Most probably she was stranded here in this oasis, Dale probably having driven back to Los Angeles hours ago.

She washed her face, changed her wet shirt, and made her way down the gravel path to the parking area. Wondrously, the Jaguar was still parked where they had left it. He had to be still in the area then. Susan combed the riding trails and the hiking paths, but could find no sign of him. After several hours of inconclusive search, she dragged her weary feet back to the cabin. She wondered if something had happened to him. She wondered if she should alert the park ranger. Maybe there were bears in the area. Maybe he had fallen and was lying hurt somewhere, far from a well-traversed path. Maybe he had been the victim of foul play.

She didn't realize that she had fallen asleep. Until she heard the heavy footsteps on the front porch and squinted through the screen

431

door into total blackness. The man who pushed the door open was dirty and bedraggled, dry leaves sticking to his boots and pine needles covering his clothes.

Susan sat up wide-awake as he lowered himself onto the bed beside her. Dale touched her hands and held them, and then moved against her and took her in his arms.

"Susan," he said with a pain in his heart that she could hear and feel, "there's a lot of things in this world that I would do for money. I take shit from stupid, self-important customers all day every day, and I smile and pretend I like it, because that's what I have to do to earn a living. But there's a limit to the amount of shit that I'm willing to take, for money, from a woman. And frankly, Lady, you passed that limit a long time ago."

She couldn't understand why she was smiling. "Then why did you come back?"

His eyes were the clearest she'd ever seen them, so lucid that the tiniest speck of deceit could not have hidden itself. "Because there's no limit to what I'm willing to take for love."

Twenty-three

"So what was the upshot of this little heart-to-heart?" Barbara asked, as they shelled peanuts on her beach house veranda. "You bought him the cabin. You probably even put it in his name, didn't you?"

"I *did* put it in his name," Susan answered defensively. "I want him to be able to use it without me. There are lots of times that I can't get away that he might want to go up there alone. Or with Randy. His son is staying with him now. The two of them might want to go fishing or riding some weekend."

Barbara popped a peanut into her mouth. "How idyllic," she said sarcastically. "And how naive. Susan, I hate to sound like a broken record—"

"Then don't."

Barbara placed the peanut bowl aside and settled into the glider that hung from the porch by two chains. She began to rock rhythmically in the swing, scraping her feet against the sandy wooden floor as she gathered her words together. "Susan, I don't hate Dale. In fact, I like him. And I'm glad that things seem to be working out with you and him, because I think you deserve this happiness. I just think you should keep your head screwed on to your shoulders instead of leaving it next to the bed with your underwear."

She ignored the angry glare Susan shot her. "Just keep your eyes open, Susan. If this were one of your clients, you would be warning her about putting her trust in a man like this. You know all the danger signs. But you can't see them when it applies to your own life."

"Maybe I can't see them because there aren't any there. Maybe this man who seems to be so warm and sincere on the outside is, deep down, really warm and sincere." Susan kicked off her shoes and sat down on the porch steps, digging her toes into the soft sand that lay beneath. "Barbara, don't you think I know everything you're trying to tell me? Don't you think I've thought about it a million times, wondered and worried and wondered some more? All this time I've been waiting for some kind of sign, some kind of proof that Dale is not after my money. Or," she added darkly, "that he is."

Barbara moistened her lips with her tongue. "And now you've found it?"

"No. But I found something else. The realization that I'm never going to have that assurance."

It had come to her suddenly like a flash of lightening. She had been putting the burden of proof on Dale, expecting him to demonstrate the sincerity of his intentions. As if he could. The judicial system, in its infinite wisdom, didn't require the accused to prove himself innocent. There *was* no way to prove Dale's innocence. The cynic could find an ulterior motive in every nice thing he did. The skeptic could twist every action to appear as its opposite. Guilt could be proven, maybe. Maybe if she stalked him constantly, listened in secretly to his phone conversations, intercepted his mail, she could catch him in a slip. It would only take one slip to prove he didn't really love her. But if she watched him for years and never saw or heard anything to corroborate her suspicions, it still would not prove conclusively that he did love her. It might only prove that he was an extremely skillful con man.

"I won't ask him to crawl, Barbara. And I'm not going to spend the rest of my life looking over my shoulder. I believe Dale loves me. It may be the biggest mistake of my life to believe that, but I have to take that chance. Dale is worth it."

"I see." Barbara's smile was not exactly a smirk, just a guarded approval to which still clung an obstinate touch of cynicism. "I guess I don't need to ask what he did to convince you of that."

"It wasn't anything he did. Or anything he said. It was something *you* said, Barbara. You said I had to trust him. And you were right. Some things just can't be proven with evidence you can see and touch. I guess, when it comes to love, you just have to take it on faith."

Twenty-four

In May, Jennifer Clemens quit her job in New York's fashion district and relocated to San Francisco. Dale and Susan drove up for the weekend and helped her settle her belongings into Joel's small Victorian apartment. Susan wasn't altogether happy about the living arrangements, but she knew there was nothing she could say about it. She was hardly in a position to counsel her son about morality or decorum.

"Don't be upset, Mom," Joel said gently, sensing her dilemma. "We probably will get married eventually. But you have to remember, Jenny and I have never spent more than a week together since we met. We love each other, but we need time to get to know each other, to learn each other's habits. I wouldn't want to marry a stranger."

What he said made sense. Joel always made

sense: he was slow and steady, like his father had been. Susan realized that this wasn't just about sleeping together, it was about living together. About learning to understand and adjust to the lifestyle of another human being. And if she were totally honest with herself, Susan had to admit that her feelings about Joel and Jennifer moving in together were not totally disapproving. Part of her was actually envious.

As she emptied Jennifer's suitcase and hung her dresses into Joel's walk-in closet, Susan wished it were Dale's clothes she was hanging in her own bedroom closet. Since Randy's arrival, Dale rarely spent more than two consecutive nights at her house. Susan was getting tired of that situation. She wanted Dale with her every night. She wanted his clothes in her closet and his toothbrush in the holder beside hers, not in the portable cosmetic bag that he kept beside her sink. She wanted to wake up every morning to find him lying beside her. If he would only move in with her, she would never complain again about the windows he left open when she wanted them closed, the smelly socks he left under the bed, or about his taking an eternity in the shower, steaming up the bathroom mirror just at the time she needed to put on her makeup.

On the other hand, she thought with just a

touch of glee, maybe the act of living together and learning each other's bad habits would drive Joel and Jennifer apart. Susan felt terrible for hoping that, but she still wasn't comfortable with the idea that her son might marry a *shiksa*. Especially since it was her fault.

Guilt, the legacy of every Jewish mother, flooded her soul. If she hadn't been dating Dale, Joel would never have met Jennifer in the first place. If he hadn't met her, he wouldn't have fallen in love with her. If he hadn't fallen in love with her . . . it was endless. Susan blamed herself for having caused the situation, yet she felt guilty for wishing that Jennifer and Joel would break up. She felt guilty in general about the resentment she felt toward Dale's children. She resented Jennifer because she had stolen her son's affections. And she resented Randy—well, because he was Randy.

Try as she might, Susan just could not make a connection with that boy. Dale brought his son with him often after work, and Susan found herself so uncomfortable in his presence that she often wished that Dale would stay away himself, rather than bring Randy with him. The boy was seldom rude; in fact, he was usually excruciatingly polite, but his sullen silences implied his disapproval of her and her lifestyle more eloquently than could words. Randy's eyes were narrow slits that seemed to observe everything and enjoy nothing. His mouth was always curled up in a sort of sneer. His hair, which had grown long again on one side, was unkempt and unwashed. He was usually preoccupied with his thoughts and often had to be spoken to twice when Susan did attempt, in an effort to be a good hostess, to draw him into the conversation. Most of the time he excused himself right after dinner and retired to another room to watch a video in solitude and in darkness.

She was glad, at least, that things were righted between her and Andrea. She and Dale had visited Andrea and Mark's new home several times, and the children came over often for Friday night dinner or a Sunday afternoon visit. Susan even invited Mark's family to dinner the next time they came to Los Angeles.

"It's so nice to see you again, Mrs. Riesman." Mark's mother had a pleasant face and a congenial smile. "I'm glad to see that you're feeling better."

"I'm glad you could come," Susan said warmly. "Feeling better than when?"

Mrs. Berman patted Susan's hand confidentially. "Andrea told us about the back problems you were having last year. She said that was why you were unable to make a wedding for her and Mark. We tried to do our best on short notice to provide a little reception for them. We were sorry that you weren't able even to come up for the wedding, but when Andrea told us that it was too painful for you to fly on an airplane, of course we understood." She smiled kindly. "I'm happy you're feeling better now."

Back problems? Susan glared at Andrea, but her daughter cringed and hid her head, begging her mother silently to hold her peace. "Oh, yes," Susan said out loud, warmly pumping Mark's mother's hand, even as she gritted her teeth in anger, "I'm feeling *much* better now!"

"I'm sorry, Mom," Andrea whispered when Susan caught her alone in the kitchen. "I was so angry at you, I made up that stuff about your back."

"You weren't just angry at me," Susan reminded her. "You were mortified at the thought of their meeting Dale. You were afraid he would embarrass and disgrace you. Well, is he embarrassing you now?"

She cocked her head toward the living room. Mr. and Mrs. Berman were sitting with Dale on the couch, chatting happily, apparently perfectly at ease. Mark's parents weren't snobs at all, Susan decided. They were very nice. It had been Andrea who was the snob all along.

"I already admitted that I was wrong about him, Mom. He's forgiven me; why can't you?"

Susan kissed her daughter on both cheeks. It was true that in the past few months Andrea had practically become Dale's biggest fan. She had taught him to play chess, perhaps initially guessing that she would easily trounce him in that game of intellect, but after he'd learned the fundamentals, Dale had begun to systematically beat her every time. Andrea didn't seem to mind. Their games together had become a backdrop for long, comfortable talks. Andrea had always been close to her father. Susan hadn't really realized how much Andrea missed her confidential talks with Mike or how much she needed a strong paternal presence in her life. Dale seemed to fill that need very well and Susan was grateful to him for it.

Although she enjoyed the visits of her children, the weekends Susan enjoyed most were those she spent at home alone with Dale. Sinking into the cushions of the living-room couch one Sunday and linking her arm through his, Susan felt blissful and serene. She surveyed the paintings on the walls and the knickknacks on her shelves, evoking memories of the past as pleasant as her hopes for the future. A statuette of an Aztec god represented her honeymoon with Mike in Mexico. A blue and white Delft vase was a souvenir of a trip to the Netherlands and northern Europe. A copper Seder tray was a purchase from their last visit to Israel.

Suddenly Susan sat up straight and scrunched up her nose in concern. The figurines on the third shelf seemed farther apart than normal.

"Maybe the maid moved something," Dale suggested, when she mentioned it.

"Cora hasn't changed anything on those shelves in fifteen years," Susan asserted. "If I ever try to rearrange anything, it's back the way it was the next time she comes. And she doesn't steal," she added in anticipation of his next comment, "and if she breaks something, she tells me right away." Susan walked closer to the shelves, scrutinizing and counting. Something was definitely missing. "Oh!" she screamed as she realized what it was. "My Chinese lion!"

Mike had bought her the lion as a fiftieth birthday present while on a business trip to China. It was solid gold and sat on a black lacquered stand. Susan's eyes combed the shelves in a panicky search. "You haven't seen it anywhere, have you, Dale?"

Dale looked over the shelves, then at Susan. He pursed his lips together, then lowered his head to his hands. "Damn," he muttered. "Damn. Damn."

Susan turned around. "What is it? You do know something about this, don't you? You know where it is."

He raised his head slowly. "No. Not for sure. But I have a good idea where it might be."

"Well, where?"

Dale shook his head sadly. "It could be in any pawnshop between here and my house. I'm sorry, Susan. I'm so sorry. Randy must have taken it when we were here for dinner the other night. I should have watched him better." He slammed his fist onto the sofa arm. "Damn! I thought he must be getting money from somewhere. I haven't been giving him very much, only what he needs to live on, because he just throws it away on booze or maybe drugs." He leaned his elbows on his knees and propped his cheeks inside his palms. "I'm really sorry, Susan. I'll find your lion for you. I'll get it back for you, whatever it costs. Whatever it takes, I'll do it."

She moved into his lap and knocked his hands away from his face, replacing them with her own hand and cheek. "You don't have to do that, Dale. If your son is stealing to buy drugs, then you have more than enough troubles already."

In June, Jennifer flew down to southern

California to visit with Dale and Randy and to attend her mother's wedding. It was Diane's third trip down the aisle. Susan was astonished when Dale asked her to drive down to San Diego with them.

"*You* were invited to the wedding?" she asked him in surprise. It seemed a little strange to invite an ex-husband to one's wedding. "I don't think you ought to go, Dale. I'm sure Diane just invited you to be polite."

"I don't think so. She wants me to give her away."

Susan stared in disbelief.

"I did it last time, too," he explained. "Although it didn't take very well the last time. I'm hoping this time it will be better."

"You're hoping? Does that mean you like this guy better than you did the last one? I assume you've met him?"

Dale nodded. "I picked him."

"What?!"

"I introduced them. Gray is a customer of mine. He's a computer serviceman; he travels all around the southern part of the state. He said he wanted to meet a nice woman and settle down, so I said, 'Take my wife. Please.' "

Susan shook her head, frowning, but a smile lit up her eyes. "Dale, you really are something. You go behind my back to fix an argument between me and my daughter, and now you're fixing up your ex-wife with a new husband." The smile moved to her lips and filled her face with tenderness. "You really are a meddler."

"Only in matters of love, Lady."

It was a cozy wedding, pleasant but plain, not at all like the extravagant Jewish weddings Susan was used to attending. After a simple church ceremony, the guests drove to the bride's home for a small reception. Susan dutifully made the rounds of the important people, pumping the hands of the groom and Dale's former mother-in-law and sister-in-law, but she was most interested in finally meeting Diane.

"I wish you all the happiness," she said as she reached the head of the reception line, pressing the bride's hand in what she hoped was a friendly gesture.

"Thank you, Susan," Diane said warmly, although Susan had not introduced herself. "I'm glad that you could come. I'm glad we're finally getting to meet each other." Diane had a face like a flower, albeit a slightly faded flower. Although the woman was barely forty, worry lines were noticeable on her forehead and in the creases of her cheeks, and the subtlest of crow's feet defied even the skillful application of eye makeup. Susan observed with well-concealed but decided pleasure that Diane didn't look a day younger than herself.

But she was lovely, just the same, like a modest, unassuming princess, and Susan couldn't help liking her. Diane took Susan's hand in both of hers and squeezed it, as if proffering a special message understood only by the two of them. "I want to wish *you* happiness, too, Susan." Her voice was earnest and sincere, and Susan detected not the slightest rancor or jealousy as she added, "Take good care of my Dale. He's really something special."

"I know," Susan whispered.

Dale, standing beside Susan, blushed in embarrassment. When he wandered away to talk to his friends and family, Susan looked around the house at the spacious rooms and the tasteful furnishings. The living-room furniture was chrome and glass, the curtains looked custom made, and the dining-room table was solid walnut. The carpeting looked new. It was a very lovely home, not as large or as nice as her own, but much nicer than Dale's house and much bigger. For some reason that disturbed her. Diane was a secretary; she couldn't possibly make as much money as Dale did. How could she afford to maintain that home? Randy couldn't have contributed much to the household when he lived there; Dale often complained that he ate more in food than he was worth in work.

Diane didn't come from a wealthy family; her father was dead, and her mother, whom Susan had just met, was a night auditor for a motel chain. Dale had often described Diane's second husband, Bill, as a lowlife and a deadbeat. Presumably he had drained more out of Diane's finances than he had put in. So what was she living on?

"You're awfully quiet," Dale remarked, as he and Susan drove back to Los Angeles alone. Jennifer was going to take a flight back to San Francisco the next day, and Randy had decided to stay in San Diego as well, to house-sit and visit with friends while Diane and Gray were on their honeymoon. "You haven't said a word for the last twenty miles. You didn't like the wedding, did you? You thought it was boring and dull."

"No, of course not. Of course I liked it. It was . . . interesting. It was just . . . different. Different from the weddings I'm used to. Different as night and day. Different as . . . you and me."

She reached into her purse for a tissue and dabbed it at the corner of her eye. Out of the corner of *his* eye, Dale noticed her action and pulled the car over into the right lane. As the Jaguar slowed down to within ten miles of the speed limit, he put his arm around her. "What's the matter, Suse?"

"Nothing," she sniffed. "Everything. You and me, Dale. We're too different. This afternoon convinced me. Despite everything, despite how much we love each other, I'm still Jewish and you're still Christian."

Dale shifted gears again on the Jaguar and gradually eased it onto the highway. "I'm hardly a Christian, Susan. Today was the first time I'd been inside a church since Diane's last wedding."

The last time they'd talked about it, he had said it was his own wedding. "It doesn't matter. You were comfortable at the ceremony today and I wasn't, and when you go to services with me, you're very polite and courteous, but I can tell that you're bored as hell."

"Well, so are you."

She had to laugh at that. "Granted," she conceded. Then her eyes became serious again. "You're a Christian at least once a year, Dale. At Christmastime."

"Now just what is that supposed to mean?"

"It evokes special feelings for you that you've had since your childhood. You have a Christmas tree in your house, don't you? You goddamn slept with your ex-wife because of the sentimentality of Christmas."

"I've already explained to you about that, and I'm not going to apologize again. And as for my Christmas tree, you didn't seem to be particularly bothered by that. You helped me decorate it, for God's sake. And seemed to have a wonderful time doing it, I might add."

"I did. I love decorating Christmas trees. I love sitting around fireplaces and drinking egg nog and listening to Christmas carols. In somebody else's house. Not mine."

Dale looked at her strangely, disturbed by the hostility in her voice. "Nobody's forcing you to have a Christmas tree, Susan. It's your house. Decorate it any damn way you want."

A stony silence ensued over the next ten miles. Finally Dale reached over and placed his hand on Susan's. "Susan, you know as well as I do that this isn't about Christmas trees. What's really bothering you?"

She turned her hand over and squeezed his. She always took comfort from his hands; they were strong and bolstering. Susan kept her fingers touching his as she turned to him. "Dale," she said pensively, "your youngest child is over eighteen. And he doesn't even live with Diane anymore, he lives with you."

"Yeah. So?"

"So you don't have to pay child support anymore, do you?"

He hesitated only a fraction of a second, but it seemed much longer. "No. Not officially."

"But you do unofficially, don't you? You still send her money every month."

The pause was a little longer this time. "Yes. Does that bother you?"

Susan wasn't sure how she felt about it. She wanted to feel jealous. Dale and Diane had been divorced for eleven years, almost as long as they'd been married, but they still maintained a financial, emotional, and sexual relationship.

That wasn't quite fair, Susan chided herself. Dale wasn't sleeping with Diane anymore; he had apologized for his one infraction. And if she were honest with herself, she hadn't really been all that angry about it. Then what *was* she angry about? The fact that he still had a relationship with her? She herself still had a relationship with Mike, and even Jeff, as well, though they were both dead.

But Diane was alive and well, and she still loved Dale, Susan was sure of it. She had seen it in the loving, proprietary way she had looked at him. If Dale had spoken up when the minister asked, "Does anyone object to this marriage?" Diane would have undoubtedly left the groom's side and run off with her ex-husband.

But Dale hadn't done that; he wouldn't. He had had plenty of chances to go back to Diane if he'd wanted to. It was obvious that he didn't want to.

"I don't love her anymore, Susan," Dale said suddenly, as if reading her thoughts.

"Then why do you still support her? That's what you've been doing all these years, isn't it? Supporting two households? That's why she lives in that nice house and you can't afford to move any closer to the city. That's why you're always short on cash, even though I know the garage must do a great business. You send her most of your income."

He didn't respond directly to her allegation. He didn't need to. "Susan, I'm the one who walked out," he said after a few minutes. "I left her with two kids to raise and plenty of bills to pay. Diane's life hasn't been easy since I left, and she's had no one to help her." Dale glanced out the window at his rearview mirror as he signaled to change lanes. "Gray is a good man, and he makes a good living. I don't think I'll need to help her out much anymore."

Susan couldn't speak. What she had been feeling before, she realized, was petty jealousy and insecurity. What she was feeling now was a swelling of love so strong and so intense that she couldn't express it in English.

Dale looked at her earnestly. "You think I'm a real sap, don't you?"

"No," she said softly, tears filling her eyes as she finally found her voice. "I think you're a real *mensch*."

Twenty-five

"A man?" Dale asked curiously, as he donned his glasses and peered into his Yiddish-English dictionary that evening at his house. "A person? That's what you called me this afternoon? A person?"

Susan smiled, amused at his use of the dictionary. He must have been looking up every Yiddish word she had let slip out, and some she hadn't. "It means a lot more than that in Yiddish," she explained. "It means a man as opposed to being an animal. Or a robot. It means a person with higher capabilities, with sensibility, with a conscience. It's someone who does the right thing by his fellow man. We don't have saints in our religion, Dale. People aren't expected to be perfect. But a *mensch* is someone who tries very hard to behave according to the image in which he was created. It's one of the few Yiddish expressions in common use that isn't a curse word or an insult. In fact, I would say that in Yiddish it's the highest compliment you can give somebody."

He was obviously touched. He was especially attentive in his lovemaking that night. And the next morning, although it was a weekday, he got up even earlier than usual to fix Susan a hot breakfast.

"What'll it be this morning, Lady?" he asked as he served her coffee. "Eggs? Pancakes?"

"Just toast'll be fine. I'm not very hungry." Susan struggled with the plastic price tag on a blouse she had recently bought and not yet worn. "Don't you have a scissors?" she mumbled, trying to break the thread with her teeth.

"In the study. If it's not in the drawer, it's somewhere on that desk. Be careful; it's a mess. Don't cut yourself."

The third bedroom that Dale used for a study was small but efficient. Usually he kept his desk fairly neat, but today there were papers spread all over the top of it, stacked in orderly piles, but covering the entire surface just the same. It was the end of the first summer school session, and Dale had been studying hard all week for his final exams.

Susan was so proud of him for having the guts to go back to school, with a lot of kids his son's age, just for the love of learning. The very first class he'd signed up for, besides the required freshman English, was Western Civilization. That figured. Dale had always been hungry for knowledge about ancient and modern civilizations. He thrived in that course. His pleasure with his studies was obvious from the copious notes he took in his lecture classes and the time and care he took researching and writing papers.

Susan glanced through the piles of handwritten notes and typewritten compositions, looking for the missing scissors. As she carefully lifted and moved the piles of paper, her hand fell on a stapled collection of notes that looked different from the others. Susan gasped as her eyes read the heading: *Rabbi Silver, Conversion Class Notes.*

She stood and looked at it for a long time. Her eyes widened in curiosity, and then her face broke into a smile. She put the papers back onto the pile and carried her broad smile out with her to the kitchen.

"Dale, you devil," she smiled coquettishly, "you've been holding out on me."

He was just placing her plate of toast next to her coffee. "What are you talking about?"

"About your surprise. I thought you acted a little mysterious yesterday in the car. Oh, Dale, what made you change your mind?"

The expression on his face was too blank for even Dale to fake. "About what?"

Susan reached around his broad back and hugged him fondly. "About converting to Judaism. I found your notes. Oh, Dale, I'm so happy."

He pried her arms off his shoulders and placed them together in front of him. He stared straight into her eyes. "Susan, I'm sorry to disappoint you, but I haven't changed my mind. Those notes aren't mine."

He was teasing her again, as usual. He was so good at that. Of course they were his. Who else's could they be?

"They're not mine," he repeated, taking her face in his hands as if to burn the words directly into her brain. "They're Jennifer's."

"Jennifer's?" A whole jumble of thoughts and emotions pressed against Susan's skull, vying for her attention. Disappointment, first of all. And then embarrassment at making the assumption and acting so happy about it. And then curiosity. And then realization. And then pleasure, a wary pleasure, one that started slowly and gradually warmed up to sincere happiness. "How long has she been studying? Why didn't you tell me?"

"About six months. She didn't want me to tell anyone. Joel doesn't even know yet."

"Well, I am surprised. I never would have guessed. You knew about it and you didn't try to discourage her?"

"Of course I didn't try to discourage her. I'm the one who encouraged her."

Now she really was surprised. "How come? I thought you were totally against the idea."

"For me. For me it would be a hypocrisy. I would be doing it only to please you and not even for you, but to pacify your tight-assed friends."

"And Jennifer? Isn't she doing it just for the formality? Just to please Joel?"

"In the beginning she was, yes. But now she's really into it. And for Jennifer it's not so terrible to do something just to please the man she loves. They want to spend their whole lives together. They want to raise a family. I think it's important that they have something to offer their children besides confusion. I think they should have a united religious front. For us it's not important, Susan. We've raised our children. We don't need a religious bond between us. We don't need a lot of things that we needed when we were younger."

Susan started. His words sounded just like Barbara's. "What do we need, then, Mr. Know-it-all?"

"Two things," Dale said categorically. "Love. And trust."

In late summer, Susan's mother suffered a

stroke. "How long are you going to be gone?" Dale asked, as Susan packed her suitcases fo the trip to Houston.

"At least two weeks. Maybe longer." Mayb a lot longer, Susan thought to herself. He mother had hired a nurse to care for her dur ing the day, but as an only child, Susan ex pected to be the major caregiver for a long time. "Do you want to stay here at the house while I'm away?"

"No." Dale dumped most of his own belong ings into the small suitcase he kept at the bacl of her closet. "Not with Randy. I wouldn't wan to be responsible for the shape your house might be in when you got back. I'll check or it every few days, though. If you need you plants watered or your mail picked up, I'm your man."

Susan stood on her toes and planted a warm kiss on his lips. "You *are* my man, Dale. Anc don't you forget it while I'm gone.

"Yes, ma'am. I mean, no, ma'am, I won't." Dale's eyes twinkled. "I'll have your name en graved on my chest." He pulled up his shirt "Which side would you prefer, left or right?"

Susan moved her hands fondly over his chest. "Don't you dare have anything else tat tooed on your body! Maybe Diane liked tha stuff, but I don't."

Dale grinned. "Diane hated it, as a matter

458

of-fact. She always said it was one of the stupidest things I ever did." He slipped his hands under her cotton sweater and caressed her back. "Stay as long as your mother needs you. I'll take care of things here."

"I'll miss you."

"I'm going to miss you, too, babe. But in a way, this is good for me. I need the time to work on straightening out my son."

"What do you mean?"

Dale let go of Susan's body and sank back on her bed. "I think Randy's been doing coke, Suse. Or something. He won't admit it, and I haven't found any on him or in the house. But I figure if I can sit on his ass twenty-four hours a day, at the shop and at home, I can shake him down from whatever he's into or at least keep him away from it long enough to sober him up."

Susan frowned. "I don't think you realize what you're getting into, Dale. What you're trying to do is not that simple. You're not a psychiatrist or a therapist. What qualifies you to try to do this?"

Dale's answer was straightforward and resolute. "I'm a parent."

Susan found her mother weakened, but still full of indomitable spirit. She was able to speak slowly but had trouble formulating the words. She had difficulty as well focusing her eyes, so Susan spent a good part of every day reading aloud to her.

"Who . . . was that . . . on the . . . phone, dear?" Mrs. Singer asked after Susan had finished a lengthy conversation with Dale.

"A friend." Susan sat at the edge of her mother's bed and smoothed her hair back against the pillows. There was a small princess phone on the nightstand beside the bed. She took the older woman's hand. "I've been dating somebody, Mom. For a long time now." She took a deep breath. "His name is Dale Clemens."

Mrs. Singer didn't answer, but Susan knew she had heard her by the way her eyes blinked and closed.

"No, he's not," Susan added bluntly. She might as well save her mother the trouble of asking the question.

"Not what?"

"Not Jewish. That was what you were about to ask me, wasn't it?"

It was a long time before her mother spoke, and when she did, the words came slowly and laboriously. Susan wasn't sure how much of that was due to the stroke, and how much to her determination to say the right thing and make every word count.

"I . . . wasn't . . . about to . . . ask you . . . that. If . . . I were . . . going . . . to ask . . . you . . . anything, it . . . would be . . . just . . . two . . . questions: Is . . . he . . . good to you? And . . . do . . . you . . . care for . . . him?"

Easy questions. Pitifully easy. "Yes, Mom. He's very good to me. And I do care for him. Very much."

Even with the modifier "very much" tacked on to the end of it, the phrase, "care for him" still sounded woefully insignificant, pathetically understated. Dale had been right about that. Susan didn't just "care for" him. She carried Dale's image in her thoughts all the time. Her loins ached for him. Her arms longed to stretch around him and hold him close. Her breasts yearned for the stimulating caress of his lips. No, she more than cared for him. Even though she'd only been away from him a few days, she hungered for him and missed him more than she ever thought she could.

Mrs. Singer patted her daughter's hand with her free one. "That's . . . good. I'm . . . glad you've . . . found . . . somebody. It's . . . not good . . . to be . . . alone." She turned her head to the picture framed on her dresser. "Your father . . . was . . . one of a . . . kind. When he . . . passed away . . . God rest his soul . . . I never even thought . . . of looking for . . . someone else. Now . . . of course . . .

it's too late. But then . . ." She paused as if letting the years of the last decade pass over her eyelids. She looked at Susan earnestly. "I . . . realize . . . that . . . I didn't need to find . . . someone to . . . replace your father. I realize that . . . it just would have been . . . nice . . . to have a . . . companion . . . someone to . . . share my last years with." She fell silent, apparently tired from so much talking.

Susan pulled the covers up to her mother's chin and moved to sit in the chair next to the wall. A companion. Someone to share your last years with. That was all that was necessary at this stage in life. Barbara had told her that, and now her mother had said it, too. But Dale was so much more than that.

Mrs. Singer improved steadily, but slowly. It was eight weeks before she was able to stand or get around by herself. The nurse had long since been let go, and she was managing now only with Susan and a housekeeper that came in twice a week. "It's time for you to go home, honey," she said to her daughter the day she was able to cook dinner by herself.

"Are you throwing me out?" Susan teased. "Now that you're finally well enough to offer me some of Mom's home cooking that I've been missing?"

"I'm not throwing you out," Mrs. Singer assured her. "I would love to have you stay longer, but I know that you need to get back."

"Yes," Susan admitted. "I've probably overburdened the others in the office with my cases long enough."

"I wasn't thinking about your workload," her mother said wisely. "You have a man back there waiting for you." Her eye twitched in a gesture remarkably like a wink. "And I know you're anxious to get back to him."

Maybe her mother *hadn't* assumed that she and Dale had just a platonic relationship. Susan couldn't deny that she was ready to go home. She missed Dale so much. Tremors ran through her body just at the thought of seeing him and feeling his hands on her again.

When her plane touched down at L.A.X., Susan could hardly contain her excitement. Although there were dozens of people in the waiting area, her eyes found Dale immediately. "Excuse me. Excuse me," she said repeatedly, as she doggedly and determinedly stalked her way through the crowd. When she reached him, she felt her feet literally lifted off the floor as Dale grabbed her in his strong arms and hugged her. She couldn't help noticing the jealous stares of several of the women whose toes she had just trod.

He smelled so good. His arms felt so good. He looked wonderful, of course. Susan could hardly wait to get home, to lie in bed beside him and show him how much she had missed him.

Usually she loved the slow, tantalizing way that Dale made love to her. Tonight, however, she was eager for him to get on with it. She couldn't wait for him to be inside her, couldn't wait for the ecstatic pleasure that she knew his body would bring her. When he finally climbed on top of her, though, his penis lay lifeless and flaccid against her body. After he had made several unsuccessful attempts at penetration, Susan took his limp member in her mouth and tried to cajole it into firmness. To no avail. Finally Dale rolled over on his side and away from her. He didn't turn back again.

Susan lay in frustration and confusion. She knew that she should say something reassuring to him, but she couldn't bring herself to speak. Of course she knew it wasn't that uncommon for a man to have difficulty, on occasion, getting an erection. It had happened to Mike several times in the thirty-odd years they had been together. It had even happened to Jeff once when she'd been with him. She and Jeff, though, had been making love practically nonstop for days; his faculties had obviously been overworked.

But Dale had no such excuse. It had been more than two months since they had been together. Her own body was overripe and impatient for his touch; she would have assumed that after nine weeks of celibacy his organ would be bursting with eagerness. Unless.

Susan didn't even want to think about the possibility that word suggested. But she couldn't keep the thought from crashing through her brain. What a stupid, naive fool she'd been. How quixotic of her to think that a young, virile man like Dale would and could forego sexual pleasure indefinitely just because his usual partner was unavailable.

She tried to blink back the tears that formed in her eyes as she thought of Dale in somebody else's arms. Even if it hadn't meant anything to him, even if he had just been satisfying his lust with some other woman's body while remaining faithful to her in his mind, it still hurt. It hurt worse when she realized that he must have satisfied his lust pretty well and pretty often. Why else would he be unable to perform with her tonight?

Susan leaned over and looked at Dale's face, lit up by the moonlight streaking through the partly opened venetian blinds. He appeared to be sleeping, although fitfully. Usually Dale slept like a heavy log. The restlessness in his body suggested a troubled mind. Perhaps a guilty mind.

He had found somebody else. That was why

he couldn't make love to her. He had met somebody; one thing led to another; they had ended up in bed; he had spent the night. He didn't want to tell her on her first night home. He had tried to pretend, but his body had given him away.

Susan couldn't stop the tears from coming now. They flooded her eyes, but she couldn't bear to let Dale see them or let him hear the wailing sobs that rose now from her throat. She grabbed her pillow and dashed downstairs to the living-room couch, where her heart split open into a thousand wet, anguished pieces.

Twenty-six

"Susan." Dale's hand gently touched her shoulder. "It's almost seven o'clock."

The sunlight streaming in through the living-room curtains and the clock on the VCR confirmed Dale's statement. Susan turned her head away from him. "I don't have to get up," she mumbled. "I told Ron I wouldn't be back in the office until Monday."

He shrugged and left her alone. Susan could hear him making coffee in the kitchen. She curled her knees up into fetal position and tried to bury her head inside the covers, but the day wouldn't go away. The percolating coffee insisted on ushering in the morning.

Sighing, Susan stretched and slung her legs over the couch. She trudged upstairs to wash up. The face in the mirror didn't look like hers, and the cold water she splashed on it felt neither cold nor wet.

When she came back down, Dale silently handed her a cup of coffee. He didn't say good morning or anything else. Instead, he sat quietly opposite her, his eyes focused on his own cup.

Jeff had always looked like that when he had something on his mind and was trying to determine the best way to say it. Susan thought about making it easy for Dale, but decided against it. If he was about to say what she thought he was, she wanted to make it damn hard for him.

Dale looked up at her at last. "Susan," he said quietly, "when's the last time you had a mammogram?"

It was not at all what she had expected to come out of his mouth. Her own mouth dropped ungracefully open. "A few months ago," she said, totally taken aback. "Why?"

He took her hand. "Susan, last night when I was touching you, I felt a lump in your left breast. It wasn't there before." His voice cracked. "I didn't say anything then, because I knew you'd just worry all night and there wasn't anything you could do about it until this morning. I want you to call your gynecologist today and get tested."

She took his hand and placed it inside her gown, on the underside of her left breast. "Here?"

He closed his eyes and nodded.

Susan breathed a sigh of relief. "Dale, it's nothing. It's a fibroma; I've had it for years. My doctor said I can remove it if I want to, but it's not necessary. I'm surprised you never noticed it before."

The relief that flooded Dale's face lit up the room like the morning sun. "You're sure it's nothing?"

She nodded.

"Thank God." He grabbed her by the shoulders and buried his face in her neck. "Suse, I was so scared. I was afraid I was going to lose you."

He had been worried to death all night. Suddenly another kind of relief filled Susan's heart. "Dale," she asked quietly, "was that why last night . . . why you couldn't . . . you know?"

He nodded. "Yes."

She burst into tears. "I was so afraid. I thought . . . I thought you'd found somebody else. I thought that was the reason that you didn't want me anymore."

He kissed her on the neck and rubbed her back. "Of course not. I haven't been with anyone else, if that's what you've been worrying about." He kissed the top of her head. "I missed you, Suse. I missed you like crazy. I'm sorry about last night. I'll make it up to you now, if you feel up to it."

Susan looked at him questioningly, and reached her hand down to feel his crotch. The obvious bulge that she felt there grew ever larger under the warmth of her hand. "Do you want to go upstairs?" she whispered.

"No," Dale answered. "I don't think I can wait that long." Hurriedly he removed the coffee cups from the table and ran a towel over it, sweeping the crumbs to the floor. Then he thrust his hands under her nightgown and pulled it over her head, exposing the whiteness of her breasts and the fleshiness of her thighs. Lifting her in his strong arms, he laid her gently down on the table. Susan raised her head to watch him undress. She had heard about people doing it on the kitchen table, but such antics had so far been out of the realm of her experience. She wasn't even sure how he was going to do it.

After a minute she lay back down and decided to let him just take charge. After another minute, she raised her head again. Dale was looking at her sheepishly. "I never tried this before," he admitted. "It's not as easy as it looks in the movies." He slid his arms under her back and lifted her off the table. "Come on, let's go upstairs."

It felt so good to be back in his arms. All of

the silly apprehensions she'd ever entertained—about age difference, religion, education—seemed now to be so insignificant. None of that was important. All that was important was being with him.

After they'd made love, Dale rolled her over and above him, then rolled her to her back again. Pinning her arms to the mattress and holding them outstretched, he kissed her on her lips, her eyes, her chin, her neck. Her breasts.

"Dale," she said, suddenly uncomfortable about the issue he'd raised, "what if it *had* been something to worry about? What if I did have to . . . lose a breast?"

He raised his head. "Susan, I'm not in love with your boobs. I'm in love with you."

God bless him, he always knew the right thing to say. But she needed more than platitudes right now. "That's easy for you to say. Now," she emphasized. "But what if something like that were to happen a little later down the line? I'm no spring chicken, you know."

"No kidding?" Dale chuckled. "How come you never told me that before?"

"Dale, I'm serious. I'm going to be sixty years old in a few years. You're still a young man. You could find somebody younger. Somebody who could give you children. Somebody who could . . . satisfy your needs . . . better than I can."

He grinned. "Interesting suggestion. Maybe I should get two thirty-year-olds. Or even three twenty-year-olds." He sat up and engaged his arms in a lewd juggling gesture. Susan didn't know whether to laugh or cry.

Dale dropped his hands to his sides. "Susan," he said seriously, "I don't want any more children. And I'm not just interested in sex. I *love* you." He shook her gently by the shoulders. "How many times do I have to tell you that before you believe it?"

She decided to cry. She wrapped her arms around him and hugged him with all the love she'd stored for months. Dale moved his arms across her back, massaging her tenderly. "Even if that was all I was interested in," he said, "I'd have a hell of a time finding somebody that could 'satisfy my needs' any better than you can. Frankly, Susan, you're the best lay I've ever had."

She stopped hugging and glared at him through dried tears. "Dale, that's not very funny. In fact, I think it's a rather cruel joke."

"I wasn't joking. I meant it."

Susan stared at him suspiciously.

"Okay," he said with a begrudging smile, "I admit I've been with a lot of women whose sexual technique was far superior to yours. If you want to know the truth, I've had some real prize-winners. But it was all physical, just bodies performing. It was great sex, but it wasn't making love." He turned her head toward him so he could look in her eyes. "I've never enjoyed sex with anyone as much as I have with you."

She knew she should stop there, but she couldn't help herself. "Not even Diane?"

"Diane?" He seemed completely taken aback by her question. "Diane was lousy in bed."

She didn't believe it for a minute. She had always considered Diane to be her toughest rival. "That's not what you said before. You said you couldn't complain about your sex life." She had remembered his words exactly.

He shook his head in amusement. "I *couldn't* complain. In all the years we were married, she never once refused me. She was always the dutiful wife, always willing to perform what she felt were her marital responsibilities. But half the time, I felt like she was doing me a favor. Like she was humoring me, allowing me to satisfy my 'animal needs' which she was somehow above. Sometimes I think she made up her grocery lists in her head while we were in bed together."

Susan wasn't totally convinced. "What about after your divorce? She used to come on to *you* a lot then, didn't she?"

Dale smiled sheepishly. "I guess she missed me. Look, I didn't say it was *never* any good. There were times when we were wonderful together. But," he said, touching her cheek gently, "it wasn't like it is with you. You turn me on ten times my normal sex drive, Suse, because *you* enjoy it so much. I love you, Susan. I want to spend the rest of my life making you happy."

Her fingers moved over his lips tentatively. She needed his words so much, and yet she was afraid to believe them. "Dale, are you sure? Are you sure you want to stay with me?"

"Susan, nobody has a perfect body forever. Bodies change and deteriorate. I'm getting older, too. I might lose my hair or my teeth. Or even—" he shuddered "—my potency." He turned back to her eyes. "How would you feel about that, Suse? Would you still love me if I couldn't make love to you anymore?"

She laughed and kissed him. But he didn't respond to her kiss, and when she looked up, she realized that he was waiting expectantly. "Do you really need me to answer that?" she asked, surprised that he could have the slightest doubt.

"Damn straight. I know you love me for my body, Susan. I want to know if that's all you love me for."

She took her face away from his and looked

at him objectively. She had never seen this insecure side of him. Couldn't he feel when she touched him how much love was behind her passion? "Dale, I liked you before I loved you. You're a wonderful man—kind and supportive, a good father, a good businessman. A wonderful friend. I noticed those things about you before I ever thought about sleeping with you." She took his hand and kissed his fingers. "I can't deny that I feel intense physical attraction for you," she said as her eyes caressed him all over. "But I don't love you just because I crave your body. I crave your body because I love you so much."

He laid his head against her shoulder. She caressed his head and his neck. "It's your own fault," she murmured, "that I'm so crazy about your body. You're just so good."

He was not seduced by the compliment. In fact, she felt his body stiffen, and when he moved away from her, she saw that his eyes were cold and hard. His words were crisp and brittle. "Am I as good as my father was?"

Susan gasped. She had always known that he would eventually get around to asking that question, and she had deliberated many hours over how to answer it. Still, when he just shot it out so unexpectedly, she was caught by surprise.

"Well?"

She looked up at him. "Do you want me to be polite or honest?"

"Never mind," Dale said dourly. "I think you just answered the question."

"No, I didn't." She reached for his arm before he could turn his body away from her. "You're better than he was, Dale. Not technically. Physically he was just about the best there was. But when he made love, he was on automatic. It was like you said about your own experiences. When we were together, I felt like he was just making love to my body. When you make love to me I feel like you're loving all of me. Like all of your soul is involved in it."

"Well, of course that's how I feel." His response was full and heartfelt, and he seemed surprised that she could ever have thought otherwise. But his face was still troubled. "Do you still love him, Suse?"

"I'm always going to love him, Dale. But not the way I did. The picture of him in my memories is fading faster now than it did in all the years since his death. When I first met you, I always used to see him in your eyes, even before I realized what I was seeing. Now when I look at you, I see you." She pressed her face to his chest. "I love you, Dale. Jeff isn't in bed with us anymore. I've let him go."

When she'd described him as loving her with all his soul, she had thought it a poetic metaphor. But Dale made it reality. He cradled her in his arms and made love to her with such intensity, she couldn't tell where her body ended and where his began. She felt as though he'd penetrated her flesh and crawled inside her skin.

When at last he drew away from her, Dale looked different. His clear green eyes were fresh and new. They were still Jeff's eyes, but there was something in them that Susan had never seen in Jeff's troubled orbs. It was a look of serenity and contentment and peace with oneself.

"Let's go up to the cabin tomorrow," Dale suggested as he zipped up his pants. "We've been away from each other too long. I want to spend the whole weekend alone with you, just the two of us."

"Sounds great to me," Susan acceded. "But what about Randy? Can you leave him alone that long?"

"I think so. I think he'll be all right. He's been straight and sober for six weeks now."

"Dale, that's wonderful. How did you manage that?"

He sat down and pulled on his boots. "By never letting him out of my sight for the past forty-two days. We work together; we live together. If he has to go to the bathroom in the middle of the night, I'm right there on his ass

until he comes out and gets back in bed. He'
cleaned up and straightened out. And he's got
ten to be a pretty good worker, too. Some o
the customers have even started asking fo
him."

Susan kissed his shoulder lovingly. "I hope
he realizes how lucky he is to have a father like
you."

"No chance. He hates my guts right now. He
can't stand me being around all the time. No
that it's been a lot of fun for me, either. Bu
if it straightened him out, it was worth it."

He snapped the buttons on his shirt and
leaned over to kiss Susan goodbye. "Let's leave
from my house tomorrow night. I need to get
home and get my riding gear. Can you leave
your office a little early? Meet me at my place
at six o'clock?"

"I can make it. Not that *you'll* be on time."

"I will. I promise. I will be home no later
than six o'clock."

Despite Dale's emphatically expressed intentions, Susan was not at all surprised when she
drove up the gravel road at five after six and
did not see the Jaguar parked in his driveway.
The truck was nowhere around, either. Susan
was relieved not to have to make small talk with
Randy while she waited. She was glad that he

478

was straightening out his life or at least having it straightened for him, but she had never felt comfortable with him, and she certainly didn't want to be alone with him.

She knocked, just in case, at the front door, but when there was no immediate answer, Susan opened it with her key. She helped herself to a Dr Pepper from Dale's refrigerator and went into the den to wait.

After flipping through the evening news on several TV channels, she decided to go for a walk. It was already after seven and the late-fall sun was about to set. Locking the house again, Susan strolled down the gravel road to its junction with a smaller path that led to a high bluff. She and Dale often strolled this way at this time in the evening. It was a good place to watch a sunset, and, as the bluff overlooked the main highway, it was a good place to watch for Dale's arrival.

After ten minutes, Susan saw the Jaguar approaching as it crested to a high place in the highway. Actually she heard it before she saw it. The engine must have been revved up to almost a hundred miles an hour.

"Damn, slow down," Susan said out loud as the car screeched into the outside lane to make its exit. "So you're already over an hour late. For you, that's not even a record. Five more minutes won't make any difference. Slow down!'' she screamed, as the Jaguar careened perilously close to the drainage ditch that ran beside the feeder. Her heart flew into her mouth and then settled down again as the car veered away from the ditch and slowed down just a little. But it was still swerving all over the road.

Susan concentrated on keeping the red convertible straight in its path, as if the power of her mind could keep the car centered on the road and steer it safely to its destination. As it hit the gravel road, the Jaguar swerved for the last time. There was the smell of rubber and the sound of crunching tires and glass as the car hit a pothole, nose-dived, and spun around and around on the narrow gravel road. With its last spin it broke the bushes that lined the outside of the road and plunged into the ditch. Susan watched in horror as the Jaguar flipped over twice, crashed at the bottom of the steep ditch, and immediately burst into flames.

Twenty-seven

The funeral was held two days later. Diane was inconsolable, weeping copious tears into her husband's shirt as the minister gave his sermon. Jennifer was quieter and more subdued, one hand clutching Joel's, the other reaching to soothe and comfort her mother. Dale was silent and immobile. He had hardly spoken at all in two days. He just kept staring straight ahead past the face of the minister, staring intently at nothing. There was no viewing of the casket. Randy Clemens's body had been so badly charred it was not even recognizable.

"It was my fault," Dale mumbled to Susan, as they walked together to the gravesite. "I should never have let him drive alone. Not on Friday night. Too many places to stop, too much trouble waiting to happen. I should have made him ride with me."

She didn't know if he wanted her to ask or not. "Why didn't you?"

"He said he wasn't feeling well that morning, so I let him sleep in. He showed up all right at work a few hours later, and he seemed okay. But then we had two vehicles to drive home that night. I had to take them both because, with you and me planning to go out of town for the weekend, I didn't want to leave Randy without transportation."

"So you let him drive the Jaguar."

Dale shrugged. "There was no reason not to. He'd been doing just fine. Randy's a good driver when he's sober. *Was* a good driver." Dale's voice broke, but he let no tears escape his eyes. "He'd been doing just fine."

"It wasn't your fault, Dale. You did everything you could. You can't save a person from himself if he doesn't want to be saved." She felt no need to mention the obvious: that Randy had been left on his own all day and all night while she and Dale had made wild, impetuous love and that they had been planning to leave him for the weekend when they went to the cabin.

The sun shone brazenly and cruelly, laughing at the grim expressions on the faces of those gathered at the gravesite. Susan's eyes lingered on Joel as he patted Jennifer's hand consolingly. He looked just like his father.

Susan remembered how supportive Mike had been at her own father's funeral. How supportive Mike had been all his life. Joel was just like him, she thought proudly. He was warm and likable and a steady rudder capable of steering his family through the most troubled waters. She hoped that Jennifer appreciated what she was getting.

Diane was still weeping uncontrollably. Gray stood staunchly by her side, literally holding her up. But not even the most steadfast husband could soothe the grief or comfort the soul of a mother who has just lost her son.

Dale walked over to Diane and took her in his arms. It was the first time Diane's sobs subsided all day. Holding each other tightly, the two bereaved parents shared their grief together.

After the funeral, the mourners went back to Dale's house. The house seemed unusually still as Dale prepared coffee and served cakes to the family. Jenny and her mother talked together in hushed whispers. Gray and Joel conversed uncomfortably, while Susan sat at the edge of their conversation. Dale didn't speak again to Susan or to anybody else.

"We're going to take off, Dale," Joel said at last. "It's a long drive back and I want to make at least part of it tonight."

Dale nodded silently. He clasped his daugh-

ter in his arms and whispered in her ear. Jenny
didn't speak, but when she broke away from
her father, the tears were streaming down her
cheeks.

Diane and Gray were going to stay overnight.
Dale offered them his bedroom. "I don't
mind," he assured them. "I'd kind of like to
stay in Randy's room tonight."

Randy's room, which had formerly been
Jenny's room, had only a small single bed. Dale
hadn't mentioned where Susan was to sleep.
"I'll sleep on the couch in the study," she sug
gested. "I know you want to be alone tonight."

"No. I don't." He reached his hand out for
her. "Please stay with me."

Dale undressed quietly, down to his under
wear. Usually he slept in the nude. Susan had
been doing the same since she had been sleep
ing with Dale, but that didn't seem like a good
idea tonight. She was sure that Dale wasn't go
ing to be interested in sex and she felt the need
to be more modest. But she hadn't brought any
nightclothes with her. "Can I sleep in one of
your shirts?"

Dale walked to the doorway and peered
across the hall. The door to his bedroom was
closed. "They've gone to bed already. I guess
you'll have to wear one of Randy's, if that
doesn't bother you. Unless you want to wear
this."

He handed her the shirt he had just taken off. It was crumpled and wrinkled and smelled of perspiration. Susan didn't mind the odor. It was his scent, and she liked the way it mingled with the scent of her own skin as she slid the silky shirt over her body. Carefully she buttoned the buttons and got into bed beside Dale.

It felt like *déjà vu*. It was like the first time they had ever shared a bed together, the night they had slept together at his office, the night of that earlier tragedy. Or near tragedy. That night, like tonight, she had slipped into bed quietly facing Dale's back.

But tonight, as soon as she entered, he turned to face her. As he put his arm around her and pressed his face against her bosom, the buttons of his own shirt cut into his cheeks. Susan helped him undo the buttons and cradled him against her. Dale lay his head in the crevice between her breasts. They were ample breasts, but in no way large enough to absorb the tears that Dale wept into them that night. Susan held him and rocked him and caressed him as he clutched at her and expelled his grief into the warmth of her body. It was the first time she had ever seen him weep openly.

"It wasn't your fault," she kept repeating soothingly, as his convulsive sobs rocked her body. "You did all you could." She opened the

silk shirt and spread it wide, trying to encom
pass him in a protective tent within which h
could could feel safe and loved.

It was a hot, humid evening, and the breez
which wafted in through the open window wa
stifling rather than cooling. When they finall
fell asleep in the early predawn hours, Susan'
hair was dripping with sweat. The sheets wer
dank from the perspiration of their bodies an
the salt of Dale's tears.

Sometime later, Susan felt the warmth o
morning touch her eyelids, but she didn't ope
her eyes. She was having a beautiful dream
and she didn't want to leave it. She felt hersel
invaded by an ethereal spirit, a spirit tha
moved over her body and opened it gently t
receive the clear light of its presence. Susar
felt weightless in its embrace, an embrace o
pure love, yet endowed with a passion stronge
than Susan had ever known. She opened he
arms, her legs, and her heart to meet her love
rejoicing in the passion, burning herself in th
painless fire. She had never felt so whole be
fore.

When she finally opened her eyes to see th
sun, it was a different sun from the one tha
had brazenly mocked them at the gravesite th
day before. It was clear and innocent, tenta
tively peeking through clouds of fog like th
rainbow after a thunderstorm.

Dale raised his face from Susan's body. "You know," he said, with the first smile she had seen from him in three days, "you'd better be careful who you sleep with, if you're going to shout out names while you're making love."

It hadn't been a dream then. "No!" she gasped. "I didn't!" She couldn't have called out Jeff's name. Not again. Not now. And if she had, then why the hell was Dale smiling? Her voice broke to a whisper. "God help me, please tell me I didn't cry out Jeff's name."

He took her in his arms, still smiling. "No," he said quietly. "You didn't. You called out *my* name, Suse." He lowered her to her back again so he could look into her face. "You mean you didn't know? You mean I was making love to you and you slept through the whole thing?"

She had to hold him, touch him, connect with him. "I wasn't asleep. It was the most beautiful experience of my life. But I thought I was dreaming. I'd never felt so . . . fulfilled before, not from Jeff, not from Mike, not even from you, Dale."

He buried his face in her neck. "I love you, Susan," he said, through a voice of choked-up tears. "I don't know how I would have made it through the past few days if it weren't for you. You understand me so well. You knew just what I needed."

Susan didn't respond. She had spoken very

little in the past few days, an unusual situation for her, precisely because she *hadn't* known what he needed. She hadn't known whether he wanted to be alone in his grief or whether he wanted to be surrounded by soothing chatter. She hadn't even known if he wanted to be touched or not. So she had remained silent away from him but nearby, waiting for his shell to crack, wanting to be there for him if he decided he needed her. Apparently that had been exactly what he wanted.

Dale stroked her face lovingly with his fingers. "You've always known what I needed. When I thought I was looking for 'class,' you knew what I was really looking for. I was looking for the courage to be myself, to express myself in ways I had always been afraid to before. I thank you for giving me that courage." He smiled wanly. "We fit together very well. I know you've never believed that; I know you think we have so many differences we couldn't possibly really love each other. But we don't need to be a carbon copy of each other, Susan. We understand each other. We always have. You knew what was missing from my life. And I know what was missing from yours."

"What?"

He kissed her cheek and placed his lips near her ear. "Passion. That desperate feeling that defies all logic and common sense. Mike gave

ou security and commitment, but passion you
ot only from Jeff. You've always needed some-
ne who could give you both."

Susan rolled into his outstretched arm and
uddled up to his body. "You know anybody
ike that?"

He smiled modestly. "Maybe."

Twenty-eight

It was the wedding of Susan's dreams. Ou
of respect for the deceased, they waited si
months to hold it, but Susan didn't mind th
delay. It gave her the opportunity to plan an
execute every aspect of the affair down to th
most minute detail. The selection of the hal
the hiring of the caterer, the choice of menu
the music, even the flower arrangements. All th
pleasure and anticipation she had been denie
from Andrea's wedding, she now poured int
this prodigious undertaking. And on the bi
day, she was well-satisfied with the results o
her efforts.

The room was festively decorated in a mar
ner that was elegant but not overdone. Th
tables had been set with fine china and wel
polished silver. The peach and aqua colo
scheme beautifully complemented the tuxedo
of the groomsmen and the swirling, feminin

gowns of the bridesmaids. An aura of restrained gaiety pervaded the room as the guests mingled quietly before the ceremony.

Weddings and funerals, Susan thought to herself. When families come together for better or for worse.

The ceremony itself was perfect, performed in meticulous accordance with traditional Jewish wedding custom. Susan's eyes fastened in turn on each of the other participants in the marriage ceremony. The groom was handsome and serious, but looked a little too young to be embarking on this permanent adventure. The bride stood out like a goddess of unblemished loveliness. Her beautiful blond ringlets cascaded over the delicate lace of the antique wedding gown that had belonged to her maternal grandmother. The shining blue eyes glistened with even more beauty than usual, shimmering with excitement and happiness. As she stood between her mother and father, Jennifer looked like a delicate porcelain doll.

The father of the bride looked handsome enough to be the groom. No surprise there, Susan thought. Although she had never seen him in a tuxedo before, she had known instinctively how he would look: like a Master of Ceremonies at a Hollywood awards presentation. Dale always looked wonderful when he was dressed up. Not that he wasn't every bit as attractive in his birthday suit, Susan thought wryly.

Dale winked at her from across the chapel. Susan stood on the opposite side of the rabbi, next to Joel. A touch of sadness entered Susan's heart at the regretful thought that Mike was not here to witness the marriage of his son. If Joel was thinking about it as well, he didn't show it. He smiled brightly and clasped Susan's hand, but his eyes were focused on Jennifer.

They really were a beautiful couple. So obviously in love. Jennifer had been the one to insist on a Jewish ceremony, and she looked extremely comfortable with her newly chosen religion.

The rabbi had been surprised that Jennifer's divorced parents had agreed to walk down the aisle together with their daughter. To Susan, of course, it was just one more example of Dale and Diane's extremely amicable relationship. She felt the old jealous feelings rising inside her but immediately thrust them aside. There was no cause for her to feel threatened, especially not now that Diane was apparently quite happily married to her third husband, the husband that Dale had practically chosen for her. Dale the Matchmaker, Susan smiled to herself.

When the ceremony was over and most of

he guests had left the chapel for the grand ballroom, Susan lingered behind. She needed the brief moment of quiet and solitude before bracing herself to go out and face again the legion of friends and family at the dinner reception. Wistfully she remembered a moment like this over thirty years ago when she and Mike had met together in a small room, as Joel and Jennifer were doing now. The beautiful moment just after their own wedding ceremony, when Mike had sworn his lifetime commitment to her.

"How is the second most beautiful lady at the wedding?" Dale's voice intruded. She hadn't heard his footsteps behind her. Susan turned to him, trying to present a composed face, but Dale detected the tears in her eyes. Wordlessly he offered her the handkerchief out of his breast pocket. "You're missing Mike right now, aren't you?"

She dabbed the handkerchief at the corners of her eyes. "How did you know?"

Dale smiled kindly. "It's not that hard to figure out. It's only natural you should be feeling that way tonight, at this special *simcha*. It should have been his *naches* as well."

She was only a little surprised at his use of the Yiddish words. Dale's mind was like a computer; everything he heard or saw went into random access memory. He was like Mike in that respect: he noticed everything and forgo[t] nothing.

A tear that the handkerchief had misse[d] trickled down her cheek. "Would you rathe[r] be alone?" Dale asked considerately.

"No. Please stay with me." Susan raised he[r] hands to his shoulders and was immediatel[y] comforted by the feel of his large hands as h[e] pulled her to him. She knew that he was sti[ll] deeply saddened by the loss of his son, but sh[e] didn't want to bring up that tragedy on thi[s] joyous day. "I love you, Dale. I do wish tha[t] Mike could be here. But in some ways, I fee[l] like you and I are the parents at this wedding[,] like it's *our* children getting married."

Dale smiled. "We are. It is. You and I ar[e] in-laws now, Susan." He kissed her on the lips[.] "Are you ready to go out now? I'll introduc[e] you to Paula."

She stared in surprise. "Your mother? She'[s] here?"

She had only sent a telegram to Randy's fu[-] neral. But there she was, as large as life. Paul[a] Clemens Scott Evans Gerland was a formida[-] ble-looking woman. She was easily five-foot[-] eight without her two-inch heels, and he[r] mane of red hair was at least seven rinses awa[y] from its natural color. Although she was onl[y] a few years older than Susan, her bearing and manner made her appear quite intimidating.

"So you're Dale's girlfriend," she said accusingly, looking Susan up and down as if she were a bug that needed squashing.

Susan would have replied that she was hardly a girl, but the woman didn't appear to have a sense of humor. Susan examined Mrs. Gerland thoroughly, but more subtly, she hoped, than the manner in which she had been inspected. She tried to imagine this hardened woman as an innocent sixteen-year-old girl, but the image eluded her. Dale's mother seemed as worldly-wise as any woman she had ever met. She wondered what Jeff could have possibly seen in her.

Mrs. Gerland opened her large purse and took out a pack of cigarettes, offering one to Susan. She didn't seem surprised when Susan refused. She took one out for herself and lit it with a match from a book that lay on the table next to her. She put the book of matches, engraved with *Joel and Jennifer*, into her large purse, and then scooped up half a dozen other souvenir matchbooks and dumped them in as well. She took a drag of her cigarette. "Dale told me that you knew his father."

Susan nodded cautiously. "I knew him very well. He was my best friend for thirty-five years."

Dale's mother stared at her without speaking, a cold, forbidding stare. Susan wondered what was behind those hard eyes, hostility or kinship. Had Dale told his mother that she and Jeff had been more than friends? Did this woman see her as a rival for the affections of a man she had once loved or as a compatriot in female solidarity, a fellow victim of love? As their eyes met, the older woman's slowly melted, relaxing into an expression of curious interest, even confidentiality.

"I've always had a soft spot in my heart for that boy," she said wistfully. "He was special, not like all the others. He had a kind of understanding about him, like he knew what you were feeling, and maybe even cared." Paula Gerland's eyes clouded over slightly and suddenly, Susan didn't feel intimidated by her anymore. She took a picture out of her small purse, *the* picture, and showed it to Dale's mother.

"Is that Jeff?" Paula whispered.

Susan nodded.

"He really was a handsome son-of-a-bitch, wasn't he? Dale looks just like him. Dale got his brains from him, too; that's for sure." She chortled loudly. "He sure as hell didn't get any from me." She punched her cigarette out into a nearby ashtray.

"Dale *is* very smart," Susan agreed. "And he's a wonderful person. You should be very proud of yourself for raising a son like that."

"Wasn't me that raised him," Paula Gerland said candidly. "My mama and daddy did that. If my boy came out pretty good, it's because of them. I never was no good with kids."

Susan was beginning to feel a little warmer, even sympathetic toward Dale's mother, but she was still relieved when Dale reappeared and hooked his elbow through hers, urging her to join him in the reception line.

"Sorry to leave you alone with her so long," he apologized, as they made their way to the center of the room. "I thought you two might have things you'd want to discuss privately."

Susan looked up at him. "We both decided that you and your father are the two most wonderful men ever." Susan squeezed his elbow with her other hand as they edged their way toward the front of the line.

"Jennifer looks absolutely beautiful," Susan commented, observing Jenny and Joel shaking hands and proffering kisses. "Even more so than usual."

"Doesn't she?" Dale beamed agreeably, with a father's pride. "I'm glad she got her looks from Diane's side of the family."

"Bullshit." She decried his false modesty. "Jenny looks exactly like you and you know it." And she looks like Jeff, too, Susan thought.

Dale grinned and pulled her into the line. Susan smiled with equal geniality at friends, relatives, acquaintances, and people she had never laid eyes on in her life.

"It's a perfectly beautiful wedding, Susan," Beverly Werner gushed when she came through the line. "You've done a wonderful job."

"Tell that to the man who paid for it," Susan smiled. "I'd like you to meet the father of the bride, Dale Clemens."

Dale kissed Beverly's hand and smiled at her engagingly. "Your compliment went to the right party," he said. "I may have paid for it, but Susan did all the work." Beverly was obviously impressed by Dale's looks and charm. Susan wondered how she could ever have been embarrassed or ashamed to introduce Dale to anyone. Proudly she steered him to meet her colleagues from the office, including Ron Davis and the new Mrs. Davis.

"Your boss is not a half-bad guy," Dale remarked as he and Susan danced together later. "I'm really glad I didn't punch him in the jaw."

"As if you would," Susan smiled. "You wouldn't hit anybody if your life depended on it. Or mine. If we were attacked by a teenage gang as we leave tonight, I know I'd be on my own."

Dale stopped dancing and looked at her

with an incredulous expression on his face. "Do you really believe that?"

Susan didn't answer.

Dale pulled her over to the side of the room and put both hands on her shoulders. "Susan, I only fight when it's necessary. I don't believe in violence if there's a choice. I'd rather walk away from a fight. But if you were ever really in danger, believe me, you wouldn't be on your own. I'd give my life for you, Suse."

His eyes were sincere and beautiful. Jeff's eyes. They reminded Susan of something she had to do. "I'd better go talk to Joel," she said. "It's time he knew the truth." Dale nodded and let her go.

When she found her son, she ushered him into the small sanctuary where he and Jennifer had met in private after the ceremony. "If this is about the birds and the bees, Mom," Joel said as he saw her serious face, "you're a little late."

"I am a little late," Susan admitted, "although, of course, it's not about that. Not exactly." She sighed, wondering how to begin. "I'm sorry to wait until the eleventh hour to tell you this, Joel. I was hoping not to have to tell you at all, but now that you and Jenny are married and planning to start a family, it's important that you know about your family background and genealogy."

"What are you about to tell me, some deep, dark family secret?" Joel grinned.

"Yes," Susan said, with no trace of a smile. "I am."

The twinkle in Joel's eyes faded slowly, then disappeared altogether. His brow furrowed and the lines in his cheeks hardened into a very serious expression. "You don't have to tell me anything, Mom," he said softly. "I already know."

Susan looked at him suspiciously, questioning.

"This is about Uncle Jeff, isn't it?"

How did he know? Had Dale, without consulting her, told Jennifer? Or had he figured it out for himself? "Yes," she said weakly, sinking into a chair. "When did you find out?"

"I've known about it for years," Joel said seriously. "Ever since I was little. I didn't know then exactly what I knew, it was just something in the air that didn't feel exactly right. Uncle Jeff was always so good to me. Not that he wasn't good to Andy, too, but with me it was special. I knew that he loved me more than just as an uncle. When I was a teenager and Dad and I started having run-ins about practically everything, Uncle Jeff always understood me and took my side. I understood that he couldn't go up directly against Daddy, but I knew he jerked his arm a little in private and got Dad to ease up on me. Those weeks I spent with Uncle Jeff every summer were always a special time for me. But the most special was the summer we went to Israel together. I think that was when I really began to understand; that's when I put the pieces together. No, Mom, he never told me. I just knew."

Susan was staring at him in horror. "Knew what? What the hell are you talking about?"

Joel didn't seem surprised by her denial of understanding. "That Uncle Jeff was my father. Isn't that what we're talking about?"

Susan's face went white. "Oh my God, is that what you think? That's what you've always thought?"

He nodded.

"Joel, it's not true! He wasn't your father!"

"Don't lie to me, Mom. We're in the presence of God. There's a rabbi here and everything."

"I'm not lying!"

Joel glared at her. "Mother, I know what I'm talking about. We've been through this once before and you wouldn't admit it then. But now there's more at stake than just your stupid determination to protect your reputation at all costs. I know you wanted to look like the perfect wife. But I have a right to know whose genes I'm carrying and passing on to my children. You owe me that much. Now admit the truth: you and Uncle Jeff were lovers!"

Susan fought back tears in an effort to remain composed and calm. "Joel, listen to me. I'm not trying to hide anything from you. This *is* a subject that normally would not be any of my son's business, but since it does affect you children, you do have a right to know. Jeff and I *were* lovers. But he was not—*not*" she repeated "your father."

Joel stared at his mother, not knowing whether to believe her or not.

Susan lowered his voice to a whisper. "There was a time," she said, "nine long months of agony in which I thought that maybe he was. I was so worried about it that I asked the doctors for your blood type immediately after you were born."

Joel looked up at her expectantly.

"You have the same blood type as your father, Joel. Your *real* father, Michael Riesman, my husband. Jeff's blood type was completely incompatible with yours. There was no way he could have been your father."

Susan leaned back against the chair she was sitting on. "There were many times I wished he had been your father," she said wistfully. "And I know he felt the same way. He did have a special love for you, Joel. He did love you like his own son. But he wasn't your father,"

502

she said emphatically. "You don't have any of Jeff's genes in your body." She gulped and took a deep breath before her next sentence. "But your children will."

Joel looked dazed and confused. "What?"

Susan sighed and pursed her lips together. "You're not Jeff's son, Joel," she said slowly. "But he did have a son." She took another deep breath. "Dale."

She watched his face as it registered surprise, shock, and realization. "Then Jennifer is . . ."

"Jeff's granddaughter," she finished for him.

"Jesus," Joel gasped. "We're having his great-grandchild!"

Now it was Susan's turn for shock and realization. "You mean Jennifer is . . . right now— how far along is she?" she demanded.

"Three months. No, that's not the reason we're getting married," he said quickly, as Susan's face blanched. "We were going to get married about six months ago. We were just going to call you to tell you when Dale called us to tell us about Randy." He hugged his mother fondly. *"Mazel Tov,* Grandma."

I'm going to be a grandmother, Susan thought in dazed delight as she wandered out to rejoin the others in the reception hall. And she realized, as she felt her eyes widen with shock, Dale's going to be a grandfather. To the same child. We're going to be grandparents together. She grabbed a tissue out of her small evening purse to stop the joyful tear that wanted to mar her carefully applied eye makeup. She was suddenly so happy she felt she would burst. She and Dale could never have children together; she would never know the pleasure of carrying his baby and bringing it into the world. But she would get to watch him bounce his grandchild on his knee—her grandchild and his.

"Come on, Mom." Andrea pulled her in close to a circle of ladies. "Jennifer's about to throw her bridal bouquet."

Susan extricated herself from her daughter's grasp. "That's not for me," she said, embarrassed by the faces fixated on her. "That's for the young girls."

"It's for all unmarried ladies," Jennifer said firmly, personally walking out to her and escorting her forward. "Come on, Susan, be a sport."

"Do it, Susan," Dale urged, suddenly appearing at her side. "Who knows," he winked, "you might get lucky."

She should have known by the way they manhandled her and pressed her forward toward the stage. She should have suspected something when Dale suddenly moved away and

Jennifer placed her in the front row of the aspiring ladies, conspicuously to the far left. She should have heard something in the giggle as Jenny leaped up onto the stage and held the bouquet poised over her head.

Jennifer's aim was true. The bouquet of flowers zeroed in squarely in front of Susan's head. As she caught it, dozens of women surrounded her, clapping joyfully.

"Look!" one exclaimed. "There's something in it!"

Susan examined the bouquet more carefully. Taped to one of its branches was a small gray velvet box. She released it from its mooring and, as dozens of eyes fastened on her in fascinated curiosity, opened the box.

Inside was a ring with two small heart-shaped diamonds, flanked by a small bright ruby on either side. Susan gasped and looked up. Dale, sitting at a table a few feet away from her, was grinning from ear to ear. As tumultuous applause filled the room, he stood and made his way to her side.

"You really have a flair for the dramatic, don't you?" Susan said, as attention finally, turned away from them and back toward the bride and groom, who were preparing to leave for their honeymoon. "What if I hadn't caught the bouquet?"

"If you hadn't caught it, *I* would have caught

it," he assured her. "You've never seen me jump over a wall of three-hundred-pound linemen before."

"It's beautiful, Dale," she murmured, admiring the clarity of the diamonds. "I know this had to cost a hell of a lot of busted BMWs. Was this your money, my money, or our money?"

"*My* money," he said emphatically. "I dipped into Jenny's nest egg. Now that she's married into a 'good' family, I don't have to worry so much about her financially anymore. I figure I'll let her rich mother-in-law bail the kids out if they get in trouble. I'd rather spend my money on the lady I love." He beamed at her. "Try it on."

She removed the ring from its berth and held it tentatively over the outstretched fingers of her right hand.

"Nuh-uh." Dale shook his head, pointing to the ring finger of her left hand. "There."

It fit perfectly. "Does this mean what I think it means?" Susan asked significantly, admiring the shimmering of the stones as she turned her hand from side to side.

"It means whatever you want it to mean. For my part, it means that I intend to love you and be faithful to you for the rest of my life. I don't need a piece of paper to prove that commitment—nothing could make me feel stronger about you than I do right now—but if you need it or want it, I'm willing. I mean it this time, Suse."

Tears formed in her eyes, but she ignored them. "That's not what I want. Not anymore. I don't need that piece of paper either. I just need you." She reached for his arms as he held them out to her. "I've been Susan Riesman over thirty years," she explained. "That's my professional name and the name I'm known by to all my acquaintances. I'm not planning to change my identity by joining my life with yours. The part that we're joining is inside, where only you and I can see it. We know what we mean to each other; it's not necessary to put on a label for anyone else's benefit."

Dale smiled, obviously pleased by her speech. He planted a chaste kiss on her cheek. "I love you, Grandma."

She stared at him. "How did you know?" she demanded. "How come you always know everything before I do?'

He laughed and folded her tightly within his arms. "I hope you're not disappointed."

"Disappointed? Oh, Dale, I couldn't be happier. I want to grow old with you. I want us to play with our grandchildren together."

They walked arm in arm toward the main doors of the hall, where young people were collecting confetti to throw at the departing newlyweds. Susan kissed and hugged Joel, and kissed and hugged Jennifer as well. Dale took his daughter in his arms, then turned to Joel with the same words with which he had admonished him when they'd first met a year ago. "Take good care of my baby," he cautioned.

Joel grinned. "You bet I will, Dale. You take good care of my mom."

After they'd left and the remainder of the guests were either dancing or packing up to go home, Susan turned to Dale. "You don't have to marry me, Dale," she said. "I told you I don't care about that. But if you were willing to do that and you truly want to be with me forever, I think it's time that we lived together. Will you move in with me, Dale? Please?"

He leaned back against the wall and stroked his mustache, as if this were a subject that required a great deal of contemplation. But Susan detected in his eyes the twinkle that usually overrode his inscrutable expression. He had something up his sleeve to tell her, she just knew it. But she also knew she was going to have to wait until he was damn good and ready to say what it was.

Finally he spoke. "I'm glad you asked me that, Susan. Real glad, in fact. Because in a month or so I won't have anyplace to live." The small twinkle in his eye grew into a wink, and he slight puckering around his lips grew into a broad grin. "I sold my house this week."

"Oh, Dale!" She flung her arms around him, oblivious to the crowd of people who were now staring at them curiously. This was what she had been waiting for. This act, more than anything else, more even than the ring he had just given her, signified the depth of Dale's commitment to her. "I love you, Dale. I love you." She hugged him tightly, not caring a bit about the damn eye makeup, just letting the tears stream from her eyes without restraint.

"I can start moving in this week," he offered, "if you like. Just me and my stuff," he added with a grin. "No Christmas trees, I promise."

Susan smiled. "How about Monday? I'd like you to be there to supervise the construction crew when they start tearing up the backyard."

"What construction? What are you talking about?"

Now it was her turn to give him a Cheshire-cat grin. "Monday," she said sweetly, as she watched Dale's eyes fill up with happiness, "is the day we break ground for the swimming pool."

Author's Note

An accountant in her daytime life, Linda Steinberg began writing when she was living in Lagos, Nigeria—in longhand on a children's school tablet, the only kind of paper she could find. She has also lived in Tel Aviv, Israel; Hickory Valley, Tennessee; Houston and Midland, Texas. *September Spring,* her first published novel, takes place in Los Angeles, which she once passed through on her way to Anaheim. Linda is married to a certified public accountant who failed auto mechanics twice. They currently live in Plano, Texas with their two lovely daughters.